DARK WATCH

DIRK PITT® ADVENTURES BY CLIVE CUSSLER

Trojan Odyssey
Valhalla Rising
Atlantis Found
Flood Tide
Shock Wave
Inca Gold
Sahara
Dragon
Treasure
Cyclops
Deep Six
Pacific Vortex
Night Probe
Vixen 03
Raise the Titanic!
Iceberg
The Mediterranean Caper

FICTION BY CLIVE CUSSLER WITH DIRK CUSSLER

Black Wind

FICTION BY CLIVE CUSSLER WITH PAUL KEMPRECOS

Polar Shift
Lost City
White Death
Fire Ice
Serpent
Blue Gold

FICTION BY CLIVE CUSSLER AND JACK DU BRUL

Dark Watch

FICTION BY CLIVE CUSSLER AND CRAIG DIRGO

Sacred Stone
Golden Buddha

NONFICTION BY CLIVE CUSSLER AND CRAIG DIRGO

The Sea Hunters II
The Sea Hunters
Clive Cussler and Dirk Pitt Revealed

DARK WATCH

CLIVE CUSSLER

WITH JACK Du BRUL

MICHAEL JOSEPH
an imprint of
PENGUIN BOOKS

MICHAEL JOSEPH

Published by the Penguin Group
Penguin Books Ltd, 80 Strand, London WC2R 0RL, England
Penguin Group (USA) Inc., 375 Hudson Street, New York, New York 10014, USA
Penguin Group (Canada), 90 Eglinton Avenue East, Suite 700, Toronto, Ontario, Canada M4P 2Y3
(a division of Pearson Penguin Canada Inc.)
Penguin Ireland, 25 St Stephen's Green, Dublin 2, Ireland (a division of Penguin Books Ltd)
Penguin Group (Australia), 250 Camberwell Road,
Camberwell, Victoria 3124, Australia (a division of Pearson Australia Group Pty Ltd)
Penguin Books India Pvt Ltd, 11 Community Centre,
Panchsheel Park, New Delhi – 110 017, India
Penguin Group (NZ), cnr Airborne and Rosedale Roads, Albany,
Auckland 1310, New Zealand (a division of Pearson New Zealand Ltd)
Penguin Books (South Africa) (Pty) Ltd, 24 Sturdee Avenue,
Rosebank, Johannesburg 2196, South Africa

Penguin Books Ltd, Registered Offices: 80 Strand, London WC2R 0RL, England

www.penguin.com

First published in the United States of America by The Berkeley Publishinng Group 2005
First published in Great Britain by Michael Joseph 2005
1

Printed in Great Britain by Clays Ltd, St Ives plc

A CIP catalogue record for this book is available from the British Library

978–0–718–14800–3
0–718–14800–2

1

THE aging Dassault Falcon executive jet drifted smoothly from the sky and touched down at the Sunan International Airfield, twelve miles north of Pyongyang. The MiG that had flown a tight escort from the moment the aircraft entered North Korea's airspace peeled off—twin cones of flame from her engines cutting the night. A truck was sent to lead the Falcon to its hardstand, and in its bed stood a machine gunner who never took his aim off the cockpit windows. The plane taxied to an open expanse of concrete at the far side of the airport complex, and even before its wheels were chocked a squad of fully armed troops had formed a perimeter around it—their AK-47s held ready for the slightest provocation. All this despite the fact that the passengers on board were invited dignitaries and important clients of the reclusive Communist country.

Several minutes after the engines spooled to silence, the passenger door cracked open. The pair of guards positioned closest shifted in anticipation. Then the door was lowered, showing the integrated steps that formed its internal side. A man wearing an olive uniform with a flat cap stood at the doorway. His features were harsh and uncompromising, with near-black eyes and a hooked nose. His skin was the color of weak tea. He stroked a finger along his dense black mustache and cast an unimpressed eye at the ring of soldiers before stepping lightly from the aircraft. He was followed by two more hatchet-faced men, one wearing traditional Middle Eastern robes and a head scarf, the other in an expensive suit.

A trio of North Korean officers marched through the cordon and approached. The highest ranking officer gave a formal greeting and waited for another, a translator, to render his words into Arabic.

"General Kim Don Il welcomes you to the Democratic People's Republic of Korea, Colonel Hourani, and hopes you had an enjoyable flight from Damascus."

Colonel Hazni Hourani, the deputy head of Syria's strategic rocket forces, bowed his head in acknowledgment. "Thank the general for meeting us personally at this late hour. Tell him our flight was indeed enjoyable since we flew over Afghanistan and were able to dump the contents of the aircraft's septic system on the American occupiers."

The Koreans shared a round of laughter once they heard the translation. Hourani continued, speaking to the translator directly, "I applaud the skill in which you use our language, but I think our dealings would go smoother if we spoke in English." Hourani switched to that language. "I understand, General Kim, that we both speak the language of our common enemy."

The general blinked. "Yes, I find it gives me an advantage over the imperialists to know their ways better than they know mine," he replied. "I also speak some Japanese," he added, trying to impress.

"And I some Hebrew," Hourani answered quickly, playing the game of one-upmanship.

"It seems we are both dedicated to our countries and our cause."

"The destruction of America."

"The destruction of America," General Kim echoed, sensing in the Arab's intense stare that the same fires burned in his belly, too.

"For too long they have pushed their influence into all corners of the globe. They are slowly smothering the planet by first sending in soldiers and then poisoning the people with their decadence."

"They have troops on your borders as well as mine. But they fear attacking my country, for they know our retribution would be swift and final."

"And soon," Hourani said with an oily smile, "they will fear *our* retribution as well. With your help, of course."

Kim's smile matched that of the Syrian. These two men, from different sides of the globe, were kindred spirits, devout haters of all things Western. They were defined by this hate, shaped and molded through years of indoctrination. It didn't matter that one worshiped a bent view of a noble religion and the other a warped faith in the infallibility of the state, the results were the same. They saw beauty in savagery and found inspiration in chaos.

"We have arranged transportation for your delegation to the Munch'on Naval Base near Wosan on the eastern coast," General Kim told Hourani. "Will your pilots need accommodations in Pyongyang?"

"That is most generous, General." Hourani stroked his mustache again. "But the aircraft is needed back in Damascus as soon as possible. One of the pilots slept most of the way here so he can fly back to Syria. If you could arrange for refueling, I would like them to leave immediately."

"As you wish." General Kim spoke to a subaltern, who passed the order to the head of the security detail. As Hourani's two assistants finished unloading their luggage, a fuel tanker arrived and workers began to unreel the hose.

The car was a Chinese-made limousine with at least two hundred thousand miles on the odometer. The seats sagged deep enough to almost swallow the slightly built North Korean general, and the interior reeked of cigarettes and pickled cabbage. The Kumgang Mountain highway linking Pyongyang with Wosan was one of the best in the nation, yet it taxed the limo's suspension to the breaking point as the vehicle ground its way around tight switchbacks and along precarious gorges. There were few guardrails along the highway, and the car's headlamps were little more than dim flashlights. Without the moon's cool glow the drive would have been impossible.

"A couple of years ago," Kim said as they ascended higher into the mountains that ran like a spine down the length of the country, "we gave permission for a company in the south to arrange tourist trips into these mountains. Some consider them sacred. We demanded they build the roads and trails as well as the restaurants and the hotels. They even had to construct their own port facility to dock their cruise ships. For a while the company had many people making the trip, but they had to charge five hundred dollars per passenger to recoup their investment. The pool of nostalgia seekers turned out to be a small one, and business quickly dropped off—especially after we posted guards along the routes and harassed the tourists any way we could. They no longer come here, but they are still paying us the one billion dollars they guaranteed our government."

This elicited a smile from Colonel Hourani, the only Syrian who spoke English.

"The best part," Kim went on, "is that their hotel is now an army barracks, and their port is the home to a Najin-class Corvette."

This time Hourani laughed aloud.

Two hours after leaving the airfield, the limousine finally descended the Kumgang Mountains and crossed the coastal plane, swinging around to the north of Wosan, and arrived at the outer perimeter fence for the Munch'on Naval Base.

Guards saluted the limo through the gate, and the car crawled across the facility, passing several impressive maintenance buildings and over a half mile of wharf space. Four sleek gray patrol craft were tied to the quay, and a single destroyer lay at anchor in the mile-square inner harbor, white smoke from its stack coiling into the night. The driver swung around a rail-mounted derrick and parked alongside a four-hundred-foot cargo ship at the end of the wharf.

"The *Asia Star*," General Kim announced.

Colonel Hourani checked his watch. It was one in the morning. "And when do we sail?"

"The tides are mild here in Yonghung-man Bay so you can leave anytime. The ship is loaded, fueled, and provisioned."

Hourani turned to one of his men and asked in Arabic, "What do you think?" He listened to the long reply, nodding several times, then turned back to the general, who sat opposite him in the limo. "Assad Muhammad is our technical expert on the Nodong-1 missile. He would like to take a look at them before we depart."

Kim's expression didn't change, but it was clear he didn't like the idea of a delay. "Surely you can accomplish your inspection at sea. I assure you that all ten missiles your country has purchased are aboard."

"I'm afraid Assad does not do well on boats. He would prefer to inspect the missiles now, because he will likely spend the voyage in his cabin."

"Odd that you would have such a man accompany the rockets back to Syria," Kim said coolly.

Hourani's eyes tightened. His country was paying nearly a hundred fifty million sorely needed dollars for the medium-range strategic missiles. Kim had no right to question him. "He is here because he knows the rockets. He worked with the Iranians when they purchased their Nodongs from you. That he has trouble on the sea is not your concern. He will inspect all ten, and we will sail at first light."

General Kim was under orders to stay with the Syrians until the ship departed. He'd told his wife he wouldn't return to Pyongyang until morning, but by remaining with the Middle Easterners, he would forfeit several hours with his latest mistress. He sighed at the sacrifices he made for the state. "Very well, Colonel. I will have the harbor master informed that the *Asia Star* won't leave until first light. Why don't we get on board? I will show you to your cabins so you can stow your luggage, then Mr. Muhammad can inspect your new toys."

The driver opened the rear door, and as Kim slid over to exit, Colonel Hourani placed a hand on his uniformed sleeve. Their eyes met. "Thank you, General."

Kim's smile was genuine. Despite their cultural differences and the inherent suspicion and secrecy surrounding this mission, he felt he really did like the colonel. "It is no problem."

The three Syrians each had their own cabins, but only a minute after being shown their accommodations, they met in the one occupied by Colonel Hourani. Assad Muhammad sat on the bunk with a briefcase beside him while Hourani placed himself at the desk below the room's single porthole. The oldest of the trio, Professor Walid Khalidi, leaned against a bulkhead, his arms crossed over his chest. Hourani then did a very strange thing. He touched the corner of his eye and shook his head, then pointed at his ear and nodded in the affirmative. He indicated the ceiling-mounted light fixture in the center of the cabin and the cheap brass-plated lamp attached to the desk.

"How long do you think the inspection should take, Assad?" he then asked.

Assad Mohammed had taken a miniature tape recorder from his suit jacket and hit Play. A digitally altered voice, actually that of Hourani himself, since he was the only member of the team who spoke Arabic, replied, "I think no more than a few hours. The most time-consuming part is simply removing inspection covers. Testing the circuits is simple."

By this time Hourani had also drawn a recorder from an inside jacket pocket and set it on the desk. As soon as Assad finished speaking, he, too, hit the Play button, and the conversation continued as the men remained silent. At a predetermined moment in the script, Walid Khalidi added his own recorder to the ruse. Once the three recorders playing altered versions of Hourani's voice were working, the trio of "Syrians" moved silently to the far corner of the cabin.

"Only two bugs," Max Hanley mused quietly. "The Koreans really do trust their Syrian customers."

Juan Cabrillo, the chairman of the Corporation and the captain of the merchant ship *Oregon*, tore the fake mustache from his upper lip. The skin beneath was lighter than the layers of self-tanning cream he'd used to darken his complexion. "Remind me to tell Kevin in the Magic Shop that his appliance glue is worthless." He had a bottle of the suspect glue and reapplied a line to the back of the mustache.

"You looked like Snidely Whiplash trying to keep that thing in place." This from Hali Kasim, the third-generation Lebanese-American who'd been newly promoted as the *Oregon*'s Security and Surveillance director. He was the only member of her crew who didn't need makeup and latex inserts to pass as Middle Eastern. The only problem was he didn't speak enough Arabic to order a meal in a restaurant.

"Just be thankful the Koreans left their translator at the airport," Cabrillo said mildly. "You mangled the little soliloquy you'd memorized and delivered during the car ride. Your proposed examination of the missiles sounded more proctologic than scientific."

"Sorry, boss," Kasim said, "I never had an ear for languages, and no matter how much I practice, it still sounds like gobbledygook to me."

"To any Arabic speakers, too," Juan Cabrillo teased.

"How are we on time?" Max Hanley asked. Hanley was the Corporation's president and was in charge of all their ship's operations, especially her gleaming magnetohydrodynamic engines. While Cabrillo negotiated the contracts the Corporation took on and was responsible for a great deal of their planning, it fell on Max's capable shoulders to make sure the *Oregon* and her crew were up to the task. While the crew of the *Oregon* were technically mercenaries, they maintained a corporate structure for their outfit. Apart from his duties as the ship's chief engineer, Hanley handled day-to-day administration and acted as the company's human resources director.

Under his robes and head scarf, Hanley was a little taller than average, with a slight paunch. His eyes were an alert brown, and what little hair remained atop his reddened skull was auburn. He had been with Juan since the day the Corporation was founded, and Cabrillo believed that without his number two, he would have gone out of business years ago.

"We have to assume Tiny Gunderson got the Dassault airborne as soon as he could. He's probably in Seoul by now," Chairman Cabrillo said. "Eddie Seng has had two weeks to get into position, so if he's not alongside this scow in the submersible now, he never will be. He won't surface until we hit the water, and by then it'll be too late to abort. Since the Koreans didn't mention capturing a minisub in the harbor, we can assume he's ready."

"So once we plant the device?"

"We have fifteen minutes to rendezvous with Eddie and get clear."

"This is gonna hurt," Hali remarked grimly.

Cabrillo's eyes hardened. "Them more than us."

This contract, like many the Corporation accepted, had come through back channels from the United States government. While the Corporation was a for-profit enterprise, the men and women who served on the *Oregon* were for the most part ex–U.S. military and tended to take jobs that benefited the United States and her allies, or at the very least, didn't harm American interests.

With no end in sight on the war on terror, there was a never-ending string of contracts for a team like the one Cabrillo had assembled—black ops specialists without the constraint of the Geneva Convention or congressional oversight. That wasn't to say the crew were a bunch of cutthroat pirates who took no prisoners. They were deeply conscientious about what they did but understood that the lines of conflict had blurred in the twenty-first century.

This mission was a perfect example.

North Korea had every right to sell ten single-stage tactical missiles to Syria, and the United States would have begrudgingly let the sale proceed. However, intelligence intercepts had determined the real Colonel Hazni Hourani planned on diverting the *Asia Star* so that two of the Nodongs and a pair of mobile launchers could be off-loaded in Somalia and given to Al-Qaeda, who would launch them hours later at targets in Saudi Arabia, notably the holy cities of Mecca and Medina, in a twisted plot to oust the Saudi royal family. It also appeared, but couldn't be verified, that Hourani was acting with the tacit approval of the Syrian government.

The United States could send a warship to intercept the *Asia Star* in Somalia; however, the vessel's captain would only have to claim that they were diverted for repairs, and the ten missiles would end up in Damascus. The better alternative was to sink the *Star* en route, but if the truth came out, there would be an international outcry and swift retaliation from terrorist cells controlled by Damascus. It was Langston Overholt IV, a high-ranking official in the CIA, who came up with the best alternative: using the Corporation.

Cabrillo had been given just four weeks to plan how to get rid of the problem as quietly and with as little exposure as possible. Cabrillo had intuitively known that the best way to prevent the missiles from reaching their customers, be they legitimate or otherwise, was to stop them from ever leaving North Korea.

Once the *Oregon* was in position off Yonghung-man Bay, Cabrillo, Hanley, and Hali Kasim headed to Bagram Airbase outside of Kabul, Afghanistan, in a Dassault Falcon identical to the one used by Colonel Hourani.

CIA assets on the ground in Damascus confirmed the flight time for Hourani's trip to Pyongyang, and a dedicated AWACS had tracked the corporate jet as it flew halfway around the world. Once it entered Afghan airspace, an F-22 Raptor stealth fighter that had been flown expressly to the theater for the mission had taken off from Bagram. The Corporation's own Falcon had left a moment later, heading south, away from the Syrians. While the U.S. controlled all of the radar facilities capable of monitoring what was about to happen, it was imperative that there be no evidence of the switch.

In one of the few zones where radar coverage was nonexistent, Tiny Gunderson, the Corporation's chief pilot, began to turn back north. Only this time the Dassault Falcon wasn't alone. She'd been joined by a B-2 stealth bomber from Whiteman Air Force Base in Missouri. Because the bomber was larger than the Falcon, yet undetectable by radar, Tiny kept his aircraft fifty feet above the flying wing. No ground-based radar on earth could track a B-2, and by shielding the Falcon, the

Corporation's jet remained hidden as they began to close on Hourani's plane.

At forty thousand feet, the Syrian Falcon jet was at her maximum ceiling, while the Raptor fast approaching her could have made the intercept four miles farther into the sky. The timing was critical. When the B-2 was a mere half mile behind Hourani's aircraft, the Raptor opened her weapons bay and unleashed a pair of AIM-120C AMRAAM missiles.

Had the Syrian jet carried threat radar, the missiles would have appeared out of nowhere. As it was, the older French-built aircraft didn't have such a system, so the two missiles impacted the Garrett TFE-731 turbofans without the slightest warning. Even as the Dassault exploded in midair, the pilot of the B-2 dove away from Tiny Gunderson's Falcon. At that altitude anyone on the ground who saw the brief fireball would have assumed it was a shooting star. And anyone watching a radar screen would have noticed the Syrian aircraft suddenly vanish for an instant, then reappear a half mile to the west before continuing on normally. They might have guessed their system had glitched, if they gave the incident any thought at all.

Now that Cabrillo, Hanley, and Kasim were safely aboard the *Asia Star*, all that remained was to plant the bomb, avoid detection getting off the ship, rendezvous with Eddie Seng in the minisub, slip out of the best-protected harbor in North Korea, and reach the *Oregon* before anyone realized the *Star* had been sabotaged.

Not a typical day for members of the Corporation. But not all that atypical either.

2

A scream woke Victoria Ballinger.

It also saved her life.

Tory was the only female aboard the Royal Geographic Society's research ship *Avalon*, after her cabin mate was transported to a hospital in Japan for acute appendicitis a week ago. Having a cabin to herself also contributed to her salvation.

The ship had been at sea for a month, part of a coordinated international effort to fully map the currents of the Sea of Japan, an area little understood because Japan and Korea fiercely protected their fishing rights and felt any cooperation could jeopardize them.

Unlike her roommate, who'd brought suitcases loaded with clothes and personal items, Tory lived a spartan existence aboard ship. Other than her bedding and a week's worth of jeans and rugby shirts, her cabin was empty.

The scream came from the passageway outside her door, a male cry of agony that snapped her awake. Even as her vision cleared of sleep, she heard muted gunfire. Her senses sharpened, and she heard more automatic weapons fire, more shouts, and more screams.

Everyone on the *Avalon* had been warned that a band of modern-day pirates were preying on ships in the Sea of Japan. They'd attacked four vessels in the past two months, scuttling the merchantmen and leaving any crewmen alive to make their own escape on lifeboats. To date only 15 out of 172 had survived the attacks. Just yesterday they were told that a container ship had simply vanished without a trace. Because of the pirate threat, an arms locker had been placed on the bridge, but the pair of shotguns and the single pistol were no match for the assault rifles cutting through the group of scientists and professional mariners.

The fight-or-flight instinct kicked in, and Tory quickly got to her feet. She wasted two precious seconds making a choice she didn't have. There was no place for her to go. The pirates were somewhere in the corridor outside her cabin, shooting into the rooms, from the sound of it. She'd be gunned down the moment she opened her door. She could not flee, and there was nothing in her room to use as a weapon.

The light of a full moon shining through the porthole fell on the stripped bed opposite Tory's and gave her inspiration. She whipped the blankets and sheets from her bed and bundled them under the frame. Then she pulled her clothes from her locker, making sure to leave its door open, just like her absent roommate's. She didn't think she had the time to empty the bathroom of toiletries. She crawled under the bed, pressing into the deepest corner, and packed her clothes around her body.

She fought to hold her breathing steady as the first wave of panic nibbled at the edge of her mind. Tears leaked from the corners of her blue eyes. She stifled a sob just as her cabin door was thrown open. She saw a flashlight beam slice the room, tracking first across Judy's empty mattress before sweeping her own, pausing for a second on the pair of barren lockers.

The pirate's feet became visible. He wore black combat boots, and she could make out that the cuffs of his black trousers had been stuffed into them. The pirate crossed to the tiny bathroom, sweeping it with his flashlight. She heard the shower curtain ripple as he checked behind it. He either didn't see Tory's soap, shampoo, and conditioner or didn't think they were important. He slammed the cabin door on his way out, apparently satisfied it was vacant.

Tory remained motionless as the sounds of the struggle faded down the hallway. There were only thirty people on the ship. Most of them were asleep in their cabins because at night the engine room ran on automatic, and only two stood watch on the bridge. Because her cabin was one of the last on the corridor, she was certain that the pirates were about finished with the crew.

The crew. Her friends.

If she wanted to get out of this alive, she couldn't let that thought seep any deeper into her brain. How long would they take to loot the vessel? There was little of value to pirates. All of their expensive equipment, their scientific gear, was too large to steal. The underwater probes were worthless to anyone outside the scientific community. There were a few televisions and some computers, but it hardly seemed worth the effort to take them.

Still, Tory figured the pirates would need a half hour to scavenge the 130-foot *Avalon* before opening the sea cocks and sending her to the bottom. She counted out the minutes by the luminous dots on the men's Rolex she wore, allowing herself to fall into the tiny galaxy of phosphorescent points in order to keep from panicking.

Only fifteen minutes passed before she felt the ship's motion change. The night was calm, and the *Avalon* rolled with the gentle swells, a normally comforting motion that lulled her to sleep each night. Tory began to sense the ship's sway had changed, slowed—as though she'd become heavier.

The pirates had already opened the sea cocks. They were already sinking the research vessel. She tried to see the logic in their action, but it didn't make sense. They couldn't have possibly ransacked the ship so quickly. They were scuttling the *Avalon* without even robbing her!

She couldn't wait. Tory slithered out from under her bed and bolted for the porthole. On the horizon she could see what at first appeared to be a low island, but she realized it was a huge ship of some kind. There was another smaller vessel near it. It looked as though the two were going to collide, but it had to be a trick of the moonlight. In the foreground she made out the stern and wake of a large inflatable craft. The sound of its outboard engines faded as it raced from the stricken oceanography ship. She imagined the pirates aboard it and felt her anger flare.

Tory whirled away from the porthole and bolted from her cabin. There were no bodies in the passageway, but the deck was littered with spent shell casings, and the air had a raw, chemical stench. She tried not to look at the blood spattered against the long wall. From her orientation when first coming aboard, Tory knew there were survival suits in the Zodiac life raft near the *Avalon*'s bow, so she didn't care that she wore only a long T-shirt. Her bare feet slapped against the metal decking as she ran with one arm clamped over her chest to keep her unsupported breasts from bouncing.

She climbed a set of stairs to the main deck. At the end of another corridor was the door leading to the outside. Between her and the exterior hatch was a body. Tory whimpered as she approached. The man lay facedown, a shiny slick of blood dampening his dark shirt and drizzling onto the deck. She recognized his shape. It was the second engineer, a high-spirited Geordie, whose flirtations she had begun to encourage. She couldn't bring herself to touch him. The volume of blood told her everything she needed to know. She kept herself pressed to the cold corridor wall as she stepped past the corpse. When she reached the end of the hallway, she looked out the hatch's small window, straining to see if anyone remained on the dim foredeck. She saw nothing and cautiously turned the handle. It wouldn't budge. She tightened her grip and tried again, pressing all her weight against the jammed mechanism, but it remained frozen.

Tory kept calm. She told herself that there were four other ways out of the superstructure and that she could always smash the glass in the bridge if the wing doors were also sealed. She first examined the other doors on the main deck before climbing another set of steps to the bridge. She knew she would get out of this, but as she approached the door leading to the command deck, a deep dread welled up. Although they'd killed the entire crew, the pirates had taken the time to seal the ship like a coffin. They wouldn't have left such an obvious means of escape. Her long fingers trembled when she touched the knob. It turned.

Tory pushed against the solid steel door, but it wouldn't open. It didn't even creak. There were no large windows she could crawl through, no porthole big enough for her to wiggle out. She was trapped, and that realization destroyed any composure she'd been able to maintain. She threw her body at the door, slamming her shoulder into it again and again until her arm was bruised down to her elbow. She screamed until her throat was raw, then fell back against the door and allowed herself to slide to the deck. She sobbed into her hands, her dark hair falling around her face.

The *Avalon* shifted suddenly, and the lights flickered. The water pouring into her lower compartments had found someplace new to flood. The shudder sent a jolt through Tory. She wasn't dead yet, and if she could stop the ship from sinking, she'd have the time to figure a way out. She'd seen a cutting torch in one of the workshops. If she could find it she would burn her way out.

Now as energized as she was in those first desperate seconds when she heard the scream—she was certain now it had been Dr. Halverson, a genteel oceanographer nearing seventy—Tory launched herself from the floor and ran back the way she'd come. She passed through the crew's accommodation block and reached a set of stairs that descended into the engineering spaces. She felt the first cold rush of air as she reached the bottom landing. The sound of flooding was like the roar of a waterfall.

She stood in a small antechamber with a single watertight door leading into the engine room. She put her hand to the metal. It was still warm from the big diesels. But when she placed her hand low down, next to the bottom jamb, the steel was icy to the touch. She'd never been to the engine room and didn't know its layout. Still, she had to try.

"Here we go." Her voice quavered as she undogged the hatch.

Water gushed across her bare feet, and in seconds she was standing knee-deep, with the level rising perceptibly. An open set of steps led down to the floor of the well-lit engine room. Beyond the tangle of pipes, ducts, and conduits, Tory could see that the giant motors, each the size of a minivan, were already half-submerged. Water sloshed against a generator housing.

She stepped over the coaming and started down. She gasped when the water reached her chest. It was probably sixty-five degrees, but she began to shiver. At the bottom step she had to get on her toes to keep her head above the flood. Half walking, half swimming, she struck out across the cavernous space with a vague plan to find how the water was entering the ship.

As the *Avalon* continued to sink on a more or less even keel, she still pitched with the waves. That slight motion made it impossible for Tory to feel currents in the water and pinpoint where they were strongest, where she guessed open pipes led to the sea. The water in the flooded engine room seethed like a boiling cauldron. In just a few minutes of frantic searching, her toes lost their tenuous grip with the deck plating. Tory swam fruitlessly for a minute more. There was nothing she could do. Even if she found the sea cocks, she had no idea how they operated.

The lights flickered again, and when they came back on, they were only half as bright. It was the signal for her to leave. She'd never find her way out of the labyrinth-like space in the dark. She cut smooth strokes through the water and swam directly into the antechamber. Getting to her feet, she found the water had risen to the level of her waist. It took all her strength to close the door. She prayed that once it was sealed the ship might remain buoyant enough to stay afloat until another ship passed by.

Cold and shivering, Tory climbed back to the second deck and padded to her cabin. She toweled off in the bathroom, bound her shoulder-length hair in a ponytail, and threw on her warmest clothes. The air was markedly chilly. She hadn't noticed, but somewhere in the engine room she'd cut the corner of her mouth. She wiped the watery trickle of blood from her lip. Under normal circumstances, the sharp planes and angles of her face were arresting, especially with her startlingly blue eyes. Looking at her reflection in the mirror above the sink, what Tory saw was the haunted look of someone on the way to the gallows.

She turned away quickly and went to the porthole. She could no longer see the moon or even its milky glow, nor could she see the pirates' boat or the big ships she'd glimpsed on the horizon. The night had gone completely black, yet she would not turn away from her only window to the outside.

Maybe if she got some grease or cooking fat she could lube her body and squeeze through the porthole. She thought the windows in the mess hall upstairs were a little bigger. It was worth a shot. She was about to turn away when something dark flashed by outside. She peered closer, her eyes watering with the strain.

She thought she saw it again, maybe ten feet from the ship. A bird? It moved like one, but she wasn't sure. And then it loomed in front of her, taking up the entire porthole. Tory stumbled back with a scream. Outside her cabin, a large gray fish stared at her with its mouth agape, water pumping through its gills. The giant sea perch watched her with its yellow eyes for a moment longer, attracted to the light in the cabin, before finning away into the depths.

What Tory Ballinger couldn't see from her cabin low in the hull was that the deck of the research ship *Avalon* was already awash. Waves lapped at the stern and bow cargo hatches. In a few minutes the water would climb the bridge, swamping the ship so her stern-mounted crane would stick from the sea like a spindly arm clawing for rescue. A few minutes after that, the ocean would close around the top of her single funnel, and the *Avalon* would begin her plunge toward the sea floor nearly two miles down.

3

WHEN a pair of North Korean agents from the brutal State Safety & Security Agency came to fetch their Syrian clients, two were quietly reading their Korans while the third studied spec sheets for the Nodong missile. A guard made a gesture for the trio to follow that also showed off a pistol in a shoulder holster. Cabrillo and Hali Kasim tucked away their Korans while Hanley slipped the schematics back into his bulky briefcase and thumbed the locks.

They threaded their way through the *Asia Star*, a Panamanian-registered bulk carrier converted to the container trade. While worn, the interior spaces were well maintained, and the bulkheads were glossy with new paint. The ship also appeared deserted except for the pair of spies on escort duty.

At a hatchway below the main deck, one of the guards undogged a hatch. Beyond loomed a darkened steel cavern that smelled faintly of bilgewater and old metal. The man snapped on banks of overhead lights, and the fluorescent glow revealed the ten Nodong missiles settled into special cradles, their outlines blurred by thick plastic sheeting.

Each missile was sixty-two feet in length and four feet in diameter and weighed fifteen tons when loaded with liquid fuel. Based on the venerable Russian Scud-D, the Nodong could carry a one-ton payload nearly six hundred miles.

In the dank hold of the freighter, the shrouded rockets didn't lose any of their aura of menace or death. And knowing what was planned for two of these missiles deepened the resolve of the Corporation members.

The three men descended a set of metal stairs to the cargo hold's floor. Max Hanley, in the guise of the missile expert, stepped boldly to the first rocket. He barked at the government minders holding back at the hatchway and indicated that he wanted the plastic removed from the Nodongs.

General Kim arrived just as Max had removed an access panel from the first missile and was bent over the opening with a circuit tester. "I see you couldn't wait to inspect your newest weapons."

"They are formidable," Cabrillo replied for lack of anything else to say.

"Our experts have greatly improved on the old Soviet design, and the warheads are much more powerful."

"Which two are to be offloaded in Somalia?"

The North Korean repeated the question to one of the guards, who pointed out a pair of the rockets near the back of the hold. "Those two under the red plastic. Because of the primitive facilities available in Mogadishu, the warheads have already been mounted. Fuel for those two can be loaded from the tanks in the forward hold in order to meet the tight schedule for firing, provided you don't add the corrosive mixture too soon. Three days from Somalia is soon enough."

"I think one day is safer," Juan countered. He knew that Kim's statement had been a test of his knowledge of the missiles. Loading the liquid fuel three days before launch would cause it to dissolve the rocket's thin aluminum tanks and likely blow the *Asia Star* out of the water.

"Where is my head? Forgive me. Any more than one day would be disastrous." There was little warmth in Kim's apology.

Silently, Cabrillo hoped the general would remain on board when the missiles blew. Max Hanley called him over to see something within the Nodong's electronic brain. Hali Kasim stood at his other shoulder and for fifteen minutes the three men mutely stared into the tangle of wires and circuits. As they'd intended, they could hear Kim impatiently shifting his weight from foot to foot and muttering to himself. "Is there something the matter?" he finally asked.

"No, all seems in order," Cabrillo answered without turning.

They played the game again for another fifteen minutes. Occasionally Max would consult a detail from the plans he carried, but other than that, the men remained as statues.

"Is this really necessary, Colonel Hourani?" Kim asked with ill-disguised impatience.

Cabrillo ran a finger along his false mustache to make sure it was in place before turning. "I am sorry, General. Mr. Muhammad and Professor Khalidi are very thorough, although I believe once they satisfy themselves that the first missile is in working order, they will be quicker with the others."

Kim shot a look at his watch. "I can take this opportunity to attend to some paperwork in the captain's cabin. Why don't you find me when you have completed your inspection. These men will remain with you, should you need anything."

Juan suppressed a grin. "As you wish, General Kim."

The three members of the Corporation moved on to the second missile ten minutes later. The two guards had sat themselves on the stairs overlooking the hold. One smoked a continuous chain of cigarettes while the other watched the Arabs without seeming to blink. Both kept their suit jackets opened enough to reach their weapons. Kim might have grown bored with the operation, but the pair of secret policemen maintained their vigilance.

There was no set time to rendezvous with Eddie Seng. If everything had gone according to plan, he would have the minisub positioned a short way from the *Star*'s stern, close enough for the craft's sophisticated passive sonar to detect the sound of the three men hitting the water. The time constraint Juan felt came from his desire to get the *Oregon* as far into international waters as he could before first light.

Dawn was three hours away. He calculated the time it would take to board the minisub, make their escape from Yonghung-man Bay, and link up with the *Oregon*. From that point on, it would depend on the ship's magnetohydrodynamic engines, in which Cabrillo placed his full trust. The technology of using free electrons extracted from seawater to power the vessel was still in its experimental stages, but in the two years since taking delivery, the complex system of cryo-cooled magnets that generated power to feed pumps for her four pulse aqua jets had never let him down.

It was time. Cabrillo felt a slight twinge in his stomach, not fear exactly but a tension brought on by his old nemesis, Murphy's Law. It was almost a religion to him. He was a superb tactician and strategist, as well as a master planner, but he also recognized the vagaries of chance, an obstacle that can never be overcome entirely. The operation had gone smoothly to this point, which only increased the possibility of something fouling now.

He had no doubt they could maintain their ruse until the ship reached Somalia, where they could easily escape. But that would mean failure, another of Cabrillo's old adversaries, one he hated even more than Mr. Murphy's famous precept. But he knew that once they committed, there would be no turning back. If the dice fell the wrong way, he and Max and Hali would die. Eddie Seng might stand a chance to escape, but it wasn't likely. However, if Lady Luck held, in a couple of hours ten million dollars would appear in the Corporation's Cayman Island account courtesy of Uncle Sam's black budget.

Cabrillo tapped his watch, their prearranged signal, and suddenly the anxiety vanished. Juan went on automatic, relying on skills first learned in the ROTC, then honed at the CIA's training facility in rural Virginia before being perfected by fifteen years in the field.

Hali shifted his position slightly, blocking the guards' view of Hanley as Max snapped a hidden set of locks in his case. Juan turned from the missile, caught the eye of the guard with the nicotine addiction, and made a universal gesture of wanting to borrow one of his cigarettes. He started across the hold as the North Korean pulled a nearly depleted pack from his coat.

Out of view of the distracted guards, Max Hanley eased the bomb from the false bottom of his valise. The explosive device was smaller than a compact disc case, a marvel of miniaturization that packed the detonative force of a claymore mine.

Five feet from the staircase, the smoker got to his feet and descended to the deck level. Juan had banked on the man remaining seated next to his partner. Damn Murphy. He accepted the proffered cigarette and held it for the guard to light with his prized Zippo.

Juan took a measured drag, held the smoke in his mouth for a second, then exploded in a wrenching cough, as if the tobacco was harsher than he'd anticipated. The guard chuckled at Cabrillo's discomfort and flicked his attention to his partner to make a comment.

He never saw that Cabrillo's coughing fit had allowed him to torque his body like a coiled spring so when Juan threw the punch, it contained every ounce of strength in his six-foot-one-inch frame. The blow landed on the point of the guard's jaw and corkscrewed him to the deck as though he'd been shot. Juan couldn't believe the reflexes of the second guard. He'd anticipated at least two seconds for him to even realize what was happening.

Instead, the man was already up at the top of the short flight of steps and was just reaching into his shoulder holster when Cabrillo dove for him. Juan jumped for the stairs, reaching for the man's ankles. The automatic's barrel had just cleared the holster when Cabrillo's hands closed around the Korean's shins. Cabrillo fell heavily onto the steel steps, gashing his chin on a sharp edge, but his momentum pulled the North Korean off balance, sending him tumbling backward. The gun clattered onto the upper landing.

Cabrillo scrambled to his feet, blood running from his chin, adrenaline surging in his veins. Even if the Korean couldn't aim the pistol, the sound of a single shot would alert Kim and call an army of security guards to the vessel. Behind the grappling men, Max Hanley had raced to the missile destined to blast the holy city of Mecca. He had to set the bomb close enough to the warhead to cause a sympathetic detonation. Hali Kasim pulled a stiletto hidden in the binding of his Koran and ran for the stairs, knowing the fight would be over before reaching his boss, but making the effort nevertheless.

Juan tried to smash his elbow into the Korean's groin as he clawed his way up the stairs. The blow missed as the lithe guard twisted, and he felt his right arm go numb from the elbow down as it smashed into the deck plate. He cursed and managed to grab the man's right wrist just before his fingers curled around the gun. Even with his superior size and strength, Cabrillo was in an awkward position, and he felt the Korean draw closer to the weapon.

Hali was ten feet from the steps when the guard made a lunge for the pistol. Juan allowed himself to be thrown with the man's desperate grab, and his useless right arm arced like a pendulum into the side of the Korean's head, stunning him for a moment. The guard shook off the blow and kicked at Juan's right leg, slamming it against a railing. What sounded like the crack of broken bone echoed over the labored breathing of the combatants. The guard was sure the Syrian was finished and turned his attention back to getting the weapon. But Cabrillo wasn't even fazed. As the Korean grabbed the barrel of his pistol, Juan grasped his wrist and smashed it repeatedly against the deck. On the third blow the automatic flew from his grip and bounced down the steps. Hali scooped it up, mounted the stairs three at a time, and clipped the guard on the side of the head with the butt. The Korean's eyes fluttered, and he was out.

"You okay, boss?" Kasim asked, helping Cabrillo to his feet.

Max bounded up the stairs with the speed of a man half his age. "Ask him later. Bomb's ticking, and we have fifteen minutes."

Familiar with all manner of ships, the three men ran unerringly to the main deck where they paused for just a moment to make sure there were no guards patrolling the area. They could see the sleek destroyer in the middle of the bay, her turret-mounted 100 mm guns trained on the outer harbor. There was no one on deck, so the three rushed to the railing and unceremoniously tossed themselves overboard.

The water was cold and tasted like kerosene soup. Max spat a mouthful as he slid his robe over his head. Beneath it he wore a pair of swim trunks and a tight thermal top. Juan struggled out of his boots but left his uniform on. He'd grown up in the surf of Southern California and was as comfortable in the water as on dry land. Hali, the youngest of the assault team, shed his jacket and kicked off his brogans, forcing them under the black surface. They swam silently to the ship's fantail and ducked under her curved hull so as not to be spotted from above.

There was a balance between speed and stealth. Eddie could have kept the thirty-two-foot Discovery 1000 submerged, and the men could have cycled through the airlock, a time-consuming process even in the best circumstance. Juan had decided that Eddie should broach the sub so the men could climb through her topside hatch. They would be visible for no more than thirty seconds, and surfacing near the acoustical clutter of waves striking the *Asia Star*'s idle prop and rudder would mask any sounds from Korean detection gear.

The wait was no more than a minute before bubbles erupted directly astern of the *Asia Star*. They were in motion even before the minisub's flat upperworks broke through the waves. Hali reached the sub first and swung himself aboard. He was working the hatch cover as water sluiced off the sub's matte-black hull. The seal broke with an audible hiss, and he threw himself down into the dark confines of the sub, followed closely by Max and Juan. Cabrillo and Max had the hatch resealed an instant later, working by feel more than sight, since the only light in the Discovery 1000 came from the faint glow of electronics in the forward cockpit.

Juan hit a switch midway up a bulkhead, and a pair of red blackout lights snapped on. The Discovery wasn't designed to dive much below a hundred feet and could operate for no more than twenty-four hours without recharging and replacing the CO_2 filters. For this mission her seating for eight had been removed to make room for racks of batteries, bulky industrial boxes joined with a snaking nest of wiring conduits. Crates of filters were crammed in the other available spaces as well as provisions for Eddie Seng. A chemical toilet sat amid a clutter of empty food cartons. The air was heavy with humidity and carried a locker room funk.

Eddie had been alone on the sub since launching off the *Oregon* fifteen days earlier. With the harbor ringed with underwater listening stations and routinely swept with active sonar, it had taken that long for Seng to drift into the heavily defended port. He had grounded the sub during the slight ebb tide and allowed her to drift when the tidal surge washed into the harbor, only chancing to run the electric motors under the cover of an inbound ship or patrol boat. There was no other way to get the sub into the naval base without being detected.

While there were other sub drivers among the *Oregon* crew, as director of Shore Operations, Eddie wouldn't let anyone else take the risk. Seng was another veteran of the CIA, although Juan hadn't known him when they were in the Agency. He'd spent most of his career working the Middle East, while Eddie had been attached to the American embassy in Beijing running several successful spy networks. Budget and policy shifts following September 11 had seen him transferred to a stateside desk. Still hungry for what he called "the teeth of the trade," Seng had joined the Corporation and quickly established himself as an indispensable member.

Cabrillo crawled over batteries and empty crates and slid into the copilot's seat to Eddie's right. Eddie's black hair was lank from going so long without washing, and stubble marred his otherwise sharp features. The emotional and physical strain of the past two weeks had dimmed his normally bright eyes.

"Hiya, boss." Seng grinned. Nothing could diminish his easygoing charm. "Welcome aboard."

"Thanks," Juan said, noting that the sub had already descended to thirty feet. "The clock's ticking, so set a course out of the harbor and punch it. We've got eleven minutes."

The Discovery's motors ramped up, and the single prop bit into the water. There was nothing they could do about the noise. They had to get as far from the *Asia Star* as possible, because water does not compress, making the coming shock wave doubly brutal.

Cabrillo kept his eyes on the sub's sonar, and only a minute after they began pulling away from the doomed freighter there was contact. "Mr. Murphy's rearing his ugly head."

"What do you have?" Hanley stood just behind Juan and leaned over his shoulder.

The computer analyzed the acoustical signal, and Cabrillo read the grim facts. "Sinpo-class patrol boat. Crew of twelve. Armed with a pair of 37 mm autocannons and tilt racks for depth charges. Top speed is forty knots, and our contact is already churning twenty and headed straight for us."

Eddie turned to Juan. "It's routine. They've been doing this ever since I entered the harbor. Every couple of hours a single patrol boat races along the dock. I think they're searching for sailors trying to jump ship."

"If he maintains his course, he's going to pass right over us."

"Does that class of boats carry sonar?" Max asked.

Juan checked the computer again. "Doesn't say."

"What do you want me to do?" Eddie's voice remained calm and professional. "Keep running, or settle onto the bottom and let him pass?"

Cabrillo checked his watch again. They'd traveled little more than a quarter mile. Too close. "Keep going. If he hears us or detects our wake, he's going to have to slow and turn back to try to find us again. We only need six minutes."

A moment later the four men inside the minisub could hear the thrash of the patrol boat's props through the water, an angry sound that rose in pitch as the craft drew closer. As it roared overhead the din filled the hull, and the men waited expectantly to hear if it would come back for another pass. The moment stretched as time turned elastic. Max and

Hali let out their breaths as the patrol boat continued on. Cabrillo kept his eyes glued to the sonar screen.

"They're turning," he remarked a second later. "Coming back for another look. Hali, check the radio, see if he's transmitting." Hali Kasim headed the *Oregon*'s communications division and could play radios like a concert pianist.

The communications suite aboard the *Oregon* was sophisticated enough to scan and record a thousand frequencies per second and had a language program that could translate fast enough for an operator to hold a conversation close enough to real time to fool most listeners. With the Discovery 1000's limited electronics they would be lucky just to pick up a broadcast, and since none of the men spoke Korean, they wouldn't know if the patrol craft was asking permission to depth charge or commenting on the weather.

"I'm not getting anything," Kasim answered after a few moments.

The North Korean patrol boat crossed over the minisub again, and the men heard her engines throttle back.

"They're pacing us," Eddie said.

The powerful sonar picked up a pair of splashes too small to be depth charges. Juan knew immediately what was about to happen. "Brace yourselves!"

The grenades were knockoffs of the Soviet RGD-5, and while they only contained four ounces of high explosives, the water amplified their explosive power. The two grenades went off nearly simultaneously just yards behind the Discovery. The sub pitched up by the stern, knocking Hali Kasim against a bank of batteries. Eddie fought to bring her nose up as the murky bottom suddenly loomed outside the large acrylic view port. With their ears ringing, no one heard a second pair of grenades hit the water. They blew just above the minisub, slamming her into the mud just as Eddie got her on an even keel. Billows of silt exploded around the Discovery, cutting visibility to zero. Electricity arced and snapped from a loose connection in dazzlingly bright flashes that temporarily blinded the men.

Eddie quickly powered down the sub to give Max a chance to fix the connection. By the glow of a miniature flashlight clamped between his teeth, the engineer worked to bypass the affected row of batteries, but the damage had been done. The flashes of electricity could be seen from the surface through the sub's portholes and looked like an eerie blue glow from the depths.

"They've got us now," Hali said. "They're transmitting something. Just a short message, but I think the jig is up."

"How's it coming, Max?" Cabrillo inquired with no more concern than if he were asking when coffee would be ready.

"Just a few more seconds."

"Anything from shore yet, Hali?"

"Negative. The brass must be mulling over the report from the patrol boat."

"Got it," Max announced. "Eddie, turn her back on."

Eddie Seng hit a button, and the display screens lit with their muted glimmer.

"Okay, Eddie, emergency blow. Bring us to the surface."

"The patrol boat's right above us, boss."

Cabrillo's response was a dark smile.

"There goes our warranty," Eddie muttered, then blew ballast from the Discovery's tanks with compressed air. The little sub seemed to launch itself from the bottom. He watched the depth gauge and called out the numbers. When he said there were only five feet of water over the Disco's top deck, all four men instinctively ducked lower in their seats.

The steel hull slammed into the underside of the North Korean craft with a deafening screech. The sub was several tons lighter than the patrol boat, but her upward momentum tipped the Koreans until their starboard rail was in the water. One crewman had his legs crushed when he was pitched over the side by a rolling fuel drum. Juan reached across Eddie and punched the command for a crash dive before the upper deck broke the surface.

High-speed pumps filled the ballast tanks in under fifteen seconds, and the Discovery dropped like a stone.

"That ought to keep 'em busy for a few minutes." Max said.

"We only need a few. Okay everyone, get your earphones on and strap in."

The men donned bulky headsets that they jacked into a piece of electronics specially installed for the mission. Built by Sound Answers, the experimental noise-canceling device took in sound waves, evaluated their frequency and amplitude, and played back the exact opposite sound, nullifying 99 percent of the decibels. Such devices, once perfected and miniaturized, would soon make it possible for silent vacuum cleaners and end the anxiety of listening to a dentist's drill.

ABOARD the *Asia Star* one of the North Korean spies sent to guard the Syrians had come to. He wasted precious seconds checking on his partner. The lump where he'd been clipped with the pistol was as tight as a drum. The man wouldn't awaken. The guard knew his duty. He ran from the hold, shouting at the top of his lungs, ignoring the pain it caused in his head. He ran up to the main deck, checking doors along the corridor behind the bridge until he found the captain's. He considered knocking, but what he had to report was too important. He burst through the door. General Kim was on the telephone.

"And then what will you do to my little lotus?" Kim snapped to his feet when the door crashed against the cabin wall. He roared, "What is the meaning of this?"

"General," the guard panted. "The Syrians, they attacked us. I did not see them in the hold. I think they might be trying to escape."

"Escape? Escape what?" Kim no sooner asked those questions when he realized the answer. He cut the connection to his mistress, pounding on the Reset lever to alert the shore operator. "Come on, you damned thing," he cursed, then addressed the guard. "They weren't Syrians; they were American saboteurs. Search the hold for a bomb."

Finally a voice sounded in the telephone. Kim knew that even if he died, getting a warning out would make sure the Americans would pay for their treachery. "This is General Kim aboard the *Asia Star*—"

At the back corner of the hold, Max's bomb wound down to zero.

The bomb blast tore through the missile where it had been hidden and an instant later caused a secondary explosion of the warhead. Overpressure built inside the hold until the four-ton hatches blew into the night sky as though a volcano had erupted. The *Star*'s old hull plates split at their welds like peels from an orange as the tons of rocket fuel stored in her forward hold detonated.

The ship disintegrated.

A seven-hundred-foot wedge of the concrete dock shattered, and chunks of it were thrown miles inland. The two massive loading cranes along the wharf toppled into the water, and every window along the harbor was blown to pieces. Then the shock wave spread. Warehouses were blown flat for a quarter mile, and those farther away were stripped of their siding so only their skeletal steel frames remained upright. The concussion stripped the first six feet of water from the bay and piled it into a wave that slammed the destroyer lying at anchor, breaking her keel and capsizing her so fast that none of her harbor watch had time to react.

Night turned to day as the fireball climbed to eleven hundred feet, and sheets of rocket fuel fell like burning rain, setting fires all around the navy yard, while bits of the *Asia Star*'s hull scythed through the base like shrapnel, leveling buildings and wrecking vehicles.

The concussion plucked the floundering patrol boat from the sea and sent it tumbling across the surface of the bay, rolling it like a log down a mountainside. With each revolution more of her upperworks tore free. First it was her fore gun mounts, then the pair of .50 calibers at her stern, and finally her small cabin came apart, leaving just her hull to barrel roll atop the waves.

The noise dampener did its job, but still the concussion wave rang through the Discovery 1000 as though she was a bell. The whole hull shook as the shock wave passed over and the plucky little sub lurched forward, then ebbed violently, straining the safety straps and scattering loose equipment from storage bins. Eardrums were brutally assaulted by the blast, and had it not been for the counterfrequencies channeled into the headsets, the four men would have been permanently deafened.

As it was, Cabrillo had to shout at the top of his lungs to inquire about his men. Eddie and Hali were unscathed, but Max had taken a bump on the head from a falling battery. The skin hadn't broken, and he hadn't been knocked out. He'd suffer a headache for a while, and it would take days for the knot already forming to subside.

"All right, Eddie, take us home."

The minisub slipped out of the harbor undetected and was two miles from the coast before they picked up helicopters thundering toward Wonsan. The choppers were flying too high and too fast to be ASW (antisubmarine warfare) birds. They were most likely rescue helos ferrying medical supplies and personnel to the devastated base.

Like all other coastal nations on earth, North Korea was afforded twelve miles of ocean as sovereign territory. Just to play it safe, Juan Cabrillo had scheduled the rendezvous for twenty miles out, a long slog in the reeking confines of the Discovery that took nearly three hours longer than planned. The Discovery had to stay deep as dawn approached in case the North Koreans did send out aerial reconnaissance.

At last they came to the spot of ocean, and Eddie eased the craft up from eighty feet where she'd remained hidden. The underside of the *Oregon*'s hull was coated with red antifouling paint and loomed over the small sub. Juan noted with pride that the hull was clear of barnacles and looked as new as the day he'd taken possession of her. In order to take advantage of the tremendous power generated by her revolutionary engines, the *Oregon* utilized an MDV design as perfected by high-speed European express ferries. Her monohull, deep V arrangement allowed her to knife through the seas at unheard-of speeds. To maintain stability she sported several retractable T-foils and fins, undersea wings that kept her planing smoothly at up to forty knots. Beyond that speed the wings produced too much drag. They were drawn back to the hull, and the crew had to strap themselves in like offshore hydroplane racers.

Eddie grabbed a device the size and shape of a garage door remote, pointed it up at the *Oregon*, and pressed the single button.

Splitting at the keel, a pair of eighty-foot-long doors hinged downward. Bright light from inside the ship filtered through the water and bathed the underside of the ship in a green glow. Eddie nudged the thrusters and adjusted the ballast, centering the Discovery in the opening. He held station just below the hull as two men in scuba gear jumped from inside the ship and attached lift cables to hardpoints fore and aft. The minisub and its larger sister, a Nomad 1000 also kept aboard the *Oregon*, could surface directly into the moon pool, but the maneuver was risky and used only in emergencies.

The frogman swam in front of the view port and gave Eddie and Juan a wave, then slashed his hand across his neck. Eddie killed the motors. A second later the sub lurched, then began to rise smoothly into the flooded moon pool. As it cleared the surface, Seng opened valves so the ballast tanks could drain.

Juan spotted Julia Huxley, the *Oregon*'s medical officer, standing at the edge of the pool with a pair of orderlies. He shot her a thumbs-up, and her concerned frown turned into a smile. She'd joined the Corporation after a career in the navy, finishing with a four-year stint as the chief medical officer at San Diego Naval Base. Under her lab coat, the five-foot-three-inch Julia was curvaceous without running to fat. He rarely saw her dark hair out of a ponytail, and the only makeup she used was to highlight her soft, dark eyes.

The overhead crane lowered the sub onto a cradle, and a workman clambered on top to crank open the outer hatch. When it finally released, the crew inside heard him gasp. "Whoa."

"Try being sealed inside for two weeks," Eddie called, pulling himself from his seat. He'd already unzipped the front of his jumpsuit in preparation for his first shower in fifteen days. His chest and stomach were so lean that individual muscle fibers were visible. Eddie was built like famed martial artist Bruce Lee, and like Lee was a master in several Eastern fighting techniques.

Juan allowed his men to precede him out, but as soon as he'd taken his first deep breaths he called to a sailor nearby, "Get these doors closed, and contact Eric in the control room. Have him set a course due east, say twenty knots. As long as the threat board remains green, there's no need to draw attention to ourselves by opening her up." Eric Stone was a control room operator, the ship's best, and the only man Juan wanted at the helm during critical operations.

"Aye, sir."

When the doors were closed, pumps came online to drain the moon pool, and workers laid decking grilles over the hole. Technicians were already assessing the damage caused when the Discovery rammed the patrol boat, while others were bringing gallon jugs of bleach to sanitize the interior.

Julia approached Juan when he came down the ladder from the top of the minisub. "We heard the explosion out here, so I don't need to ask how it went."

"You don't sound too happy about it." Juan stripped off his Colonel Hourani uniform coat.

"Just bored, Mr. Chairman. Other than a few strained muscles, I haven't had much to do in months."

Juan smiled. "I thought that was a good thing for a doctor."

"For a doctor, yes; for an employee, it's dullsville."

"Come on, Julia, you know us. Give it a few days or a week, and we'll get into some sort of trouble."

Cabrillo would soon regret those words. In just ninety-six hours, Dr. Julia Huxley was going to be literally up to her elbows in work.

4

"COME," Cabrillo called at the sharp knock on his cabin's door.

The *Oregon* was safely beyond the range of all but North Korea's best fighter jets and, according to intercepted communications, it seemed unlikely any would be scrambled before the vessel was outside their range, too. He had allowed himself an hour-long soak in the copper Jacuzzi tub in the adjoining bathroom and was just finishing getting dressed. Not one to stand on formalities aboard ship, he wore cotton trousers and an open-neck shirt.

Unlike his Colonel Hourani disguise, and despite his Hispanic name and background, Juan Cabrillo's eyes were blue, and his spiky hair was white-blond from a youth spent in the sun and surf. His features, too, looked more Anglo than Latin, with an aristocratic nose and a mouth forever poised at a smile from some joke only he knew. But there was a hard edge to Cabrillo, one formed over years of facing danger. While he masked it well, people meeting him for the first time could still detect an intangible quality that commanded immediate respect.

Linda Ross, the Corporation's newly promoted vice president of Operations, stepped through the door, a clipboard held against her chest. Linda was another navy veteran, having spent time as an intelligence officer aboard an Aegis cruiser followed by a stint at the Pentagon. Trim and athletic, Linda possessed a soft-spoken demeanor and a razor-sharp mind. When Richard Truitt, the Corporation's former VP, unexpectedly resigned after the Sacred Stone affair, Cabrillo and Hanley knew that Linda was the only one who could fill Dick's shoes.

She paused at the door, mesmerized by the sight of Juan adjusting his prosthetic right leg and rolling down his pants cuff. He slid into a pair of Italian moccasin-style boat shoes. It wasn't that she wasn't aware of the fake limb, but it was always a shock to see it, since Cabrillo never seemed bothered that he was missing a leg below the knee.

Cabrillo spoke without looking up. "On the *Asia Star,* a North Korean guard smashed the leg against a railing and cracked the plastic. He was sure surprised when I kept fighting with what he assumed was a broken shin."

"You just proved North Korean propaganda," Linda said with a low chuckle.

"How's that?"

"That we Americans are just robots of our imperialist government."

They shared a laugh. "So what's been happening since we left for Afghanistan?" he asked.

"Do you recall Hiroshi Katsui?"

It took Cabrillo a moment to place the name. "Hiro? God, I haven't thought about him since UCLA. His father was the first billionaire I ever met. Big shipping family. Hiro was the only guy on campus with a Lamborghini. I will give him this, though; the wealth never went to his head. He was real down to earth and generous to a fault."

"Through some cutouts he approached us representing a consortium of shipping owners in these waters. In the past ten months or so, piracy has been on the rise from the Sea of Japan all the way down to the South China Sea."

"That's a problem usually confined to coastal waters and the Strait of Malacca," Cabrillo interrupted.

"Where natives in small boats attack yachts or board freighters to make off with whatever they can handle," Linda agreed. "It's a billion dollar a year enterprise and growing every year. But what's happening around Malaysia and Indonesia is nothing more than thugs mugging old ladies on darkened streets compared to what's been happening farther to the north."

Cabrillo crossed to his desk and removed a cheroot from an inlaid box. He listened to Ross as he prepared the fine-leafed Cuban cigar and lit it with a gold and onyx Dunhill.

"What your friend Hiro is reporting sounds more like the bad old days of the mob hijacking trucks at Kennedy Airport. The pirates are well-armed, well-trained, and highly motivated. They are also as brutal as hell. Four ships have vanished completely. No sign of the crew at all. The most recent was a tanker owned by your friend's company, the *Toya Maru*. Several others have been hit with significant, and I might add unnecessary, loss of life since none of the crew reported putting up any resistance."

"What are the pirates taking?"

"Sometimes the ship's payroll." It was customary for cargo ships to carry enough cash to pay their crews at the end of a voyage in case some men didn't wish to continue on. To Cabrillo this sounded like overkill for fifteen or twenty thousand dollars. "Other times they take shipping containers, transferring them to their own vessels, which, from the sketchy descriptions, sound like converted fishing trawlers mounted with cranes. And like I said, sometimes entire ships just disappear."

Juan let that sink in, watching jets of smoke bloom against the teak coffered ceiling where he blew them. "And Hiro and his consortium want us to put a stop to it?"

Linda glanced at her clipboard. "His words are, 'Make them pay like a quarterback facing the Raiders defense.' "

Cabrillo smiled, recalling Hiro's fondness for American football and especially for the Raiders when they played in L.A. Then his smile faded. Because of the Corporation's structure, each crew member was an owner, their percentages determined by their rank and years of service. Dick Truitt's unexpected retirement had put a dent in the Corporation's cash reserves. The timing couldn't have been worse, because the Corporation was heavily invested in a real estate deal in Rio de Janeiro that wouldn't show a return for another two months. He could bail out of the deal now, but the expected profits were too great to ignore. The just-finished job for Langston Overholt would cover what Dick was entitled to, but that left Cabrillo in a bit of a cash crunch to keep up with payments on the *Oregon,* insurance for his people, and all the other myriad expenses that any company must meet month to month. Just because they operated outside the law didn't mean he could avoid the financial realities of a capitalistic world.

"What are they offering?"

Linda consulted her clipboard once again. "One hundred thousand a week for a minimum of eight weeks and a maximum of sixteen, plus a million dollars for each pirate ship we destroy."

Cabrillo's frown deepened. The pay structure would cover expenses, barely. What bothered him was that by agreeing, he was stuck for two months and would be unable to take off if something more lucrative should arise. But it did buy him the time he needed before his Brazilian investment paid out, and once that was in, the Corporation would be deep into the black once again. Also, Juan held every mariner's contempt for piracy and would like nothing more than to help put an end to the scourge of the sea.

From reports he'd read, he knew that modern-day pirates bore no resemblance to the swashbuckling legends of old. There were no more bearded captains with eye patches and parrots on their shoulders. Today's pirates, at least the ones he'd read about operating in the Straits of Malacca, were usually poor fishermen armed with whatever they could scrounge. They attacked at night and vanished just as quickly, taking whatever they could carry in their dugouts and pirogues. There had been murders, surely, but nothing on the scale Linda described.

Juan had always harbored a fear that one day a leader would come along to organize pirates the way Lucky Luciano had formed Murder Inc., turning a ragtag band of criminals into a well-oiled machine. Had that day come? Had a mastermind entered the picture, convincing others that by organizing they could double or triple their profits, and elevated piracy to an act as deadly as terrorism? It certainly wasn't inconceivable. And as he sat at his desk, Cabrillo wondered if the two weren't linked. In the years since 9/11, terrorist funding had dried up over much of the world. It was possible, no, he thought, it was likely that groups like Al-Qaeda would turn to piracy and other illegal enterprises to fill their war chests once again.

That link cinched it for him. It was true that Cabrillo and his crew did a great deal of covert work for the U.S. government. This would be one of those times that a private sector operation would also benefit American interests and save Uncle Sam from picking up the tab. He turned his gaze back to his VP of Operations. "Did he say how many pirate ships they suspect are operating out there?"

"There are no firm numbers, but they're believed to have at least four converted trawlers because of distances and the timing of some of the attacks."

That would translate into four million dollars. It sounded like a great deal of money, but Cabrillo knew well just how quickly the Corporation could eat up that sum. If they'd done structural damage to the Disco minisub, a replacement would set them back two million dollars. He considered the proposal for another moment. "Contact Hiroshi, tell him we'll take on the contract with two provisions. Number one is that the bonus for each ship sunk is two million and that we reserve the right to sever the contract at our discretion with one day's notice." A single ship-to-ship missile from the *Oregon*'s launcher cost just under a million dollars. "Then get in touch with Overholt at Langley and tell him what we're up to and let him know I'll have a detailed after-action report to him in a couple of days."

"What about Eddie Seng?" Eddie had been promised two weeks' vacation for having to endure the same amount of time locked in the minisub.

Cabrillo flicked on the plasma monitor on his desk and moused through a few screens before finding the one that showed the *Oregon*'s location. He calculated distances and the range of the Robinson R-44 helicopter stowed in a concealed hangar under an aft hatch. "We can fly him to Seoul sometime tomorrow. He can catch a commercial flight from there."

"That's not the problem. He told Julia that he doesn't want to leave."

Juan wasn't surprised. "You can lead a man to vacation; you can't make him relax."

"I'm just concerned that he's pushing himself too far. He's been through hell since we cut him loose two weeks ago."

As chairman, Juan Cabrillo was the only member of the Corporation to know every detail of his crew's files. He wondered if he'd be breaking a confidence by telling Linda how back in his CIA days Eddie had spent two months under double cover, first as a Taiwanese traitor eager to sell the Red Chinese information about Taiwan's military disposition along the Formosa Strait and then as a counterspy with the ultimate goal of discrediting the group of Chinese generals who had bought his information. He'd pulled off the coup brilliantly, and four of China's best battlefield commanders were transferred to an outpost in the Gobi Desert while the government wasted millions of dollars building fortifications for an invasion that would never come. It had been his last mission before his transfer to Washington. Juan left the story untold and merely said, "If Eddie wants to stay on board, I'm not going to argue with him."

"Okay."

"Did Hiro provide details of the attacks?"

"His communiqué said that he'd transmit them if we took the assignment."

"As soon as they arrive get Mark Murphy and Eric Stone working on a computer model of where the pirates are likely to strike next and have them come up with a cover story to make us sound like a juicy target." Young Murph was the *Oregon*'s weapons specialist and a dogged researcher with an uncanny eye for pattern recognition.

Linda made notes on her clipboard. "Anything else?"

"That should do it. Once Mark and Eric have their position, set a course and get under way."

Cabrillo finished his cigar while working on his report to Langston Overholt, deciding to get it over with now rather than prolong the tedium. As the cheroot burned down to a stub, he dumped the report into an encryption program as powerful as those used by the NSA and e-mailed it to his old friend at CIA headquarters. Still buzzing with adrenaline and despite lunch being served in the main dining room, he decided to take a tour of the ship.

From her gleaming engine room where the magnetohydrodynamic engines purred to her high-tech operations center located below the bridge where just about every wall was covered in plasma screens, and through her multiple weapons bays, Magic Shop, armory, hangar, and the lavish crew accommodation areas, he skulked his ship, greeting crewmen as he roamed. He visited the stainless steel galley where a team of Le Cordon Bleu chefs prepared meals fit for the finest restaurants of New York or Paris. He looked in on the spa with its ranks of exercise machines and free weights as well as the popular saunas. He laid a hand on one of the four black Sun/Microsystem supercomputers, sensing its raw power and knowing no problem was too complex for it and its operators.

He was fully aware that every detail, each inch of wiring and ductwork, her deck layout, and even her interior color scheme had been born in his mind and transformed into steel and plastic and wood on his order. The *Oregon* was both his castle and his refuge.

But what gave him the most pride was the moment he stepped out onto the deck. For it was outside that the *Oregon* showed off what made her the greatest espionage platform ever devised. The Russians had been too slavish at disguising spy ships as trawlers, making them somewhat a cliché whenever they arrived off a coastline. The U.S. Navy made use of undetectable submarines for their spy operations, an impossible option for what Cabrillo and his crew did. No, the Corporation needed anonymity at the very least or outright ridicule at best.

For that reason from the outside the MV *Oregon* looked like a derelict on borrowed time from the breaker's yard.

Juan had entered the ship's bridge using the elevator in the operations center located just below the main deck. From there he'd stepped out onto the starboard wing bridge and surveyed his ship. The *Oregon* was 560 feet long, 75 wide, and had a gross tonnage of 11,585. Her superstructure stood a little aft of amidships, so she carried three cargo cranes fore and a pair of them aft. The cranes were rusted wrecks festooned with frayed cables, and two of them actually worked. The deck was a scabrous patchwork of rust and various colors of marine paint. Her rails sagged dangerously in places, and several of her cargo hatches appeared sprung. Oil had leaked from drums stowed along the front of the wheelhouse into a gooey slick, and rusted husks of machinery lay scattered about, everything from broken winches to a bicycle with no tires. Looking along the outer hull, Cabrillo saw smears of rust below every scupper, and steel plates that had been welded as if to cover cracks. The hull's main color was a turbid green, but there were splashes of brown, black, and midnight blue.

He threw his customary one-fingered salute at the Iranian flag on the stern jackstaff before glancing around the bridge. The once-polished deck was scarred and littered with cigarette burns. The windows were coated with equal mixtures of grime and salt, while her consoles were coated in dust. The brass of the engine telegraph was so tarnished it looked black and was missing one indicator needle. Some of her electronics, such as her navigation aids, were old enough to be museum displays. Behind the bridge was a chart room littered with poorly folded maps and a radio with no more than a few miles' range.

The crew's accommodations in the superstructure were also in disarray. Not a bed was made in any of the cabins, and not a single piece of crockery or silverware matched in the filthy galley. Cabrillo was especially proud of the captain's cabin. The room reeked of cheap cigarettes and was decorated with tacky velvet paintings of sad-faced clowns with liquid, mournful eyes. In the desk was a bottle of South American Scotch laced with syrup of ipecac and two glasses that had never been cleaned. The adjoining bathroom was dirtier than a men's room in a West Texas roadhouse.

All this detail was designed to encourage inspectors, harbor officials, and pilots to get off the *Oregon* as quickly as possible and ask the fewest questions. The record for the shortest stay so far went to a customs inspector in Cape Town who refused to even step foot on the ship's wobbly gangway. The wheel and the engine telegraph could, with computer assistance, maneuver the ship and operate her engines. This was for the benefit of harbor pilots and those who guided the freighter on her trips through the Panama Canal, but the vessel was actually run from a digitized workstation in the state-of-the-art operations center.

It was her dilapidated condition that allowed the *Oregon* to enter any port in the world without drawing attention. She was quickly overlooked as just another tramp steamer slowly rusting away as ocean commerce turned to containerization. Anyone who knew ships could tell that her owners had pretty much written off their vessel and no longer replaced worn-out machinery or even sprang for a few gallons of paint. And when the need arose, her crew could appear as decrepit as their ship.

A noise disturbed Cabrillo's inspection. Max Hanley rode up the elevator from the op center and joined him on the wing bridge. Max had scrubbed the makeup from his face, revealing a florid complexion and a bulbous nose. He wore coveralls, and Juan suspected he'd gone straight from a shower to inspect his engines. The wind danced through Hanley's sparse auburn hair as the two enjoyed a companionable silence.

"Thinking about Truitt?" Max finally asked. Juan hadn't spoken much of their partner's retirement.

Juan turned so his back was to the sea and rested both elbows against the fore rail. He had to squint against the bright glare reflecting off the waves. "I was just walking around, touring the ship," he said after a moment, "feeling mighty pleased with what we've accomplished."

"But?"

"But the *Oregon* is a means to an end. Dick knew that, and for a few years I thought he believed in it the way you and I do."

"And now you're doubting that, and doubting Dick Truitt, because he pulled stakes and hit the road."

"I thought so at first, but now I think I'm doubting myself and our mission."

Max slowly filled a pipe and lit it, shielding his match from the wind as he considered his friend's response. "I'll tell you what I think is going on. We've been working for a few years now, squirreling away money with each assignment. We all knew there was a pot of gold at the end of the rainbow, only now with Dick's retirement we both got to see just how big it was. He's cashing out to the tune of forty-five million dollars, tax free. I'm worth even more than that, and you've accumulated even more than me. It's hard to ignore that kind of money when you're putting your butt on the line for an ideal and a paycheck."

Juan said, "A big paycheck."

Max conceded the point. "True. Let me ask you, when you were doing duty for the CIA, twisting in the wind in places like Amman and Nicaragua, did you do it for a measly GS-17 salary and a government pension?"

"No," Cabrillo said sincerely. "I would have done it for free."

"Then why feel guilty that we're making good money now, doing what you used to do for a pittance and having the power to turn down operations we don't feel right about? You couldn't do that working for Langley or when the pressure came down from the Pentagon E-ring. They said jump, and you landed in the shit." The outermost ring of the

Defense Department building was the home to all the top brass and their civilian overseers.

Cabrillo opened his mouth to reply, but Max continued speaking. "Actually seeing that we've got enough money to retire to a private island someplace and live the good life has made you understand just how much we risk every day. You and I have always put our lives on the line. It's what makes us who we are. Only now we both know our lives are worth a little more than we thought."

"And our mission?"

"You have to ask? We're the last line of defense, my boy. We agree to the jobs Langley and the E-ringers need done but can't touch. The gloves have come off in the twenty-first century, and we've become the iron fist."

Cabrillo absorbed the words before asking with a smirk, "When did you become such a poet?"

Hanley grinned as if he'd been caught. "That actually just sort of came out. Sounded damn impressive, if you ask me." He turned serious once again. "Listen, Juan, what we do is important, and I for one am not going to feel guilty because we're getting rich doing it. There's no shame in profit, only in failure.

"And as for doubting Dick Truitt, you can forget about it. Dick put a lot of sweat and blood into the Corporation. He was there at the beginning and believed just as strongly as you and I. But he'd reached his limit. He'd had enough. Him leaving wasn't about the money; it was about Dick listening to that little voice inside his head that we all have, and it was saying he'd run his course with us. You can best believe, though, that Dick Truitt hasn't given up the fight. I wouldn't be surprised if he poured his money and expertise into a security company or intelligence think tank. I bet—"

Max stopped in midsentence. He'd noticed the spark in Cabrillo's eye and the crooked, almost piratical smile that played along his lips. As always, Juan Cabrillo had been one step head of his corporate president. Juan had been testing Max, getting a sense of how he felt about Truitt's leaving. Cabrillo had never doubted his mission or himself, but this was a pivotal time for the Corporation, and Juan needed to make certain Hanley was still 100 percent behind their goals. Juan had set the trap perfectly by acting unsure, and Max had wandered blindly in. This was why no one played poker with the chairman.

"You're a crafty one." Max said with a throaty chuckle.

Just then, a high-pitched hiss sounded from the *Oregon*'s water line. They peered over the rail. Special tanks along her outer hull were filling with seawater to ballast down the tramp freighter and make her look like her holds were full. Juan looked along her wake line and detected a subtle change in course. The long line of white on the otherwise empty sea arced ever so slightly to the east.

"Murph and Stone must have found the spot of ocean for us to play staked goat," Max said offhandedly and checked the time on an old pocket watch looped with a chain to his coveralls.

Cabrillo thought about the awesome arsenal of weapons secreted about the *Oregon* and the men and women trained to use them. "Staked tiger, my old friend, staked tiger."

A day later the *Oregon* reached the grid that Mark Murphy and Eric Stone had calculated would be the most likely to attract the pirates. Hiro Katsui had agreed to Cabrillo's negotiations, replying, "It takes a pirate to catch a pirate. Good hunting." And he had transmitted everything his consortium had on the recent attacks. Murphy and Stone had dissected the information, finding commonalties in the attacks overlooked until now. They cross-referenced weather, the phases of the moon, size of the ships, cargo manifests, crew numbers, and a dozen other factors to find a spot in the Sea of Japan where it was most likely the pirates would attack the *Oregon*.

A legend had been created concerning the ship and her cargo and was hacked into various databases in case that was how the pirates found their marks. The ship was purportedly carrying a mixed cargo of timber and electronics from Pusan to Nigata, Japan, but what made her a tempting target was the presence of a passenger on her manifest, an eccentric American author who wrote while tramping around the globe on cargo ships.

Richard Hildebrand was a real person, and his fondness for working at sea was well documented in the media. He was currently working on his next best seller aboard a supertanker deadheading back to the Persian Gulf from Rotterdam, a detail the Corporation doubted the pirates would verify. Between book royalties and the price his books commanded in Hollywood, Hildebrand was one of the wealthiest writers in the world and ripe for kidnapping. While the pirates had yet to attempt such an act, Murph and Stone, with Juan agreeing, believed snatching Hildebrand was a logical escalation of their criminal activities.

In case they wouldn't risk ransoming a hostage, Murph and Stone had also listed the *Oregon*'s complement at fifty-seven, large by the standards of modern merchantmen, and to the pirates she'd be a tempting target because of the correspondingly large payroll in the ship's safe.

The sunset's palette of reds and rose and purple had been made even more spectacular by the volcanic ash pumped into the atmosphere by an erupting volcano far to the north on the Kamchatka Peninsula. Now the bloodred moon cast a hellish reflection off the calm sea while the stars had dimmed to pricks. The crew was at battle stations. Julia Huxley and her staff were ready in the medical bay to treat anything from a wood sliver to multiple gunshot wounds. The ship's armaments were primed and ready in their concealed redoubts. Like the German K-boats of World War One, plates along each side of the *Oregon*'s hull could be lowered to reveal 120 mm cannons utilizing the same fire control and ranging system as found on the M-1A1 Abrams tank. She also carried three 20 mm radar-controlled multibarrel Gatling guns. Each weapon could pump out three thousand rounds per minute. While primarily an antimissile system, the Gatlings could also take out aircraft, and a barrage against the waterline of an unarmored ship would punch enough holes in its hull to send it to the bottom.

The *Oregon* also sported concealed machine guns on her decks with thermal and IR sights. Gunners with video displays controlled these remotely from the operations center. One of her forward hatches could be blown off to launch four Exocet ship-to-ship missiles, and another hatch hid a pair of Russian-made land-attack cruise missiles. Although Langston Overholt at the CIA had paved the way for the Corporation to acquire some American military hardware, he'd drawn the line at missiles, thus forcing Juan to search elsewhere. Overholt had also vetoed the Corporation from getting Mark-48 ADCAP torpedoes. No other nation on earth used them, so they could be too easily traced back to the United States. The fish in the pair of forward-facing tubes had also been bought with hard currency from the same corrupt Russian admiral who'd procured the cruise missiles and supplied the end user certificates for the French Exocets.

It was nearly midnight when Juan entered the operations center. He regarded his people under the red glow of battle lights and the muted shine from their display screens.

Mark Murphy and Eric Stone occupied the workstations closest to the forward bulkhead. Stone had come to the Corporation from the navy, while Murphy had never spent time in the military. The young prodigy had earned a Ph.D. by the time he was twenty and joined the Corporation straight from private industry, where he'd designed weapons systems. Juan had been suspicious of him at first, fearing he lacked the mettle to cut it as a mercenary. In truth, his fear was that Murphy would turn out to be a psychopath who thrived on killing, but a battery of tests and psychological profiles showed that Murphy would have excelled in the military, provided the people around him were on the same intellectual level. Because Juan recruited only the best and brightest, Murph had settled in perfectly, even if no one else shared his joy of punk rock and skateboarding.

Behind and off to the sides of their stations were Hali Kasim monitoring the communications gear and Linda Ross on the radar and the waterfall sonar display. Along the back wall of the op center were stations for the remote deck guns, as well as fire and damage control coordinators. The rest of the crew had their positions, some suited up to fight fires, others to act as corpsmen, and still others who made sure the rapacious guns had enough ammo. Eddie Seng was in charge of the tactical troops on deck, ready to repel boarders. Juan could hear Max on a comm link from the engine room talking to Eric, announcing that the ship's propulsion system was green across the board.

What had brought everyone to battle stations was an announcement from Linda that a contact thirty miles from the *Oregon* had suddenly changed course and was heading for the ship. In the world of maritime operations, efficiency was the name of the game. A deviation of a degree or two could add hundreds of miles to a journey and thus cost more money. Unless there was an emergency, and with the radios quiet there wasn't, the approaching vessel was up to something. And because they'd been warned what to expect, the crew of the *Oregon* knew what was coming.

Cabrillo took his command station in the middle of the room and surveyed the high-tech equipment around him. He believed when he'd designed the op center he'd been subconsciously influenced by the bridge on the old TV show *Star Trek,* right down to the large flat-screen monitor above Stone's and Murph's heads. But it wasn't the weapons or the sensors or the computers that made the *Oregon* such a formidable opponent. It was the people in this room and those supporting them throughout the ship. That had been Juan's greatest accomplishment, not the steel and electronics and guns, but assembling the finest crew he'd ever had the pleasure of knowing.

"Sit rep," he called, turning on the computer screens near his centrally placed chair. The Kirk Seat, as Murph called it.

"Contact bearing oh-seventeen degrees and closing at twenty knots. Range is twenty-one miles." Linda Ross answered without looking up from her screen. Like the others, she was dressed in black battle fatigues, a SIG Sauer pistol belted around her waist.

"What do you make of her?"

"Approximate size is seventy feet, and I can tell she has a single screw. She'd been running at four knots, as though she were trolling, before turning on us. It sounds like one of the fishing boats the pirates are using."

"Anything on the radios, Hali?"

"Nothing from the target, Chairman. I've got regular chatter from a pair of bulk carriers well outside our grid."

Juan dialed in the *Oregon*'s hangar bay. "This is Cabrillo. I want the pilot suited and the Robinson on five-minute alert for takeoff." He then punched up the shipwide channel. "This is the chairman speaking. We have a target closing in that looks like the real thing. It's unlikely that the men aboard her are very high on the food chain, so we need prisoners not corpses if we're to cut off the head of the organization. Don't, I repeat: Do not take unnecessary risks, but if it's a choice between a kill or a capture, try to take them alive. Good luck to all."

His eyes swept the room once again. There was neither grim fatalism nor any expectant gleams in the faces around him. The next move belonged to the pirates, and the crew waited with cool efficiency.

"Conn, slow us to eight knots. Let's make us too tempting to ignore, but have the ballast pumps ready in case we have to lighten up and run."

"Aye."

"Range?"

"Ten miles," Linda answered crisply, then her voice took on an odd tone. "What the . . . ?"

"What have you got?"

"Damn! Sonar contact directly below the ship, depth seventy feet." She looked up from her display, catching Juan's eye. "They have a submarine."

5

THE op center crew had no time to digest her words before Mark Murphy at the weapons control announced, "I have a missile launch from the trawler. Time to impact forty-seven seconds. Gatlings are coming online."

The tactical situation had spiraled out of control in only a few seconds, leaving Cabrillo little time to react. He relied on his mind and not the expensive equipment around him to visualize the battle and seek a solution. "Hold your fire for my signal. Conn, pump us dry and prepare for full power. Wepps, be ready to launch countermeasures and depth charges. Sonar, what's the sub doing?"

"She's seems dead in the water, no propulsion and no indication she's going to fire."

"Time to impact?"

"Thirty-one seconds."

Cabrillo waited, feeling how the *Oregon* rode differently as the waist ballast tanks drained. At maximum speed the magnetohydrodynamic engines could move the ship her full length in just a couple of seconds. Even if his plan didn't work, the freighter wouldn't be where the missile thought it would.

"Sonar?"

"If anything, I'm getting the sound of escaping air, but the sub isn't submerging."

That cinched it for him. The sub wasn't a threat, yet. Cabrillo wanted to blow the missile as close to the *Oregon* as possible to make the pirates think they'd scored a hit. "Okay, Wepps, when the missile is ten seconds out, smoke it with the Gatling. Conn, ballast us back down, but be ready on those throttles."

Mark Murphy, also wearing dark fatigues but over a black T-shirt with the saying "Never Mind the Bollocks We Are the Sex Pistols," brought up an external camera on the main screen. From out of the darkness a streaking corona of light raced for the *Oregon* a few dozen feet off the surface of the sea. The rate of closure was astronomical—at least a thousand miles per hour. The missile appeared to have been fired at an oblique angle so it would impact on the *Oregon*'s stern. The pirates' intention was to take out their victim's steering gear and propellers and leave them unable to run. Not a bad plan if they wanted to kidnap a hostage or plunder the ship's safe.

With eleven seconds to go, Mark released the trigger safety on the Gatling gun. It was as though the weapon was eager to prove itself, like a police dog held back on its leash while its master was being mauled. The electronic brain, slaved to a dedicated radar system, found the missile in a microsecond, calculated trajectory, windage, humidity, and a hundred other factors.

The plate hiding the gun emplacement had automatically lowered when the master radar had first detected the missile launch. The autocannon adjusted its aim slightly as electric motors spooled up the six rotating barrels. The instant the computers and radar agreed it had a target, foot-long twenty-millimeter depleted uranium shells fed into the breach at three thousand rounds per minute.

The Gatling sounded like an industrial buzz saw as it cranked out a five-second burst. Forty yards from the ship the missile hit the wall of slugs. The explosion rained fire onto the sea, illuminating the side of the *Oregon* as though it had been caught in a miniature sunrise. Pieces of the rocket fell, carving trenches into the ocean, and a few smaller ones even rained against the ship's hull.

"Conn, all stop, steer ninety-seven. Hali, give it a few seconds, then send a mayday on the emergency frequencies, but keep the power setting low so only our friends out there hear us." Cabrillo dialed the engine room. "Max, lay a small smoke screen. Make us look like we took damage."

"They'll think they hit us and the ship's dead in the water," Eric Stone said with admiration. "You're going to sucker them all the way in."

"That's the plan," Juan agreed. "Sonar, anything on that sub?"

"Negative. We've now put her a mile astern. I can't hear any machinery noises or anything else but a slow air leak."

"Did you get her dimensions?"

"Yes, and they're odd. She's a hundred and thirty feet long and nearly thirty-five wide. Short and squat by conventional standards."

Juan considered a possibility. "A North Korean minisub that somehow followed us here?"

"The computer couldn't find a match, but it's not likely. We're four hundred miles from the Korean Peninsula, and I get the sense that sub's been sitting here for a while. No way they could have beat us."

Cabrillo didn't doubt Linda's assessment. "Okay, keep an eye on her. For now our priority is the pirates' trawler. We'll come back to investigate later." Across the room Hali Kasim was calling out his mayday and giving an Academy Award–winning performance.

"Motor vessel *Oregon,* this is the trawler *Kra IV*, what is the nature of your mayday?" The voice over the radio was scratchy, and the output was weak, as though the pirate was transmitting at low power. No one could place his accent.

"*Kra IV*, this is the *Oregon,* we appear to have had an explosion in our steering gear. Helm is not responding, and we're adrift."

"*Oregon, Kra.* We are six miles away and closing at maximum speed."

"I bet you are," Hali muttered under his breath before keying the mike. "Thanks be to Allah you are here. We will lower our boarding stairs on the starboard side. Please bring all the firefighting equipment you have."

"*Kra* acknowledges. Out."

Juan switched frequencies to the tactical radios carried by Seng and his handpicked team. "Eddie, can you hear me?"

"Five by five, Chairman." Eddie waited with his five men in a passageway in the deserted superstructure. The soldiers wore Kevlar armor over black fatigues, and all had third-generation night vision visors. Each carried sound-suppressed MP-5 machine pistols and SIG Sauer automatics. Their ammo was short loaded in the armory, meaning it had a reduced powder charge. It was powerful enough to put down a man but wouldn't overpenetrate and potentially cause a friendly fire incident in the confines of the ship. From combat harnesses hung flash-bang grenades and enough spare magazines for a ten-minute firefight.

Only Eddie Seng wore civilian clothes and sported a bulky rain slicker that disguised two bulletproof vests. He was the point man, charged with meeting the pirates as they came up the stairs now lowering to the sea. His was the most dangerous job. He had to lure as many pirates as possible onto the ship for his team, mostly SEAL veterans, to take out. He carried a single pistol in a slim rig at the small of his back. The vests were to buy him a few seconds if the pirates came up with guns blazing.

"What have we got?" Seng asked.

"Trawler calling itself the *Kra IV* coming up the starboard stairs to lend firefighting support," Cabrillo answered. "If I were them, I'd send over at least nine men. Two for the bridge, two for the engine room, four for flexible duty, plus one leader."

"We said the *Oregon*'s sailing with a complement of fifty something," Eddie countered. "They'll send at least a dozen."

"Good point. Do you have enough men?"

"Roger, as long as the deck machine guns can take out the cannon fodder while we concentrate on capturing officers."

"Sounds good," Cabrillo responded. "Call me when you have visual." The ops team watched the trawler approach the *Oregon* through low-light cameras mounted high atop a deck crane. The *Kra IV* matched the description given by the few survivors of pirate attacks. She was seventy-three feet long and beamy, with a blunt bow and an open aft deck. She sported a tall A-frame derrick over her fantail, and they could see a single cargo container lashed just aft of her pilothouse. The distortion of the night optics couldn't prevent the crew from seeing that the trawler was well-worn. Her machinery looked as dilapidated as that aboard the *Oregon,* and Juan decided the pirates used the same ruse the Corporation utilized to lull their adversaries.

"Target is twenty yards to starboard," Eddie radioed. "I can see a dozen or so men on her deck. They're dressed mostly in shorts or jeans. A few are wearing foul weather gear. They look like they're carrying equipment, but I bet it's cover for weapons."

"Acknowledged." Cabrillo called down to the engine room to tell Max to cut the smoke screen. With their forward speed down to almost zero, the thick smog blew across the decks and would make visual identification difficult for Seng, as well as the operators of the remote machine guns.

Eddie watched one of the "fishermen" raise a bullhorn to his mouth and hail the *Oregon.* He stepped from the shadows and took a position at the head of the gangway stairs. A bead of sweat trickled down his rib cage. "Are we glad to see you," he called back with the right tinge of fear and relief. He noted that the curtain of smoke began to thin. "I think we have contained the fire but don't know what damage we've sustained."

"We will offer any assistance we can," the pirate replied. Eddie could hear the mocking tone in his voice through his accent.

As the two boats came together, deckhands on the *Kra IV* secured their ship to the gangway, and two of the pirates started up the stairs. If the first shot was to come, now was the time. Eddie tensed, his pistol out of its holster but held out of view.

Several things happened in the space of the next few seconds. Unseen searchlights on the trawler snapped on, bathing the side of the *Oregon* in stark white light and overloading most of the crew's night vision capabilities. Just short of the deck, the leading pirate raised an automatic and put two quick rounds into Eddie's chest and motioned to his companions. They charged up the gangway, shouting incoherent challenges as another dozen men rushed from the *Kra*'s pilothouse.

Eddie felt as though he'd been hit in the chest with a sledgehammer. He staggered back, his body numb. He heard more than felt his pistol fall from his deadened fingers.

Four of the pirates had gained the deck by the time Eddie's men reacted. Two of them were cut down in the first burst of gunfire from their concealed positions, but five more reached the *Oregon* to take their place. That they were meeting resistance sent the boarding party into a frenzy. They came on like berserkers eager for battle. In another few seconds the odds were five to one against the Corporation fighters and lengthening with every tick of the clock. Red beams from laser sights crisscrossed in the smoke as the firefight turned into a frenzy.

As soon as the screens in the op center whited out under the luminous onslaught of the arc lamps, Cabrillo understood the pirates' strategy. It had been called shock and awe during the second Gulf War—overwhelm your enemy in the first few moments of battle by creating the maximum confusion. An untrained crew on a merchant vessel would be so paralyzed by the lights, the screams, and the sheer number of men storming their ship that they wouldn't even get off a mayday.

And while the tactic was designed to defeat an unarmed crew, it also happened to negate the Corporation's advantage. The night vision gear was worthless, and there was still too much smoke blanketing the deck to use regular sights. The infrared system couldn't discern friend from foe, so for the moment the remote gunners were useless.

Cabrillo launched himself from his chair, snatching a pair of night vision goggles and a machine pistol from the rack along the aft bulkhead. He was in the elevator before anyone knew he'd moved.

"Lock down the elevator when I reach the bridge," he called as the hydraulic lift whisked him five stories to the bridge.

Even from high above the deck, the sound of the gun battle was ferocious. The former SEALs were making a good show for themselves, but it was only a matter of time. Cabrillo raced out along the wing bridge, taking a second to peer down. At least twenty pirates had taken defensive positions all around the forward deck and poured blistering fire into the superstructure. He spotted a figure slowly crawling away from the head of the gangway. He had his weapon up and his finger an ounce away from firing when he recognized Eddie's rain jacket. His gaze swept the pirates again just as one popped up from behind a winch, taking aim at Seng with an AK-47.

Cabrillo swung his weapon and put a bullet through the pirate's face, adjusted slightly, and dropped another with a double tap to the chest. He ducked behind the solid curtain rail as bullets whizzed by like angry hornets and sparked against the steel. He clicked the selector on the MP-5 to auto, raised it over the railing, and let loose with a long barrage, hosing the deck with fifteen rounds. In the seconds-long pause in counterfire, he got to his feet, flipped the selector back to single, and took aim at the searchlights aboard the trawler.

His heart was beating like a trip-hammer, so the first two rounds missed. He took a steadying breath, let half out, and fired twice more. The pair of lights exploded in a shower of glass, and darkness descended once again.

Almost immediately he heard the staccato bark of the hidden .30 calibers and the pinging rain of spent brass ejected onto the deck. The remote gunners were back online.

Cabrillo's machine pistol had a spare magazine taped to the one in the receiver. He changed them over, settled the goggles over his head, and got to work. In the eerie green cast of the night vision device, muzzle flashes looked like fireflies while men appeared like radiant ghosts. He dedicated himself to be Eddie Seng's guardian angel.

Eddie was still pinned in the open, and judging at how slowly he was moving, Juan knew he'd been hit. There was no trail of blood, so it was likely the vests had saved his life; however, Juan had taken a hit once through a vest and knew it would be hours before Eddie could even catch his breath. It took several agonizing minutes for Eddie to reach the hatchway into the superstructure, where a pair of hands hauled him to safety.

Through the cordite smoke drifting like a dense English fog, Cabrillo identified potential targets and fired with mechanical efficiency. Until the crew gained the upper hand in the battle, he couldn't worry about taking prisoners.

Blood ran thick across the deck as bodies piled up, but fire from the SEALs had withered to an occasional desultory burst. They'd taken losses. Cabrillo spotted two pirates dashing forward, moving from a hatch cover where they'd hidden to the base of one of the cranes. One pulled something from the knapsack worn by his partner. Juan recognized the satchel charge and cut them down before they had time to arm the device. Another tried to race for the superstructure. As Cabrillo swung to fire, one of the remote machine guns turned on its gimble. The sustained burst cut the man nearly in half.

That seemed to break the back of the pirate horde. The ten or so survivors ran for the gangway just as the big diesel on the *Kra* bellowed out of idle. They ran into devastating fire from the superstructure. By holding back, Eddie's men had fooled the pirates into thinking their avenue of escape was clear. Two dropped to the deck, their corpses skidding in their own blood.

The *Kra* began to pull away, abandoning their boarding party. Cabrillo stitched the trawler's deck, but there were no targets. The lines securing the gangway to the fishing boat were still secure, so it was slowly torn from its mounts. Two pirates were halfway down it when the *Kra* began to move. The gangway stretched like a bridge from one ship to the other until the ropes on the *Kra* parted under the strain. The eighteen-hundred-pound set of stairs twisted, then pulled free from the *Oregon,* dumping the men into the sea, then crushing them when they surfaced.

The *Kra* changed angle slightly, narrowing the gap to give their men on the *Oregon* a chance to jump for it. Eric Stone at the helmsman's station in the op center recognized the maneuver and turned the *Oregon* to port and gave her some speed just as the remaining pirates leapt for the rails. One landed on the *Kra*'s main winch. High above on the wing bridge, Cabrillo heard bones shatter and saw his body tumble to the trawler's deck. A second gunman smashed into the *Kra*'s hull, fell into the water, and never resurfaced. The remaining six landed in the narrow space between the two ships.

Juan didn't know if the helmsman on the fishing boat didn't see what had happened or just didn't care. He continued to turn into the *Oregon.* Eric Stone hit the bow thruster in an attempt to shove the *Kra* aside, but the prop's athwartships tunnel was well forward of the trawler, and its powerful wash merely rippled the waves.

The two hulls came together in a grinding crash of steel, smearing the men struggling in the water, turning flesh and bone into a pink paste that washed away when the ships separated.

Juan fetched a walkie-talkie from a drawer at the back of the wheelhouse. "Wepps, Cabrillo. As soon as you have a sight picture, hole her at the waterline. Let the sons of bitches know they aren't going anywhere."

"Roger," Mark Murphy replied.

As the distance between the two vessels grew, Cabrillo saw a deckhand aboard the *Kra* attach the cable from the A-frame derrick to lines already secured to the shipping container sitting aft of the wheelhouse. The chairman squeezed off a few rounds from his H&K, but hitting a target that's bobbing with the swells from an unstable platform was next to impossible. The man didn't even look up from his task as bullets ricocheted around him. An unseen winchman cranked up the derrick. Because the A-frame angled out over the trawler's stern, the large container was dragged across the *Kra*'s deck, leaving deep scars in the wood planking. The bottom edge caught on a bollard, but the winch drum continued to revolve. The container teetered for a moment before flipping on its side with an echoing clang. When it was finally under the crane, it was hauled into the air and swung free over the transom. The winchman released the brake, and the container smashed into the sea, bobbed for a moment, then began to fill with water.

Cable stripped away from the freewheeling winch drum as the *Kra* continued to increase the distance. Whatever contraband the trawler was carrying was doubtlessly in the container, and Cabrillo felt if they were quick enough, they could disable the fishing boat and tie on to the unspooling line before it vanished forever.

As if reading his thoughts, Mark Murphy loosened a one-second burst from the Gatling gun hidden in the *Oregon*'s bow. Fifty depleted uranium slugs punched into the *Kra* at the waterline just fore of the pilothouse at a spot Murph assumed was clear of hitting her fuel tanks.

The tanks were well aft of the gaping hole, but the rounds impacted the pirates' weapons cache. The first explosion was relatively small and contained. Only a lashing tongue of fire belched from the gash cut into the hull by the Gatling. The second blast punched through to the deck and blew out an eight-by-eight section of hull. Fire and smoke rolled from the trawler as she heeled over like she'd just fired a broadside of cannons. Cabrillo watched helplessly as more explosions ripped apart the fishing boat. It looked as though she'd been rigged to blow by Hollywood effects masters. The pilothouse vanished in a splintering pall of flame, and then her aft deck erupted when her main tanks detonated, slamming her stern so deeply into the water that her bow lifted clear. Shrapnel and debris peppered the side of the *Oregon,* forcing Cabrillo to duck behind the rail. The trawler's stern winch flew right over the freighter's rear deck, trailing cable that looked like gossamer in the moonlight. The *Kra*'s keel split where the explosions had weakened it. The smoking bow settled back on the water as the stern sank from view, and then the fore section lifted free again before it, too, was dragged under the waves.

The entire sequence of events, from the first impact of 20 mm rounds to the final hissing plunge, took nineteen seconds.

Juan got back to his feet, wiping a smear of blood from where a piece of hot steel had nicked the back of his hand. A wide circle of smoking flotsam coated the sea, no piece larger than a garbage can lid. The quiet roar of oily fires burning on the swells was the only sound once the concussion waves dissipated across the uncaring waters. There were no moans from the injured, no cries from the stranded. No one had survived the conflagration.

He remained rooted for ten seconds, perhaps for as long as thirty, before he realized there was hope of salvaging what had turned into a debacle. The cable securing the pirate's container lay across the *Oregon*'s deck, slowly slipping into the ocean as the weight of the container pulled it down.

"Deck party to the aft deck for cargo detail," he barked into the radio. "Security to the foredeck. Check for survivors."

He raced through the deserted superstructure, taking stairs four at a time in a race to the aft deck. He burst from a hatchway just as a team of deckhands reached the slithering cable. Because the winch spool had unwound as it sank on the far side of the ship, there was little counterweight to the rapidly sinking container. The cable rasped across the deck, and smoke from blistering paint coiled into the air.

Juan grabbed a length of chain from a pile left haphazardly at the base of a derrick. He looped it several times around the cable where it rose over the rail, then snapped the links into the hook of a small cargo winch. While the winch looked as though it hadn't worked in years, its two-cylinder engine fired at the press of a button. He threw the lever to draw on the hook, and the chain tightened around the cable. The friction of steel against steel created an acrid stench as the links clenched further. The cable slowed enough for the deckhands to create a loop long enough for them to wrestle over a capstan. The cable came taut, vibrating with the strain, but it held.

It took several more minutes for them to rig a more secure system to hold the cable steady and attach it to the one operational crane on the *Oregon*'s aft deck. Eddie Seng and Linda Ross joined him just as they started to haul up the container. Seng was pale and walked with a slight stoop, a hand pressed to his chest where he'd taken the two shots.

"How're you doing?" Cabrillo asked.

"It only hurts when I laugh," Eddie said gamely.

"Then let me tell you the one about the hooker who walks into a bar with a parrot and a roll of quarters."

Eddie held out a hand and groaned. "Please don't."

Juan turned serious. "How bad was it back there?"

"Believe it or not, I'm the worst of the injured. My boys suffered a grand total of one concussion and a single flesh wound among them."

"And the pirates?"

"Thirteen dead and two injured," Linda answered. "Julia doesn't think either's gonna last an hour."

"Damn." They might get something from forensic autopsies, the ages and ethnicities of the pirates for example, but nothing to lead them to who was behind the attack.

"Clear the rail," a deckhand shouted.

The trio stepped away from the ship's side as the container was lifted from the sea. Water poured from its top and jetted from holes drilled along its sides. The twenty-foot container swung over the rail, and the crane operator settled it onto the deck as though it was as fragile as an egg. Juan was handed a pair of bolt cutters, which he used to shear the padlock securing the doors. Everyone crowded around, each with their own private thoughts about what they'd find inside. It was inevitable that some believed the pirates' trove would contain gold and precious gems, as though this was the eighteenth century.

Cabrillo held no such illusions, but he wasn't prepared for what spilled from the container when he unlatched the doors. A crewman retched when he realized what he was seeing, and even Juan had to clench his jaws as acid surged up his throat. Borne by several tons of water still trapped inside the steel box, a tangle of thirty naked bodies tumbled onto the deck of the *Oregon*.

6

THE chateau sat in a valley near the base of Mount Pilatus just south of Lucerne and only a short train ride from Zurich. Although the forty-room mansion looked as if it had dominated the landscape for generations, it had been constructed only five years earlier. With traditional steeply pitched slate roofs and countless gables and chimneys, the structure was storybook beautiful. The circular drive curved around an enormous marble fountain decorated with a dozen nymphs who poured water into the clear pool from filigreed urns.

Around the main house were several stone outbuildings to make the estate look like it had once been a working farm. In the surrounding alpine meadows, brown Jersey cows sporting bronze bells kept the fields trimmed and fertilized.

Seven dark limousines were ranked in a parking annex next to the garage, and behind it lay an enclosed field where a pair of Aerospatiale Gazelle helicopters sat, their pilots drinking thermos coffee in the cockpit of one of the executive choppers.

The summit meeting of European finance ministers in Zurich drew little media attention, since nothing much was expected of the gathering. However, it provided an excuse for the men meeting at the chateau to be in the same city at the same time. They met in the mansion's great hall, a lofty two-story room paneled in oak and decorated with boar and stag heads and large Swiss horns crossed over the walk-in fireplace.

As Switzerland is one of the world's great banking centers, it was little wonder that with one exception the fifteen men represented some of the largest banking concerns in Europe and America.

At the head of the table sat Bernhard Volkmann. Raised Catholic in a strict household run by his banker father, Volkmann had forsaken his religion early in life for another, that of wealth. Currency had become his god, cash his Eucharist. He was a high priest in the world of finance, respected for his dedication and a little feared for his uncanny instincts. Every action of every day went toward the accumulation of more money, for his bank and for himself. Volkmann had a wife because it was expected of him and three children because he'd allowed himself to sleep with her on a half-dozen occasions. He considered them a necessary distraction from his professional life but could not recall any of their birthdays or the last time he'd even seen his youngest, a twenty-year-old student he believed was at the Sorbonne.

Volkmann arrived at his office on Zurich's Bahnhofstrasse at six each morning and left at eight each night. This routine varied begrudgingly on Sundays and holidays when he would work out of his home for at least twelve hours a day. Volkmann neither drank nor smoked and would be no more likely to enter a casino than a Muslim would become a swineherd. At sixty, he was paunchy and almost uniformly gray. His skin was the same washed-out shade as his hair, and behind his glasses his eyes were the murky color of dishwater. He even took to wearing gray suits, and though his shirts were white, they invariably took on his gray cast.

Those who worked for him had never seen Volkmann smile, much less laugh, and only a severe financial upheaval would elicit a slight downward tug at the corners of his mouth.

Around him were similarly severe men whose dedication to money was no less intense. They were presidents of banks whose decisions affected billions of dollars and millions of lives. And today they were gathered because the very foundation of the world's economy was about to crumble.

On the table in front of Bern Volkmann a simple black cloth covered a small rectangular object. When the men were settled around the table, water poured, and attendants withdrawn, Volkmann reached out and pulled away the cloth.

The bankers and their guest were among a handful of people in the world who wouldn't noticeably react to the object on the table. Yet Volkmann saw that even these seasoned professionals couldn't mask all emotion. A few drew shallow breaths, one contemplatively stroked his chin. Another's eyes widened for an instant, then the person glanced around as if he'd given a tell in a poker game. The six billion other people on the planet would have gasped in wonder and rushed to touch the object as their minds filled with possibilities.

The trapezoidal bar weighed twenty-seven pounds and was known as a London Good Delivery. Its facets radiated a warm buttery yellow, and it possessed an almost oily sheen in the subtle lighting of the great hall. Refined to 99.9 percent, the ingot of pure gold was worth approximately one hundred sixty thousand dollars.

"Gentlemen, we have a crisis," Volkmann began in accentless English. He spoke crisply, enunciating every word so there could be no confusion or misinterpretation. "As you are all aware, the world will run out of gold very shortly. In fact, demand far outstrips supply for a very simple reason. Some of you became greedy.

"Starting more than a decade ago many of you approached your country's central banks with a proposition that at the time seemed profitable for everyone concerned. You, as bankers, would borrow the gold held on deposit with the promise to repay at one-quarter percent interest. The gold, as it sat in vaults in New York, Paris, London, and elsewhere, had no value so long as it was kept out of circulation. By paying a quarter point you would make the gold work for the central banks as it never had in the past.

"Had it ended there, we would not be facing a crisis. But it did not end. You turned around and either sold the gold on the open market or used the value of your holdings as leverage and collateral for other ventures. In essence you pledged or sold a commodity you had only the right to borrow. The central banks gave tacit approval to this action yet maintained the right to recall the gold at any time. Had this scheme taken place in only one country or on a small scale, there would remain enough surplus gold on the market to cover such a call.

"However, your greed got the best of you all. As it stands today, twelve thousand tons of gold valued at one trillion euros is on the books of central banks but is, in fact, on the fingers and around the necks of women all over the world. In a word, gentlemen, it is beyond redemption.

"Several central banks are aware of the situation and continue to accept their quarter percent on the gold's value, but some are asking for the gold's return. Two years ago the French national bank announced they were going to sell some of their reserves. We got together to finance the purchase of enough gold to replenish their treasury so the sale could go through. As you recall, the price of gold rose fifty euros in just a few weeks when traders realized such buying was taking place. The French then sold their gold, and the price stabilized once again. Our scramble to cover the call cost us nearly a billion euros. We told our stockholders it was a one-time charge-off, but in truth it is a charge-off we will face any time a central bank calls in their assets."

"Bern, we don't need a history lesson," a New York banker said testily. "If you look around you'll see there's a few familiar faces missing because they were canned by their boards of directors."

"Being 'canned by their boards' as you put it, Mr. Hershel, is now the least of our worries." Volkmann gave the American a stare that silenced any follow-up rejoinder.

"Banking is a business of trust," he continued. "A worker cashes his paycheck, spends what money he needs to survive, and trusts a bank to hold the rest. What happens to it afterward is frankly beyond his understanding or threshold of interest. He has done his job of converting labor to capital and trusts us to do our job of maximizing that capital. We lend it to entrepreneurs who build new businesses to employ more workers to transform more labor into more capital in a system that has worked well for centuries.

"But what happens when that trust is abused? Surely there have been banking scandals in the past; however, what we now face is a crisis of confidence of unprecedented proportions. The store of capital that governments use to assure their people of the country's strength, their gold reserves, has been sold off for what is in essence an IOU that can no longer be paid. We can not honor our promise to the central banks. Even if we had the money to buy the gold to return to the central banks, there isn't enough of it in the world to cover what we owe."

"Production can be increased to buy us the time to fill a call order." This from an Englishman in a Savile Row suit.

"It can't." The answer was short and blunt, like the person who gave it. He, too, had an accent, somewhat British in nature but with a Colonial twang.

"Mr. Bryce, would you care to explain."

Bryce stood. Unlike the others, he had tanned, weathered skin, and his blue eyes were hidden behind a permanent squint. His hands were large, with swollen knuckles. He was someone who'd worked to obtain his wealth, toiled in ways the bankers could never understand.

"I've been chosen to represent South Africa's mining concerns here," Bryce said. "Mr. Volkmann told me what we were to discuss, so I talked with my people beforehand to give you accurate information. Last year South Africa produced about thirty-four hundred tons of gold at a cost of around two hundred and eighty dollars an ounce. This year we project the same tonnage but at a price of three hundred and eighteen dollars an ounce. Labor costs have risen since the end of apartheid because of the power of the trade unions, and we're under heavy pressure to sign a new contract that's even more generous."

"Don't give in to them," the president of Holland's biggest bank interjected.

Bryce shot him a look. "Hard rock mining isn't assembly line work. It takes years of training to become proficient. A strike now would cripple us all, and the unions know it. They see gold trading near five hundred an ounce and know the mines aren't losing money."

"Can you increase production?" Another at the table asked.

"Our mines are two miles deep now. Every level we sink farther is a geometric increase in cost. It's like building a skyscraper. To make it taller you can't simply add a floor to the top. You must first reinforce the foundation and the structure. You must make sure the elevators can reach and that your water and sewer lines can take the additional capacity. Adding a floor to the top, architects say, costs as much and is as difficult as slipping a new floor under an existing building. Every new level we dig in our deepest mines costs two to three times as much to excavate as the one above it. We could get the gold, sure, but the expense far outweighs the profit."

"Then we need to find alternative sources of bullion. Russia perhaps? Canada? The United States?"

"Not enough capacity to make a dent in the shortfall," Volkmann answered. "Also, environmental protections in North America add a thirty to forty dollar premium per ounce."

"What about exploration? We develop new mines, maybe bring order to the chaotic gold mines of Brazil so they can increase production."

"Even with the latest equipment and management, the veins in Brazil aren't big enough to fill an armored car in a year," Bryce replied. "And as for exploration, there are gold reefs out there. We even know where some of them are. It would take years just to cut through the bureaucracy to stake claims, and then you'd need to invest billions of dollars to bring any of them up to the production levels you gentlemen require."

"Then the solution is simple," a Frenchman said into the short silence following Bryce's gloomy assessment. "We must convince the central banks to never call in their reserves. Perhaps we could promise them a greater interest rate to ensure their cooperation."

"That's just a temporary fix," said another New Yorker. "We can't run from our obligation forever."

"But if we have time to refill the central banks' coffers, we can maintain price stability and avoid what happened when my country announced their sale."

"And when the *Wall Street Journal* breaks this story," the New Yorker countered, "what then? People are going to demand to see the gold their government promised them existed. Joe Six-Pack thinks there's a vault at Fort Knox brimming with the stuff. He's not going to be too happy when he learns it's empty except for a bunch of worthless promissory notes. He's going to panic because his government lied about the one thing it never had in the past, the surety of the greenback."

"Which is precisely why I said earlier this is a crisis of unprecedented proportions," Volkmann said. "We have removed the foundation of the capitalist system, and as soon as the public learns of this, it is going to crash down like a card house."

The Swiss banker paused, scanning the room. He saw that he had their attention, and he could tell by the dour expressions that some of them already anticipated what he was about to say, even if they didn't know the specifics. He sipped from a glass of water before continuing. "For the past six years Germany has embarked on a series of failed economic policies. The result has transformed the country from Europe's industrial engine into something akin to a welfare state. Productivity is down, unemployment is at the ceiling allowed by the EU, and shortly the government will face the likelihood that it will default on their overly generous pensions. In a word, Germany is about to go bankrupt. I learned two weeks ago that they are going to sell all of their gold stock."

The collective gasp was the sound of men realizing they were facing the abyss.

"That is six thousand tons, gentlemen—or roughly two years' worth of South Africa's production. As it stands there are only two thousand tons on reserve in Berlin and Bonn. We have to make up a four-thousand-ton shortfall."

"How soon?" the Frenchman asked, having lost his earlier bluster.

"I'm not certain," Volkmann replied. "In order to keep prices stable I suspect it will be over some time."

"But not enough," the New Yorker muttered.

"And keep in mind," Volkmann went on doggedly, piling disaster on top of disaster, "if commodity traders realize the bind our banks are in, they will gouge us, and prices might double or even triple."

"We are ruined," the banker from Holland cried. "All of us. Even if the Germans accepted currency, we could not repay. The money we made selling the gold has already been lent to others. We would have to recall loans, all of our loans. It would ruin the Dutch economy."

"Not just yours," the banker named Hershel said. "We bought and sold twenty billion dollars' worth of German bullion, and a good chunk of that evaporated during the dot-com implosion. We would have to deplete our savings-holders' accounts to pay it back. There would be runs on banks all over the United States. It would be the Great Depression all over again."

A despondent silence enveloped the room as they considered those words. These men were too young to recall the Depression that enveloped the world in the 1920s and '30s, but they'd heard firsthand accounts from grandparents and other relatives. But this time would be much worse, because the global economy was so interconnected. A few even thought beyond their own losses and those of their home countries. With nations struggling to provide for their own people, international aid would end. How many people in developing nations would die because the men at this table had sold borrowed gold in order to fatten their profit ledgers?

Suddenly the sleek corporate high rollers were as gray as Bernhard Volkmann.

"Is there any way to dissuade the Germans?" one asked after a few moments.

"We can try," another answered, "but they have to look after their own interests. They need their gold back, or they'll face insolvency and possible rioting, maybe insurrection."

Volkmann allowed the conversation to continue for a few minutes on its own as the bankers bandied ideas of how to save themselves, their banks, and the world. In the end they had no answers. It was as the talk died down to silence once again that he asked the South African mine representative, Bryce, to leave the room.

When the door closed behind him, the bankers gave their undivided attention to Volkmann. He remained silent until someone finally asked the question they all prayed he could answer.

"Did you call us here because you have a solution?" asked the English CEO of the world's sixth-largest bank.

"Yes," Volkmann replied simply and almost felt their relieved sighs on his skin. He tapped a text message on his PDA and a moment later the great hall's doors swung open again. The man who entered strode in with a sense of confidence that the bankers would never admit they only possessed as a front, camouflage to hide their insecurities. He moved loose-limbed and with his head high. He was their age, early fifties, perhaps a little younger. It was hard to tell. His face was unlined, but his eyes seemed old and his bristle-cut hair was more silver than brown. Unlike the bankers, he didn't have the self-satisfied smugness of entitlement, the sense of superiority that came with the illusion of wealth and power. He was simply a presence, an undeniable force that had entered their meeting and seemed the center without having to utter a word.

"Gentlemen," Volkmann said as the stranger took a seat next to the Swiss. "This is Anton Savich, formerly of the Soviet Bureau of Natural Resources. He is now a private consultant."

No one said a word or made a move. None could fathom the presence of a former Russian functionary.

"I've known something like this was coming for some time and secretly made plans," Volkmann continued. "There can be no argument about what I propose, nor any dissent. This is our only option, and when I am finished, each of you will agree to it without reservation. Mr. Savich will outline the particulars."

Without getting to his feet, speaking casually with an arm draped over the back of his chair, Anton Savich told them how he was going to save their banks. It took ten uninterrupted minutes and left the faces of the other men with a mixture of shock, anger, and outright revulsion. The Dutch banker looked like he was going to be physically ill. Even the tough New Yorkers, one of whom Volkmann knew had fought in Vietnam, had gone ashen.

"There is no other way, gentlemen," Bern Volkmann said. No one could actually agree orally. Volkmann passed his gaze from man to man, meeting their eyes, and knew he had their assent when they either looked away or gave an almost imperceptible nod. The last was the Dutchman. He gave a weak moan at the thought of what he was agreeing to and dipped his eyes.

"I will make the arrangements," Volkmann concluded. "We need never meet like this again."

The New Yorker who'd spoken of Fort Knox said, "Oh, I'm sure we will. In hell."

7

CABRILLO crossed himself.

The victims were of all ages, though they were predominantly in their twenties, from what he could tell. Some had been dead for quite some time. Their bodies were black with lividity, and several were bloated with internal gas. Others had apparently drowned when the pirates dumped the container over the side of the fishing boat. They appeared sickly pale under the deck lights. It was hard to tell in the jumble of limbs, but it looked as though there were more men than women. The one thing they all had in common, other than their gruesome deaths, was that every one of them was Chinese.

"Snakeheads." Cabrillo spat with disgust, looking out to where an oil slick still burned on the dark ocean.

Eager to seek work outside China, peasants and even moderately well-to-do workers paid upwards of thirty thousand dollars to be smuggled out of the country. Of course, even a wealthy Chinese couldn't come up with that kind of cash, so a system was put in place whereby the illegal immigrant would work for the gangs who smuggled them, paying off the debt by toiling in sweatshops or restaurants in every city from New York to New Delhi. The women were generally prostituted in "massage parlors" that sprang up even in small towns across America and Canada. They labored for years, living in overcrowded apartments owned by the gangs, until the entire debt was repaid. If they tried to run away, their families back in China would be tortured or killed.

In this way more than a million Chinese a year left one bitter, dead-end existence for another, all believing the promise that things would improve if only they worked harder.

The immigrants had a name for their journey to a new life. It was called riding the snake, and those who ran the gangs were called snakeheads.

Cabrillo and his crew had intercepted a shipload of illegals most likely on their way to Japan, or the pirates had hijacked such a boat and were planning on selling the laborers back to the gang or to some third party. Either way, they had stumbled onto a human trafficking ring. Past his horror at what lay on the deck of his ship, beyond the grief that built behind his eyes, Juan Cabrillo felt a spark of anger flare in his chest. He nurtured it, fanning it with hate until it roared and threatened to consume him.

He turned to Linda Ross, his eyes glacial hard. "Get Dr. Huxley up here as soon as she's able. There's nothing she can do for these poor people, but autopsies might shed some light on what happened." He motioned to the deckhands. "As soon as orderlies empty the container, check it for any kind of ID numbers, then heave it over the side."

"Are you okay, Juan?" Linda asked with concern.

"No. I'm pissed," he said as he strode away. "And I still have a submarine to deal with."

He took his seat in the operations center. Word had already spread, and the mood was subdued. Mark Murphy was running systems checks on the shipboard weapons in case they were needed again, while Eric Stone sat quietly at the helm station awaiting orders.

"Mr. Murphy," Cabrillo called sharply.

Mark turned in his seat, a grave look on his face. It had been his shot that blew up the *Kra* and ruined any chance of interrogating prisoners. "Yes, sir?"

The chairman's voice softened. "Don't blame yourself. I would have plugged her in the same place. We're in this for the long haul. There'll be others."

"Yes, sir. Thank you."

"Mr. Stone, make your speed thirty knots and put us over that submarine."

"Aye, sir."

Linda was still on deck, doubtlessly helping Julia and her medical team. Juan monitored the passive sonar array and called course and speed corrections to Stone until they had the *Oregon* directly over the mysterious sub. It had settled to seventy-five feet in the half hour since they'd first detected it. He washed the acoustical signal through the computer, filtering out extraneous sounds, until all he heard was the slow escape of air from the craft. He couldn't tell if the sub was just playing dead or if it was having a problem. But if there were some sort of emergency, surely he'd hear alarm Klaxons and crewmen working within the pressure hull. Even without the sophisticated listening devices, the sound of metal banging on metal would carry right through to the *Oregon*. Yet all that came through was the burbling hiss of the slowly sinking sub.

Juan pulled up a chart of the region on the computer. There were nearly two miles of water under the keel. It would be days before the sub hit bottom, although by then she would have long since collapsed after passing her crush depth.

He went back to his own seat and called down to the moon pool, "Dive master, this is Cabrillo. Open the hull doors and prepare an ROV for a shallow-water recon. Also have two divers standing by and lay out some gear for me."

Fifteen minutes later Cabrillo stood behind the ROV's pilot wearing an orange wet suit. His goggles were strapped around his left arm.

There was no need for him to dive on the sub but for his own desire to feel the freshening calm of the ocean's embrace. His shoulders and neck ached from tension and rage.

The underwater probe was a small, torpedo-shaped craft with three variable-pitch propellers along its axis for propulsion and maneuverability. In its domed nose was a high-resolution video camera, and mounted on its back were enough lights to illuminate a ten-foot swath in even the murkiest water. The craft had just been launched, and two workers made sure its unspooling tether ran free from the ship.

The huge doors that were opened to the sea allowed a chill to creep into the cavernous amidships hold while underwater lights attached to the hull cast a wavering green reflection along the bulkheads. The big Nomad 1000 submersible loomed over the pool like an airship, ready just in case they needed her powerful manipulator arm.

"Passing fifty feet," the operator announced, his attention fixed on the screen showing a live feed from the ROV's camera. All it revealed was blackness. His fingers rested on a pair of joysticks that controlled the probe.

"Sixty feet."

"There." Cabrillo pointed.

From out of the gloom came the faintest trace of an outline. It was murky and indistinct at first but resolved itself as the ROV approached. The probe had come upon the sub from the stern. It was her bronze propeller that glinted in the powerful lights. Then they could discern her rudder. It looked like no sub Juan had ever seen.

"Bring us up five feet and forward another ten."

The operator followed his orders, and the prop slid under the camera's view. They could see steel hull plates, but these weren't in the cigar shape of a typical submarine. Linda had said the craft was odd when she'd hit it with active sonar to check its shape.

Suddenly they could see the word HAM painted in white against the black hull.

"Back us off," Cabrillo said.

The little undersea robot eased in reverse, and the word expanded into gibberish. UTHAMPTO.

"What the hell is an Uthampto?" one of the divers asked.

"Not what," Juan replied. "Where. Southampton, England."

And as he spoke, the full name of the vessel's home port came into view as well as her name: *Avalon*. And she wasn't a sub at all.

"Do you think this is the ship where the pirates pulled the refugees?"

"I doubt it." Cabrillo stared at the screen as the probe sailed over the ship's stern rail and across her aft deck. A few fish swam amid the tangle of gear. "But I'm sure she was one of their victims. I bet she was attacked just before we got into radar range." He called up to the bridge to have Mark Murphy run a check on the British-flagged ship.

"Wouldn't we have heard an SOS?" the diver asked.

"Not if the pirates jammed them or boarded using some trick that allowed them to take out her radios before a warning could be sent."

"Chairman, it's Murph. The *Avalon* belongs to the Royal Geographic Society. Launched in 1982, she's a hundred and thirty feet long, displaces—"

Cabrillo cut him off. "When was she last heard from?"

"According to a press release from the RGS, all contact was lost with her four days ago. American search and rescue units out of Okinawa didn't find a thing."

"That doesn't make any sense," Juan said for his benefit and not for those around him. He puzzled aloud. "If she was boarded and the pirates cut communications, the SAR crews should have spotted her in no time."

"Not if they sank her right away," the ROV pilot answered.

"There's no way she would have sunk only seventy-five feet in four days." Cabrillo paused. "Unless . . . unless someone managed to stop her from taking on more water."

"She'd still keep sinking," the diver said. "If she'd lost enough buoyancy to sink this far, she'd have lost enough to keep going down."

Cabrillo regarded the man. "Good point, unless she became trapped in a halocline, a band of highly saline water. Salt water is more dense than fresh, so an equal volume displaces more weight. The ocean is layered like a cake with striations of water with differing salt levels and temperatures. It's possible the *Avalon* sank into a layer of superdense water that's maintaining her equilibrium for the time being." He was aware that the ship was still taking on water, so eventually she would slip through the band of water, then plunge like a stone.

The men watched in silence as the probe glided over the sunken vessel. There were no outward signs of a struggle, no bullet holes or evidence of explosion. It was as though she'd just slid beneath the waves without a fight. Once the probe reached the *Avalon*'s bow, Cabrillo had the pilot swing her along the superstructure and see if they could peer into any of the windows.

"Do you think anyone's still alive on her?" the diver suddenly blurted.

Juan had already considered and discarded the idea. He'd seen firsthand how savage the pirates were and knew they wouldn't have left behind any witnesses, even on a scuttled ship. Further proof was the derelict's silence. If he'd been trapped on a sunken vessel, he would have done something to attract attention, no matter how futile. He would have banged on the hull with a wrench until he could no longer move his arms. Then he would have shouted until his dying breath. No, he was certain no one was left alive aboard the *Avalon*.

The ROV swept back across the *Avalon*'s deck, heading for the bridge. In the tight cone of light they could see the big windows had all been smashed, either by the pirates or when the research vessel slipped into the sea. The pilot eased the probe through one of the empty window frames, mindful that the armored tether could easily tangle. The ceiling looked like a shimmering wall of liquid mercury. It was an air pocket fed by a string of bubbles leaking up from a small hole in the floor.

There was ample evidence of the attack on the bridge. Stitched lines of bullet holes crisscrossed the room, and brass shells littered the deck.

A pile of what looked to be rags or a tarp in one corner revealed itself to be a body. Tiny fish darted at the tendrils of blood still leaking from the numerous wounds. The pilot tried to maneuver so they could see the dead man's face and maybe make an ID, but the little probe didn't have the power to roll what had once been a large man.

"See if you can find a way to access the rest of the superstructure," Cabrillo ordered.

The pilot tried, but they found the door at the rear of the bridge jammed with a metal bar across the latches.

"Never mind. Back us out and check the portholes. Maybe we can see inside her."

The probe ran first down the *Avalon*'s port side, pausing at each porthole, but they couldn't see anything within the hull. Inside was stygian black. The operator swung around her stern and started up the starboard. The light cast a perfect circle along the black hull, and each round window glittered like a jewel. The instant it shone into one of the cabins there came the sharp sound of metal banging against metal. It was a frantic, staccato tattoo. The men monitoring the screen recoiled as a pale face suddenly appeared at the window. It was a woman. Her eyes were huge with fear, and her mouth moved as she shouted a scream they could not hear.

"Dear God! She's alive."

Cabrillo had already moved to a bench seat and was snugging the straps of his twin air tanks over his shoulders. Next came the buoyancy compensator that looped around his neck. He struggled to his feet to cinch a weight belt around his waist. The two other divers were quickly following suit. He snatched up a pair of swim fins and a powerful flashlight.

"Alert Huxley," he said as he waddled to the moon pool, burdened by sixty pounds of gear. He adjusted his mask, checked his airflow, and fell back into the water.

As he dropped through a curtain of bubbles, Cabrillo slid his feet into the fins, then purged some water that had seeped in around his mask. The water wasn't that cold, and his body heat quickly warmed the thin layer trapped inside his wet suit. He waited just long enough for the two other divers to hit the water before dumping air from his BC and dropping into the darkness, one hand on the probe's tether as a guide.

How had she survived? he wondered. Judging by the damage fish had done to the corpse on the bridge, the pirates had scuttled the *Avalon* shortly after taking her. Was there that much air trapped inside her hull? Obviously, the answer was yes. The question was if it would last until they could get her out.

Below him he saw the corona of light from the probe and shadowy details of the research ship. Air spilled from at least a dozen spots around her hull, as though she were bleeding. Juan felt a superstitious chill down his spine. The *Avalon* had become a ghost ship, but unlike the *Flying Dutchman,* she'd been cursed to sail through the darkness below the seas, a forlorn wanderer on borrowed time.

When he reached the main deck, Juan checked the depth gauge on his dive computer. He was down to eighty-three feet. The *Avalon* was sinking faster. Her borrowed time was running out.

He finned down to where the ROV hovered motionless outside the porthole where they'd spied the survivor. When he peered in through the small, round window, the trapped woman jumped back in fright. She quickly came forward again so an inch of water and a thick pane of glass separated their faces. If Juan didn't come up with something quick, the gulf would remain insurmountable.

She wore two jackets and several sweaters. Her hair was covered in a wool watchman's cap. The air inside the ship would be the same temperature as the water. A quick check told him fifty-one degrees. Her eyes were bright blue, and now that he'd arrived, they had lost their edge of madness. As desperate as she was, she still retained some semblance of humor, because she tapped her watch as if to say, *About time.* Juan admired her courage.

Then he took in the subtle details and noticed her lips were blue and her face an unnatural white. Her body quivered with uncontrollable paroxysms. He looked deeper into the cabin. Water completely covered the small room up to the level of the bed frames. One mattress floated free while the woman kept the other anchored with her weight. Yet even her refuge hadn't remained dry, and neither had her clothes. With her kneeling on the mattress, her weight formed a depression that pooled with seawater. No doubt her feet were soaked as well. Unable to know how long she'd been in this condition, he was certain she'd be hypothermic soon.

Juan removed his regulator and mouthed, "Are you all right?" The seawater against his lips was bitterly salty, confirming his earlier supposition about how the *Avalon* had delayed her plunge to the bottom.

She gave him a flat stare as if to say he was nuts to ask, given the circumstances, then nodded to tell him she wasn't injured. He pointed at her and held up a finger, then pointed to other places on the ship, holding up more fingers. It took her a moment to realize he was asking if there were others with her. She shook her head sadly. Then she held up a finger and disappeared for a moment. When she returned she had a pad of paper and a black marker. Her hand shook so much her writing was barely legible. "I'm the only one. Can you get me out?"

Juan nodded that he could, although he had no idea how. They could attach lines from the *Oregon*'s cranes to the research vessel and try to haul her to the surface, only the cranes had nowhere near the power to deadlift a sinking ship, and if they got the balance wrong, she could tilt and fill even faster than she was now. However, it would be worth getting some lines down to the *Avalon* so they could at least stabilize her for the time being.

The other divers reached Juan. He wrote out instructions on a slate one of them carried and sent the man back to the *Oregon*. He turned back to the trapped woman and winked. She wrote something on her pad and held it to the glass. "Who are you?"

He wrote out his name. She flashed him a look of frustration and wrote "Are you with the navy?"

Uh-oh. How could he explain their presence? He wrote back that he headed a private security company hired to bring the pirates to justice.

She seemed satisfied. He asked her to describe where water hadn't yet flooded the *Avalon*. She wrote that the bridge deck was flooded and the bilge and engine room. Water had been climbing her deck for the past twelve hours. He asked if there were any exterior doors that he could open that would only flood a small room, an antechamber of some sort that could be isolated from the rest of the ship.

She wrote that she wasn't sure, then fell back onto the bed. Water welled up through the mattress around her backside and shoulders. The woman didn't seem to notice or no longer had the strength to do anything about it. Juan pounded the butt of his dive light against the hull to rouse her. She opened her eyes but barely registered his presence. She was slipping away. He pounded his light again, and the woman crawled to the porthole once more. Her eyes were glassy, and her jaw chattered like she was holding the business end of a jackhammer. He couldn't get her out without her help, and she was maybe five minutes away from unconsciousness.

"What is your name?" he wrote.

She stared at the words for a moment then mouthed something Juan couldn't understand. He shook his writing slab to remind her how they were communicating. It took her twenty seconds of intense concentration to write "Tory."

"Tory, you must stay awake!!! You sleep, you die. Is there a small room you can seal that has an exterior door?" He was afraid she was too far gone to understand the question, but her shoulders suddenly straightened, and she managed to clamp her jaw tight. She nodded and began to write. It took four minutes by Cabrillo's stainless Concord chronograph because she had to erase many of the words and start over.

She finally held her notebook to the porthole. The letters looked like a child's first attempt. She had written, "Tne att port doon one dek op opons to a stoinwll thot can be sealecl." It took Juan another precious minute to decipher the illegible scrawl. "The aft port door one deck up opens to a stairwell that can be sealed."

"You must go there and seal yourself in. Do not leave, no matter what. Trust me."

Tory nodded and heaved herself off the bed. As she stood in the knee-deep water, agony etched itself across her features. Juan could almost feel the icy fingers of cold cramping her muscles and sending jolts to her brain. She lurched across the room, lost her balance, nearly caught herself against a bulkhead, then fell heavily. If he could have squeezed through the porthole, Juan would have done so and gathered her up in his arms. As it was, he hung helplessly in the water as Tory slowly dragged herself to her feet. She was drenched. She staggered to the door without a backward glance, moving stiff-limbed like a zombie in a horror movie.

As soon as she was out of sight, Juan swam up to find the door she'd described. As he cleared the rail he saw four other divers working to attach a cable sling to the *Avalon*'s stern bollards. They had set up big underwater lights and worked efficiently in their glare. He imagined a team doing the same fore. The ship had now settled to a hundred feet. Even if the cranes couldn't lift the research vessel, having her secured to the *Oregon* would prevent her from sinking any deeper for a while.

But depth wasn't the problem. Tory's endurance was.

Unbeknownst to Cabrillo and his crew, the *Avalon* had large holds both fore and aft that stretched from her bilge to her main deck and almost the entire breadth of the ship. So far, they had remained dry, thanks to tightly dogged hatches and servo-controlled louvers on the ventilation system that sealed it nearly airtight. It was their buoyancy that aided in keeping the survey ship from free-falling into the depths. While Juan was scrutinizing the door, one of the tightly closed vents began to buckle under the increasing pressure of water that was bottled within the ventilation ducts behind it. A flat jet of water sprayed from a gap between two of the louvers. It fell in a fine mist almost all the way across the hold. The slit between the louver's metal fins was tiny, and only a few gallons per minute entered the hold—but every second saw the gap widening, and it was only a matter of time before the louver failed entirely, and a three-foot-square column of water roared into the hold.

The door, Juan noted, was a solid slab hinged from the outside. He could turn the handle freely once he'd removed a steel clamp that had been locked to prevent anyone from escaping during the initial raid. Only the pressure of the surrounding water kept him from drawing it open. To do that he needed to equalize the pressure on both sides. And to do that, he had to flood the antechamber on the other side with Tory trapped inside. It was a straightforward concept, and while Tory was in for the fright of her life as the room filled with water, Juan would have her out and breathing off a spare scuba tank before she was in any real danger.

He motioned over one of his divers and wrote what he needed on his slab. This man wore a full helmet with an integrated communications system that allowed him to talk with the dive master aboard the *Oregon.* Juan tapped the beat of "Shave and a Haircut" on the door while he waited for both Tory and his delivery from the ship. Waiting for either was interminable, but when the basket of tools and dive equipment was lowered from above and Tory still hadn't arrived, Juan began to fear the worst.

Being trapped anywhere with the bodies of her friends littering the hallways was bad enough. Adding to the psychological stress was the fact that her prison was a hundred feet underwater and continuing to sink. It was amazing Tory hadn't gone catatonic days ago. She was frightened, near hypothermic, and now soaking wet. Did she have it in her to reach the antechamber and remember to seal the room from the rest of the ship?

Cabrillo had his doubts. But there was no other way. Her cabin door would have burst and flooded the ship had they cut their way into the room. She would have drowned long before they could have made a hole big enough to even pass her a regulator. No, he thought, this was the only plan that could work.

He tapped his rhythm against the steel with his light again and again. Then he thought he heard something from within the ship. He tapped again, "Shave and a Haircut," pulled off his hood, and pressed his ear against the door.

There. The unmistakable reply. Tap tap. *Two bits.* She'd made it.

He reached into the basket of tools he'd requested from the *Oregon*. First, he checked that the spare scuba tanks were ready. Next came the drill, which fed off two compressed air cylinders slung under the wire-mesh cage and attached by a long hose. The tip was specially hardened and at the RPMs generated by the air tanks would cut through the door in seconds. Cabrillo looked around. The divers at the stern must have finished securing the cable sling to the *Avalon*. A pair of them went to help those working at the bow while another two came over to help him.

Cabrillo braced his back against the heavy basket, pressed the drill bit near the bottom of the door, and pulled the trigger. The piercing whine was like actually standing on a tooth while a dentist went after a particularly nasty cavity. It drove spikes through his ears that met in the middle in a blinding point of pain. He ignored it and watched silver slivers of metal curl away from the drill point. In just a few seconds the tip bored through, and Juan carefully removed the drill from the hole. Water and bits of the shavings were sucked into the ship. He didn't know the size of the antechamber and couldn't guess how long it would take to fill, so all he could do was wait until the pressure had equalized enough for him to open the door.

He used a metal pry bar to tap at Tory and tell her he was with her. Her reply came instantly and angrily. She hadn't expected that this was how she'd be rescued.

After four minutes, Juan pulled at the door with the pry bar, but it remained sealed tight, so he drilled two more holes and tried again every minute afterward with the same result. He was about to drill a few more to hurry the operation when something happened.

A sudden gush of bubbles exploded from someplace ahead of the superstructure. The louver in the fore hold had given way, and thousands of gallons a minute poured into the derelict. The quick rise in pressure had popped an inspection hatch on the main cargo hatch. The six divers working at the bow appeared from over the *Avalon*'s squat funnel, fighting their way through the maelstrom of bubbles and surging water. One of them made a cutting gesture across his throat as soon as he was within the circle of light cast by the undersea lamps. They hadn't completed securing the forward sling.

In moments the *Avalon* began to drop by the head. And then she started to roll to port. The divers had managed to secure only the starboard side of the sling. The *Avalon* was held to the *Oregon* by three cables, two aft and one forward. For a few moments the ship appeared to stabilize, but her off-kilter angle allowed water to enter from other places. The crane operators on the *Oregon,* no doubt supervised by Max, gamely tried to hold the ship steady for as long as they could, but it was a losing battle.

Cabrillo had floated free from the deck in those first frantic seconds but quickly dropped back to the door. The basket of tools had slid all the way to the scupper. He motioned for one of his men to retrieve it while he hauled on the unyielding hatch.

Tory would have been tossed around inside the antechamber when the ship torqued over, and her new angle meant she'd have to tread water until he could get the door open. It was a race against the clock, and time had just accelerated.

The cable sling at the bow was looped to one of the ship's mushroom-shaped cast-steel bollards. The free end was caught in a jet of air bubbles and danced around the rigging holding the *Avalon*'s forward mast. Because of the uneven load, the cable pulled at the top of the bollard and started to slip off. The steel strands rasped as they were drawn over the top of the bollard, a pitiable cry like a mountain climber at the moment his grip slips from a rock face.

With water gushing into the forward hold, the cable remained taut for a few seconds more before sliding off the bollard. The *Avalon*'s bow plummeted, tilting the ship through ninety degrees until she dangled nose down from the straining crane aboard the *Oregon,* her knife-edged prow pointing into the abyss. Rated for sixty tons, the crane was probably fighting to hold three times that weight, and every second increased the strain.

Because of water resistance, the ninety-degree rotation had taken a few seconds, long enough for Juan to clutch the door as the deck became a wall and the aft bulkhead became the floor. Then there came a scraping sound, one that tore through the water and seemed to come from every direction. Juan frantically looked around for the source. The light towers his crew had erected were still tumbling across the deck, creating a nightmare effect of glare and blackness. The sound grew louder. Juan glanced up to see a lifeboat that had pulled free from its davits hurtling down the length of the ship. He dove to the side as it raced past, its momentum pulling at him like a whirlpool. The davit cables trailing the lifeboat were a thick tangle of inch-thick rope that caught him just as he looked back to see if his people had avoided the speeding projectile. The knot of rope slammed into the back of his head, tearing off his face mask.

He fought the pain and disorientation, groping for the mask as it swirled in the back eddies. He opened his eyes, the sting of salt worse than any he'd ever felt. But there, just beyond his fingers, the orange mask was slipping into the depths. He grabbed it, snapped it back over his face, purging it by tilting his head and allowing air from his regulator to expel the water. He swam back to the door, checking his wrist computer. The *Avalon* was sinking at ten feet a minute and accelerating. He knew Max would run out every foot of cable on the *Oregon* to slow her descent, but there were limits to how deep they could breathe off compressed air.

The other diver had been thrown violently when the ship upended. It took him a few moments to clear his head and find the tool chest where it had lodged against the rail near the ship's jack staff. He didn't bother with the drill and instead concentrated on taking the spare air tank and a dive bag up to the chairman.

Together they heaved against the door with the pry bar. A curtain of bubbles exploded around the seam for a second. They'd managed to open it a crack, but pressure slammed it closed again. They pulled harder. Juan felt as though the muscles of his back were being stripped from his bones, and black stars exploded behind his tightly closed eyes. Just as he was about to stop and shift to a new position, the door swung open, instantly flooding the last of the interior space.

The powerful lights they'd set on the aft deck had either smashed themselves to pieces or were lost over the fantail, so all he had was his trusty dive light. He swung the beam around the antechamber. The space was cramped, painted a drab white. A set of metal stairs dropped to a solid-looking hatch that had once led to the bridge deck. Another door to the right that gave access to the interior of the main deck had also been secured. Then he saw Tory, a dark drifting shape of sodden clothes and loose limbs. Her hair fanned around her head like an anemone on a tropical reef.

In two swift kicks Juan was at her side. He slid his regulator past her slack lips and upped the airflow, trying to force the precious gas into her lungs. The other diver joined him and ripped open his dive bag. As fast as he could work, he plucked fistfuls of chemical warming packs from the bag, shook them violently to start the reaction, and stuffed them under Tory's clothes. They had several decompression stops to make on their ascent, and this was the only way Juan could think of to protect her from the biting cold.

He took back his regulator to take a quick breath before again feeding it to Tory. A third diver joined them. A knot was forming on her head from where she'd struck it against something, most likely when the ship rotated, and a fine feather of blood stained the water around the welt. He had the spare tanks and a dive helmet. Juan placed it over Tory's head and gave her sternum a sharp rap. Tory coughed into the helmet, a small amount of water pooling around her neck. Her eyes fluttered open, and she retched again. Juan used his regulator to purge the water from her helmet and kept his eyes locked on hers as she slowly came back. He knew she was going to be okay when she realized a stranger had his hand down her pants.

Other divers appeared. They guided Tory and Juan out of the room. One checked Cabrillo's tanks. He'd been down the longest and working the hardest. He was okay for now but would need fresh tanks during the decompression. Once they had swum far enough from the dangling survey ship, one of the men sent word to the *Oregon* that they could release the doomed vessel. A moment later, her slow downward plunge turned into a runaway plummet, and the *Avalon* slipped from view. The severed ends of cable trailed behind her like steel tentacles.

The team ascended in a tight group centered around Tory and Juan. The dive master shaved as much time as he dared from their stops, but it was still ten minutes before the freshest divers could guide Tory up into the moon pool and another fifteen before Juan and the others allowed deckhands to drag them onto the metal deck plating.

Juan stripped off his mask and dive hood, taking great gulps of air. The moon pool smelled of machinery oil and metal but tasted as sweet as a clear mountain morning. Max appeared at Juan's side, handing over a mug of steaming coffee. "Sorry, old friend, no booze until all the nitrogen has dissolved out of your blood."

Cabrillo was about to tell Hanley he would risk it for the worst case of bends in history, but he tasted the coffee and savored the sting of Scotch Max had laced it with.

He let Max help him out of his gear. Then he tried to get to his feet. "How is she?" he asked, his voice weak and thin from the cold.

Max put a restraining hand on his shoulder. "She's with Julia. We'll know for sure soon, but I think she's going to be okay."

Juan sagged back against an equipment rack with a tired and satisfied smile. At least they'd snatched one of the pirates' victims from certain death. Then he noticed several deckhands eating premium ice cream from pint containers. He knew why. Julia needed room in the big freezer for the victims they were too late to save.

8

CONSCIOUSNESS slowly congealed for Tory Ballinger through the haze of pain. She first became aware that every inch of her body ached, but it was a shin and her head where the agony appeared centered. The rest was low-grade throbbing. She levered open her eyes, blinking rapidly to clear them of sleep. Above her a fluorescent light shone with indifferent intensity. More light streamed through a nearby porthole. Three people were leaning over her. She didn't recognize them but somehow knew they were not a threat. The woman wore a doctor's white coat, and her dark eyes were filled with compassion and competence. One of the men was older, early sixties, and looked kindly. His features were weathered, and his bald head was blotchy, as though he'd spent a great deal of time outdoors. The unlit pipe at the corner of his mouth reminded her of her grandfather, Seamus. It was the second man who held her attention. The lines etched into the corners of his eyes and along his wide mouth weren't the inevitable effects of age. They had been chiseled into his skin by hard-won experience. They were the marks of someone who had struggled with life, someone who treated it as a day-to-day battle. Then she noted his eyes, blue and bottomless, with just a hint of humor, and she knew he won more of life's battles than he lost.

She felt as though she knew the man or should know who he was. He wasn't an actor. Perhaps he was one of those billionaire adventurers who flew hot-air balloons around the world or paid to be launched into space. He certainly had that roguish presence about him, a confidence born out by a history of success.

"Welcome back," the female doctor said. She was American. "How do you feel?"

Tory tried to speak and managed only a hoarse croak. The older gentleman produced a cup and tenderly held the straw to her lips. The water soaked into her tongue like the first rain on a desert. She sucked greedily, relishing at how the liquid sluiced away the sticky coating in her mouth.

"I think—" Tory began but started to cough. When she was finished, she cleared her throat. "I think I'm okay. Just cold."

For the first time she realized she was under a mound of blankets, and the one closest to her body was electrically warmed. It made her skin prick.

"When you were brought here, your core temperature was about two degrees colder than the charts say you can survive. You're very lucky."

Tory looked around.

"This is a shipboard infirmary," the doctor answered her unasked question. "My name is Julia Huxley. This is Max Hanley and our captain, Juan Cabrillo." Again Tory felt she knew the man. His name seemed so familiar. "It was the captain who rescued you."

"Rescued?"

"Do you remember what happened?" the man named Hanley asked.

Tory thought hard. "There was an attack. I was asleep. I heard gunfire. That's what woke me. I remember hiding in my cabin. Then I . . ." She lapsed into frustrated silence.

"It's okay," Captain Cabrillo said. "Take your time. You've been through a hell of an experience."

"I remember wandering around the ship after the attack." Tory suddenly buried her face in her hands, sobbing. The captain placed a hand on her shoulder. It steadied her. "Bodies. I remember seeing bodies. The whole crew was dead. I don't recall anything after that."

"It's not surprising," Dr. Huxley said. "The mind has defensive mechanisms that act to protect us from trauma."

The captain spoke. "After your ship was attacked, the pirates scuttled it. We happened along before it sank too deeply for us to rescue you."

"It was a near thing," Max Hanley added. "A couple of days had passed since the attack. Your vessel was held steady in a highly saline band of water."

"Days?" Tory exclaimed.

"Think of yourself as Jonah," Juan Cabrillo said with a warm smile. "Only we had to rescue you from the whale's belly."

Tory's eyes widened. "I remember you now! I saw you in my porthole. You swam down to get me."

Cabrillo made a self-deprecating gesture as if to say it was no big deal.

"It was you who told me to go to the aft hatchway and close the watertight doors. And it must have been you who drilled holes into the hatch. I thought you were going to kill me, and I almost ran back to my cabin before I realized you had to equalize the pressure so you could get me out. That was the worst. The water level rising inch by inch. I climbed the steps up to the bridge deck to stay out of it for as long as I could, but then there was no place to go." She paused as if feeling the agony of the freezing water all over again. "I waded in when it was already up to my chest. It took forever. God, I've never been so cold in my life. I'm surprised my teeth didn't shatter from chattering so hard." She looked up at the trio standing around her bed. "The next thing I knew was just now, waking up here."

"Your ship began to sink much faster, and it tilted in the water as the bow section flooded. You must have been tossed against a railing or pipe and hit your head. When I finally got the door open, you weren't breathing, and you had a gash in your scalp."

Tory touched for the spot on her head and felt a thick bandage.

"We've already contacted the Royal Geographic Society," Cabrillo went on, "and I'm sure they've told your family that you're okay. A charter helicopter is standing by in Japan to get you to a proper hospital as soon as we're in range. Are you sure you don't remember anything else about your attack? It's very important."

Tory's face scrunched with concentration. "No, I'm sorry, I don't." She looked to Julia. "I think you're right. My brain has blocked it all out."

"Last night when you were brought aboard you spoke to the ship's third officer. Her name is Linda Ross. Do you remember talking to her?"

"No," Tory replied a little testily. "I must have been delirious."

Cabrillo went on despite a warning glance from Julia. "You told her your name and said you were a researcher. You went on to talk about the attack and said one of the pirates searched your cabin while you were hiding. You told Linda he wore a black uniform and black combat boots."

"If you say so."

"You also told her that you saw two other ships nearby. You said that you thought one of them was an island at first because it was so big. You described it as being perfectly rectangular. The other ship was smaller, and it appeared the two were going to collide."

"If I don't remember being trapped on the *Avalon* for four days, I certainly don't remember what happened minutes after the attack. I'm sorry." She turned to Julia. "Doctor, I think I'd like to rest now."

"Of course," Julia said. "My office is just outside your room. Call if you need anything."

"Thank you." Tory gave Juan an odd look. It passed quickly, and she said, "And thank you for saving my life."

He touched her shoulder again. "You're very welcome."

"Helluva looker," Max remarked when he and Cabrillo were in the corridor outside the medical bay.

"Helluva liar," Juan said.

"She's that, too." Max tapped his pipe stem against his big teeth.

"Why, do you think?"

"That she's a good liar or that she lied to us at all?"

"Both."

"Haven't a clue," Max said. "I'm just glad Linda had the foresight to debrief Miss Ballinger last night."

"I wouldn't have thought of it," Juan admitted.

"The shape you were in, I'm amazed you even found your cabin."

"Linda said the way Tory described the ships and the pirates' uniforms made her think our passenger might have some military training."

"Or she's a researcher, just as she and the Royal Geographic Society claim, and she applies her scientific observation skills to everything she encounters."

"Then why lie and say she doesn't remember what happened to her when she was trapped on the *Avalon*?" Juan's gaze turned somber. "No one told her how long she was down there, and yet she knew exactly how many days. There's something more to her than she's letting on."

"We can't force her to tell us, and we can't hold her. The chopper that the RGS chartered is going to be here in a few hours."

Juan went on as if he hadn't heard Hanley's comment. "And uniforms. She said her pirates wore black uniforms. The guys we tangled with last night wore mostly jeans, shorts, and T-shirts. None of this adds up."

They entered the operations center. Linda Ross was the officer on duty. She was seated at the command station munching on a bagel sandwich. "How'd it go?" she asked around a mouthful of food, realized the gaffe, and tried to cover her mouth with a napkin. "Sorry," she mumbled.

"Put yourself down for employee of the month," Juan said. "Talking to Tory last night was a stroke of genius. Today she claims she doesn't remember anything, not the ships, not the uniforms, not even how she passed the time after the *Avalon* sank. Which reminds me, she didn't get a good look at the moon pool, did she?"

"No, Julia was quick with a hot towel to wrap her face as soon as she was lifted from the water. She really didn't start talking until we were in medical and Hux had started to warm her up. She was still the color of a blue jay and shaking like a leaf, but she was pretty damned sure about what she saw. She made me repeat that the big ship had a rectangular silhouette. Now she doesn't recall any of it?"

"We're pretty sure she remembers all right, only she's not telling," Max said.

"Why not?"

Juan checked a duty roster clipboard. "That's the million dollar question. Answer it, and you'll get an employee parking spot."

"Nice perk except my car's about ten thousand miles away at a garage in Richmond." Linda turned serious. "Like I told you when we spoke this morning, I got the sense that Tory was trying to brief me as though I were her case officer."

Juan didn't question her assessment. With her background in naval intelligence, Linda had been in on many such debriefings and would recognize the situation. "She wasn't sure if she was going to live, so she had to tell someone what she knew."

Linda nodded. "That's what it felt like."

"And now she knows she's going to be okay, so she clams up. Sounds to me like Miss Ballinger is much more than a humble marine researcher."

"Which would explain how she managed to survive her ordeal without losing her mind," Max added.

Far from a simple operation to rid the Sea of Japan of piracy, Juan realized they were in the middle of something far larger. If Tory was to be believed, and there wasn't anything much more sincere than a deathbed confession, there were two sets of pirates in these waters: those that belonged to the ragtag band they'd engaged the night before and the men in the black uniforms who had assaulted the *Avalon*. Tory had told Linda they had been systematic and quick. That made them sound more like commandos than the undisciplined thugs who'd tried to overwhelm the *Oregon*. Then there were the mystery ships Tory spotted at the moment of her attack. He didn't know their role in all of this. And what of the hapless Chinese immigrants locked in the cargo container? Had they paid the ultimate price for being in the wrong place at the wrong time, or were they somehow involved?

He couldn't understand why Tory refused to cooperate. If she was as lucid during her rescue as he thought she was, then she'd remember what he'd written on the dive slate. He'd told her he was part of a security firm tasked to combat piracy. Did that agenda somehow interfere with whatever she was doing? It didn't seem likely, but how could he not consider it? None of it made sense.

He decided it was best that they get her off the *Oregon* as soon as possible so they could resume the hunt on their own. He had every confidence that his people would unravel this mystery and get to the bottom of what was really happening.

Mark Murphy wasn't on watch, but Cabrillo was glad to see him at the weapons station. Today he wore a concert shirt from a band called Puking Muses. Given Mark's taste in music, Juan wasn't surprised he'd never heard of them and was again thankful his cabin was nowhere near that of the young weapons specialist. Juan caught his eye. Murph took off his headphones, and even from across the room Cabrillo could hear his music, some techno-industrial sound played at a volume that could crack plaster.

"Up for a little research, Murph?"

"Sure thing. What have you got?"

"I'm looking for a ship that's large enough to be mistaken for an island and has a completely rectangular silhouette."

"That it?" Murphy was clearly looking for something a little more to go on.

"It would have been in this area four days ago."

Cabrillo misunderstood Murphy's disappointment. He wanted more of a challenge. "So I'm looking for either a big container ship, a supertanker, or perhaps an aircraft carrier."

"I doubt it's a carrier, but punch it into the search parameters anyway."

Any station on the bridge had access to the *Oregon*'s mainframe computer, so Mark remained at his seat as he pulled up a maritime database for tracking shipping in the Sea of Japan. He remained hunched over his keyboard, his foot tapping the rhythm of the music pouring in over his headphones.

"What's the status on the chopper from Japan?"

"ETA is three hours," Linda answered. Because there was so much traffic in the area—five ships were within the *Oregon*'s one hundred mile radar—they couldn't risk exposing themselves by fully exploiting her mammoth engines. The tramp steamer was only making twenty-two knots, delaying the rendezvous with the chartered helicopter.

"Okay, I'm going back to my cabin to inform Hiro Katsui that his consortium owes us two million bucks. Call me if Mark gets a hit or when the chopper's ten miles out."

"Aye, Chairman."

THE screen saver had been pinging geometric shapes across the liquid crystal screen for an hour and a half as Juan sat at his desk, staring sightlessly at his computer. So far he had written exactly eleven words of his report to Hiro. Even discounting Tory's reticence, nothing fit the way Juan expected. Had a commando team attacked the *Avalon,* and if so, why? The most likely answer was to prevent the crew from seeing what was taking place on the other two ships. Could Mark be right about an aircraft carrier, and this was a government operation?

The problem was the only naval force in the area that had any carriers was the United States. China wanted to buy an old Russian flattop, but as far as Juan knew, they were still negotiating, and there was no way pirates could have gotten their hands on one. He was sure it was some other type of vessel that Tory saw. He didn't discount the possibility that her ship was attacked by trained commandos, only he had no idea how they fit with the pirates Hiro had hired the Corporation to wipe out. Were they working together?

His intercom buzzed. "Juan, it's Julia. Can you come down to my office?"

Thankful to escape the answerless questions swirling round and round in his head, he left his cabin and made his way down to medical.

He found her in the trauma bay, an equipment-packed room as modern as any level-one ER. The temperature was a cool sixty-five. A sheet-draped body lay on a gurney under brilliant lights. Julia wore green surgical scrubs. Her gloved hands were smeared with blood. Powerful ventilators prevented odors from building up inside the room, yet Juan could still sense the lingering smell of decay.

"One of the Chinese immigrants?" he asked, nodding at the shrouded form.

"No, one of the pirates. Want to take a look?"

Juan said nothing as Julia peeled back the sheet. Death never looked more ignoble, especially with the large sutured Y-incision Julia had cut to examine inside the chest and abdomen. The pirate was young, twenty at most, and skinny to the point of starvation. His hair was lank black, and his fingers and the bottoms of his feet were thickly callused. The pair of sneakers he'd worn when boarding the *Oregon* were probably stolen during a previous raid and were the first he'd ever owned. There was a single neat bullet hole in the middle of his forehead, an obscene third eye that was puckered around the edges.

Cabrillo couldn't discount the brutality of what the pirates had done, but he also couldn't help feeling a little pity as well. He had no idea what circumstances drove the boy to crime, but he felt the kid should have been with his family, not laid out on a slab like a dissected specimen.

"So what have you learned?" he asked after Julia drew the sheet back over the corpse's head.

"This guy's dead."

"Well, since you performed an autopsy, I assumed he would be."

"What I mean is if he hadn't taken a shot to the skull, he would have died anyway, probably within the next few months." She waved him over to a computer workstation. On the screen were spectrograph lines of a sample Julia had run. He had no idea what he was looking for. His puzzled expression prompted an explanation.

"Hair sample run through optical emission spectrometer." The Corporation had bought the million-dollar piece of equipment not only for Julia's medical bay but also for analyzing trace evidence. It had been key a year earlier tracking a missing shipment of RDX explosives. "During my exam," Julia explained, "I noticed some pretty significant symptomatology. For one, he was about to suffer complete renal failure. Also, he's anemic as hell; his gums are severely inflamed with late-stage gingivitis. I noted lesions all along his digestive tract and bloody crusts in both nostrils. It made me think of something, and the hair sample proved it."

"What's that?"

"This guy had had long-term exposure to toxic levels of mercury."

"Mercury?"

"Yep. Without treatment, the mercury, like other heavy metals, builds up in tissue and hair. It eventually shuts the body down, but not before causing madness as it deteriorates the brain. I bet if you recheck the video of the pirate attack, you'll see these guys fought with little regard for their own lives. The level of mercury contamination would have impaired this one's judgment to the point where he'd fight on, no matter what."

"Some of them tried to escape," Juan pointed out.

"Not all of them had such elevated or prolonged exposure."

"What about the Chinese?"

"I only checked one for toxicity, and she came up clean."

"But this guy's riddled with mercury?"

"You could fill a couple of thermometers off him. I checked two of his compatriots quickly and found the same thing. I bet they're all suffering to one degree or another."

Juan ran a hand across his jaw. "If we find the source of the mercury, we might find the pirates' lair."

"Stands to reason," Julia agreed, stripping off her gloves with a sharp snap. She removed her surgical cap and redid her ponytail with a well-practiced twist. "You can get mercury poisoning by eating contaminated fish, but the risk's mostly to children and women who want to conceive. But with the levels I'm seeing here, I'd put my money on these guys basing themselves someplace close to a contaminated industrial site or an old mercury mine."

"Any idea if there are such mines in this area?"

"Hey, my job's medical mysteries and patching you cutthroats back together," Julia teased. "You want geology lessons, call on someone else."

"How about their ethnic background? That might help narrow the search."

"Sorry. The fifteen pirates I have on ice are a veritable United Nations. This one looks Thai or Vietnamese. Three others are either Chinese or Korean, two Caucasians, the others are Indonesian, Filipino, and a mix of everything else."

"Super," Juan said acidly. "We have the luck to run across a bunch of politically correct pirates who believe in diversity. Anything else?"

"That's it for now. I need a few more days to finish up everything."

"How's your other patient?"

"Sleeping. Or at least pretending to so she doesn't have to talk to me. I get the feeling she wants off this tub ASAP."

"Why am I not surprised? Thanks, Hux."

Juan had only just gotten back to his cabin and ordered a lunch of steak and kidney pie when Mark Murphy knocked at his door. "What do you have, Murph?"

"I think I found her."

"Have a seat. So is it a bulk carrier of some kind or a container ship?"

"Neither." Mark handed over a thin file. Inside was a single photograph and a half-page description.

Juan glanced at the picture and gave Murphy a questioning look. "You sure?"

"She's on her way to Taiwan from Oratu, Japan, where she was used for a refit of a Panamanian tanker that threw a prop during a storm."

Juan looked at the picture again. The vessel was 800 feet long and 240 feet wide. Just as Tory had described, the ship was completely rectangular, with no rake to her bow or stern and nothing protruding from her deck to alter her flat profile. Juan read what Mark had managed to learn about the odd craft. She was the fourth-largest floating drydock in the world. Built in Russia to service massive Oscar II–class submarines like the ill-fated *Kursk,* it had been sold to a German salvage firm a year ago but had then been sold again to an Indonesian shipping company who chartered it out like a service station wrecker.

Juan's pulse quickened.

Using a drydock to hijack an entire ship at sea was truly inspired but also frightening in scope and sophistication. His deep fear about a leader uniting pirates across the Pacific into a coherent group might well be the tip of the iceberg. With a drydock this size, they could snatch nearly any ship they wanted.

He pictured how they'd pull it off. First a team of pirates would need to board their intended target in order to subdue the crew. Then they would sail their captured ship to rendezvous with the drydock. Under the cover of night, and only when weather conditions were favorable, because it would be dicey work, the drydock would ballast down so the bottom of its open hold was lower than the keel of their stolen ship. Big winches at the stern of the drydock would then reel in the vessel. The bow doors would swing closed, ballast pumped out, and the tugs towing the drydock would continue on their way. Without a direct overflight, no one would ever know that inside the drydock was the booty of the most audacious pirate ring in history.

"Pretty slick, hey boss?"

"Yeah."

"They come along and swallow up their victim." Mark gave an animated pantomime of the action as he spoke. "Haul it to their secret base. They'd have all the time in the world to offload the cargo before dismantling it. Rather than scavenge like hyenas, these guys are taking down their prey like lions."

"Why dismantle the ship?" Cabrillo mused aloud. "Why not make some changes to it, alter a few characteristics, paint a new name on her stern, and either sell her off or sail her for themselves?"

"I hadn't thought of that, but that makes even more sense."

"So what do we know about the company that owns the drydock? Wait, what's it called?"

"The drydock?" Murphy asked and Cabrillo nodded. "*Maus.*"

"German for mouse. Cute. So, the company?"

"Occident and Orient Lines. O&O. They've been around for like a hundred years. Used to be publicly traded, but in the past decade most of the shares have been bought up by entity or entities unknown."

"Shell companies?"

"So hollow even their names ring false. D Commercial Advisors LLC. Ajax Trading LLC. Equity Partners International LLC. Financial Assay—"

"LLC," Juan finished for him. Then a thought struck. "Wait. *Assay* is a mining term. Julia said the pirates were dying of mercury poisoning, and we both think they might be based near an abandoned mercury mine. I wonder if this Financial Assay owns mines in the region."

"I haven't even started digging into the shell companies yet. I thought you'd want to know about the drydock right away."

"No, you're right, but you've got a lot more to research. I want to know who owns the *Maus*—not the corporate veil but the actual guy who holds the pink slip."

"What are we going to do about the drydock? If what that British woman said is true, there might be a stolen ship in her hold and maybe some crew held hostage."

"The most powerful tugs in the world can't tow a vessel the size of *Maus* at more than six or seven knots. How long do you think their head start's gonna last when we're pushing fifty?"

Murph grinned like a teenager given the keys to a Ferrari. He got up to leave.

Juan came to a quick decision. He knew at some point he was going to have to split his forces. The *Oregon* was a perfect platform for espionage operations, but he needed the flexibility of people on the ground with access to jet travel. He had no idea where this case was going to take him. Most likely Indonesia, if that was where O&O still kept an office, so now was the time to get assets en route.

"Do me a favor and find Eddie Seng. Tell him to pack up some gear. We'll be going international, so nothing that can't pass airport security. Have him pick two of his men. We're hitching a ride on Tory Ballinger's helicopter to go hunting hyenas and lions."

"But where?"

Juan tapped Mark's report. "Have an answer by the time we land in Japan."

9

ANTON Savich would have preferred meeting Shere Singh at his office in a downtown Jakarta high-rise, but the stubborn Sikh demanded they meet at the site of Singh's latest venture, across the Sunda Strait on Sumatra. Savich had developed a healthy fear of flying after crisscrossing the Soviet Union for years on Aeroflot and would have taken a ferry despite Indonesia's dismal maritime safety record but was saved when Singh offered him use of his company helicopter.

He looked out the yellowed Plexiglas at the strip of beach below the chopper that seemed to guard the jungle from the sea. It was a primeval landscape, and the villages that flashed under him looked as though they hadn't changed in generations. The wooden fishing boats clustered in secluded bays had likely been built by the grandfathers of the men who sailed them today. The land to his left was hidden by an impenetrable canopy of vegetation that had yet to fall to slash-and-burn farming or industrial timber cutting. To his right, the sea was clear blue and pristine. A double-masted schooner, a coastal freighter he assumed, cut through the light swells with her sails bellied taut by the trade winds. She looked as though she'd sailed out of the nineteenth century.

How could a people who had known such a paradise as the archipelago create a city like Jakarta with its eighteen million people, gridlocked traffic, crime, poverty, disease, and smog as thick and noxious as a World War One mustard gas attack? In their rush to modernize, the Indonesians had embraced the worst of what the West had to offer and then abandoned the best of their own culture. They'd created a patchwork of consumerism, corruption, and burgeoning religious fanaticism that teetered on the brink of collapse. Through contacts, Savich had learned that the United States had clandestinely stationed more than a thousand soldiers on the islands to help train local forces to fight the twenty-first century war.

The pilot tapped Savich's arm and pointed ahead. He grudgingly looked away from the peaceful sailing ship and focused his attention on their destination. The complex was hidden in a bay by a rocky promontory, so all he could see was the flotilla of ships lying at anchor. Even from this distance and altitude he could tell they were derelicts, the steel husks of once-proud vessels that had outlived their usefulness. Several were wreathed in shimmering halos of their own spilled bunker fuel, like murdered corpses surrounded by their own blood and waste. One had lain so long here that her keel had succumbed to corrosion. Her bow and stern both pointed skyward with her crushed stack vised in between like a nut in a giant cracker. A quarter way to the horizon a line of oil containment boom cut a wide arc around the bay. There was an entrance gate manned by a pair of small tenders that could open the floating boom to allow the ship's entrance. No ships ever left the facility, at least by sea.

The chopper banked around the headland, and the Karamita Breakers Yard came into view. More ships of every size and description were moored within the bay like cattle in a chute headed for slaughter. A pair of supertankers, each at least a thousand feet long, had been dragged up the sloping beach by a combination of tidal surges and huge winches.

An army of men swarmed over the hulks, tips of glowing flame sparking whenever their cutting torches touched metal. A crane on wide crawler treads sat just at the surf line and plucked steel sections of hull as soon as they were sliced free. It swung them farther up the beach, where even more workers were ready to cut and beat the slabs into manageable chunks. Other teams of men ripped piping and electrical cables from within the ship's hull, eviscerating the supertanker as though they were dissecting a carcass for consumption

And in a sense they were. The smaller pieces of metal were transferred to railcars for the short journey northward to the Karamita Steel Works. There, the scrap was melted down and remilled into steel reinforcement bars for the never-ending construction boom going on in southern China. Behind the modern steel mill shimmered the artificial lake backed up behind Indonesia's largest hydroelectric plant, the engine that allowed for such heavy industry in an otherwise inhospitable jungle.

The once pristine sand that ringed the bay had turned into a black, tarry porridge that clung to the men's feet like clay. Beyond the oil boom the sea was reasonably protected, but inside the floating containment wall, the water was a toxic soup of oil, heavy metals, PCBs, and asbestos. Acres of land had been turned into storage yards littered with ships' boilers, mounds of lifeboats, an assortment of anchors, and hundreds of other items that could be resold on the open market. Behind the fenced lots rose dozens of drab dorm buildings little better than tenements. A squatters' camp of prostitutes, con men, and crooks had sprung up along the rail line to drain the workers of the few pennies a day they earned turning retired ships into scrap.

Savich noted that the forest behind the facility was slowly receding as thousands of workers cut the trees for their cooking fires. While the air was free of pollution because the mill ten miles north ran on hydro rather than coal or oil, an industrial pall hung over the breaker's yard, the miasma of its own corruption and filth.

But there was one modern element to the process, and this was doubtlessly what Shere Singh wanted Savich to see. On the far side of the tankers was a gleaming corrugated metal building nearly as large as the ships, with dozens of translucent panels on the tin roof to provide light within. Two-thirds of the eight-hundred-foot building was constructed out over the water on large pilings. Four sets of train tracks met the inland side, and as the chopper thundered over the facility Savich saw two pairs of small diesel engines haul a five-foot-long portion of a ship out of the building. He recognized the curve of the hull, the thick keel, and could see interior passages as though peering into a cutaway model. No, he thought, it reminded him of a slice taken from a loaf of bread. The cuts were straight, and the metal shone silvery in the tropical light. He couldn't fathom how something as large as a ship could be carved so perfectly.

The helicopter pad was several miles from the breaker's yard, protected from the din and smell by another promontory of naked rock. Around it were tended lawns and breezy bungalows for the supervisors, clerks, and skilled workers. An open jeep was waiting next to the landing zone, the driver standing by to help Savich with his luggage. The Russian had no desire to stay in Indonesia longer than necessary, so all he carried was a briefcase and a battered leather grip. The bulk of his luggage was in an airport locker. He allowed the driver to put the bag in the back of the jeep but kept the calfskin case on his lap as they drove toward the breaker's yard.

It took a few moments for his hearing to return after an hour's flight in the helo, and when it did, his ears were assaulted by the racket of pneumatic cutting chisels, spadelike jackhammers, and the piercing throb of countless generators. The crane dropped a ten-ton slab of metal onto the beach with a dull thump, and seconds later men were hacking at it with sledgehammers and handheld electrical saws designed to cut steel. They wore little more than rags, and Savich could see their legs, chests, and arms were covered with dark scars from contact with hot, sharp metal. He saw more than one missing an eye, fingers, or part of a foot.

And then from the enclosed building came an unholy shriek that cut the air like a diamond being cleaved. It rose in pitch until Savich thought his head would shatter and continued on for a minute, then two. The driver offered him a pair of ear protectors, and he gratefully snugged them over his head. The noise was still there but low enough now that his eyes cleared of tears. To his amazement, the workers continued their tasks as though the screaming wasn't even there, and the driver seemed equally unfazed.

The jeep stopped outside the large warehouse structure just as the sound came to an abrupt end. Savich hadn't realized he'd held his breath. He let it out with a grateful whoosh and motioned to the driver if it was okay to remove the plastic and foam protectors. The Indonesian nodded.

"I am sorry," he said formally in English. "We are used to it."

"What was that?" Savich asked.

"The ship saw," he said and motioned Savich over to an exterior scaffold elevator that ran up the side of the ten-story building.

The driver handed Savich over to another worker. He was given a plastic hard hat with ear protectors that could be snapped into place. The worker slammed the elevator door closed, pressed a button, and waited patiently as the lift ascended the building. While not as impressive as the view flying in, Savich was amazed by the scale of Singh's operation. It looked as though the next ship to meet its fate after the rusting tankers had been rendered was a small white cruise ship that looked like a virgin bride amid a group of indigent hookers. A square hole had already been cut in her side, and a floating crane was transferring the vessel's desalinization unit to a waiting lighter.

The elevator reached the top, and the worker slid open two sets of doors. Savich recoiled at the stench of burned metal. When his eyes adjusted to the gloomy interior and he'd blinked away the effects of the fumes, he saw that the building was one huge open space with massive doors at both ends. Despite the size, it felt cramped because a large ship took up most of the volume. Or what was left of the ship.

The catwalk where they stood was almost directly in line with her bridge. Before being admitted into the shed, workers had cut away the ship's funnel and masts so she could fit inside. Nearly half the vessel had been lopped off, a neat line as though a giant guillotine had cut her clean. Large winches at the front of the building strained to drag the carcass up the inclined floor. Once in position, a mechanism on an overhead track lowered from the ceiling and tightened what looked like a large chain around the entire hull. Savich looked more closely. The chain was embedded with metal teeth like a flexible band saw.

"What do you think, my friend?" Savich's host called from the bridge of the derelict freighter.

Like all Sikhs, Shere Singh wore a long beard that covered the lower portion of his face that he tucked into his tightly wound turban. The hard hat perched precariously atop the white cloth looked like a child's toy helmet. His hair and beard were streaked with silver and discolored around his mouth from years of heavy smoking. His skin was nut brown and weathered, and he had intense, almost maniacal hazel eyes with a disconcerting tendency to stare unblinking. Singh was also at least six inches taller than Savich's five ten, with a barrel chest, shoulders as wide as a gallows' arm, and a heavy gut as solid as oak.

From a dossier provided by Bernhard Volkmann, Savich knew that the fifty-two-year-old Singh had raised himself up from a Lahore slum where from an early age he'd used his size and strength as tools of intimidation. He didn't have his first legitimate job until the age of twenty-six, when he purchased controlling interest in a Pakistani import-export company at the time the United States was funneling money into the region to counter the Soviet invasion of Afghanistan. Despite the conflict raging in that mountainous country, steady streams of opium smugglers still managed to get their product to Karachi, and Singh was more than willing to forward on their raw product to the heroin-producing centers in Amsterdam, Marseilles, and Rome.

Singh understood that American support guaranteed an Afghan win, so by the time the Taliban came into power and eradicated the opium trade, he had shifted his focus elsewhere. He diversified, using bribery to secure timber rights in Malaysia, Indonesia, and New Guinea. He bought a fleet of his own ships to haul the lumber. He sold private hunting rights to wealthy Chinese so they could harvest tigers on his land and have their bones ground into aphrodisiacs. Nearly every legitimate venture he embarked upon had an illegal angle to it. Four of the twelve apartment buildings one of his companies built in Taiwan collapsed during a mild earthquake because he'd ordered the use of substandard materials. So long as his wealth continued to increase, Shere Singh didn't care how or where he made his money.

No doubt, Savich thought as the Sikh stepped across to the catwalk, there was an illicit side to the Karamita Breakers Yard.

"Very impressive," the Russian answered, looking at what the driver had called a ship saw and not bothering to meet Singh's reptilian gaze.

Singh lit a cigarette in front of a No Smoking sign. "Only one like it in Asia," he boasted. "The trick to it is the teeth. Even carbon steel would wear out. The metal in the teeth was produced in Germany. Strongest in the world. We can cut ten ships before teeth need to be replaced. Have technician come from Hamburg to show us how. We call him dentist." When Savich didn't laugh, Singh plowed on. "You know, fix teeth. Dentist. Is very funny."

Savich waved a hand to encompass the echoing shed. "This must have been expensive."

"You have no idea. But Indonesian government gave me tax credits if I modernize. Of course they don't think that I can fire a thousand workers because of this. Which is good thing. These monkeys are clumsy. Cost me a hundred thousand rupia to family every time some fool gets himself killed breaking ship. Fifteen die last week when a cutter didn't vent a bunker fuel tank and blew up a container ship in the bay.

"But now that I have the ship saw, government inspectors won't be around so much. I can start dumping all the asbestos we've stripped off ships back in ocean rather than haul to special dump. With the price of scrap ships down and the value of steel up, and a thousand Indonesian monkeys off my payroll, this will pay for itself in two years. So yes, expensive in short run. Profitable in long run." Singh tried another smile. "And I always say life is marathon."

An alarm Klaxon sounded. Singh flipped the ear protectors down, and Savich just managed to get his into position when the eight-inch-wide saw blade began to rotate. It spooled up smoothly, rattling only when it ran around the two large sprocket gears near the ceiling. Like a boa constrictor squeezing its victim, hydraulic rams began to tighten the saw around the freighter five feet aft of the previous cut. When the chain reached its required speed, the rams choked back even farther, and the teeth bit into the ship's keel. The sound filled the metal shed, rebounding off the walls so it assaulted the two men on the catwalk from every direction. Water cannons on either side of the hull automatically tracked the toothed belt as it sliced the ship and kept the cuts lubricated and cool. Steel shavings and steam exploded from where the teeth ripped into the ship's keel, turning the metal red hot. The smoke coiling from the cut was dense and rank. Once through the solid keel, the saw shredded the much thinner hull plating like a chain saw cutting through rotted wood.

In just ten minutes the rotating chain had cut up to the main deck. Savich watched spellbound as the deck began to glow from the heat of the teeth cutting the metal, and then the chain emerged in an eruption of torn steel and cut through the freighter's railings as though they weren't there. A sophisticated braking system stopped the chain, and the entire mechanism retracted toward the ceiling. The dismembered section of hull had already been secured to a rolling crane that spanned the shed. The crane lifted the hull slice as the forward doors opened and the four small locomotives backed in to accept the load.

"They will lay the piece on its side out in the yard," Singh explained. "Men with hand cutters will chop it up to send to the steel plant. The only parts we can't cut with the saw are the ship's main diesels, but they are easy to remove once we cut our way into the engine room. By hand it takes two weeks to scrap a ship this size. We can do it in two days."

"Very impressive," Savich repeated.

Shere Singh led the Russian back toward the elevator. "So what is it Volkmann sent you around the world to tell me?"

"We'll discuss it in your office."

Fifteen minutes later they were seated in an office attached to the largest bungalow. Framed pictures of Singh's eleven children were arranged along one wall dominated by a studio portrait of his wife, a heavyset dowager of a woman with a bovine expression. Savich had declined a beer and drank bottled water instead. Singh drank through a bottle of Filipino San Miguel and was on his second by the time Savich had his briefcase opened.

"The consortium accepted everything Volkmann and I proposed." Savich said. "It's time to expand what we already started."

The Sikh laughed. "Was there any doubt?"

Savich ignored the sarcasm and slid across a file. "These are our projected needs for the next year. Can you fulfill them?"

Singh perched a pair of reading glasses on his large nose and scanned the list, mumbling the salient figures. "An additional thousand immediately, two hundred a month first two months. Four hundred next two. Six hundred after that." He looked across at the Russian. "Why the increase?"

"Disease. By then we expect typhoid and cholera to run rampant."

"Ah."

Their discussion of specifics over the next several hours was Savich's way of making certain Singh fully understood the plan he and Volkmann had perfected since learning of the German central bank's intention to sell off their gold reserves. To his credit, or perhaps discredit, the Sikh had an inherent grasp of criminal enterprise and was even able to contribute a few inspired refinements.

Satisfied that everything on this end was handled, Savich said his good-byes two hours before sunset so as to have ample time to chopper back to Jakarta. There was no way he'd fly in the small helicopter after dark. He planned on staying in the city overnight before commencing the next leg of his journey, a roundabout odyssey of a half dozen flights to get him back to Russia. He wasn't looking forward to it.

Ten minutes after Savich left his office at the Karamita Breakers Yard, Shere Singh was on the phone to his son, Abhay. Because of the nature of his work, the senior Singh trusted only his sons to know the full scope of his business, which is why he had had six of them. His five daughters were merely a financial drain, one of whom hadn't yet married, meaning he still had her dowry to consider. She was the youngest and marginally his favorite, so he'd have to top the two million dollars he'd given the horse-faced Mamta.

"Father, we haven't heard from the *Kra IV* for two days," Singh's eldest said after a brief exchange of pleasantries.

"Who is her captain?"

"On this voyage it was Mohamed Hattu."

Singh was a reprehensible figure of a man, but that didn't mean he wasn't shrewd. He kept a tight rein on his enterprises and made it a point to know all his senior people. Hattu was a pirate of the old school who'd preyed on shipping in the Malacca Strait for twenty years before Singh made him an offer. He was audacious and reckless but also dogmatic about procedure. If he hadn't checked in for two days, something must have happened. And with that thought, Singh wrote off the *Kra IV*, her captain, and her crew of forty. "There are others eager to take his place," Shere Singh told his son. "I will look into a replacement. However, alert your contacts to listen for any mention of a thwarted pirate attack. Whoever fought Mohamed Hattu and lived will want to tell the tale."

"Yes, Father. I've thought of that. So far there have been no such reports."

"On to other business. Anton Savich just left my office. The plan is in motion. I have his list of requirements. It's about what I anticipated."

"On your order we've already begun to collect."

"Yes, good. What about your men? Will they do what is necessary when the time is right?"

"Their loyalty is absolute. Savich and his European bankers will never know what hit them once we strike."

The confidence in his son's voice sent a proud thrill through Shere Singh. His boy was so much like him. He was sure that had Abhay not been born with wealth, he would have created his own fortune, clawing his way up like Shere had done in his youth.

"Good, my boy, good. They maneuvered themselves into a vulnerable position without even realizing it."

"No, Father. You maneuvered them. You turned their fear and greed into action, and now it will consume them all."

"No, Abhay, we don't want them destroyed. Remember always, you can continue to eat the fruit from a dying tree but not from one that is dead. Savich, Volkmann, and the others will suffer, but we will leave enough so we can feast on them for a long time to come."

10

"YOU'RE going to wear a trail into the carpet," Eddie Seng said from an overstuffed chair in the corner of the hotel room.

Juan Cabrillo remained silent as he paced to the plate glass window overlooking the dazzling lights of Tokyo's Ginza District. He paused there with his hands clasped behind his back, his broad shoulders rigid with tension. The *Oregon* was fast approaching the floating drydock named *Maus* and would be going into action soon. His place was on her bridge, not stuck in a hotel suite waiting for Mark Murphy to come up with something about the vessel's owners. He felt caged.

A driving rain blurred the view of the city from their thirtieth-floor room. It matched his mood.

Twenty-four hours had passed since stepping off the helicopter sent to fetch Victoria Ballinger. A representative from the Royal Geographic Society was on the windswept pad to meet the rented helo, a bearded man in a tan trench coat. From their body language it was clear to Juan that Tory and the representative had never met before. The man introduced himself as Richard Smith. While he thanked Juan for saving Tory,

Cabrillo sensed he was reserved, almost wary. Tory was obviously grateful and gave Juan a kiss on the cheek as an orderly guided her to the private service ambulance Smith had arranged for her.

She had held up her hand just as she was about to be placed into the ambulance, her blue eyes steady on Juan's. "Last night I remembered something from the rescue," she'd said.

Uh-oh, thought Cabrillo.

"When I was trapped in my cabin I asked if you were the navy, and you wrote back something about being a private security company. What was that all about?"

Smith was already settled on a jump seat in the back of the ambulance and had to lean out somewhat to hear the answer.

Juan paused, looking from her over to him, then back to Tory. "I lied."

"Excuse me?" She crossed her arms over her chest.

Cabrillo smiled. "I said I lied. Had I told you I was the master of a rust-bucket freighter who happened to have fish-finding sonar and a few crewmen with scuba gear, would you have trusted me to get you out?"

Tory didn't speak for several long seconds, her gaze penetrating and doubting. She arched an eyebrow "A fish finder?"

"The cook uses it when we're in port to catch dinner once in a while."

"Then why was it on in the middle of the ocean?" Smith asked, his tone edged with accusation.

Juan kept his smile in place, playing the role. "Just dumb luck, I guess. It went off when we passed over the *Avalon*. The watch stander happened to notice the dimensions of the target, realized we'd either discovered the biggest whale in history, or something wasn't right. I was called to the bridge and decided to turn about. The *Avalon* hadn't moved, so we discounted our monster whale theory. That's when I threw on my tanks and had a look."

"I see." Smith nodded. He wasn't entirely convinced, which made Juan even more certain that neither Tory nor the stiff Englishman were members of the Royal Geographic Society. His first thought was that they were Royal Navy and the *Avalon* was a spy ship, most likely in these waters monitoring North Korea or Russia's Pacific Fleet out of Vladivostok. But if that were the case, it meant the pirates were capable of approaching a modern combat vessel loaded with sophisticated electronics, take out the crew in a lightning raid, and escape undetected. Cabrillo just couldn't bring himself to believe that. Ex–Royal Navy then, perhaps using a ship belonging to the Society, but still out here on a mission of some kind.

"Then you must also thank the cook for me," Tory said, nodding to the orderly to settle her in the ambulance.

Juan, Eddie, and the two former SEALs Eddie had selected were left on their own to arrange transportation. Rather than deal with hiring a car or finding a train station, they'd chartered the same helicopter that brought them from the *Oregon* to fly them to Tokyo, where Max Hanley had reserved a four-bedroom suite under one of the Corporation's front companies. And that is where they waited. The SEALs spent most of the time in the hotel's extensive fitness center, while Cabrillo paced the room, willing his cell phone to ring. Eddie took up guard duty, making sure his boss didn't damage the room out of frustration or boredom.

"They can bill me for a new rug," Juan finally said without turning from the window.

"What about the ulcer you're giving yourself? I don't think Doc Huxley packed you any antacids.

Cabrillo regarded Eddie. "That's the pickled octopus I ate, not the stress."

"Riiight." Eddie returned to his English-language paper.

Cabrillo continued to stare out into the storm, his mind a million miles away. That wasn't entirely true. His mind was six hundred miles away, at his seat in the *Oregon*'s operations center. This wasn't the first time his ship had gone into battle without him, and it wasn't that he didn't trust his crew. He just felt a personal need to be part of the action as they went after the snakeheads.

God, he thought, *how old was I when I saw it?* He couldn't have been more than seven or eight. They were coming back from an aunt's house in San Diego. His dad was driving, of course, and Mom was in the other front seat: he remembered her shouting a warning to his dad about the traffic jam several seconds after he'd applied the brake. She'd immediately turned to check on him in the backseat. The quick deceleration hadn't even locked his seat belt, but she acted as though he had almost been launched through the windshield.

And for what seemed like forever, traffic inched along the highway. He remembered that for a while they were next to a car with a Saint Bernard in the backseat. It was the first time he'd seen one, and he'd been captivated by its size. To this day he still vowed that when he finally retired he'd own one of those huge dogs.

"Have you picked a name?" Eddie asked softly.

"Gus," Juan answered automatically before realizing that he'd been telling the story out loud rather than in his head. He lapsed into an embarrassed silence.

"So what happened?" Seng prompted.

Juan knew he couldn't leave it there. His unconscious mind was telling him that this story had to come out. "We finally approached the accident site. A car must have swerved and caused an eighteen-wheeler to jackknife. The trailer had detached and lay on its side, the rear doors facing the road. Only one police car had made it to the scene. The cop had already locked the truck's driver into his cruiser.

"One of the trailer's rear doors had popped open when it tipped, and the patrolman was helping the other victims of the crash. I have no idea how many, maybe a hundred Mexican workers had been in the trailer when it went over. Some were only slightly injured and helped the officer with the others. A few were better off and could walk from the wreckage. Others they had to drag. There were already two areas set aside. In one, women tended to the wounded. In the other, the bodies had been lined up in a straight row. My mother was very protective and told me not to look, but she said it softly as she stared at the carnage, unable to tear her eyes away. We passed the accident and soon were back up to speed.

"No one spoke for a few minutes. My mom was crying softly. I sat there not quite understanding what I'd seen, but I knew that people weren't supposed to be in the back of a semi. I remember my father's words when Mom finally stopped sobbing. 'Juan,' he said, 'no matter what anyone tells you, there is evil in this world. And all it takes for it to triumph is for good people to do nothing.' "

Juan's voice lost its soft tone as his mind returned to the present. "When I was old enough, we talked about that day again. My parents explained how smugglers snuck people up from Mexico and how some never survived the journey. They told me the truck driver pleaded guilty to thirty-six counts of vehicular homicide and that he'd been killed in prison by a Latino gang."

Eddie said, "And when that cargo container was opened on deck and you saw those Chinese—?"

"I was back on that hot interstate and felt just as powerless. That is, until I remembered my father's words."

"What did he do for work, if you don't mind my asking?"

"An accountant, actually, but he had fought in Korea and believed there was nothing more evil on earth than Communism."

"If he had as much influence on you as I think he did, you doubly want these guys—smugglers and Communists."

"If it turns out that China's behind it, damn right." Cabrillo gave Eddie an appraising look. "I don't need to tell you about that. You were in their backyard for years."

Eddie nodded gravely. "I've seen firsthand evidence of entire villages being wiped off the map because someone spoke out against a local party official. The cities may be opening up to the West, but the countryside is ruled as ruthlessly as ever. It's the only way the central government can control a billion people. Keep them on edge, near starvation, and grateful for whatever handouts they get."

"Something tells me," Cabrillo said, "that this isn't a Chinese operation."

"It makes sense to me if it were," Seng countered. "They have a population crisis, and I'm not talking about overcrowding, though that is a problem. No, what China faces today and over the next twenty years or so is something far worse."

"Worse than trying to feed a quarter of the world's population?" Juan asked skeptically.

"In fact it's a direct result of the one-child policy enacted in 1979. Today China's birthrate is 1.8 children per woman. The rate's even lower in the cities. For a sustainable population, a country needs a fertility rate of at least 2.1. Falling birthrates in the U.S. and Europe are mostly offset by immigration, so we're okay. But China is going to see their population ratios age dramatically in the next decades. There won't be enough workers to man the factories nor enough people to care for the elderly. Add to that the cultural bias against girls, select-sex abortion, and infanticide, and right now China has one hundred and eighteen boys under the age of ten for every one hundred girls."

"So what's that going to do?"

"Unless a significant segment of the male population is gay or chooses celibacy, there are going to be about two hundred million men with no chance of having families of their own by 2025."

Cabrillo followed through to the logical conclusion of Eddie's lecture. "So you think they're shipping excess men overseas now?"

"It's a theory."

"A plausible one," the chairman agreed. "And something I hadn't considered—the wholesale export of people."

"About a million Chinese immigrate illegally a year," Eddie told him, "with the tacit approval of local governments, I might add. It's not much of a stretch for the leaders in Beijing to actually start their own program to get rid of what's already being called the 'army of bachelors.' " Eddie's voice turned bitter. "Despite the propaganda spin over the last few years, China remains a brutal dictatorship. They invariably take the hard approach to any problem. They want to build a dam, they move thirty million people out of the way, show Western reporters the new towns they're building, but ultimately dump the population on collective farms."

Juan let Eddie Seng's accusation hang in the air for a few seconds. He was well aware of how much Eddie hated the Beijing government. "But there were only a few dozen people on the *Kra*," he finally said.

"But what's on that ship Tory Ballinger saw?"

"You mean who?"

"Exactly."

Juan's encrypted cell phone chimed. "Cabrillo."

"Juan, it's Max."

"What's up?" He tried to sound nonchalant, but there was an edge to his voice.

"We're about twenty miles behind the *Maus*. We've already talked to them, establishing procedure for passing a drydock under tow. In about ten minutes we're going to launch an unmanned aerial drone with a low-light camera to take a peek into her open hold. I do have a boarding party standing by if we need to send over some Mark-one eyeballs."

"Sounds good. What's the weather? It's raining here."

"Fine. No moon at all. Seas are only a couple of feet, and the wind's light. Listen, the reason I called is we have some information for you."

About time, Cabrillo thought but kept it to himself. "Murph tracked down who owns the *Maus*?"

"No, he's still working on it. Julia came up with something during her autopsies of the Chinese folks we plucked from the container. I'm passing her off to you."

"Thanks. E-mail the feeds from the UAV to my phone. I'd like to take a look at the *Maus* during the flyover."

"You got it. Here's the doc."

"Chairman, how's Tokyo?"

"It's all warm sushi and cold geishas."

"I bet. I think I found something about our immigrants. They're all from the same village, a place called Lantan in Fujian Province. Most of them are part of the same extended family."

"Did you do a DNA test?"

"No, I read the parts of a diary that hadn't been destroyed when the container went into the drink. A lot of the journal was illegible, but I scanned everything into the computer and let the translator take a crack at it. The guy who wrote it's last name was Xang. With him were two brothers, a bunch of cousins, and distant blood relatives. They had been promised work in Japan by a snakehead who called himself Yan Luo. Each of them had to pay this Yan Luo about five hundred dollars before leaving the village and would have to pay back about fifteen *thousand* once they reached a textile mill outside Tokyo."

"Does he talk about the *Kra*? Was that the boat taking them to Japan?"

"He doesn't say, or that part of the journal was too damaged to read."

"What else were you able to get?"

"Not much. He wrote about his dreams and how one day he would be able to afford bringing his girlfriend to Japan with him. Stuff like that."

"What was the name of that town?"

"Lantan."

"If we can't backtrack the *Kra* or the *Maus*, maybe we can backtrack the immigrants." Cabrillo glanced at Eddie. His chief of Shore Operations had heard enough of the call to understand what was coming. It was in his eyes. "I'll call you right back," Cabrillo said to Julia and cut the connection.

"China, huh," Eddie said with an air of the inevitable. "I had a feeling it would come to this as soon as I saw them."

"Can you do it?"

"You know my cover was blown just before I got out the last time. I've already been sentenced to death in absentia. I can name a dozen generals and party officials who would like nothing more than for me to step foot in China again. It's been a few years, but last I knew, my picture had been sent to every police department in the country, from Beijing and Shanghai to the smallest provincial outpost."

"Can you do it?" Cabrillo repeated.

"My old network is long gone. I was hustled out of China fast after everything went down and couldn't get a warning out. I'm sure some of them were rolled up by the state police, which means the rest are compromised. I can't use any of them."

He went silent. Cabrillo didn't ask a third time. He didn't need to.

"I've got a set of credentials in a safe-deposit box in L.A., one the CIA doesn't even know about. I had them made before Hong Kong was handed over to China in case I needed to get back in to help a couple of friends. They've since immigrated to Vancouver, so the identity is still viable. I'll contact my lawyer first thing tomorrow and have them sent by courier to Singapore. From there I can catch the Cathay flight to Beijing."

"Shanghai," Juan corrected. "Julia said the village is in Fujian Province. If my geography is sound, the closest big city is Shanghai."

"Oh, this gets better and better," Eddie said as if his mission wouldn't be difficult enough.

"Why's that?"

"The people of Fujian have a dialect all their own. I don't speak it very well."

"Then we'll call it off," Juan decided. "We'll just have to get some leads from the *Kra* or the *Maus*."

"No," Eddie said sharply. "It might take you weeks to track these bastards through shipping records and corporate pyramids. If illegal immigrants somehow fit into the pirates' scheme, we need answers now. You and I both know that the ones dumped over the side of the *Kra* aren't the only ones who've been taken."

Juan nodded, a curt, decisive gesture. "All right. Make your arrangements."

* * *

ON the main display screen along the front wall of the operations center, the picture was a weirdly distorted view of the ocean, where the foam topping the low waves looked like green lightning forking across the black water. The camera's optics made the rhythmic pulse of the sea look like a beating heart. The image jerked slightly, and George Adams swore.

Adams was the pilot of the *Oregon*'s Robinson R-44 helicopter as well as the pair of matching UAVs, or unmanned aerial vehicles, that could be launched from an open space along the freighter's port rail. Although the U.S. military spent millions on their Predator drones, the Corporation's UAVs were commercially available remote-control airplanes fitted with low-light cameras. George could sit at a computer workstation inside the operations center and fly the model plane using a joystick within a fifteen-mile radius of the ship.

One of the few aboard the *Oregon* from the army, George "Gomez" Adams had earned his reputation flying special ops teams into Bosnia, Afghanistan, and Iraq. Unmarried at forty, Adams cut the figure of a fighter pilot. He was dark-haired and dark-eyed, tall and lean with a charming cockiness that never failed to make him a center of attention with women. His good looks had been used in more than one past Corporation mission. He'd earned his nickname after one such mission when he seduced the mistress of a Peruvian drug trafficker who bore a striking resemblance to the television character Morticia Addams.

The telepresence given to Adams through the video link allowed him to see what was in front of and below the gimballed camera in the UAV's nose, but he couldn't feel the subtle updrafts or crosswinds that affected the five-foot-long airplane. He adjusted for the sudden gust that hit the plane and eased back on the stick to gain a bit more altitude.

"What's the range?" he asked Linda Ross, who was monitoring the radar picture.

"We're four miles astern the *Maus* and three miles to port."

The UAV was too small to be seen by even the *Oregon*'s powerful search radar, but the massive drydock and the pair of tugs towing her showed crisp on her repeater screen.

Adams used a thumb control to pan the camera mounted in the model plane's nose. The ocean was still streaked with eerie green lines of sea foam, but a few miles ahead of the UAV a bright emerald slash cut the otherwise dark water.

"There," someone called unnecessarily.

The glowing wedge was the *Maus*'s wake as she was hauled southward. Just ahead of her were bright, glowing points, searchlights mounted at the stern of the towboats to illuminate their ponderous charge. The thick hawsers securing the vessels looked as fine as gossamer from five thousand feet. There were a couple less powerful lights along the side of the drydock, but her cavernous hold was completely dark.

"Okay, George. Take us in," Max Hanley ordered from the command station. He then pressed a cell phone to his ear. "You getting this, Chairman?"

"Kind of," Juan Cabrillo said from his Tokyo suite. "I can't make out much on this one-inch screen."

"I'm going for a high pass first," Adams said as he worked the joystick. "If we don't get anything, I'll cut the engine and glide in for a closer look." He took his eyes off his screen to glance at Hanley. "If the engine doesn't refire, the UAV's a write-off."

"I heard that," Juan said. "Tell George that we can't lose the element of surprise if we have to send over boarders. Tell him it's okay to ditch the drone."

Max relayed the message, saying, "George, Juan says that if you crash the UAV, it's coming out of your paycheck."

"You tell him," Adams said, fully concentrating on his screen once again, "that I'll cut him a check as soon as Eddie pays for that submarine he banged up."

George slowed the UAV to just above stall speed, but it still overtook the slow-moving caravan of ships. There was no chance the black airplane could be spotted from either the drydock or the tugboats; however, it was possible that an attentive crewman could hear the high whine of the UAV's engine. He kept the drone five hundred feet to the starboard side of the convoy and panned the camera as it flew down the eight-hundred-foot length of the drydock.

It looked more like a fortress than a vessel designed to travel across the ocean. Her sides were sheer vertical walls of steel, and there was only the barest hint of streamlining at her blunt bows. The pair of hundred-plus-foot tugs looked like toys compared to the behemoth in their charge.

Even as the pictures came in, Eric Stone and Mark Murphy were filtering the video through computer software to enhance the image. The pair of tech geeks cycled the feed to increase contrast and eliminate distortion caused by the UAV's engine vibration. By the time George had completed his run and peeled the drone away from the *Maus,* they had sharpened the raw data and played it back on the main screen.

"What the hell am I supposed to be looking at here?" Juan asked through the cell phone.

"Damn," Max said, staring at the big plasma display. He held his cell phone in one hand and his unlit pipe in the other.

"What is it?"

"The lights along the *Maus*'s rail make it impossible to see into her hold. It's just a black hole in the middle of the ship. We need to make a run directly over her."

"Coming around now," Gomez Adams said, his body unconsciously leaning as the UAV swooped in a tight turn.

A few minutes later he had the drone lined up behind the drydock at two thousand feet. Rather than bleed off speed, he pressed the throttle to its stop, hurtling the tiny plane directly at the *Maus* on what he was sure would be a suicide run. The UAV's ignition system was temperamental at best, and a crewman usually had to hand crank the little propeller on deck prior to launch.

The bulk of the *Maus* filled the view screen as the drone bored in. George killed the engine when he was about a quarter mile out, and the picture lost its annoying jumpiness as the plane became a silent glider sliding out of the night sky. He checked the altimeter. The drone was at a thousand feet, and he deepened the angle of attack. It was now arrowing at the drydock like a Stuka dive bomber, but as silent as a wraith.

Eric and Murph double-checked that the recorders were burning the images onto disc just before the UAV crossed over the *Maus*'s vertical transom. Adams leveled the drone a hundred feet above the floating drydock and soared the little craft down the vessel's dark length, making sure the camera caught every detail of her murky hold.

Fifty feet from the bow, he heeled over the UAV, diving once again to gain airspeed. At an altitude of thirty feet he hit the starter toggle on his controls. The sea grew on the plasma screen monitor. When nothing happened, he calmly reset the toggle and tried again. The plastic prop turned once, but the engine refused to fire.

It was as though the plane accelerated in its final moments or perhaps the ocean reached up to pluck it from the sky. The team in the control room winced as the UAV augered in, and the screen went blank.

Adams got to his feet and cracked his knuckles. "You know what they say: any landing you can walk away from is a good one."

A few people groaned at the old joke as Murph put a replay of the aerial pass back on the screen.

"What did you see?" Cabrillo asked over the satellite link.

"Hold on a second, boss," Max replied. "It's coming up now."

While the image was dark, Adams had done a superb job controlling both the UAV and its camera. The shot was steady and clear and not at all what they wanted to see. There was a cover of some type over the entire length of the drydock's hold. The cover wasn't solid, because sections of it rippled in the wind, but it completely blocked their view of anything the drydock might have been transporting.

"Well?" Juan's voice was insistent in Hanley's ear.

"We have to send over a recon team," Hanley told the Chairman. "They've got the entire hold covered with sections of dark cloth. We can't see diddly."

Linda Ross was already at the control room's rear door. As the senior intelligence officer aboard the *Oregon,* it was her job to lead the team over to the *Maus*. She wore a black combat uniform and had slipped into the flak vest she'd had draped over her chair. Her fine, honey-blond hair was covered by a black watch cap.

Despite the determined set to her narrow jaw and the accoutrements of war, she still managed to look young and vulnerable. It didn't help that she had a high-pitched voice, not shrill but almost pubescent, and her cheeks were dusted with freckles. At thirty-seven, Linda was still carded at bars on her infrequent trips back to the States.

Although she had spent her naval career as an intelligence analyst, Linda was well practiced at the art of intelligence gathering, too. Because of her background, she usually spent less time on a particular covert mission than others simply because she knew exactly what information was needed. She could make quick assessments in the field, innately knowing what was crucial. For that she had more than earned the respect of the SEALs she was to lead.

"Tell Juan we'll be careful," she said to Max and left to make her way down to a door at the waterline on the starboard side where they'd launch a Zodiac inflatable boat.

Three commandos were waiting for her in the aqua garage. They were similarly outfitted, and one handed Linda a combat harness. She checked that the silenced Glock she preferred was loaded. She liked that the pistol didn't have a safety that could be inadvertently activated on a quick draw. Because this was a reconnoiter, a sneak and peek, and they doubted there would be guards posted on a ship under tow, none of the team carried anything heavier than handguns, but these weapons were hot-loaded with mercury-tipped hollow points, a round packing enough kinetic energy to incapacitate with even a glancing blow. She settled the throat mike of her tactical radio next to her skin and secured the earpiece. She and the team did a quick test, making sure they could hear each other and Max in the op center.

The garage was lit by red battle lights, and in their glow Linda applied black camo paint to her face before slipping on tight no-shine gloves. The Zodiac was large enough for eight, powered by a big black outboard. Next to the four-stroke engine was a smaller battery-powered trolling motor that could silently propel the Zodiac at nearly ten knots. A few items they would need had been secured to the floorboards.

A cargo master checked each team member again before flashing the thumbs-up to Linda. She threw him a wink, and the deckhand doused the lights. A cable system opened the outer door, a ten-by-eight-foot section of hull plating just above the waterline. The hiss of the sea passing by filled the garage, and Linda could taste the salt in the air. While there was virtually no moon, the *Maus* stood out against the darkness, her forward sections lit by floodlights on the pair of tugs, and sodium arc lamps along her top deck cast her silhouette in strong relief.

The Zodiac pilot fired the engine with a press of a button, and with a pair of people along each side, the team shoved the inflatable down a Teflon-coated ramp and jumped aboard as soon as the craft hit water. They shot away from the *Oregon* in a burst of foam to escape the turbulent water running along the tramp steamer's flank before throttling back to eliminate their own wake.

The gap between the two ships seemed small when seen from the cameras mounted on the *Oregon*'s deck, but down in the trough of water between the vessels, the distance appeared enormous. The seas were light, and the inflatable rode the swells easily, gliding up the face, hanging for the barest moment before dropping back in a smooth rhythm. Even muffled, the outboard sounded loud in Linda's ears, though she knew that the craft was silent at full speed from a mile away.

Five minutes after launching from the *Oregon,* they had knifed through three-quarters of the way. The pilot cut the outboard and engaged the silent electric motor, taking a cue from Linda to circle around the stern of the *Maus* in order to find a suitably dark area to board.

The drydock was only making three knots, so they had little trouble passing behind the vessel and easing their way along her starboard side. The hull was a featureless wall of gray steel that stretched from stem to stern. The lights mounted high atop her rail washed down the plating, but amidships there was a patch of darkness where one of the bulbs was burned out. The pilot eased the Zodiac over, running right outside the wake zone next to the darkened section of hull. He had to constantly adjust the motor to keep the vessel stable in the choppy wash.

"Grapple," Linda called over her throat mike.

One of the SEALs raised an odd weapon to his shoulder. It looked like an oversized rifle, but a hose ran from the pistol grip to a cylinder strapped to the floor of the Zodiac. He activated a laser range finder slung under the ungainly rifle and pointed it skyward, centering his sights at a spot just above the *Maus*'s rail.

"Sixty-seven feet," he whispered.

By the light of a small red-lensed flashlight, his partner dialed the number into a valve at the top of the cylinder. He tapped the shooter on the shoulder.

The man centered his breathing, feeling the gentle rise and fall of the Zodiac, and waited for the exact moment the craft reached the zenith of a wave. He eased the trigger.

A precise amount of compressed nitrogen exploded from the tank, launching a stubby rubber-coated arrow from the grappling gun. Behind the arrow trailed a millimeters-wide nanofiber line. At the apogee of flight, the arrow peeled apart to become a grappling hook. The hook cleared the rail by scant inches and fell silently to the deck.

Back in the Zodiac, the shooter pulled back on his weapon, dragging the hook high above so it locked around a rail stanchion. "Secure."

His partner unhooked the reel from the grappling gun and used a snap link to splice a nylon climbing rope to the nanofiber line. In smooth hand-over-hand motions, he hauled the line through a small pulley at the back of the grapple so the climbing rope rose into the night sky. It took barely thirty seconds for him to loop the rope around the pulley and recover the end. He secured one end of the rope to cargo straps at the bow of the Zodiac while the pilot did the same at the stern. Using sheer muscle power, the men pulled on the ropes, and the Zodiac lifted free of the water. They heaved again, and the little inflatable rose another foot. They did this three more times until there was no danger a wave would come along and capsize the craft. Had they left it bobbing in the wash while they were reconnoitering the *Maus,* the boat's rubber skin would have shredded against the drydock's steel hide.

All the lines were locked down, and one by one the team climbed the thick nylon rope, first making sure they had chambered rounds in their pistols. Linda climbed third in the stick, trusting the first team member would clear the rail under the cover of the number-two man. She heard the shooter call "*Clear*" through her miniature earpiece and looked up to see him slither between the metal railing.

She glanced down as she neared the top. The Zodiac pilot was right below her, and far down in the shadows she could see the inflatable snuggled up against the drydock like a seal pup nursing from its mother. The sea was a surging presence a littler farther down.

She accepted the hand from above and was dragged over the rail, thankful that the heavy flak vest protected her breasts. She doubted Doc Huxley with her 38-Ds could have done it.

The three of them formed a defensive perimeter around the rail until the last man clambered over. The shooter took a second to remove the grappling hook and secure the rope holding the Zodiac with a coupling device that could be disengaged once they were safely back on their boat.

The top deck of the *Maus* appeared deserted, though technically it wasn't a deck but a ten-foot-wide catwalk that circled the entire ship. Had huge sheets of stiff material not been drawn over the hold, the deck would have been like the parapet of an iron castle. Linda approached the protective covering. The material felt like woven plastic fibers. It had been pulled taut across the hold so it was stiff, like the canvas of a large tent. She pressed against it and felt no give.

One of the men had pulled a blued Gerber knife from a boot sheath and was about to cut the fabric. Linda held up a hand. Wordlessly, she pointed to the shooter and his partner and indicated they were to search the perimeter headed aft while she and the pilot would head forward. She pointed across the 240-foot hold to where she wanted to meet up.

Linda eased her Glock from its holster. There was too much light around the deck to use night vision gear but too little to see clearly. Fortunately, there didn't appear to be many places a sentry could hide on the catwalk. There were few ventilators or machinery housings to provide cover. Backed by the pilot, she stalked silently along the starboard rail, her pistol held steady near her waist while her eyes darted from shadow to shadow. Her breathing came easy and light, but she could feel her pulse in her throat and wondered briefly if her team could hear it through the tactical radio.

There was a structure near the bow, a blockhouse that probably housed the ballast and door controls. At first it appeared dark and deserted, but as they approached, Linda could see seams of light outlining several blacked-out windows. She pressed her back against the structure's cool metal, then cocked her head to place her ear to the steel. She couldn't make out words, or even the language, but she definitely heard voices inside. She heard four distinct voices, all male, and held up four fingers for the pilot. He nodded.

The pair of them eased past the blockhouse, keeping a wary eye on the single door. Just as they reached cover behind a massive ventilation hood, the door was thrown open, and a single man emerged into the night. Linda checked her watch. Two thirty. Time for a bihourly patrol. A second guard joined the first. Both wore black uniforms similar to the ones the Corporation team sported, but these men carried compact submachine guns on slings around their necks. Linda didn't recognize the model, though it didn't make any difference. She and her entire team were outgunned. The guards had the air of the military. Mercenaries, she guessed, hired by whoever headed the pirate ring. She also suspected that these men, or others like them, had been responsible for killing the crew of the *Avalon* and scuttling the research ship.

The first to emerge said something to his partner. To Linda it sounded like Russian or some other Slavic language. She wished Juan were here. He had an ear for languages. He spoke four fluently and understood enough of several others to at least get by.

Linda and her teammate ducked deeper into the shadow cast by the ventilator and let the guards pass. They moved at a brisk pace, their eyes following the beams of flashlights each carried in their left hand, leaving the right free for the wicked little machine pistols. They craned their necks over the rail every few feet to check the drydock's hull, then cast the beam out across the black expanse of material covering the hold. They seemed to miss nothing, so it was only a matter of time until they spotted the Zodiac dangling alongside the giant vessel.

Linda whispered into her throat mike once the guards had moved out of earshot, "Team two, we have a pair of guards headed right for you."

"Acknowledged."

Linda's orders were to leave no evidence that she and her men had boarded the *Maus*. That wasn't going to happen. She ran through some scenarios in her mind and decided there was only one way. She'd detected a whiff of cigarette smoke when the blockhouse door had opened. She could only hope that one of the guards on patrol was a smoker.

"There was a ballast tank vent thirty feet aft of where we hung the Zodiac," she whispered to her team. "We'll take them there."

"Roger."

"No guns."

Rather than backtrack all the way around the bow, Linda and the Zodiac driver chanced walking across the covered hold. The material was so tight that their weight did nothing more than create shallow dimples around their shoes. She noted that the fabric was in twenty-foot-wide strips and had been tightly threaded together with wire through ready-made eyelets. A lot of thought and time had gone into hiding whatever lay in the *Maus*'s hold.

Once on the far side, she met up with the other team in the protection of the ventilator she'd seen earlier. These vents allowed air to escape from huge tanks along the length of her hull when the drydock ballasted down for a ship to be drawn inside. When it was time to raise the vessel, pumps someplace deep inside the drydock expelled the ballast water through nozzles dotted around the ship.

They tracked the guards' progression around the drydock by the beams of their lights. It seemed to take forever. Once they rounded the stern and started up the starboard side of the *Maus,* they were headed right for the ambush. They had nearly four hundred feet to cover. The team waited. Linda's mouth had gone dry, and she couldn't make her tongue work to moisten her lips.

She could smell the adrenaline as the guards drew nearer, hers, her men's. The air seemed charged with it. They were within twenty feet when one stopped and patted his partner on the shoulder. The men spoke, shared a low chuckle, then one faced the railing and unbuttoned the fly of his uniform. He leaned over the rail to watch his arcing stream of urine.

It shouldn't have happened. They were on a moving vessel at sea. The wind of her passage should have blown the urine stream aft. But the drydock was only making a couple of knots, and she had a tailwind of eight to ten. To watch his drops fall away, he had to look toward the bow.

The guard rocked back in shock, nearly soaking himself. "Nikoli!"

He'd spotted the Zodiac.

Linda and her team had less than two seconds before the alarm went up.

The guard named Nikoli didn't even bother looking over the rail. He doused his flashlight and started running across the fabric-covered hold, leaving his partner straining to empty his bladder. In an instant Nikoli was swallowed by darkness. This must have been the standard procedure. If one saw something, the other was to get away and radio the guardhouse.

"Take him," Linda ordered without pointing to the guard at the railing. She sprinted off after Nikoli. A moment after running onto the tight fabric, she felt the vibration of the apparently Russian guard's footfalls ahead of her.

The stiff cloth flexed under the weight of her long strides, causing her knees to buckle with every pace. She was relying on this. At 108 pounds, plus the weight of her gear, she was still a good seventy pounds lighter than the guard. For him it would be like trying to run across a slack trampoline. She saw the glint of his machine pistol and the band of white skin below his hairline. Her Glock was in her hand.

The guard must have sensed her gaining. He had been struggling to draw a walkie-talkie from a hip holster. He forgot about the radio and began to turn so as to bring his weapon to bear. Linda slid flat, skidding across the fabric, her silenced pistol at full stretch. She fired as soon as she stopped.

The shot went wild, but the guard dropped flat. For a heartbeat he lay still. Linda raised herself and cycled through the clip as fast as she could pull the trigger. The distance was fifty feet. At a firing range she could put eleven of twelve shots in the center of a bull's-eye at this range. On the dark deck of a rogue ship she was lucky to connect with one bullet. The nine millimeter hit the guard on the top of his right shoulder and nearly took his arm off. The big Russian staggered to his feet, his arm dangling useless from his shoulder, blood shining like oil on his uniform. He had lost his gun but charged at Linda anyway.

With no time to reload, Linda got to her feet to meet his charge head-on. She tried to use his momentum to hip-throw him to the deck, but the guard got his good arm around her throat, and they both went sprawling. His knee had slammed into her chest when they fell, and Linda tried to reinflate her lungs, sucking oxygen while at the same time trying to get back on her feet.

Mortally wounded, Nikoli managed to lever himself upright, a four-inch knife in his left hand. Blood poured from his fingertips. He swiped at her with a clumsy underhand thrust that Linda easily dodged. She tried to back away to give herself room and time to reload her Glock, but the Russian came at her with the determination of the damned.

Changing tacks, Linda went on the offense and fired a kick into the side of the guard's knee. She both heard and felt cartilage tear, and

Nikoli went down. She rammed a fresh magazine into the butt of the Glock and racked the slide. Nikoli lay immobile as blood pooled around his mangled shoulder. Linda took a cautious pace forward.

"*Nyet, Specivo,*" the guard whispered when she came into his view.

She didn't move, realizing that his knife arm was under his body. He was still dangerous. She tightened her grip on the pistol. She should shoot him, but if she could get him back to the *Oregon* alive, they would have their first tangible lead.

"Show me the knife," she ordered.

Nikoli seemed to understand. He cautiously dragged his left arm from under him. The movement drained the color from his face. Linda was four feet away, well out of range, and she'd put a bullet through his brain if he made to throw the blade. He held the knife out as if he was going to toss it at her feet. Then before she knew what was happening, he plunged the blade into the plastic fabric. Under tension, the tiny puncture split like a seismic fault, and the Russian vanished, plunging eighty feet to the bottom of the hold.

Linda had no time to react as the rip grew. Her weight caused the fabric to sag, and the next thing she knew, she was on her stomach, sliding headfirst toward the expanding hole.

11

LINDA pressed her hands against the fabric, trying to find purchase, but her gloves could do little to slow her inexorable plunge. As her fingers reached the edge of the tear she frantically tried to grab the frayed edge. Her momentum was already too great, and a second later her head was over the hole, then her shoulders.

There wasn't even time to scream as her upper body slid through the rip and dangled high above the cargo hold of the drydock. Inside was pitch-dark, but she knew that she hung over an eighty-foot void. Her hips hit the edge of the tear, shifting her center of gravity. She was powerless as her body coiled under and her legs were lifted from the tough cloth covering.

Just as the top of her thighs slid over the precipice, strong hands wrapped around her ankles. For a precarious moment she continued to fall, and then she felt herself being drawn backward. She was plucked from the rent in the fabric and dragged back from the hole, not caring that the tough material scraped against the skin of her cheek.

Linda rolled onto her back and smiled into the face of the Zodiac driver. "Jesus, thanks. For a second there I thought I was . . ."

"For a second there you were."

"The other guard?" Linda asked.

"Taken care of."

"Okay, we only have another minute or two before these guys are going to be missed." Linda removed her combat harness as she spoke. She unclipped the suspenders from the belt, then reclipped them in a way to create an eight-foot-long rope of sorts. "Team two, bring the body out here."

"Roger."

"Hand me your harness." Linda worked this belt, too, doubling the length of her safety line.

She threaded an arm through a loop she had made, then secured a night vision monocle over her eyes. She averted her face from the perimeter floodlights to preserve her vision.

"Belay me," Linda ordered once the other team arrived and lowered the dead guard to the deck. She noted two things. One was that someone had thought to close up his trousers and the other was that his neck was at an oblique angle to his body.

She crawled toward the elongated hole. Nikoli's knife had sliced next to a seam, the area of maximum tension, which was why it had torn open so easily. Originally she had planned to burn a hole in the fabric to dispose of the bodies, hoping the other guards would assume a hastily tossed cigarette was at fault. But this gash would serve her purpose just as well. The others aboard the *Maus* would guess their comrades had taken a shortcut across the hold and were swallowed when the cloth suddenly gave way.

Linda slithered closer to the rent, feeling the fabric sag under her weight but confident that her team could haul her back. As she neared the hole, she felt herself slide a little and instantly felt pressure under her arms as the men checked her descent. "Okay, hold me here," she said.

She lowered her head into the hold and snapped on a tiny flashlight.

Her first concern was Nikoli. Had he landed in such a way as to make his bullet wound noticeable, their covert inspection would be blown. Linda peered downward. Because of the two-dimensional quality of the low-light optics, she didn't experience the sense of vertigo she expected. Directly below her was a ship, a small tanker with its superstructure at the stern. She peered aft, seeing that they had cut off the ship's funnel and masts to make it fit under the tarpaulins. From this vantage she saw nothing to identify the vessel, no name or distinctive characteristics. But now they had their proof that they were dealing with hijackers as well as pirates.

She switched her goggles from low-light to infrared. Her vision went black with one glowing exception. A smear of light appeared at the ship's rail and continued down to the bottom of the hold where she saw a growing pool of bright color. She changed back to the night optics and trained her flashlight on the spot. It appeared that Nikoli had hit the freighter's rail when he fell, blood that had shown up as warmth on IR looked black now, and his body lay on the lowest deck, covered in gore. She doubted very much that anyone but a trained pathologist would notice the bullet wound amid the carnage the fall had caused.

Satisfied, Linda called for her men to drag her back.

"There's a tanker in the hold. They hacked off her funnel to make her fit. I put her length around four hundred feet."

"Is there any way you can get her name?" Max asked from the op center.

"Negative. We have to clear out. Those guards are due back from their patrol about now."

"Okay. We'll be ready for you."

At a crouch the team ran back to where they had secured the Zodiac and climbed down the rope. The driver started the electric motor and was ready when the sniper released the rope. The inflatable smashed into the sea and immediately pulled away from the *Maus*, bobbing dangerously for a second before its speed evened out the ride.

Fifteen minutes later they approached the *Oregon* at twenty knots, the gasoline engine purring smoothly. The deckhand in the garage watched their approach through closed-circuit television and, as they drew nearer, he doused the red lights and opened the door just in time for the Zodiac to rocket up the ramp and come to a perfect stop. The doors were closing even before the pilot killed the engine.

Max Hanley was there to greet them. He handed his cell phone to Linda.

She peeled her watch cap from her head. "Ross here."

"Linda, it's Juan. What did you find?"

"She's hauling a midsized product tanker, Chairman. I couldn't tell her name."

"Any sign of the crew?"

"No, sir. And since the hold was completely dark, my bet is they're either dead or on one of the tugboats."

Neither needed to say that the second option wasn't likely.

"Okay, great job to all of you," Cabrillo said. "Put yourself down for an extra ration of grog."

"Actually, I'm going to avail myself of a couple shots of the Louis XIII brandy you keep in your cabin."

"That is to be enjoyed in a warm snifter, not shot down like cheap tequila."

"I'll warm the shot glass," Linda teased. "Here's Max." She handed back the phone and left the garage for a long shower, and yes, a snifter or two of Juan's fifteen-hundred-dollar cognac.

"So what do you want us to do now?" Hanley asked.

"According to what Murph told me, the *Maus* is headed for Taiwan. Why don't you get ahead of her and wait to see if she enters port? If she does, I'll meet you there and we'll play it by ear."

"And if she changes course and heads someplace else?"

"Stay with her."

"You realize she's making about three knots. We could be shadowing her for a couple of weeks before she makes landfall."

"I know. Can't be helped, old boy. Think of yourself as one of the cops following OJ on his low-speed chase along the L.A. freeways."

"Low speed? Hell, lobsters migrate faster than that damn drydock." Max turned serious. "You do remember that the last ship taken from your Japanese friend's fleet was a tanker. The, ah . . ."

"*Toya Maru,*" Juan provided.

"Right. Stands to reason that's her in the *Maus*'s hold. Why not just contact the navy or Japan's coast guard?"

"Oh, I'm certain it's the *Toya Maru.* But this isn't about one ship, and I doubt anyone on those tugboats can tell us much. The pirates are playing this too smart. You mark my word: about a day out of Taipei they'll get orders to go someplace else. We take down the *Maus* now, we nab one vessel and a few low-level guys. We track her back to wherever they're going to scrap the *Toya* or disguise her so they can use her themselves, we'll have made a dent in their operation."

"Sounds reasonable," Max agreed. "We'll play tortoise to their snail and see where this chase takes us."

"I'm handing the phone over to Eddie. He has a list of things he's going to need for his insertion into China. You can send someone to act as courier when you pass through the Korea Strait. The Robinson has more than enough range to make it to Pusan. From there, the courier can take a commercial flight to Singapore and meet up with Eddie at the airport."

"Hold on, let me get a pen. And some paper. And my reading glasses."

FIVE hundred miles north of where the *Oregon* steamed near the *Maus*, another drydock, her sister ship in fact, was just clearing the La Perouse Strait separating the northern tip of Japan from the Sakhalin Islands and entering the frigid waters of the Sea of Okhotsk. She, being towed by more powerful tugs than the *Maus*, was making six knots despite the fact that the ship hidden inside her hold was considerably larger than the tanker Linda had seen.

The seas were building around the vessels, high, rolling waves that alternately tightened and slackened the long towlines so one moment they were submerged and the next they were as taut as steel bars, bursting with water wrung out by tension. The tugs turned into the seas, shouldering aside the waves as they plowed northward, meeting the ocean as a ship should, nimble and responsive to her vagaries. The drydock played no such game. She took the waves square into her bow so explosions of white froth were flung almost to her top deck. Then she would throw off the water, slowly, ponderously, as though the sea was merely a distraction.

Like the *Maus*, the drydock's holds were covered over, but in this vessel's case, metal sheets had been laid over a steel framework and all the seams welded. The hold would have been virtually airtight except for several industrial ventilators mounted at the stern. These powerful machines drew in thousands of cubic feet of air per minute to circulate within the drydock's hold. The outgoing air was fed through banks of chemical filters to disguise the raw stench emanating from belowdecks, a smell that hadn't been found on the high seas for almost two hundred years.

CABRILLO was stuck in Tokyo until Mark Murphy came up with a lead, so he spent three days basically playing tourist in a city he'd never particularly enjoyed. He longed for the fresh air on an open sea, a horizon that seemed unreachable, and the peace that comes from standing on the fantail watching the wake curve into the distance. Instead he dealt with an impenetrable language, crowds that defied imagination, and constant staring by people who should be used to Westerners but acted as though they'd never seen one.

His feeling of impotence was further compounded by Eddie Seng's mission. Eddie had left days earlier, rendezvoused with the courier in Singapore, and had already gone on into China itself. He'd phoned the *Oregon* upon his arrival in Shanghai but then ditched the phone. While cell phones were ubiquitous in the cities, he was going deep into the countryside. Not only would there be no cellular service, but if he were caught with a phone, it would likely arouse suspicion. He would be completely on his own in a country that had already issued his death sentence until he'd learned the circumstances behind the villagers being aboard the *Kra*.

Cabrillo felt his phone vibrate in his jacket pocket. He slid it free and opened the line as he continued strolling the park surrounding the Imperial Palace, the only quiet location in the sprawling megalopolis. "Cabrillo."

"Juan, it's Max. Are you ready to put an end to your vacation?"

"Murph found something?" Cabrillo didn't bother to mask the delight in his voice.

"You got it. I'm putting him through, but I'm staying on."

Juan found a deserted bench so he could give the conversation his full attention. He had a small pad and a Montblanc pen ready in case he needed to take notes.

"Hey, boss, how's it going?"

"Max tells me you have some information," Cabrillo said, anxious to find a direction in which to hunt.

"It took a while, and I had to consult with Mike Halbert on quite a bit of it." Halbert was a sometimes consultant to the Corporation and also acted as their investment broker. He'd gone on a couple of missions aboard the *Oregon*, though usually he worked out of his New York apartment, a fiftieth-floor corner unit overlooking Central Park. Halbert was a whiz at the more arcane aspects of international finance, the shadowy world of front companies, tax havens, and derivatives, though right now, with the current sad state of the Corporation's financial situation, Halbert wasn't one of Juan's favorite people.

"So what do you have?" Cabrillo prompted.

"This might get a bit confusing, so bear with me." Murph paused to study the notes on his computer screen. "Okay, first what I had to do was find out who was behind all those dummy companies I told you owned the *Maus*. You remember, D Commercial Advisors, Equity Partners International, and all the rest. First off, it appears these companies were created strictly to buy the drydock. They don't have any other assets."

"That's not uncommon," Juan said. "If there was ever an insurance claim against the vessel's owners, their only asset is the drydock itself."

"That's what Halbert told me. None of these companies are based in the same place. One is Panamanian, another is headquartered in Nigeria, another is out of Dubai. I tried contacting D Commercial Advisors directly. They don't even have a phone number, so it's likely the headquarters are nothing more than a PO box with automatic forwarding to another address."

"Is there any way to find out where their mail is sent on to?"

"Not without breaking into some Third World post office and having a look at their files."

"We'll keep that option open," Cabrillo said in all seriousness. "Keep going."

"Next, we checked the corporate structure of each company. These are public records and fortunately kept on a database. My hope was we would find the same names on the boards of each company."

"You didn't think it was going to be that easy?" Juan chided.

"Well, I'd hoped. As you can imagine, no such luck. There was one common element, though. Of the seven companies that own the *Maus* and the forty people listed as directors of those companies, every one of them is Russian."

"Russian? I thought they would be Chinese."

"Nope, Russkies to a man. Which ties in with Linda's suspicion about the men guarding the *Maus* being from the land of the tsars. I have a search under way through Interpol right now. So far, I've already gotten hits on a few of these guys. They're members of the Russian mafia. No one highly placed, but they're definitely connected."

"So this whole thing is a Russian enterprise," Juan said, thinking aloud. "I can see how they'd benefit from the hijackings, but what about the human trafficking? The snakeheads are well organized and entrenched in China. I can't see them allowing competition from the Russian mob."

"I had an idea about that," Max interjected. "What if the snakeheads have a contract with the Russians? Could be they use Russian ships or allow the Chinese to use Russia as a conduit to get the illegals into western Europe."

"That could be," Juan agreed. "They could use the port of Vladivostok. Dump the Chinese there, then send 'em across on the Trans-Siberian Railway. Once in Moscow or Saint Petersburg it's a simple matter of some forged documents, and they're on their way to Berlin, London, or New York. I've heard that customs police all over the world have closed a lot of the old back channels, so this could be their new route."

Cabrillo was already thinking ahead. He didn't know many people in the cold water port city of Vladivostok, but he still had contacts in Saint Petersburg and Moscow. In fact, several of his old Cold War foes worked in private security for the new-generation capitalist oligarchs, and more than a few were wealthy oligarchs themselves.

"So I'm headed to Moscow," Juan said.

"Not so fast, Chairman," Mark countered. "You might end up there, but there could be another way."

"I'm listening."

"I thought about how hard it would be to track down forty Russian gangsters and what leverage we could use to get them to talk. Mike Halbert and I talked about it at length, and we both came to the conclusion that the Russians probably don't have a clue what these companies do. It's likely that whoever set up D Commercial Advisors and Ajax Trading and the others paid the Russians a fee to use their names, and they know nothing beyond that."

"You're talking a dummy board of directors for a dummy company."

"Exactly. Complete deniability."

"So where does that leave us?" Juan asked, slightly irritated that Murphy seemed to be leading him along.

"The guy who set up the companies."

"Wait. Guy? You said guy?"

"Yup."

"They screwed up," Cabrillo exclaimed, irritation turning to excitement as he grasped what Murph had just said.

"Sure did, boss." Mark agreed, a smile in his voice. "Every one of the dummy companies had two things in common. They all own part of the *Maus*, actually on the documents it's called *Mice*, but I think it's a translation problem. And the other thing is they were all set up by the same lawyer in Zurich. Guy by the name of Rudolph Isphording."

"Never heard of him."

"No reason you should have, at least not until a few months ago."

"What happened a few months ago?" Juan had suddenly become wary.

"Isphording was named as a star witness in the biggest financial scandal to hit Switzerland since it was discovered they had hoarded gold for the Nazis. He was caught up in a money laundering net, quickly saw the writing on the wall, and made a sweetheart deal with Swiss prosecutors. The scope of the investigation is expanding every day. A few bank presidents are under indictment, a couple of government ministers have tendered resignations, and now the investigators are looking into the Swiss representatives at the United Nations for potential bribe-taking. And there might be a link to the billions of dollars the late PLO chief Yasir Arafat hid away in Swiss banks that has yet to surface. It seems there's no limit to how high or far the scandal goes."

"All because of this Isphording character?"

"He had a very long reach into some very dirty pockets."

"If the PLO is involved, I'm surprised he hasn't been killed by now."

Max Hanley spoke up with a low chuckle. "He'll get a grateful hug by a suicide bomber only after the Palestinians find their money."

"So where's Isphording now?"

"Under protective custody at Regensdorf prison outside Zurich. The only times he's been seen in the past five months is at special prosecutorial court sessions. He's driven to the courthouse in an armored van. The media aren't allowed anywhere near him, but one telephoto shot that might be him shows a figure in a flak vest with his face covered in what looks like bandages. Rumor circulating in the Swiss press is that he's undergoing plastic surgery during the proceedings and will be given a new identity after he's finished testifying."

"An armored van?" Cabrillo asked, just to be sure.

"With a police escort. I said this was an alternative to tracking down forty Russians who may or may not know anything," Mark replied. "I didn't say it was an easier one."

"Is he allowed visitors?" Juan asked, already thinking about what he could use as leverage over the attorney. Isphording was getting a great deal from the Swiss authorities. Why would he jeopardize that by talking to the Corporation about a handful of dummy companies he'd helped establish? Juan would have to get creative.

"Just one. His wife."

That shot down his idea of trying to intimidate him in the prison's interview room. If they couldn't talk to him in jail, and he doubted Isphording would be allowed to speak to anyone in the courthouse, Juan saw his options as severely limited. He played a hundred different scenarios in his head and came up with nothing. Well, not nothing—but what sprang into his mind was one hell of a long shot.

"How sure are they about a PLO connection?" he asked.

"Reports are sketchy," Mark said, "but it fits with his pattern of corruption."

"That'll have to be good enough. Even rumor can work to our advantage."

"What's happening in that scheming mind of yours?" Hanley asked.

"I'm too embarrassed to tell you yet. It's that nuts. Are there any pictures of Isphording's wife?"

"Shouldn't be too hard to dig one up in newspaper archives."

"Okay, get on it. I'm going to Zurich, get the lay of the land to see if my idea could even work. Where are you guys now?"

"We're in the East China Sea about two hundred miles north of Taiwan," Max said.

"And the *Maus*?"

"Twenty miles ahead of us. We've determined this is the limit of her radar. We send up the UAV every twelve hours just to put some eyeballs on her and make sure nothing's changed. So far it's just a regular tow job. Nothing out of the ordinary."

"Except the ship in her hold was stolen off the high seas."

"Well yes, there is that."

With the *Maus* only covering 150 miles a day, they were only a day and a half out from Taipei, although Juan was still convinced the vessel would change course and head someplace else. Taiwan was a modern democratic country and was too well-regulated for the pirates to use it as their base of operation. He was sure they'd continue on to Vietnam, the Philippines, or Indonesia.

That meant that if he was going to get to Rudolph Isphording, it would be without the *Oregon* as a base of operation. But he would need her unique capabilities if he was going to pull off what he'd been thinking. He calculated distances and times, factoring in the range of the Robinson R-44 in her protected hangar belowdecks. If he wanted to get equipment or personnel off the *Oregon,* he had a short window as the ship steamed past Taiwan in which to do it. Once she reached the South China Sea, they'd be too far from land to make any transfers. With a sinking feeling, he figured he had just two days after reaching Zurich to determine who and what he wanted off the *Oregon* before she was out of range.

They had needed three weeks to get everything set up to pull off the job in North Korea, and even then they had been rushed. And that caper was a piece of cake compared to what Cabrillo had in mind now.

12

EDDIE had always believed in the old adage that people made their own luck. That didn't mean he discounted the blind chance of someone winning a lottery or being involved in a freak accident. What he meant was that proper planning, attitude, and sharp wits were more than enough to overcome problems. You didn't need to be lucky to be successful. You just needed to work hard.

After the first two hours of lying in an irrigation ditch, he still maintained his beliefs. He hadn't had time to properly plan the mission, so it wasn't bad luck that brought him to this predicament. It was lack of preparation on his part. But now that he was into his fifth hour, and his shivering sent waves across the stream's surface, he cursed the gods for his bad luck.

His arrival in China had gone off without a hitch. Customs barely glanced at his papers and made only a desultory search of his bags. That hadn't come as much of a surprise, since he was traveling as a diplomat returning home from a year at the Australian embassy and was therefore afforded special courtesy. The papers he'd planned to use while traveling in China were those of an unemployed office worker. He'd spent his first day in Shanghai just wandering the streets. He hadn't been in China for so long he needed to reacclimatize himself. He had to change his posture and walk—his was too brazen—and he needed to get used to the language again.

He'd learned Mandarin and English simultaneously from his parents living in New York's Chinatown, so he had no accent but rather a bland inflection that would sound foreign to a Chinese. He tuned into the conversations around him, relearning the accent he'd used when he'd been here with the CIA.

He couldn't believe the transformation in the years since he'd last been to China's largest city. The skyline was among the tallest in the world, with buildings and construction cranes crowding ever higher, and the pace of life was among the most frenetic. Everyone walking the sidewalks carried on excited conversations over ubiquitous cell phones. When night fell, the Shanghai streets were washed in enough neon to rival the Las Vegas Strip.

He vanished into society in incremental steps. After checking out of his hotel, he left his two suitcases behind a Dumpster that had just been emptied and wouldn't likely be moved for a few days, not that there was anything in the bags to incriminate him. The diplomatic papers had already been flushed in the hotel. Next, he bought off-the-rack clothes from a midpriced department store. The clerk thought nothing of a customer wearing an expensive Western suit buying clothes that didn't seem up to his standard. Wearing his new purchases, Eddie ditched his suit and bused out of the thriving downtown until finding an area of factories and drab apartment blocks. By this time, he'd gotten food stains on his shirt and had scuffed his shoes using a brick from a construction site.

He got a few looks from the poorer workers in their ill-fitting clothes, but for the most part no one paid him much attention. He wasn't one of them, but he didn't look like he was that much above them either. Again, the clerk at the clothing store where he bought two pairs of baggy pants, a couple of shirts, and a thin gray windbreaker assumed Eddie was a down-on-his-luck salaryman forced into the labor ranks. He bought shoes and a rucksack from another store and a few toiletry items from a third without raising an eyebrow.

By the time he arrived at the overland bus terminal for his trip to Fujian Province, on his third day without a proper shower, he was an anonymous worker returning to his village after failing to make it in the big city. The slow transformation not only ensured no one would remember him, it helped Eddie become the role. As he sat on a cold bench at the terminal, his eyes had the haunted look of failure and his body slouched under the weight of defeat. An old woman who'd struck up a conversation told him it was best he return to his family. The cities weren't for everybody, she'd said and told him she'd seen too many young people turn to drugs as an escape. Fortunately, her cataracts prevented her from seeing that Eddie wasn't as young as she assumed.

The trip had been uneventful, crowded onto a bus that belched great clouds of leaded gasoline fumes and stank of humanity. His trouble had started when he reached Lantan, the town where Xang and his family had begun a trip that ended with them murdered in a shipping container. Eddie had no way of knowing, again because he hadn't had time to prepare, that he'd arrived during regional elections. The army had set up a checkpoint in the town square, and everyone was required to pass through on their way to the polls.

Eddie had seen such elections before and knew that the townspeople had a choice among one candidate for each office up for election. Oftentimes the ballot was already checked, and the voter had to simply place it in the ballot box under the watchful eye of armed soldiers. This was China's version of a democratic concession to its people. Some high officials had come out from the provincial capital of Xiamen to watch the polling, and the military had even brought a tank, a massive Type 98 if Eddie's quick glimpse had been enough for an ID. He assumed it was a public relations ploy by the PLA, the People's Liberation Army, as well as a subtle reminder of where the ultimate power in China lay.

Although Lantan had a population of less than ten thousand, Eddie knew he'd attract attention. He didn't speak the local dialect all that well and didn't have a plausible reason for being in the isolated town if questioned by a curious soldier. Which was why he'd spent the past five hours under a bridge in an irrigation ditch just outside the town limits. He didn't plan on leaving his hiding place until the officials and military rolled on to the next target of their intimidation.

But once again the luck Eddie tried to make for himself had left him.

He'd been lost in his own world of cold and pain and didn't hear the voices until they were almost directly overhead.

"Just a little farther," a male voice cajoled. "I saw a spot when we entered town."

"No, I want to go back." It was a woman's voice, but young—maybe a teenager. She sounded frightened.

"No, it will be okay," the male said. He had a cosmopolitan accent. Beijing or its environs. The girl sounded local.

"Please. My parents will wonder where I am. I have chores."

"I said come on." The man had lost all pretense of civility. His voice was sharp, tinged with a manic, desperate edge.

They were on the bridge spanning the ditch, just a few feet over Eddie's head. A patter of dirt rained from the joints of the heavy wood decking. Their footfalls had become uneven. He could picture the couple in his mind. The girl was holding back, trying to slow them, as the man drew on her arm to the point of having to drag her.

Eddie gently pushed himself from the bank and sidled silently across the eight-foot ditch, listening as the man drew the girl across the structure. "It will be fun," he said. "You'll like me."

There was a dense copse of trees just beyond the village along the dirt road, a secluded spot that Eddie knew would soon become the scene of a rape. As the man and his victim gained the road, Eddie pulled himself up the embankment, exposing himself had there been a sharp-eyed observer in the nearby town. He shouldn't have even moved from his original spot. What was about to happen wasn't his concern, but he was about to make it so.

The man was a soldier, an AK-47 slung over his shoulder, his uniform clean compared to the dirty peasant clothes the girl wore. He had her by the arm, lifting her so her feet barely touched the ground in a frog march to the nearest trees, already in shadow as the sun set beyond a range of mountains to the west. She wore a skirt and simple blouse, long hair in a thick tail dangling between her narrow shoulders.

Eddie waited until they'd vanished into the woods. He peered back to the town. Electric lights were coming on in a few of the buildings, while outlying houses remained dark, their owners hoarding the candles they relied on for illumination. No one was looking in his direction, and the soldiers in the square appeared like they were making preparations to load the tank onto its special twenty-wheeled hauler.

He rose from the ditch and crossed the road, water streaming from his clothes. His feet were bare because he knew the cheap cloth and stitching would have dissolved after such a prolonged immersion. He merged into the forest, letting his sense of hearing guide him deeper into the woods. The girl was protesting, her voice pitched high before becoming suddenly muffled. The soldier must have a hand over her mouth, he thought, his feet silent amid the sparse ground cover.

He stopped at the base of a large pine. A flash of white had caught his attention. The girl's blouse. It lay on the forest floor. Eddie chanced a look around the thick trunk. The soldier had set his rifle on the ground next to where he'd pinned the girl. His upper body covered hers, but he could tell she was naked from the waist up. With one hand over her mouth, the solider used the other to pry the girl's skirts up to her hips. Her legs were thin and coltish, and they scissored in the air as they tried to throw off her attacker.

The soldier removed his hand from her mouth, but before she could cry out, he punched her across the jaw. Her head snapped to the side, and her body went still. Eddie had just moments, but there was no cover between him, the soldier, and his weapon.

He slid around the tree anyway, moving slowly at first. The human eye detects light and movement better at the periphery than straight ahead. He'd covered three of the ten paces to where the rape was about to take place when the soldier sensed Eddie's presence. Eddie burst into a run, his toes digging deep into the loamy soil like a sprinter's cleats.

Reacting fast, for he was already charged with adrenaline, the soldier twisted to grab up his rifle. He had the weapon by the grip, his fingers finding the safety in a well-practiced move. The assault rifle came up as he swung the barrel to his target. Even if he missed, the shot would be heard in the town and draw the attention of his comrades. The soldier must have known this because his finger tightened on the trigger before Eddie was in his sights.

Eddie launched himself, one arm arcing out wide to catch the barrel of the AK-47, the other knifing in with fingers extended into the soldier's windpipe. But he was too late; the soldier had applied the last bit of pressure to discharge the banana magazine. The gun didn't go off. Eddie's momentum ripped the soldier off the girl with such force her body rolled twice along the ground. Eddie ignored her as she cried out suddenly. The soldier lay atop Eddie when they stopped. Moving fast before the man could recover his senses, Eddie pressed the soldier's dead weight from his chest, used one arm to steady the man, and fired two swift strikes into the soldier's larynx. They lacked power, but hitting the same spot as his initial attack more than made up for it. The soldier's throat was crushed. He made a series of strangled gasps, then went limp.

Seng pushed the corpse aside without giving the would-be rapist a second thought. The girl lay curled on her side, clutching at her hand and moaning aloud. Eddie recovered her shirt and draped it over her. She clutched it around her frame as he gently turned her over. The punch hadn't dislocated her jaw, though she'd carry the bruise for a while. Her eyes were wide with fear and pain. He gently uncurled her hand. Her index finger was bent almost ninety degrees, and he understood why the AK hadn't gone off. She'd feigned her stupor rather than give her attacker the satisfaction of raping a conscious victim and at the last moment jammed her finger behind the rifle's trigger, preventing the bolt from releasing. She'd saved Eddie's life while saving herself from a crime most women believed was worse than death. Her finger had gotten broken when Eddie's charge had torn the weapon away.

"You are very brave," he said soothingly.

"Who are you?" She sobbed through the pain and humiliation.

"I am no one. You haven't seen me, and this didn't happen. You broke your finger when you tripped walking back from the fields. Do you understand?" Her eyes darted to the figure of the dead soldier. He knew what she was silently asking. "I will take care of him. You don't need to worry. No one will know. Now go back to your family and never speak of this day again."

She turned her back to slip into her blouse. Enough buttons remained on the thin fabric to cover herself. She got to her feet, fighting the tears that welled at the corner of her eyes. It was pride, shame, agony. It was a face of China.

"Wait," Eddie called before she vanished from the forest clearing. "Do you know a family named Xang? Several of them rode the snake not long ago."

At the mention of illegal immigration she stepped back protectively, ready to bolt. But she held firm, wanting to return something to the man who saved her. "Yes, they live in town. They own a store that sells and repairs bicycles. The family live above. Do you have news of them?"

From the way she spoke he could tell she knew the family well. Perhaps she was the sweetheart Xang had written about. "Yes," he said, sickened by what he was going to tell her. "They reached Japan, and they are all working. Now go!"

Startled by his last command, the girl vanished amid the trees. Eddie had perhaps done something far worse than the soldier just now. He'd given the girl hope.

He rifled the soldier's pockets for his identification and then pulled the dog tags from around his neck, settling the warm metal against his own chest. Using the sling from the AK-47 and the soldier's belt, he fashioned a rope and within ten minutes had the body wedged into the crotch of a twin oak tree twenty feet off the ground. Search parties looking for a deserter would take days to find the body, most likely drawn to it by the smell.

He used a branch to erase all tracks and traces of what had happened and made his way back to his hiding place under the bridge. The girl was probably back in town, most likely with her mother at the local healer's house having her finger set. Her problems were over. Eddie's had just begun.

The military presence in Lantan wouldn't leave until all the soldiers were accounted for. It looked as though they planned on staying the night, and it was doubtful the dead rapist would be missed till morning. His buddies would cover for him, assuming he'd found someone, either a professional or the proverbial farmer's daughter, whose legend of beauty and promiscuity were as popular in China as they were in America.

The trouble would start at the morning's roll call. When he didn't show up they'd search the town, then the surrounding farmland in ever widening circles. Eddie could no more abandon the mission than he could have left the girl, so that gave him until dawn to contact the snakeheads. And he no longer planned to interrogate them to learn what happened to Xang and the others. He now needed them to get him out of China.

He fingered the dog tags, knowing he had the perfect cover.

13

ANTON Savich was relieved he had only one more flight to take to finally reach his destination. It had taken days to arrive at Elyzovo Airport outside Petropavlovsk-Kamchatskiy, the regional capital of the Kamchatka Peninsula on Russia's far east coast.

Petropavlovsk-Kamchatskiy, or PK, as it was commonly referred to, had been closed to the outside world until the collapse of the Soviet Union in 1990, and the ensuing years had brought little improvement. Nearly every building was made of concrete using ash from the 1945 eruption of the nearby Avachinsky volcano, so the city of a quarter million had a drab uniformity that went beyond its boxy Soviet architecture. Its streets hadn't been paved in decades, and its economy was in ruins because the military, which had once supported the city, had mostly withdrawn. Surrounded by towering snowcapped peaks at the head of beautiful Avacha Bay, PK was a dismal stain of a place where residents stayed only because they lacked the inertia to move.

The entire Kamchatka Peninsula had once been controlled by the Soviet military. Sophisticated radar stations dotted the rugged landscape to watch for incoming American ICBMs. There were several air force bases for intercepting American bombers, and it was the home of the Pacific Submarine Fleet. Kamchatka was also the designated landing site for Soviet ballistic missiles test-fired from the west. Today the subs of the Pacific Fleet rusted away at the Rybachi Naval Base in the southern reach of Avacha Bay; several were so badly deteriorated that they'd sunk at their moorings, their tubes still loaded with torpedoes and their nuclear reactors still fueled. The radar stations had been abandoned, and planes remained grounded at the air bases for lack of parts and aviation gas. In the wake of the military withdrawal, countless sites had been left so polluted that even brief exposure would cause severe illness.

It wasn't the military presence that had first drawn Anton Savich to Kamchatka more than two decades ago. It was the geology. Kamchatka had risen from the sea two and a half million years ago, first as a volcanic archipelago like Alaska's Aleutian Islands. The sea quickly wore these mountains flat, but the land rose again, driven by endless reserves of molten rock from deep underground. Kamchatka was an arc within the Ring of Fire, a circle of volcanoes and earthquake zones that mark the boundaries of the vast Pacific tectonic plate. Twenty-nine of the more than 150 volcanic peaks on the peninsula were active, most notably Karymsky, which had been erupting continuously since 1996, and now an unnamed volcano in the center of the peninsula had started belching plumes of ash and steam.

Driven by economic necessity in the 1980s, the Soviet Union initiated a program of exploration and exploitation. To face Reagan's unprecedented military buildup, the Soviets scrambled to find the raw materials to feed the growing demand of their own military-industrial complex. These were the last salvos of the Cold War, fought not with bullets and bombs but with factories and resources. It was a fight the Soviet Union ultimately lost, but huge reserves of minerals such as coal, iron ore, and uranium were discovered in the process.

Anton Savich had been a young field researcher for the Bureau of Natural Resources, the agency tasked by the Central Committee to find all the wealth buried within the Soviet borders. He had come to prospect the Kamchatka Peninsula in 1986 with two other field men under the guidance of a geology professor from Moscow University, Akademik Yuri Strakhov.

The team spent four months scouring the peninsula from helicopters and all-terrain vehicles provided by the Red Army. Because of the active geology, it was felt there might be diamonds on Kamchatka, although they found no trace minerals to back Moscow's belief. What they found instead was just as valuable.

Savich recalled the days they'd camped at the foot of the reef, chipping samples by day and imagining the possibilities at night. They speculated as though what they found belonged to them, but of course it didn't. In likelihood they would receive commendations for their find, and maybe vouchers for larger apartments.

He wasn't sure who suggested it first; perhaps it was Savich himself, though it didn't really matter. Somehow the idea came up, mentioned as a joke at first for sure, but soon they discussed it in earnest. The rain had finally stopped that night, Savich remembered, which was unusual. They passed a bottle of vodka, which wasn't unusual. You couldn't get decent toilet paper in Moscow, but the state could keep you well-stocked in liquor five hundred kilometers from the nearest town.

Why report the find? someone had asked. Why tell anyone about it? Only the four of them knew the truth, and no one would prospect this area ever again once they filed their reports. They could return to Moscow, go about their lives for a few years, and then return and mine the reef themselves. They'd all be rich.

Savich stepped from the Ilyushin jetliner at PK's Elyzovo Airport, smiling as he recalled their naïveté. Akademik Strakhov allowed them to carry on for an hour or two before bringing them back to reality. He never told them it was wrong, what they wanted to do, for even the respected professor couldn't help his greed. But he also knew what they discussed was idle fantasy. It took just a few words to explain how they would never be allowed to return to Kamchatka, and even if they managed, how it was impossible for the four of them to mine enough material to make any sort of impact on their lives. He went on to tell them how world markets actually operated and how they would never be able to sell the ore they'd dug from the earth. He'd quickly cooled their ardor and dashed their hopes. The vodka went flat on their tongues.

Savich remembered that at that very moment the rain had started again. Strakhov doused their hissing gas lantern and for a few minutes the men listened to the rain pelt their canvas tent before crawling into their sleeping bags. He was sure the rest of them continued to think of the possibilities as they drifted to sleep. Many minutes passed before he heard their breathing settle into somnolence. All except his own. He had intuitively realized that with one additional element their plan would work: Time.

They were thinking in terms of years. He knew that it would be decades before anyone could come back. No one could return until the entire communist government had collapsed and capitalism took root in the *Rodina*. Maybe they couldn't consider such an event, but Savich already knew it was an inevitability. Propaganda couldn't shorten breadlines or produce spare parts for automobiles, and eventually the leadership would just stop trying. He predicted a quiet implosion, not revolution, but eventually the Soviet Union would collapse under the weight of its own inefficiency. If he managed to position himself for that day, then all the other pieces could fall into place.

There was one more component that the others hadn't envisioned—that Savich had no intention of sharing his eventual wealth with any of them.

Their extraction helicopter wasn't due for another four days, more than enough time for him to put his plan into action. They had been assigned a sixty-kilometer-square search area and had been autonomous since their arrival five weeks earlier. When it arrived from PK, the chopper would fly box patterns across the grid and wait until the team launched flares to pinpoint their exact location.

Savich had to get the team as far away from their strike as possible, but Strakhov would want to keep them where they were until the helicopter came, ready to bask in the glory of their find. Without a weapon to compel them to move on, Savich would have to act now in order to get away from the site.

He lay in his bag for another couple of hours. It wasn't guilt or remorse that made him wait. He just wanted the team as deep into sleep as possible. He rose at four, the night's darkest hour, and by the glow of a penlight he opened their medical case. The supplies were rudimentary: bandages, antiseptic, some antibiotics, and a half dozen syringes of morphine.

Black flies were so prevalent that the men no longer bothered to swat them away or react to their nasty stings. Each of them was so covered in angry red welts from numerous bites that their arms, ankles, and faces were mottled red.

Savich emptied the morphine from one of the syringes into the ground and drew back the plunger to fill the cylinder with air. Mikhail was the biggest man on the survey team, a heavyset Ukrainian who had once been a wrestling champion in Kiev. Savich thought nothing of it as he sank the fine needle into Mikhail's throat where the carotid artery pulsed faintly. He slowly depressed the plunger, sending a lethal bubble of air into the wrestler's bloodstream. So used to the flies, Mikhail hadn't even felt the small sting. Savich waited just a few seconds before the bubble became an embolism inside the man's brain and he stroked out silently. He repeated the procedure twice more. Only old Yuri Strakhov struggled at the end. His eyes flew open at the prick of the needle. Savich clamped his hand over his mouth and pressed his weight on the geologist's chest, pumping the air into his artery with a savage thrust. Strakhov thrashed for just a brief moment before he went limp.

By the light of the gas lantern, Savich thought about his next move. He recalled that about five kilometers closer to the coast was a tall, steeply angled slope covered in talus and scree. The footing was treacherous, and a careless man could slide nearly a kilometer to its base. A tumble down the slope would do enough damage to a corpse to dissuade even the most iron-stomached forensic doctor in the unlikely event there would be an autopsy.

That first night Anton Savich went through his teammates' notebooks and field journals. He tore out any page that made reference to the strike or any observation about terrain or geology from after they'd trekked past the gravel-strewn hillside. He excised everything that could be questioned during the investigation and made certain none of the journals mentioned anything interesting in their current search grid. He doctored his own journal to make it appear they had covered more ground than they had so no one would have reason to return here.

At dawn he began to carry the sleeping bags containing the bodies to the top of the slope. The Ukrainian, Mikhail, was too heavy to shoulder, so he fashioned a litter out of branches and straps from a backpack and dragged the corpse. He was exhausted and drenched in sweat and cursed himself for not waiting until the next day to move the last body. Rather than return to camp in the darkness, he spent a miserable night huddled next to his victims.

On the second day he broke down their tent and portaged all their gear to the slope. He had to repack the camping equipment and load it into the assigned backpacks before securing the packs to the bodies. He decided to wait until dawn the next day before tumbling the bodies down the slope. It wasn't that he particularly wanted to watch the men disintegrate against the sharp rocks but he needed to know where they landed. Only Professor Strakhov carried the flares he would need to alert the chopper coming in the next afternoon.

Mikhail went down the slope after Savich had a hearty breakfast of coffee, tinned meat, and a can of Crimean oranges. He watched through binoculars as the body first rolled, then tumbled, and as it picked up speed, began to cartwheel. Centrifugal forces caused blood to spray from numerous deep gashes, and limbs became rubbery after breaking against the stones. If possible, the other two were even more mutilated by the fall.

He took more than an hour to pick his way down the mountainside, scraping meat from his hands so they stung from his own sweat. Once at the bottom he removed gear and food from the packs and emptied a few tins so it would look like he'd been at the bottom of the hill for days.

When he estimated the helicopter was an hour away, he injected the two remaining morphine syringes into his arm and waited as the narcotic took effect. When he sensed a creeping numbness working its way up his extremities, Savich took a deep breath. To make things as authentic as possible it didn't seem right that three men died during the fall while he merely scraped up his hands.

Leaning against a rock outcrop he grasped a stone nearly the size of his head and held it as high as he could. He lay his left arm against the hunk of basalt and before he could give himself time to reconsider, he smashed the stone against his arm. The radius and ulna cracked audibly, and Savich bellowed in pain. Fueled by adrenaline and morphine he then took up a smaller stone and pounded it against his head hard enough to split the skin. Spittle drizzled from his slack lips as he fought the waves of agony and prayed for the drug to deaden the pain.

He was nearly unconscious when he heard the helicopter in the distance, and it took several tries to launch the flare. The arcing ball of white phosphorus rose on a column of smoke and must have been spotted immediately. The next thing Savich remembered was a hospital bed in Petropavlovsk.

The inquiry was perfunctory. The grisly scene the chopper crew described mirrored Savich's account of the slope giving way as the men crossed it and how they all tumbled to the valley floor. The investigator was amazed Savich had only sustained a mild concussion, a few scrapes and bruises, and a broken arm.

"Just lucky, I guess," he'd told the man as he'd closed his book of notes on the case.

* * *

SAVICH rubbed his left forearm as he crossed the tarmac to the airport terminal. In the past few years it had started to ache a bit on damp days. Maybe not quite as disquieting as Poe's Telltale Heart, but a reminder of his deeds nevertheless.

The immigration agent recognized him in the queue and motioned him to the head of the line. A few locals grumbled, but no one challenged him.

"Back again, Mr. Savich?" the friendly guard asked, pocketing the twenty-dollar bill Savich had folded into his passport.

"I could get some work done back at my office in Moscow if your damn volcanoes would stop erupting."

"It's the gomuls," the guard replied with an air of mock conspiracy. "They're the native spirits who hunt whales at night and return to the mountains to roast the meat on giant fires."

"When I find whale bones in a volcanic caldera, I'll blame the gomuls, my friend. For now I suspect it's tectonic activity."

Savich had returned to Moscow following his recovery in the hospital and lived and maintained his silence concerning his find, all the while continuing his work for the Bureau of Natural Resources. He led an unremarkable life through the waning days of the Soviet Union and managed to keep his position secure during its collapse. In the wild aftermath he had actively sought foreign contacts, cultivating some he thought would eventually allow him to see his plan to fruition.

His chance had come through a Swiss metallurgist he'd met at a symposium who in turn eventually led Savich to the banker, Bernhard Volkmann, and the current deal he had under way. Backed by Volkmann, and using the companies controlled by the loathsome Shere Singh, Anton Savich had returned to Kamchatka countless times over the past year, laying the necessary groundwork under the cover of a volcanologist. With the numerous eruptions all across Kamchatka, he had become a common sight at the airport and maintained a standing reservation at the Avacha Hotel, just a short walk up Leningradskaya Street from what was possibly the only Lenin Square in Russia still dedicated to Lenin.

He collected his bags and went straight to a counter run by a heliski company. The sport had grown popular along the rugged peaks of the peninsula, and there were several companies willing to take skiers up the mountains by chopper. The company, Air Adventures, actually did book ski trips to maintain legitimacy, but it was a dummy company Savich had funded through Volkmann in order to have rapid but unobtrusive transportation to the site. A private helicopter at Elyzovo would have drawn too much attention.

The woman behind the counter put away a Japanese fashion magazine when she saw him approach. Her smile was fake and perfunctory. He didn't recognize her, and he certainly didn't look like a thrill-seeking tourist.

"Welcome to Air Adventures," she greeted in English.

"My name is Savich," he grunted. "Where's Pytor?"

Her eyes registered surprise, then fear, as she blanched. She vanished into a curtained-off section of the kiosk. A moment later, Savich's pilot, Pytor Federov, stepped from around the curtain. He wore an olive drab flight suit and retained the cocky air he'd earned over the missile-filled skies of Afghanistan.

"Mr. Savich, good to see you. I assumed you'd go to your hotel for the night and we would fly out in the morning."

"Hello, Pytor. No. I want to see this latest eruption for myself before it gets dark," Savich replied in case anyone was paying attention.

"Say the word, and I'll file a flight plan."

"Consider it said."

Forty minutes later they were a racing down a twisting valley. The rugged mountains flanking the Air Adventure's MI-8 helicopter towered some eight thousand feet above them. Several peaks on the Kamchatka Peninsula topped fifteen thousand. The air was hazy with fine ash particles from the eruption farther north. Even with headphones it was difficult to speak in the forty-year-old chopper, so for the two hours it took to get to the site, Savich was content to let the landscape unfold around him.

He hadn't drifted off to sleep, the helo was too loud, but his mind had gone so blank he was surprised when Federov tapped him and pointed ahead. He hadn't been aware that they were about to arrive.

From above and at a distance, the area looked pristine except for the spreading brown stain that bloomed in the black waters of the Gulf of Shelekhov. A ring of containment booms had been strung along the coastline, but sediment from the workings drifted far beyond their reach. The reason the site looked so good was that much of it was hidden by acres of tarps strung atop metal poles. The tarps had been painted to look like snow, and the ash that had drifted onto the upper surface furthered the illusion. The ships had been beached and had also been camouflaged, first with dirt and rock from the workings and then with more fabric coverings to break up their shapes.

The only sign of life for a hundred miles was the thin wisps of smoke that coiled from the ships' funnels to provide heat and warm food for the workers.

Savich looked out to sea. A trawler was returning to the site, its wake a fat wedge, for she ran low under the weight of her catch.

With the ship's bunkers full of fuel, fresh water available from a nearby glacial river, and food provided by a pair of trawlers, the site could remain self-sufficient for months, perhaps years. He was rightly proud of his accomplishment, but then he'd had half a lifetime to refine every detail.

All except one, Savich thought grimly. There was one obstacle he hadn't been able to easily overcome, a commodity the site used up at a voracious pace and was the most difficult to replace.

Federov had radioed ahead, so the site manager was at the helipad to greet Savich when he stepped from the chopper into the biting cold wind. It was May, but the arctic circle was only four hundred miles north.

"Welcome back, Anton," greeted Jan Paulus, a broadly built South African mine engineer.

The two shook hands and headed for a waiting four-wheel-drive. "Do you want to go see the workings?" Paulus asked, putting the truck in gear.

Savich had seen that aspect of the project just once and never wanted to repeat the experience. "No. Let's go to your office. I have a decent bottle of Scotch in my bag." The Russian didn't much care for his site manager but knew he had to keep the man happy. Of course, Paulus's five million dollar salary did more for their relationship than the occasional drink.

The three ships they'd brought north and beached below the site were all old cruise liners that Shere Singh had provided through his shipbreaking business. Though past their prime, they were functional and served Savich's needs perfectly. Paulus had ensconced himself in the Ambassador Suite of a 380-foot cruise ship that had once plied the Aegean.

The gold and blue décor had once been considered chic, but the carpets were worn and scarred with cigarette burns, the furniture scuffed, and the fixtures tarnished. Savich used the bathroom and when he flushed, a god-awful stench erupted from the toilet. His image in the mirror appeared sepia because the glass had lost much of its backing.

Paulus was seated on the couch in the suite's living room when Savich returned. He'd already filled two tumblers with the Russian's Scotch. "There was an accident on one of the drydocks."

Savich paused in mid-sit. "Which one?"

"The *Maus*. Two of your Spetsnaz commandos decided to ignore procedure and walk across the tarp covering the hold. The fabric gave way, and both fell to their deaths."

The Russian took a sip of his drink. "Any sign they were, ah, helped?"

"No. Your men swept the drydock and the ship in her hold as soon as the pair didn't return from the patrol. No one had come aboard, and there were no signs of struggle. The only vessel nearby was an Iranian-flagged freighter, so unless the mullahs in Tehran got wind of our little operation, I doubt they're involved."

Savich cursed under his breath. All the men he'd hired to guard the ships were ex–special forces, the vaunted Spetsnaz. It went against their considerable training to deviate from a patrol route, but he could also understand why they might. Once they'd seized their prize, maintaining a high sense of alertness guarding a quiet ship at sea would be nearly impossible. He could easily imagine them cutting their perimeter patrol by crossing over the hold. It was a careless mistake that would teach the others vigilance in the future.

He considered this an unfortunate accident and put it out of his mind. "How is everything going here?"

The South African had horrible teeth, so his smile looked like a gray grimace. "Couldn't be better. The reef you found has the highest assay I've ever seen. Hell, this whole region is loaded with minerals. Production is above expectations by twelve percent, and we're still working the alluvial beds downslope. We haven't even started in on the main strike."

"When do you anticipate sending out the first shipment?"

"Sooner than I expected, actually. The *Souri* is scheduled to arrive in ten days. Because of her cargo, she's carrying a triple complement of guards, so I want to send it out when she heads back south."

"That should work out. I spoke with Volkmann two days ago. The processing center is ready. The last of the correct dies and stamps came in this week."

"And the banks will take delivery?"

"As soon as possible."

Paulus freshened their drinks and held his glass up for a toast. "Here's to greed and stupidity. Find that combination in the right group of people, and it can make you very rich."

Anton Savich could drink to that.

14

IT was nearing midnight by the time Eddie left the Xang home. It had been an exhausting emotional ordeal. They had lost their son once, when he left with the snakehead, and Eddie told them they'd lost him again to the sea. He had introduced himself as a merchant sailor for COSCO, China's military-run shipping line, and said that his ship had come across a container on its return to Shanghai. The captain had ordered it hauled aboard, thinking there might be something of value inside. He spared them the grim details of what had really been found but said he'd discovered their son's diary and vowed he would inform the family.

It had taken several hours to coax out where the snakehead, Yan Luo, had his headquarters. Eddie was relieved the family didn't ask him to explain why a merchant sailor would want to know, because there was no ready answer.

He left their house above the bicycle shop armed with directions to a bar in a warehouse district and went in search of the snakehead who had sent Xang and his extended family on a journey to their deaths. The streets were quiet. It was late, and with the military encamped in the town square, the locals had prudently decided to remain indoors.

The bar was located on Long March Street, a potholed strip of crumbling asphalt that ran parallel to a tributary of the Min River. There were few lights, and the air was heavy with the smell of decay and rust. Most of the buildings along the river side of the street were corrugated metal, and all seemed to lean against their neighbor. It made Eddie think that if the lynchpost was removed, several blocks of warehouses would tumble like dominoes. Thorny weeds grew from grease-blackened soil in the few areas not paved over.

The other side of the street was crowded with three-story apartment blocks. Every time Eddie passed the alley separating two buildings, he got a whiff of the communal dung heap. From the numerous garbage piles came the sound of cats and rats competing for food. He heard the occasional wail of a child from one of the darkened apartments.

Nearly to the end of the street, garish light spilled from a storefront, and as he approached he heard muted music coming from within. This had to be the place. His pace slowed as he approached. He was planning on retracing the steps that Xang had taken, a route that had ended in tragedy. Once under the control of the snakehead, Eddie would have few options but to go along with the tide of humanity seeking to escape China. As the light grew brighter and the pop music louder, Eddie's breath became short, and he felt sweat trickle down from under his arm.

He knew his fears, had faced them over a distinguished career in the CIA and during his time with the Corporation, but knew that each time he forced himself to overcome them it had a corrosive effect on his psyche. It took something from him, weakened him. Like the cumulative effect of concussions, there was always the risk that the next one would be fatal.

Eddie clenched his fists and forced himself to stride those last few yards to the bar. There was no bouncer, so he threw open the door and stepped in. The music blared from a pair of speakers mounted behind the bar. The fog of cigarette smoke was as dense as a tear gas attack and just as irritating to his eyes. The wood-planked floor was slick with spilled beer and was moldy in spots. The patrons were mostly young toughs in black leather and overly made-up girls in miniskirts and belly-revealing tops. Despite the infectious beat of the music, the bar's atmosphere seemed charged with something ugly.

Eddie spotted the problem as his eyes swept the men seated at the bar along the room's back wall. Three of them wore uniforms. The army had come into the local oasis of Western decadence, and no one seemed willing to do anything about it. Yan Luo, if he was here, wouldn't invite trouble for his smuggling operation by confronting a trio of drunk soldiers in town for one night. And if the snakehead wasn't going to evict the soldiers, no one else would either. The men would remain until they'd had their fill.

No one paid Eddie much attention as he moved to an open seat at the far end of the bar. He ordered a beer, making sure the bartender saw the wad of money he carried. He had the situation figured out and a plan formulated by the time he'd downed half the bottle.

If the soldiers didn't leave before closing time, Eddie was in trouble. Once the soldier he'd killed turned up missing the next day and the army began to tear the town apart, Yan Luo would fade into the background. He'd close down his smuggling ring until after the body was found and an appropriate number of arrests had been made. It might be weeks before he felt safe enough to resume trafficking people out of the area. Eddie needed to be in the smuggling conduit tonight if he hoped to discover if there was a connection between the snakeheads and the pirates preying on shipping in the Sea of Japan. His solution was simple. He had to get the three armed soldiers out of the bar before closing, which by the sour look on the bartender's face wouldn't be too much longer.

Of the three soldiers, only one was drinking heavily. He was a corporal, a couple years older than the two privates flanking him. He regaled his pals with wild stories as he drank beer after beer. His two companions had the look of peasants just off the farm and appeared overwhelmed by everything that had happened to them since stepping from behind the plow ox. The corporal sounded like he was from a city. It was possible that he was a friend of the would-be rapist; maybe they had joined up together. He held his comrades enthralled with tales of sexual excess and debauchery and made boasts that by the end of the evening his companions would have such stories of their own. He said this and leered at the closest girls.

Eddie waited for any of the locals to react. One man at the bar wearing black jeans and a motorcycle jacket made of vinyl glanced at a table in the darkest corner of the room. It was a quick flicker that the soldiers didn't notice, but Eddie did. At the table were three men and a pair of girls who could be twins. Two of the men looked like muscle, bodyguards. The third had to be the snakehead, Yan Luo. He wore a dark suit jacket over a black T-shirt and impenetrable sunglasses. He gave the barest shake of his head. It seemed he didn't want trouble with the soldiers.

The snakehead sensed Eddie's gaze. Eddie did nothing to mask his intentions. He stood. He'd finished his beer and grabbed the bottle around the neck. Yan Luo slid his Ray-Bans down his small nose to watch what was about to unfold. His expression remained neutral, and the bodyguards seemed oblivious.

Eddie moved so he was behind the soldiers and tapped the corporal on the meaty shoulder. The big man didn't react, although one of the privates shot Eddie a wary look. The din of patrons' conversations became a muted, expectant silence. Only the stereo continued to play on. Eddie tapped the corporal again, harder.

He whirled around on his barstool and shot to his feet. He was much steadier than Eddie had expected. His small, piggy eyes narrowed as he looked down at the creature who dared to interrupt his drinking.

"You owe those young women an apology, and I think it's best if you and your friends left the bar," Eddie said in his most cultured voice.

The corporal roared with laughter. "You think it best." He laughed again. "I think it best if you piss off." He put a heavy hand on Eddie's chest and shoved with all his strength.

Rather than fall back, Eddie twisted so the force of the push made the corporal take a staggering step forward. As he'd anticipated, the two farm boys remained in their seats, though they watched expectantly. The corporal threw a lightning punch at Eddie's head. Eddie barely had time to duck as another shot bored in, a left jab to his ribs that connected solidly. He had wholly overestimated the corporal's level of inebriation, or else the man was a natural drunken brawler.

The corporal grabbed up his own beer bottle and smashed it on the bar. The jagged ring of glass he waved at Eddie's head was as sharp as any knife. Eddie could have broken his own bottle to even the fight, but killing the soldier wasn't an option. He wanted the men out of the bar, not a police raid.

"I think it best if you bleed a little," the corporal snarled and swung the broken bottle at Eddie's throat. Had it connected, the glass would have torn through cartilage and arteries and nearly taken Eddie's head off. He rocked back and let the broken bottle whisk an inch from his skin. He jammed his own bottle under the soldier's ribs, digging the neck into the slab of muscle so the corporal had to step back, roaring in pain.

Both young privates got to their feet.

Eddie pegged the farm boys with a hard stare. "You don't want any part of this." His warning came in a hoarse whisper, and he refocused on the corporal. He moved into a martial arts stance, his motions so fluid it seemed his body was made of water. He let the bottle drop from his fingers.

The bigger man also crouched down, his hands weaving in front of his face, his eyes locked on Eddie's.

Big mistake.

Eddie's upper body didn't move as he threw three successive kicks: ribs, knee, and a shot to the groin that didn't properly connect. The corporal should have been watching Eddie's torso to be able to anticipate his blows.

The soldier staggered under the onslaught, but Eddie gave no quarter. He glided in close, launching a series of quick strikes, his hands almost blurring. Throat, ribs, solar plexus, head, ribs again, nose. By the time he stepped back again, five seconds had elapsed, and the corporal was a bloody mess.

One of the privates made a jerky move as if he were going to defend his comrade. Eddie had a hand to his throat before the boy was even sure he was going to commit.

"He isn't worth it," Eddie said evenly, his breathing unaffected by the adrenaline or the fight. He gently pushed the soldier back into his seat.

The corporal was still standing, barely, but there was hatred in his eyes. In his condition, the soldier would most likely return to the bar with reinforcements. Eddie spun like a dervish, firing two brutal roundhouse kicks to the corporal's head. The first bent him double and rolled his eyes back into his skull. The second drove him to the floor so hard his insentient body bounced off the wood planking. He wouldn't wake for hours, and at least a day would pass before he would be coherent enough to consider revenge.

Eddie looked back at the privates. "Do yourselves a favor and find a new buddy. This guy's got a big enough mouth to get you into trouble but no way to get you out. You understand?" One of them nodded mutely. "Take him back to wherever you're encamped. Tell your sergeant he fell down a flight of stairs, and don't come back again."

Grateful they'd been spared, the two privates scooped the unconscious corporal from the floor and slung his limp arms over their shoulders. They dragged him from the bar without a backward glance. Eddie turned to the bartender and indicated he wanted another beer. As if a dam had burst, everyone was talking at once, conversations floating over his head as the youths recounted what had just happened.

Eddie managed to take his first sip before one of Yan Luo's bodyguards ambled over. "Mr. Yan would like a word with you."

Eddie eyed the bodyguard, took another sip, and got to his feet. Once he committed himself there was no turning back. The snakehead would have complete control of his life. Yan Luo could turn him in for reward money once Eddie made his play as a deserter. He could have him killed on the spot just for the sport of it, or he could pass him along the chain that could ultimately end in a shipping container on the high seas. He squared his shoulders and followed the bodyguard over to Yan's group.

Yan ordered the teenage twins away as Eddie approached. One of them purposely pressed her backside against Eddie's groin as she and her sister moved over to the bar. Eddie ignored her and sat opposite the snakehead. Yan Luo removed his sunglasses. Eddie estimated he wasn't yet thirty, but the smuggler had an aura of world-weary disdain found in someone who'd only known life's darker side.

"I suspect there was a reason behind your demonstration," Yan Luo said.

"I couldn't speak with you with them in the bar."

"Why is that?"

Rather than answer, Eddie pulled the stolen dog tags from around his neck and tossed them onto the scarred table.

Yan Luo didn't pick them up or even touch them. His gaze turned speculative. "Are you with the troops in town for the election?"

"No. I was stationed outside Fouzou."

"And you came here?"

"You helped a friend's cousin a while back."

"I help a great many people. What did I help this person do?"

"You got him to Gold Mountain." That was the name illegals had given the United States. Eddie let the words hang in the smoky air for long seconds. "I want to go, too."

"Not possible."

"Why?"

"I get paid for favors," the snakehead replied.

At that, Eddie pulled a thick roll of money from his pocket. "I know how the system works. I give you money now and work off the rest when I reach America. Only you have no way to guarantee I'd pay since I have no family here to threaten." Eddie peeled several yuan notes from the outside of the roll to reveal an inner core of American dollars. "Five thousand right now. Another two when I leave China, and you forget you ever met me."

The corners of Yan's mouth lifted slightly, and his eyes narrowed. "And what's to stop me from taking your money now and forgetting we ever met?"

Eddie spun the table forty-five degrees with a flick of his foot and rammed a corner into one of the bodyguard's chests, just hard enough to knock the wind out of him. He launched himself to his feet and drove his elbow onto the tabletop, splitting the wood in half. As it collapsed, he kicked the spot where the leg met the top, snapping the three-foot leg free. He had it in his hand and thrust against the second bodyguard's throat before the man had even thought of going for the gun hidden behind his back.

Yan remained in his seat but couldn't hide his disbelief at how quickly his two best men had been subdued.

"I could have killed all three of you," Eddie said just loud enough to be heard over the driving rock beat from the speakers. "I'm making you a fair offer. If you don't want it, I walk away."

"I think you will do well in Gold Mountain," Yan said, breaking into an insincere smile.

Eddie dropped the stump of table leg on the floor and retook his seat. The bodyguard massaged his throat and glowered but made no retaliatory move. "How does it work from here?" Eddie asked.

"I have two others ready to make the trip with you." The snakehead checked his watch. "I wasn't planning on leaving until tomorrow night, but things might get hot if that soldier decides to make trouble. I have a truck. I'll pick you up at the end of the block in an hour. We'll meet with my contact in Fouzou tomorrow. They'll have documents made up and take you on from there." Yan paused, his stare hardening. "Let me give you a little advice. Don't screw with these people. You pull the kind of crap you did tonight, and you'll find yourself trying to stuff your guts back into your body."

Eddie nodded. He knew he could get away with intimidating Yan because he was low on the snakehead chain of command. He was a recruiter, a foot soldier with little clout. He would remain a big fish in the small pond of Lantan, while the people Eddie really wanted were much higher up. From now on he'd pretend to be a model immigrant, compliant, grateful, and a little afraid.

The fear he didn't have to fake.

15

BY the time the jumbo jet's tires screeched against the tarmac at Zurich's airport, Juan Cabrillo had filled in the outline of his plan. Admittedly it was one of the most insane he'd ever thought of, but given the mission parameters and the short timeline his instincts told him he was under, there was nothing left for him but insanity.

He'd spent most of the long flight from Tokyo in communication with the *Oregon* through a secure laptop. Max Hanley had assembled the team Juan wanted with him in Switzerland as well as the equipment they would need from the ship. The *Oregon* was running at flank speed for Taipei, the closest anchorage with an international airport. It was a calculated gamble to break the surveillance with the *Maus,* but at four knots Juan was sure his crew could find the floating drydock again. He and Max estimated that they'd be off-station for less than a day provided there were no troubles in Taiwan. Juan had pulled in an old favor with the harbormaster in Taipei to make sure there wouldn't be.

Equipment that couldn't pass an international customs inspection would have to be improvised once they were in Switzerland, but Juan didn't think it would be a problem. He had numerous contacts in and around Zurich from his days with the CIA, and they only needed a couple of guns. They could mix the explosives themselves with household chemicals, and everything else they would need was either available for rental or sale.

With his team twenty-four hours behind him, Juan's first priority was to find a safe house and reconnoiter the route between Regensdorf prison and the courthouse downtown.

Twenty minutes after clearing Customs, he was behind the wheel of a rented Mercedes ML-500 sport utility vehicle. He doubted he'd need the truck's off-road capabilities, but it was anonymous enough in the affluent city, and it came equipped with a GPS mapping system. It was a beautiful spring morning, so he had the windows rolled down and the sunroof retracted.

Unlike Tokyo, Cabrillo enjoyed Zurich, with its seamless blend of old and new. Baroque and modern architecture stood side by side, not in competition but in a calming harmony. It was in Zurich that he'd first slept with a contact while working for the Company. She was a low-level Russian embassy employee who couldn't provide any valuable information, but that didn't make Juan feel any less like James Bond. The memory brought a smile as he circled the city on the ring road and found the exit that would take him to the prison. The safe house would have to wait until he had found the best spot for what he had in mind.

Just before he reached the turnoff for the prison, Juan turned around and headed back into the city. No sense in showing off the car to the guards at the entrance gate since he was pretty sure he'd have to cover this route a few times before he knew where his team would stage their strike. He drove straight to the courthouse where Rudolph Isphording was playing star witness in the trial of the century.

The streets around the courthouse were cramped and full of traffic, mostly because there was a new building under construction next door, and the trucks hauling materials to and from the work zone blocked intersections. The new building was still just a steel frame with concrete slab floors stacked seven high. A tower crane lorded over the construction site, its horizontal boom arm able to swing far over the plywood and chain-link fence ringing the construction site. Juan paused at a red light to watch it hoist a bundle of I-beams into the air and was startled into motion when the driver behind him gave a polite tap on his horn. The light had changed. He waved an apology and drove on.

He tracked back and forth between the prison and the courthouse six more times, taking six different routes. If he were in charge of the security team that drove Isphording into the city for the trial, he would select a different route at random each day, making it much more difficult for someone to attack the armored caravan. But the problem was that the destination was the same every time. The closer the van came to the courthouse, the more predictable and vulnerable it became.

Juan found a parking spot a few blocks from the court and spent the next two hours walking the neighborhood, sipping black coffee from a Starbucks. He felt he should have bought his coffee from a local vendor instead of an international franchise, but it had been months since he'd had a taste of his favorite brew. He made a mental note to contact the company's Seattle headquarters and see if it was possible to buy their special equipment for the *Oregon*.

While traffic was heavy all around the courthouse and the adjacent construction site, the main street behind the two buildings was relatively quiet. He would need to post people here for a few days to get a better handle on the traffic patterns if this was the location they would use. So far everything looked right. He only needed to make a few changes to his original plan.

A little after noon he rented an apartment in a four-story building about six blocks from the courthouse. He explained to the leasing agent that he and a group of American lawyers were in Zurich for several months as part of an ongoing lawsuit against an insurance company. The apartment had three bedrooms and an office. The furniture was a bit threadbare, but the kitchen had been recently remodeled, and the bathroom contained a tub big enough to swim laps. Most important, it was on the building's top floor and Juan could tell that, if they needed it, they could gain roof access from the back alley fire escape. He'd been forced into a six-month lease, which meant he'd need to keep the unit occupied well after the job was done in order to deflect suspicion.

Too often a criminal would establish himself in a neighborhood, stay close to the bank he planned to rob, then vacate the area as soon as the crime had gone down. A police canvass a couple days later would reveal the person had left, and the cops had themselves a solid lead. By rotating a few Corporation operatives or outside contractors through the apartment for a couple months, no one would suspect anything was amiss. It was this level of detail that ensured the Corporation's anonymity as well as its success.

After making calls to procure weapons, Juan had nothing to do but wait for his team to arrive. He grabbed a meal at a nearby restaurant. He hadn't planned on polishing off the carafe of wine, but each sip seemed to work magic on the tension in his shoulders and neck. Juan rarely worried about his own safety; it was his people who concerned him.

He'd always had a leadership style of commanding from the front, to never ask a subordinate to do what he was unwilling to do himself. For that, his people gave him their loyalty. In return, Juan knew he could trust them in any situation. But it never got easier, asking them to put themselves in harm's way. Yes, each member of the Corporation shared in the profits of their work. Each was a millionaire at the very least, but like he'd discussed with Max back on the *Oregon,* this wasn't about money, not really. It was about the dedication to doing the right thing. It was an ideal that drove Juan and his people, an ideal that someone had to face the new dangers of the twenty-first century.

People were needed on the ramparts of freedom to stand the dark watch against any and all who were against it.

His team had taken it upon themselves to become those gatekeepers, those standers of the dark watch. And it seemed each time Juan read a newspaper or caught the news from a satellite feed and learned of some new atrocity, he realized they would need to stand their posts for a long time to come.

DR. Julia Huxley was the last to arrive the next day. Rather than have her stay in the safe house, Juan had told her to take a hotel room near Zurich's famed Bahnhofstrasse, the bank- and shop-lined street that as much identified the city as Fifth Avenue did New York or Rodeo Drive did Beverly Hills. Although Julia had proven herself on several covert operations, her primary function was as medical officer. Juan would have much rather used Linda Ross for this job, but she wasn't the right body type or height for what Juan had in mind, nor were any of the other half-dozen women aboard the *Oregon*. Julia had readily agreed to come to Zurich, yet Juan made sure she was as insulated as possible from the rest of the team.

He barely recognized her when Hali Kasim escorted her into the safe house living room. Gone were her soft, dark eyes. She wore tinted contacts that made them look watery blue behind large-framed glasses. Her customary ponytail was hidden under a wig of gray hair that curled around her head like a thinning bush. Julia normally had the curves of a 1950s pinup model, but her travel-wrinkled clothes now hid the doughy body of a prison matron. The frown lines across her forehead were deep enough to be considered corrugation, and two laugh lines alongside her mouth were like trenches.

She looked nothing like Julia Huxley, M.D., and everything like Frau Kara Isphording, wife of convicted embezzler Rudolph Isphording.

"Good God," Juan greeted her, "you're ugly enough to scare a bulldog off a meat wagon."

Julia curtsied and smiled. "You sure are a charmer, Juan Rodriguez Cabrillo. I must admit Kevin outdid himself." Kevin Nixon ran what the Corporation had dubbed the Magic Shop, a large space aboard the *Oregon* where he and his team could throw together any number of uniforms, disguises, and all manner of dirty tricks.

"We might be here for a while," Juan said as he circled his medical officer with a critical eye. "Can you re-create this effect?"

"Kevin showed me how to do it." Julia shook her ample hips. "This oh-so-flattering body suit is no big deal, but doing the makeup so you can't notice the facial appliances is tricky. I think I have it, though. It's a little creepy. Kevin knows more about cosmetics and skin care than a counter girl at Bloomie's."

"He was just nudged out for an Oscar for best makeup a few years before joining us," Juan told her. He didn't add that Nixon had turned his back on Hollywood following September 11. His sister was on her way to see him from Boston when her plane smashed into the North Tower.

"Plus," Julia added, "he packed me enough frumpy clothes to open my own secondhand shop."

"You don't need to bother with the costume until we're ready. No need to advertise there's a Kara Isphording clone running around Zurich."

"What, and deny all the men a gaze at my beauty?"

"The only head you're going to turn looking like that is the head of a screw, and even then you're going to need a pneumatic wrench." Juan called out to gather his people together. In total there were five members of the Corporation present, including himself. It was a small team, but once Julia had done her thing, she could act as backup when they made their move.

"I've had a chance to go over the ground, and think I found the perfect spot. We'll need a few days for additional recon just to be sure. I'm not married to the site, so if something doesn't feel right, don't hesitate to bring it up. We'll go over the ground together later on.

"Once we're comfortable and we have all our equipment ready, we'll move on to phase one, and that's snatching the real Kara Isphording."

"Is she guarded?" Hali asked.

"Don't know yet. That'll be part of our reconnaissance."

"What's gonna be our cover?"

"All the dummy companies Rudy Isphording set up for the purchase of the *Maus* have Russians on their boards of directors. We'll use that and pretend to be Russians out to spring Isphording from jail."

"Why would he want to go?" asked Franklin Lincoln, a SEAL vet. "As I understand from the briefing Max gave, this shyster has a sweetheart deal with the prosecutors."

"Because we're going to play up the rumor about how Isphording had his hands in the Palestine Liberation Organization's cookie jar."

"Has he?"

"I've got Murph confirming it, but it appears old Rudy might know where some of Yasir Arafat's missing billions are. Either way, we convince him that the PLO believes it, and he'll know his only chance is with us."

"And once we have him?" Julia asked.

Juan's tone darkened. "We sweat him. Hard. Eddie's still in China last I heard."

"Near Fouzou," Hali interrupted.

"So we need to learn what we can on our end and pray we're in position to intercept the boat they're using to smuggle him. I'm convinced Isphording's the key to whoever's behind the *Maus* and the pirates."

"What if he's not?" Julia asked. "What if he doesn't know anything beyond the shell companies he set up?"

As much as he didn't want to face that possibility, Juan knew he had to answer. "Then Eddie's as good as dead, and we're back to chasing individual pirates across the Sea of Japan."

For the next several hours Cabrillo laid out his ideas in detail, refining them with suggestions from his people. They all had sharp intellects and years of covert experience. No one deluded themselves that this would be a simple job, but by the time they finished, they knew they had the best possible plan. Juan gave each of them their orders for the next several days. Some would chart traffic flows and activity around the construction site. Others were to procure and modify equipment, the most critical being a ten-wheeled truck and trailer. Juan would scout out the

Isphording home and determine what, if any, security they would need to overcome as well as rent a warehouse outside the city.

Today was Tuesday. Mark Murphy had learned that Rudolph Isphording was scheduled to appear in court on the following Monday. For what Juan had in mind, they could lay a lot of the groundwork but would need the weekend to have everything in place for Monday morning. That meant they had to get to Frau Isphording no later than Thursday night if Julia was going to double her during Friday's regular visiting hours. Juan hated the tight timeline, but there was no helping it. He didn't dare wait another full week. God knew where Eddie or the *Maus* would be by then.

It was now or never.

"COM check?" Juan said into the voice-activated throat mike.

He received the ready signal from Linc and Hali Kasim. Julia merely placed a hand on his shoulder, since she wouldn't leave his side for the next twelve hours. The night was dark and moonless because of cloud cover. Dew shone silvery white on the lawn surrounding the three-story brick house. The upscale suburban neighborhood had been quiet since an elderly man had returned to his own minimansion after walking what had to be the most constipated dachshund in history.

Cabrillo knew after watching her for three days that Kara Isphording lived alone. She had a maid during the day, but at night she was her home's sole occupant. He also knew she had an alarm system. The doors and windows were all wired, and he'd once spied the maid deactivating the system when she'd shown up for work in the morning. He guessed it would have been installed after her husband had been arrested, so it wouldn't be too deeply integrated into the grounds, no motion detectors or IR cameras, but then again, all it took was Isphording's wife to push a panic button, and all hell would break loose.

"Okay, Hali, you're up. Once Linc pops the door, you have sixty seconds to deactivate." This was an estimate on Juan's part but a calculated one. Kara Isphording was in her late fifties and would doubtlessly have little experience with electronics. Whoever installed the alarm would make sure a client had ample time to shut the system down so as to avoid false alarms.

Once the ex-SEAL and the Corporation's communications specialist did their job, they were to return to the Mercedes. Juan was approaching Frau Isphording as a member of the Russian mafia here to save her husband from Palestinian terrorists. It would be a little hard explaining the presence of a Lebanese and an African-American.

"Think of it as affirmative inaction," he'd joked as they finalized the plan.

Frank Lincoln towered over Hali Kasim as they dashed from cover behind a thick hedgerow bordering the Isphording property. Both wore black. Hali carried a small duffel for his tools. Linc had his lockpicks in a slim billfold jammed into his back pocket.

They reached the heavy oak door. Curtains were drawn over the flanking sidelights. The house was completely dark. Kara Isphording's bedroom light had gone out three hours earlier, long enough to enter deep REM but not so long as to need to use the bathroom.

Hali hung back as Linc readied his picks. He'd practiced on an identical lock that he'd bought from a building supply store on the other side of the city. His fingers were large, but they moved with the delicacy of a surgeon's as he eased in the tension pick, then began to set the pins with another smaller tool. It took him eight seconds to snick back the dead bolt and a further fifteen to turn the main handle.

He shot Hali a glance. The smaller man had his bag open and wore a tiny light mounted on a headband. He nodded. Linc eased open the door. An electronic tone sounded and would continue at five-second intervals until the alarm was shut down or went active.

The entry floor was polished wood. A dark Oriental rug covered the space between the door and a massive staircase that rose to the second floor. To right and left were other rooms, a living room and a dining room large enough to seat ten. Hali saw all this in a fleeting glimpse.

The alarm panel was to the right of the door. A red light on its cover blinked accusingly.

He pried off the face with a screwdriver. Within were bundles of wires. He ignored them all. The circuit had already been cut. He needed the numerical key that would deactivate the system. He spotted two computer chips embedded on a small motherboard. He popped them both, then clamped a tiny wire to the broken leads as a bypass. The light and chime continued. Linc posted himself at the foot of the stairs, straining to hear if Kara Isphording had been disturbed.

With such a system, the owner had three tries to enter the right code in order to prevent the alarm from sounding. After the third attempt the system would automatically trip. By removing the logic circuits from the panel, the security system had no way of knowing how many attempts Hali was about to make.

Kasim dusted the alarm's touchpad with fingerprint powder. Actually, it was finely ground pencil lead and worked just as well. He let out a relieved breath when only four of the keys showed they'd ever been pressed. The fingerprints were smudged, but that wasn't the point. With just four numbers to reset the alarm, there were thirty-six possible combinations and not nearly enough time to run them all. Except that the four keys used by Frau Isphording were one, two, three, and four. It was the most common alarm code in the world, a convenience for homeowners and thieves alike. Hali pressed them in sequence. The little red light continued to wink at him and the chime sounded that another five seconds had passed.

He hit the keys in reverse order and still the alarm remained active.

"Time," Hali hissed into his microphone.

"Twenty-three seconds," Juan answered from outside.

Hali had no choice but to punch in the progression. 1243 Enter, 1324 Enter, 1342 Enter, 1423 Enter, 1432 Enter.

"What's happening?" Juan asked.

"Random number. I haven't hit it yet."

"You've got ten seconds."

2134 Enter, 2143 Enter, 2314 Enter, 2341 Enter.

"Hali," Linc whispered, "Try 3142."

"Five seconds."

Kasim didn't question Linc's guess. He hit the numbers and stabbed the Enter key.

The chime sounded again and the light began to blink at double speed.

"We gotta go," Hali said, his voice strained with the tension.

"Reverse 'em," Linc ordered. "Try 4231!"

"One second."

Linc's suggestion wasn't a reversal of the numbers, but Hali punched them in anyway: 4231 Enter.

The light stopped blinking. The alarm had been disabled. Hali shot a questioning look at his partner.

"Hey, man you should have paid more attention to Max's briefing." Linc's smile was that of the Cheshire Cat. "Isphordings have two grown children. One born on April second and the other March first. Four/two, three/one. Elementary, my dear Hali, elementary."

Hali spent a few more minutes with the alarm panel to disable the panic buttons. One on this control and no doubt one next to the Kara Isphording's bed.

"All right, clear out," the chairman whispered as he and Doc Huxley entered the foyer. "If we're still inside after twenty minutes, assume everything's okay and you can head back to the safe house. Julia will take Mrs. Isphording's car to Regensdorf tomorrow. Once she's back she'll babysit her over the weekend, and I'll borrow the car to get back to the city."

After Hali and Linc returned to the SUV, Juan stepped outside and dialed the Isphording residence from his cell. He heard the phone ring in his ear and throughout the house. After the third ring a sleepy voice croaked, "Allo?"

"Frau Isphording, my name is Yuri Zayysev," Juan said in Russian-accented English. "I am an associate of your husband. It is important that I see you tonight."

"*Was? Nein.* That is not possible," Kara Isphording groused, switching to English. "*Mein Gott*, it is two o'clock in the morning."

"This concerns your husband's safety, Frau Isphording." Juan had deepened his voice, adding menace. By now she must have realized that many, perhaps all, of her husband's clients worked the other side of the law. "I am just outside your home. Please meet me downstairs. I have already disabled your alarm system. If I wanted to harm you, I would have done so already."

"Who are you?" Fear had crept into her tone.

"Someone who is trying to help you and your husband. He is a trusted member of an organization I work for, and we have learned that he's been targeted for assassination on Monday morning."

"Assassination?"

"Yes, Frau Isphording. By members of the PLO."

"What did you say your name is?"

"Yuri Zayysev. I have been sent from Saint Petersburg to help your family."

She had to know Rudolph did a great deal of work with Russians, because after a moment's pause she agreed to meet. Juan was relieved. He could have simply bound and gagged the woman in her bed, had Julia send away the maid when she arrived in the morning, and put his plan into motion. However, that wasn't his style. The woman was an innocent in this affair, and he wouldn't put her through any more than absolutely necessary.

A light at the head of the stairs came on. Made up and properly dressed, Kara Isphording was not an attractive woman. But fresh from her bed with her hair awry and her face puffy with sleep, she was downright scary. She'd donned a heavy robe over whatever she wore to sleep in, and Juan fervently hoped it wouldn't slip open. For this meeting he was dressed in black jeans, a black shirt, and a large black leather jacket, the de rigueur uniform of an enforcer in the Russian mafia. He'd dyed his hair and five days' worth of beard a ginger red. He also wore tinted contacts that darkened his bright blue eyes.

"I am sorry to disturb you, Frau Isphording," Juan said when she reached the first floor. Neither made a move to shake hands. "There was no other way. Plans are in motion to free your husband, but we need your help. You are the only one allowed to see him at Regensdorf, and he needs to be made aware of what is happening."

"You said someone wants to kill my Rudy?" She dumped herself into a chair. Tears were already in her eyes.

"Yes. You may not be aware, but factions within the Palestinian movement believe your husband is the key to a great deal of their money. Perhaps billions of dollars."

"But . . . but he said that what he did for the Palestinians was legal."

Juan knelt in front of the frightened woman and took her trembling hands in his. "That may be true, but for these people rumor is as good as fact. They are either going to kill him on Monday or try to abduct him. We must act before they do."

"I don't . . . I don't know what to do. Shouldn't you tell the police?"

"Your husband's testimony has already ruined the careers of several prominent people in business and the government. There are even more powerful people who would like nothing more than for your husband to be silenced."

Juan could see he was being too circumspect. Kara Isphording was already at the end of her mental and emotional rope and couldn't grasp what he was saying. He couldn't blame her. A year ago she was married to a successful lawyer and enjoying the genteel life of a Swiss *hausfrau*. Today she was bombarded with reporters and dosed daily with stories about her husband's criminal activities.

"What I am trying to tell you is the police won't prevent an attack on your husband."

"But that's just not right!" she cried indignantly. "We pay taxes."

Cabrillo almost smiled at her naïveté. "As the Americans would say, your husband has stirred up a hornets' nest. I am here to make sure he isn't the last one stung."

She dabbed at her eyes with a tissue that looked like it had been in her pocket for as long as she'd owned the robe. She tried to square her shoulders. "I don't know what to do. What do I tell Rudy? What is your plan?"

"You don't have to do anything, Frau Isphording." Juan turned his head and called into the dining room. "Ludmilla."

Julia stepped into the light cast from the fixture atop the stairs. Kara gasped at seeing her twin and jammed her knuckles against her mouth. For a moment Juan was afraid she'd faint, but she gathered enough composure to get to her feet. She crossed to where Julia stood and studied her doppelganger.

"This is my associate, Ludmilla Demonova. She will go to Regensdorf in your place tomorrow. I do not mean to insult you, but it is safer operationally for her to pretend to be you than it is for us explain the details of our plan. Had we had more time, you could have gone to your husband yourself, but . . ." Juan's voice trailed off, letting the woman draw whatever conclusions she wanted. "Are you allowed to give your husband anything?"

Kara Isphording continued to stare at Julia, forcing Juan to repeat the question.

"No, not really, but I pass him little notes. The guards haven't made me stop."

"Okay, that is good. I need you to write to your husband. Tell him that we haven't harmed you and that he is to listen carefully to what Ludmilla tells him. Can you do this for me?"

"*Ja,* yes, I can." She was regaining her senses and seemed to accept that Juan and Julia were there to help her. "What happens afterward?"

"You mean once we free your husband? I do not know. I am only to take him to a safe house. After that"—Juan shrugged like a soldier just doing his job—"it is up to your husband and my boss. I'm sure they will send for you, and the two of you can retire to the south of France or the Costa del Sol."

She gave him a wan smile as if she knew that the rest of her life would never be so idyllic.

Julia left for the prison the following morning a little past nine. Juan chafed at having to wait around, but there was always the risk that Kara Isphording would lose her nerve and phone the police. After giving the maid the day off, the two of them sat in the dining room over a cold coffee service. Juan continued in his role of a Russian gangster so there was little conversation, and for that he was grateful. Only three days remained until they would snatch the lawyer, and he felt every minute tick by. The modifications to the truck weren't complete, although they'd done run-throughs in rental cars and had the timing down. What worried him most was the work they had to get done over the weekend at the construction site. Fortunately, the company overseeing the building didn't post night watchmen, so that wasn't a problem. However, they had ten tons of cement to get into position tonight if they were to make their deadline.

By eleven Juan's wrist was sore from checking his watch. He'd spoken with Linc and found they'd finished with the semi at the warehouse and were now loading the fifty-pound sacks of cement.

The sound of the automatic garage door opening launched Juan out of his seat. He was at the door to meet Julia when she stepped from the Isphordings' 740 BMW.

"Well?"

"Piece of cake." Julia smiled. "It actually took him a few seconds to see through the disguise, and none of the guards even looked twice."

"Great job. Is he all set?"

"More than all set. He's eager. I guess he really was hooked up with the PLO. As soon as I mentioned they were gunning for him, he agreed to everything."

"And you laid out the whole plan?"

"He knows where and when we're making the grab. He'll tell the prison administrator that he needs to meet with his attorney early on Monday morning. That'll put his convoy at the construction site before the work crew shows up."

"Did he give up any information?"

"About the *Maus*? No. And I didn't press. But when I told him the Russians sent me, he asked if I worked for Anton Savich. I played dumb and agreed. Isphording seemed relieved. Savich must be his principal contact."

"Savich?" Cabrillo said the name aloud as if tasting it, trying to draw out a memory. He shook his head. "New one to me. I'll contact Murph and have him do a search. Are you all set to watch the real Kara Isphording?"

"Got everything I need." Julia patted her shoulder bag. Inside was a syringe that she'd administer Sunday night after Kara went to bed. She'd be out for twenty-four hours, long after Juan and Julia were headed back to the *Oregon*.

16

NO matter how often Doc Huxley admonished him, Max Hanley refused to give up his pipe or dessert. He figured that by his age he'd earned the right to know what was best for him. The thickening around his middle added only ten or fifteen pounds, and while he couldn't run a mile in under ten minutes, his job rarely required him to run a mile. So what was the big deal?

His cholesterol was just about normal, he wasn't showing any signs of diabetes, and his blood pressure was actually on the low side.

He swirled his fork through the raspberry drizzle pooled on his plate and made sure he got the last few crumbs of the chocolate cake. The fork was spotless when he returned it to his plate and pushed back from the mess hall table with a satisfied groan.

"All finished?" the white-jacketed mess steward asked.

"Only because I'd need a microscope to find the few remaining cake molecules. Thanks, Maurice."

Max had dined alone this evening but nodded to the personnel at the other tables before leaving the mahogany-paneled mess. His sturdy brogans sank into the almost inch-thick rug. A squall had kicked up from the north over the past several hours, so he decided to take his pipe in his cabin. He'd just settled into an easy chair with a week's worth of the *International Tribune* that had been choppered back to the *Oregon* when his intercom rang. He let his cheater glasses dangle around his neck and set his pipe into an ashtray.

"Sorry to bother you on your day off." It was Linda Ross from the operations center.

"That's okay. What's the trouble?"

"No trouble, but you wanted to know if we got anything from Eddie. It appears he's left Fouzou and might be headed back to Shanghai."

Max digested the report. "Makes sense from the snakehead's perspective. Shanghai is one of the busiest ports in the world. Much easier to slip a bunch of illegals onto an outbound freighter amid the confusion than at a smaller harbor like Fouzou."

"That's what Murph and Eric Stone think, too. Do you want me to call the chairman?"

"No. Last I spoke to him he has enough to worry about. If we get any better intel, I'll have you pass it along. What's our position, and how's our wallowing friend?"

"They've picked up a current so they're now making six knots. That'll put us about a hundred miles due east of Ho Chi Minh City in another five hours."

The name always caught Max off guard. Vietnam's largest city would always be Saigon to him. But that was from another time and another war. Every so often when a chopper approached the *Oregon,* a flood of memories would leave Hanley shaken for days.

Actually, the memories were never that far from the surface. It wasn't the sound of the Vietcong's RPGs exploding or the chatter of their AK-47s that stuck with him. And the screams as his patrol boat was raked from stem to stern were just a background noise. What remained sharpest in his mind was the sound of the Huey's blades pulsating over the black jungle, homing on the stream of flares Max launched into the night with one hand as he used his other to keep his newbie bow gunner's intestines inside his body. God, the blood was hot, even in that stinking hell. The Huey's door-mounted minigun sounded like a buzz saw, and the jungle flanking the estuary peeled back under its three-thousand-round-per-minute onslaught. And when that RPG arced up at the Huey—

Max yanked himself from the past he'd never stop reliving. The newspaper was balled in his fist. "Ah, any course change?" he finally asked.

"No, she's still on one hundred and eighty-five. Projected either she's headed for Singapore, which isn't likely since they've got the most incorruptible harbor workers in this region, or she'll turn due south soon and make for Indonesia."

"Seems a better bet," Max agreed. With several thousand islands to patrol, the Indonesian Coast Guard was stretched thin. The pirates would have an easy time eluding them and finding a secluded spot to unload the ship they'd hijacked off Japan. The ship-wide betting pool had been evenly split between the Philippines and Indonesia as a final destination since before they'd reached Taiwan.

"Okay, then," Max said, "call me if the *Maus* turns or you get anything from Eddie or Juan."

"Roger."

Max straightened out the rumpled pages of his newspaper and set them aside. He relit his pipe and let smoke dribble past his lips until his cabin was perfumed with the aromatic blend. As yet he couldn't figure out why the pirates hadn't found a quiet spot of ocean to disgorge their stolen ship. They'd had enough time to give her a new name and make enough cosmetic changes that no one would recognize her, especially if they ran her in different waters, say, off the coast of South America. So why risk keeping her in the drydock this long? Unless they had a specific destination in mind. Someplace close to shore where they felt safe. Max hoped the *Maus* was leading them to the pirates' lair, but it couldn't be that easy.

There was another level to this operation, another peel to the onion they hadn't seen. He knew he wouldn't find it by merely shadowing the *Maus,* but he was confident that either the chairman or Eddie Seng would. Confidentially, he was betting on Eddie finding the key. There was no real reason, just a strong feeling of confidence in the tough, independent ex-CIA operator.

HAD Eddie Seng known at that moment that Max was placing a mental wager on him, he would have told the Corporation's president to put his money on Cabrillo and his team in Switzerland.

During his training for the CIA, Eddie had undergone a grueling program to teach agents how to deal with imprisonment and torture. It had been run by army specialists at a corner of Fort Bragg in North Carolina. Before he left for Bragg, his training instructor at the Farm had given him a random code word: aardvark. It was his job to keep it a secret and the soldiers' to get it out of him.

For a month they owned Eddie body and soul. They used hoses to beat him on a regular basis, confined him in an iron box in the sun for hours without water, and often poisoned his meager food rations so he couldn't keep them down. They tried to break his will by keeping him awake for six straight days and screaming every racial slur they could come up with. They once dumped him naked onto a fire ant nest, and one night they poured half a bottle of Scotch down his throat and questioned him for an hour before he passed out. They pulled out all the stops in their interrogation, but Eddie never gave up his code word. He was able to keep a small part of his mind focused that no matter what they did to him, it was only an exercise, and he wouldn't die.

Eddie held no such illusions now, and as the truck lurched, the throng of illegals packed in with him swayed so that those closest to the rear doors were almost crushed. He whispered, "Aardvark."

Six days in the hands of the snakeheads made that month at Fort Bragg feel like a Club Med vacation.

There were about a hundred men packed into the sweltering box truck. They hadn't been fed or been given water in at least two days, and the only reason many were still on their feet was that there was no room for them to fall. The stench of sweat and body waste was overwhelming, a cloying film that coated Eddie's mouth and seared his lungs.

It had been like this since Yan Luo had turned him over in Fouzou. The next link in the smuggling ring were members of a triad, China's version of a Mafia crew. Once they'd taken his picture for forged travel documents, he'd been locked in a cell under a cement factory with sixty others. There were no bathroom facilities. They stayed there for two days, and each night guards came down to select a couple of the more attractive women. The girls would return hours later, bleeding and shamed.

On the morning of the third day a group of South Asians arrived. They spoke to the snakeheads in accented Chinese, so Eddie couldn't tell where they were from. They could have been Indonesian, Malay, or even Filipino. But he was sure their presence was a deviation from the normal channels for getting immigrants out of China and suspected they were connected to the pirate ring.

The immigrants were brought out of their cell in groups of ten and paraded in front of the Asians. The Asians made his group strip naked and then subjected them to a humiliating scrutiny. Eddie felt like he was a slave on the auction block. They checked his teeth for decay and his genitals for obvious venereal disease. He and the others had to prove they could lift a pair of cinder blocks suspended from a bamboo pole. The Asians singled out three of the men from Eddie's group, himself included. They were the biggest of the lot, the strongest. The others were sent back to the cell.

Of the original sixty from the cell, ten were loaded into a truck. The Asian guards had to use wooden planks like bulldozer blades to pack them into the already overcrowded vehicle. The bodies were so tight there wasn't enough room to take a deep breath.

Before closing the rear door a fire hose was turned on the crowd. In the frenzy to slake their thirst, several people were hurt. Eddie managed a mouthful and was close enough to the side of the truck to lick a little more water from the hot metal. Then the door slammed shut, and the immigrants were left in total darkness.

What got Eddie, what made this so difficult, was the silence as the vehicle began its journey. No one cried or complained, no one demanded to be released. They were willing to put up with any privation if it meant they could get out of China. To them anything was worth the chance for freedom.

They drove for what felt like days but couldn't have been more than twenty hours. By the continuous swaying and jostling Eddie was sure the snakeheads kept to back roads. To compound their misery, many of the men became motion sick, adding the acrid smell of vomit to the already overwhelming stench inside the truck.

The truck squealed to a halt after a particularly smooth stretch of road. No one came to open the doors. Eddie thought he heard the sound of jet aircraft, but the noise was muffled and indistinct. It could have been thunder. They were left packed and sweating in the truck for at least another hour before someone outside unlocked the rear door.

It swung open, and glaring white light blinded the immigrants. Eddie's eyes filled with tears, but the pain was worth the first breath of fresh air he'd had in a day. They were inside some kind of huge, modern warehouse, not at all the seedy dockside facility he thought the snakeheads would use. Had Eddie not been so disorientated, he would have noticed there were no support columns for the metal building's arching roof, a clue as to his real location.

The men were allowed to jump from the truck. Many were so weak they fell to the polished concrete floor and had to crawl away to make room for the next. Eddie was proud that he managed to keep his feet. He took a few shuffling steps away from the truck and tried to squat to ease his aching knees.

There were four guards inside the warehouse. Eddie was pretty sure they were Indonesians. They wore cheap cotton pants and T-shirts, and plastic sandals on their feet. All carried the Chinese version of the AK-47. Out of habit he burned their faces into his memory.

As his sinuses cleared he became aware of another smell, not the tangy saltiness of the sea but a recognizable chemical taint. Casually, so as not to arouse the guards, he crossed back around the truck. On the far side he saw towering doors that reached nearly to the ceiling. But what gripped his attention and sent a jolt of fear to his very marrow was the functional shape of a commercial airliner. It had four engines mounted on its tail, an old Russian-built Ilyushin Il-62.

They weren't taking this group out of China on a cargo ship. They were going to fly them out. Eddie realized he was in more trouble than he'd anticipated. These people weren't connected to the pirates at all. This really was a legitimate, albeit illegal, smuggling operation. His whole trip to China was a dead end, only he had no way of contacting the *Oregon*. The jetliner's door was opened, and the guards were forming the men into a line to board. The hangar doors were still securely closed, so there'd be no escape that way.

The truck that had brought them here was quiet, its engine was off, but Eddie thought that maybe the keys were still in the ignition. The last of the immigrants were out of the cargo box and shuffling toward the Ilyushin. Eddie joined the end of the line. The truck's cab was only ten yards away to his right. He could cover that in seconds, swing himself into the seat, and try to ram his way out of the hangar.

He braced himself for the attempt, planting one shaky foot, and was about to start running when he saw that the driver was still in the cab. For another fraction of a second he thought about trying for it anyway, even though he would lose time subduing the man. One of the guards saw he'd paused and barked something that was plain to understand in any language. Eddie released a long breath, allowed his body to relax, and adopted a posture of defeat.

He took one last glance at the truck when it was his turn to mount the stairs to the aircraft's cabin. He had no idea what awaited him and the others at the end of the flight, but he saw fear in the eyes of those he passed on his way to an empty seat. They were also realizing they'd gotten more than they bargained for.

Fifteen minutes later, the Ilyushin was towed out of the hangar, and after another delay its engines fired and it began to taxi. Judging by the size of the airport complex and the time they'd driven, Eddie guessed they were near Shanghai. His theory was confirmed after the plane took off and arrowed over the city before turning northward.

"How long do you think it will take to reach America?" his seatmate whispered. He was a big farm boy who had no idea what he'd gotten himself into.

The boy still thought they were going to the United States, a land of prosperity and opportunity called Gold Mountain. Eddie didn't know where they were headed, but he knew it wasn't the States. The Ilyushin didn't have anywhere near the range. He also had a sinking feeling that before long he'd come to believe the illegals they'd found drowned in the Sea of Japan were the lucky ones.

"You'll know it when we get there, friend," Eddie said as he closed his eyes to the inevitable. "You'll know it when we get there."

CABRILLO and his team spent the weekend setting up for the snatch. They worked at the construction site under the cover of darkness. Moving the tons of cement was backbreaking labor that took all of Friday night and part of Saturday evening. The risk of their activities being detected by a foreman checking the site over the weekend was negligible, since the sacks of portland were common at the work zone. They left the placement and wiring of the explosives for Sunday night. Because of their demolition expertise, this went quickly, and by midnight they were ready to return to the warehouse Cabrillo had rented in a town about twenty miles north of Zurich.

Juan sent the others ahead in the cars they'd use during the operation while he and Linc remained behind with the tractor trailer for one final test. At this late hour there weren't any pedestrians on the street to question why the truck's driver locked his partner in the back of the box trailer. Once Linc closed the doors, Juan wedged himself into a corner of the modified trailer to keep from being tossed around. He was exhausted, and his joints creaked as he eased himself to the floor. A moment later he heard the big MAN diesel grumble, and the truck started to move. He carried a flashlight, but the echoing metal container remained mildly claustrophobic. The motor and pulley system attached to the roof looked perfect, a simple design that Linc could operate from the cab.

Juan turned on a portable radio but couldn't get a station on any frequency, and when he powered up his cell phone it couldn't acquire a signal. "Can't hear me now," he said into the mute device. "Good."

They'd installed baffles and jammers inside the trailer to isolate it from electronic signals. Linc and Hali Kasim had tested the equipment at the warehouse, but Juan wanted to make sure the system worked inside the city limits where cell coverage would be more complete. It was one more detail that he wouldn't leave to the vagaries of Murphy's Law.

Every five minutes during the thirty-minute ride he checked to make sure the phone remained useless. Linc let him out after Hali closed the warehouse doors behind the ten-wheeled truck.

"Anything?" the big man asked.

"Nada," Juan answered, noting that once he was outside the truck his phone could connect to the nearest cell tower. "We're good to go. We'll grab a couple hours of sleep. The van carrying Rudolph Isphording should be in position no later than eight fifteen. I want us ready by seven thirty. Has Julia checked in?"

Hali nodded. "She called me when you were in the truck. Isphording's wife is out cold, and she's on her way back to her hotel. She'll be waiting at the prison at seven and will report in as soon as the van leaves the gates."

"Okay, good. She'll shadow them into the city. Linc, you'll wait with the truck behind the construction site. The crash car's in position?"

"Parked it myself," Kasim said. "And I triple-checked the cables are in the back."

Juan nodded. He'd expected no less. "Now, up until tonight the only thing illegal we've done is impersonate a lawyer's wife, and even that probably isn't against the law. Come tomorrow morning, however, we're going to break about every law written into the Swiss penal code. If this operation goes south, anyone who gets nabbed is looking at a few decades in Regensdorf prison."

His people understood the danger. It was what they were paid for, but Juan always reiterated the risks before they went into action. Hali, Linc, and the other Corporate mercenary, an ex-pararescue jumper named Michael Trono, looked primed.

The following morning broke gray and cold. A light drizzle had begun to fall by the time the team reached their prearranged staging posts. The few people out on the streets were huddled in trench coats or under umbrellas. Rather than a problem, the foul weather was a blessing because it seemed to have delayed the morning traffic.

Juan had little trouble breaking into the construction site. After all, it was his third incursion, and hot-wiring the big engine that powered the crane was a snap. The climb up the tower left him wet and shivering but, fortunately, the crane's cab had a heater. He fired it up and drank coffee from a thermos as he waited. Around his neck dangled infrared goggles.

Julia checked in again, informing the team that the armored van bearing Rudy Isphording into the city would be there in another ten minutes. From his vantage high above the streets, Juan would be able to see them five blocks before they reached the construction site. Linc had parked the tractor trailer behind the muddy area. Juan could see smoke pumping from its stack as Linc waited with the engine idling. Hali and the others were in the crash car, a small van they'd bought secondhand from a moving company in Lucerne. Juan couldn't see them but knew they also had infrared goggles as well as gas masks.

The chairman scanned the work zone once more. Piles of building materials littered the site alongside overflowing trash containers the size of trucks. Excavators and bulldozers remained silent. There was no activity around the construction trailer because no one had yet shown up for their shift. If they held to the schedule the Corporation team had observed the past week, the first worker wouldn't arrive until a half hour after the snatch had gone down. The seven-story building was dark in the murky storm, a skeleton of steel and concrete. From the high vantage he couldn't see where he and his people had wired it to blow.

His cell rang. "Juan, it's me." Julia Huxley. "Isphording's van just stopped. One of the cops in the lead car got out to confer with its driver. Hold on. I think it's okay. The cop's getting back into his car. All right, they're on the move again. You should see them in a second."

Far down the street a police car came into view followed by the armored van and a second cruiser. They didn't have their bubble lights or sirens on and crawled along with the regular traffic.

"Okay people, it's almost showtime," Juan said over his encrypted phone's walkie-talkie mode.

He wiped the sweat from his hands and let them rest lightly on the crane's joystick controls. Although he'd never operated a tower crane, and the height made depth perception a bit tricky, he'd run more than his share of derricks and cranes over his years at sea to feel confident he could manage the behemoth. He'd already swung the hundred-foot horizontal boom over the street, and the trolley where the cable descended was positioned directly above the roadway. The heavy steel hook was lowered to within fifty feet of the cobbled street.

"I got 'em in my mirror," Hali announced from the crash car.

"Goggles on, everyone." Though distorted, Juan could make out details well enough, most notably the infrared strobe lamp they'd mounted on the crane's hook. Invisible without the goggles, the IR lamp glowed like a flare through the sophisticated optics. This was similar to the technology that allowed stealth fighters to drop bombs with pinpoint accuracy in any weather.

A flash of movement caught Juan's attention. He looked up the street as a Ferrari rounded a corner and shot up the road. It had to have been doing eighty miles per hour as it rocketed down the wrong lane of the two-way street. The sound of its throaty exhaust echoed up the canyon of Baroque buildings and reached Juan's perch a hundred feet up in the control cab. He calculated speed and distance and realized that the low-slung sports car would be abreast of the lead police cruiser at the critical moment. If Hali pulled out in front of it, the kinetic energy of the impact would not only destroy the Italian-built car and kill its driver, it would also push the van carrying Isphording out of the path of the police car, allowing the convoy to pass through their carefully laid ambush.

"Juan?" Hali called anxiously.

"I'm on it."

As much as he hated to move the crane from its carefully calculated position, he had to act. He flexed a joystick and the long boom arm began to swing across the horizon. He thumbed off a safety cover from a toggle, and as the boom reached what he thought was the right position, he hit the switch. The three-thousand-pound hook assembly plummeted from the sky.

The Ferrari's driver never saw the weight falling from above, so he only had seconds to react as the mass of steel smashed into the street, gouging a two-foot crater less than two car lengths in front the wedge nose of his F-40. He stood on the brakes and twitched the wheel to the right, sideswiping the trailing police cruiser. Juan activated another switch, and the hook tore free from the street, pulling up clots of dirt. The hook smashed through the million-dollar car's windshield and peeled off its roof like a sardine can as it passed below. The Ferrari's rear wheel fell into the hole, and the supercar pitched sideways, slamming into the cruiser again so both vehicles shuddered to a sudden stop.

Hali Kasim might have seen the whole thing unfold behind him in his rearview mirror, but it didn't distract him from his job. As the first cruiser passed the van, he accelerated out of his spot, barely clipping the Swiss police car's rear bumper. It was enough of a nudge to spin the vehicle so it completely blocked the narrow street.

The armored car carrying Rudolph Isphording braked hard and barely avoided hitting the cruiser. Julia Huxley, trailing the convoy, spun her car to block the van from reversing out of the trap.

Juan triggered the homemade explosives they'd laid inside the unfinished building.

The shaped charges had been carefully positioned for the maximum effect. As each went off, its force was funneled into sandbaglike redoubts of cement powder the men had stacked on every floor. From the ground level up, each sequential explosion sent a blooming gray cloud of dust blasting from the building in a scene reminiscent of the Twin Towers collapse. In seconds the fine powder had formed an impenetrable curtain of dust that lofted from street level to nearly two hundred feet and covered a two-block radius. It would take at least ten minutes for the light breeze to clear the dense fog from the area. Until then, no one would be able to see anything happening on the streets around the construction site.

Hali Kasim ignored the screaming pedestrians as he and his men dashed from the van, each carrying lengths of braided cable. The gas masks filtered out the worst of the cement dust, but he could still taste it with each breath. As for the IR masks, they allowed him to see the descending hook and the infrared lamps wired to the cable in his hand, but for the rest, it was like running through a forest fire.

The driver of the armored van would be trained to ram his way out of the accident and was probably in the process of doing so when Cabrillo kicked off the explosives. Now, like everyone else on the street, the driver and his men sat paralyzed by the enormity of the explosions that appeared to have leveled the adjacent building.

Hali fumbled to the front of the truck and looped the wire around the axle. He used a parked car to leap onto the roof with the two loose ends. Looking up, he saw the IR lamp on the hook gliding through the gray clouds like a tiny star amid the darkness of night. Kasim's men had passed their cables around both rear axles and handed the ends up to Hali. Their job done, each stripped off their gear and vanished into the panicked crowd. The fleeing pedestrians were coated with cement dust and resembled ghosts stalking a foggy moor.

Up in the tower Juan maneuvered the hook so it was directly above the multiple bundle of IR lights atop the armored van. He could see them move a bit as Hali steadied himself on the vehicle's roof.

"Okay, that's got it." Hali's voice was muffled by his gas mask. "You're right above me. Lower the hook about ten feet."

"Lower ten, roger." Juan paid out more cable, watching closely as the two points of infrared light merged. Without the lamps, finding the truck in the turbid swirl of dust would have been impossible.

"Hold there." Hali fed the eyeholes at the ends of each cable through the heavy snap hook so that all six were secured. "Okay, Chairman, she's all yours. Give me a second to get clear, and haul away."

The Lebanese-American jumped to the ground and was about to let the current of running people to carry him away when a cop from the lead cruiser suddenly reared out of the dust cloud. For what seemed like forever the two regarded each other. The officer's eyes widened in his dust-streaked face as he finally recognized the object in Hali's hand was a gas mask. That was as much a reaction as Kasim would allow him. Because he lacked Eddie Seng's martial arts training, Hali had to settle for a swift kick to the cop's groin before he took off running.

He managed just a few yards when he spotted another officer getting out of the rear-guard cruiser's passenger side. The man was dazed by the car crash and explosion but had the presence to carry his big flashlight and a blocky automatic pistol. He was halfway out of the car when he saw Hali running through the storm of cement power. He recognized Hali's Arab features despite the dust and made a snap assumption. He tried to raise his weapon above the doorframe, even though the angle for a shot was all wrong. Hali threw himself bodily against the cruiser's door, breaking one of the cop's ankles and pinning him momentarily. Hali reached for the gun, realized the cop had an iron grip on the SIG Sauer, and rammed his elbow into the cop's face until his fingers went slack. Kasim wrenched the weapon away and took off again, leaving the unconscious officer in a heap on the pavement.

High above the fight, Juan Cabrillo put pressure on a joystick to raise the hook, tensioning the cables for a moment before lifting the seven-ton armored truck from the ground. Once he'd hauled it thirty feet off the street, he flicked the joystick to rotate the tower crane counterclockwise. He watched as the bright flare of IR light turned through the roiling dust. He slowed the rotation as the truck swung over the street where Franklin Lincoln waited with the semi.

As part of their preparations back in the warehouse, Linc and Hali had cut off the top of the trailer, split it lengthwise with cutting torches, and then remounted the two pieces on long hinges so the entire box could be opened to the sky. An IR light had been mounted on each corner of the trailer. While the dust had begun to settle at his elevation and his view out the cab windows was clearing, down at the truck the cement dust still billowed. Yet Juan could clearly see the rectangular pattern of lights with his goggles, and he gently lowered the armored van once it was positioned within the grid.

Linc had been waiting atop the tractor cab, and as soon as the van's tires flattened slightly under the vehicle's weight, he scrambled to release the hook. As soon as it was free, he radioed Juan to clear out, then returned to the cab. He put the transmission into first gear and hit the remote device to seal the trailer roof.

The guards were now isolated, and even if they'd called for help during the grab, they hadn't seen anything in the dust storm, and the local police would be busy for several hours as they pieced together that this hadn't been a terrorist attack.

Juan checked his watch just before descending the long ladder that ran down the tower crane's single support column. From explosion to securing the armored van had taken one minute, forty-seven seconds. Thirteen less than he'd expected, but then he was working with the best. He could barely see to grope his way across the construction site, moving like a blind man through the dust storm. Grit filled his eyes and choked his lungs. It took five long minutes to find the gate. He climbed the chain-link fence and lowered himself to the sidewalk.

The street was at a standstill, and the curbs were empty of people. A fine, pale powder covered everything, like ash from a volcano. He had to brush his hand against the cars parked along the street to guide him out of the worst of the swirling storm, and it wasn't until he was two blocks from the ambush site that he could finally see enough to pick up his pace. Police cars were fast approaching, their lights slashing through the clouds like lighthouse beacons.

"What happened?" asked an Englishman standing outside a café. His clothes were clean as opposed to Juan's dust-covered work clothes.

"I think some sort of construction accident," Cabrillo lied, coughing.

"Dear God. Do you think anybody was hurt?"

Juan looked back at the settling cloud. "Not a soul," he said, knowing this time he was telling the truth.

RUDOLPH Isphording knew a little about how the Russians were going to pull off his rescue, so he wasn't as stunned as the guard in the back of the van with him when they heard the screech of brakes and the crash of metal from a traffic accident. The big truck came to a sudden stop. But when an instant later the building next to the courthouse seemed to collapse, Isphording's fear was genuine.

Neither he nor the corrections officer could see anything out the small view ports that had been installed into the side of the vehicle, nor could they comprehend what was happening when the truck suddenly began to sway. They could both feel the slight centrifugal force, as if they were going around a gentle curve. Then the motion stopped, the truck pendulumed for a moment, and there was a slight bump followed by a low-pitched mechanical whine and a loud crash over their heads.

Just seconds later came a new sensation of movement, only this time Isphording was sure that the van was on the road again. Outside their armored box they could see nothing but darkness. The guard tried his cell phone but couldn't get a signal and could only communicate with the two men in the cab by banging on the bulkhead that separated them.

For thirty-five minutes they could feel the motion as the van was moved out of the city. They could sense and hear the truck accelerate as it reached a highway and later slow and twist around curves as it left the major thoroughfare. Not long after, all motion stopped. Wherever the Russians, Yuri Zayysev and the woman, Ludmilla, who'd pretended to be Kara, were taking him, Isphording assumed they'd arrived.

He and his guard waited in silence for something to happen. The minutes crept by slowly.

What the lawyer couldn't see from the back of the armored van was that Linc and the others were waiting for Juan to arrive. As soon as he pulled his Mercedes SUV between the tractor trailer and Julia's Volkswagen, Hali closed the big overhead door. Because of the overcast sky, the light coming through the opaque skylights cast the big warehouse in murky shadow. Hali snapped on a few overhead lamps, but it did little to soften the building's gloomy air.

Cabrillo's SUV was powdered with cement dust, and the chairman himself was grimy. He accepted a damp cloth from Julia to wipe the worst of the dust from his face. He also drank down a half liter of water. "So far, so good," he congratulated his people. "Looks like no one had any trouble getting here, so let's open this tin can and finish it. Linc, I couldn't tell when I lowered the truck into the rig, which way is it facing?"

"It's facing the rear doors."

"That should make this a little easier." Juan grabbed a Heckler&Koch MP-5 machine pistol from a workbench and slid the strap over his shoulder. He also palmed a pair of round grenades. They were dummy practice grenades but would look indistinguishable from the real things to the guards in the van. He passed around black ski masks to everyone and lowered his over his face so only his eyes and mouth were exposed. The others had also armed themselves with an assortment of pistols and machine guns.

Once everyone was ready at the rear of the trailer, he unlatched the door. He gave his people a five-second countdown and swung open the door with a jerk. All five of them swarmed up inside the trailer, jumping onto the van's long hood, waving their weapons and shouting incoherently. The Swiss driver and the guard riding shotgun had service pistols in their hands, but through the bulletproof glass they were at a standoff. Before the driver could start the engine and try to drive out of the trailer, Juan leered into the windscreen and showed off the grenades.

He pointed at each man and then at the doors before pulling the pin from one of the grenades. There was no mistaking his intention.

The guards maintained their defiant look but knew there was nothing they could do. They laid the weapons on the dashboard and slowly reached for the door handles. As soon as the doors unlocked, a member of the team was ready with plastic-tie handcuffs, blindfolds, and gags. Hali yanked the key ring from the driver's polished belt and tossed it to Juan.

The Chairman climbed over the top of the armored van and jumped lightly to the floor of the trailer. On the fifth attempt he inserted the correct key into the lock, but before he turned it, he nodded to one of his men.

If anything went wrong there was no reason for Kara and Rudolph Isphording to be able to give the same description of Yuri Zayssev, so he had General Operations specialist Michael Trono call out in Russian-accented English, "To the guard in there with Herr Isphording. Your two comrades have already been subdued. They will not be harmed, and neither will you. I am going to open the door just enough for you to toss out your weapon. If you do not, I will be forced to use tear gas. Do you understand?"

"I understand," the guard responded.

"Herr Isphording, how many guns does the guard have?"

"Just a pistol," the lawyer replied.

"Very good. Has he removed it from its holster?"

"Yes."

"That is very wise of you," Trono said. "Herr Isphording, take the gun from him and move to the rear door. I am opening it now. Toss the weapon onto the floor."

Cabrillo cracked open the heavy door, and a black revolver clattered off the rear bumper. Hali and Julia had joined them, their weapons at the ready. Juan nodded to them and heaved the door all the way open. The frightened guard sat on a bench that ran along one wall of the van. He understood enough of the situation to have already laced his fingers on top of his head. Hali cuffed, gagged, and blindfolded him while Julia helped the paunchy lawyer from the vehicle. The other two guards were shoved into the back of the van, and Juan locked them in.

ISPHORDING saw five armed commandos, some wearing work clothes, others all in black. One had the curves of a woman, and he guessed it was Ludmilla. "Is one of you Yuri Zayysev?" he asked eagerly.

"Da," one of the commandos answered. His work clothes were streaked with gray powder, and when he stripped off his mask, his face was still streaked with dust. His hair was red, like Isphording had been told to expect, and his beard had been trimmed to a ruddy goatee.

"Mr. Savich sends his compliments, Rudolph." The man used the name Isphording himself had provided. "Of course, he couldn't meet you in person, but you will see him soon enough. There is an office at the back of the warehouse. Ludmilla will take you there. We'll leave here in a few minutes."

Julia had taken off her mask so that the attorney could see that she was the woman he knew as Ludmilla, although she wasn't wearing the disguise.

"Thank you." Isphording pumped her hand. "And my wife? What about Kara?"

"Another team is fetching her now," the woman called Ludmilla replied.

"Thank you," the lawyer repeated. "I thank all of you for saving me."

"You were not harmed?" Ludmilla asked as Isphording followed her out of the trailer. Linc had placed a stepladder at the rear door to make it easier for him.

"No. I am fine. A little frightened perhaps. Until you came on Friday I had no idea the Palestinians were after me. I'm grateful to you all."

Julia gave him a smile. "You have Mr. Savich to thank. We are just doing as he ordered."

"I knew he's a powerful man, but I had no idea he could arrange something like this."

"Here we are," Ludmilla announced.

The office was spartan, just a couple of desks and filing cabinets and a worn vinyl couch under a frosted glass window. The floors were scuffed linoleum, and the room smelled of cigarettes. Curtains were drawn over the large piece of plate glass that overlooked the warehouse floor. Isphording collapsed onto the couch and accepted the bottle of water Ludmilla handed him.

A few minutes later Yuri Zayysev strode into the office. He'd left his machine pistol out in the warehouse, but he'd belted a holster around his lean waist.

"What happens now, Herr Zayysev?" Isphording asked.

"We're waiting for some more of my people, and then we are leaving. The man who drove the truck thinks he might have been followed, so we're hurrying our schedule. We don't know if the Palestinians are on to us or not."

"They haven't operated outside the Middle East in years," Isphording said. "They must truly be desperate."

"A lot of money is unaccounted for since Yasir Arafat's death," Zayysev countered, "enough to make anyone desperate."

The lawyer was about to reply when everyone jumped at a crash outside in the warehouse. A second later came the unmistakable sound of silenced weapons fire. One of Zayysev's men gave a choking scream that was cut off by another burst of gunfire. Zayysev tore his pistol from its holster and racked the slide. "Stay here," he ordered Ludmilla. He crossed to the open door, keeping low. More gunfire echoed outside. He eased around the jamb, his pistol outstretched, probing. He cursed and fired four rounds to clear a way out of the office. Taking a cautious step out, he fired again at a dark shape running behind the semi. He turned to give Ludmilla another order when he was caught by a sustained and brutal burst of autofire that stitched him from knee to chest. The impact of a half-dozen rounds blew him back into the office, where he fell crumpled against a desk. His chest was a mass of blood.

The plate glass window overlooking the warehouse exploded in a rain of silenced gunfire. Bullets impacted all around the room, sparking off the metal furniture and tearing gouges from the cheap paneling. With the reactions of a cat, Ludmilla threw her body over Isphording, shielding him until she could unholster her own weapon. She twisted off him as a figure loomed in the shattered window frame. Around his face the gunman had wound a checked kaffiyeh like those favored by Palestinians. He spotted Ludmilla and raised his assault rifle to his shoulder. She fired first, and Isphording saw the Arab's head literally come apart. Blood and pink clots of brain matter sprayed the wall next to him in an obscene Rorschach ink blot. Another Muslim gunman took his place and raked the office with his assault rife. A chunk of Ludmilla's arm was blown off, and then she caught two more rounds to the stomach. She managed a low keen of pain as she fell to the dirty linoleum surrounded by a spreading lake of her own blood.

The attack had been so lightning fast and savage that Isphording was too stunned to move. The smell of blood and gunpowder overwhelmed the small office. The attacker, who must have been the one that killed Zayssev, entered the room. He stepped over to Ludmilla's crumpled body, using a foot to turn her corpse so he could better see her wounds. "Nice shooting, Mohammad," he said in Arabic to the gunman at the window. The terrorist leader unwound the kaffiyeh from his face and glanced at Isphording. His features were sharp and dangerous, and his dark eyes blazed with hatred. "I know you speak my language," he said to Isphording, continuing in Arabic. "You did work for the late

Chairman Arafat, hiding money that should have been spent fighting the Americans and the Jews."

"The others are all dead, Rafik," Mohammad reported from outside the office. "The building is ours."

"Did I not tell you someone would try to free this pig from prison?" Rafik gave Isphording such a superior leer that the lawyer couldn't stop his bladder from releasing. "All we had to do was wait."

Rafik snicked open a switchblade knife, its keen edge glinting in the fluorescent light. "Now, let's talk about the money."

17

RUDOLPH Isphording never gave much thought to the people whose money he laundered. He'd insulated himself from his clients so they were nothing more than pass codes on bank account ledgers or vague signatures on legal documents. He had always considered himself a numbers man, a person most comfortable behind a desk protected by a paper fortress. Now the evidence of what he'd done was sprayed across the walls of the office and pooled under Ludmilla's body. He couldn't bring himself to look at the carnage that had been Yuri Zayysev's chest.

Rafik had been called out to the warehouse before asking the lawyer any questions. Mohammad watched him from the office doorway, his eyes looking like chips of obsidian. Isphording could see that the Palestinians were maneuvering a ramp to the back of the trailer to unload the armored van. The Russians who'd snatched him had taken great pains to make sure no one had been injured or killed. He felt certain that Rafik and his thugs wouldn't be so scrupulous. Isphording's entire body trembled like he was in the grip of an epileptic seizure.

The terrorist leader called out for Mohammad to join him for a moment. He pinned Isphording with a menacing glare and stepped out onto the warehouse floor.

Minutes crawled by, allowing the lawyer's fears to kaleidoscope in ever more horrifying thoughts, so when the sound penetrated his mind, he wasn't sure what he heard. It sounded like someone was calling his name, but the voice was distorted and wheezy, like they were a great distance away or it was coming from a dream. He turned his eyes toward the doorway. No one was there. He looked around the room. Ludmilla lay faceup, her clothes sodden with blood.

"Isphording."

He heard it again, and had he not been turning his head to check on Zayysev he never would have believed the Russian's lips had moved. By some miracle Zayysev was still alive. He was ghostly white, and blood continued to drool down his chest like crimson molasses. Isphording felt hope surge inside him like a dose of adrenaline.

"Keep them talking," Zayysev mumbled, his eyes flickering from shock.

"What?" the lawyer whispered urgently. Mohammad or Rafik could be back any second.

"Tell them anything they ask. Just keep them talking." Zayysev's voice was so faint Isphording had to cup a hand to his ear and tilt his head to hear him.

"I don't understand," he pleaded.

"More of my men are on the way . . ." Zayysev's voice trailed off. His eyelids fluttered and rolled back into his skull as he fell unconscious once again. How he had survived the multiple gunshots staggered the imagination.

Rudolph Isphording recalled what the Russian had said prior to the attack, that they were waiting for more of his companions. No doubt they would be armed. His first rush of hope became a torrent. He was going to be rescued. He was going to get out of this alive!

A bellow of exhaust echoed from the warehouse, and the armored van slowly emerged from the trailer, guided by one of the masked terrorists. Rafik strode back into the office an instant later. His face was contorted in a cruel mix of hatred and self-satisfaction. He dragged a chair from behind one of the desks and sat astride it in front of Isphording. His breath smelled of carrion.

"Now, pig, you will tell me what you did with the money you stole from my people." He spoke in English, his accent somehow making him even more intimidating.

"I will tell you what you want to know," Isphording replied in Arabic.

Rafik slapped him across the face hard enough to leave a red print on his skin. "You will not defile the language of the Prophet again. Speak English, Isphording. Isphording? That is a Jewish name."

"I'm Catholic."

Rafik slapped him again, his eyes going wide with insane rage. "You will speak only when asked a question."

Isphording glanced to the motionless form of Yuri Zayysev, praying that his men would come soon.

"We know you used part of my people's money to create fake companies," Rafik began. "One is called D Commercial Advisors. Another is Equity Partners International. You used these companies to buy a large ship, called *Maus*, that is someplace in the Far East. You will tell me who controls these companies and who profits while my people suffer."

For a long second Isphording didn't know what to say. The Palestinian had it all wrong. None of the PLO money he'd hidden away had gone into that deal. That one was set up solely for Anton Savich and the Sikh, Shere Singh. Then he thought that it didn't matter if he told Rafik all about it. Zayysev's men would be here any moment, and the kidnappers would be dead.

"That is correct," he said in a scratchy voice before clearing his throat. "There were actually two ships, floating drydocks. One called *Maus*, the other *Souri*."

"Who has control of these vessels?" Rafik demanded.

"A Russian named Anton Savich and a Sikh named Shere Singh."

"You are wise not to lie." There was little praise in Rafik's voice. "We know about Savich. Tell me where we can find him."

"I—I do not know," Isphording admitted miserably. "He travels all the time. I don't think he has a home, only a post box in Saint Petersburg."

Rafik made to strike the lawyer again.

"It is true, I swear," Isphording cried. "I have only met him once, over two years ago."

"We will return to him in a moment. What about this Sikh? Who is he?"

"Shere Singh. He is Pakistani but now lives in Indonesia. He is a wealthy man. His holdings are vast—timber, shipping, real estate. The largest company is the Karamita Breakers Yard on the west coast of Sumatra. I believe he controls the two drydocks through it."

"Have you ever met this man? What does he look like?"

"I've met him through a video conference last year. He appears to be a big man and like all Sikhs has a long beard and wears a turban."

Mohammad suddenly burst into the office, jabbering in almost incoherent Arabic. "Rafik!" he shouted. "Rafik, the police arrest Fodl. He knows our, our, eh . . ." He drew silent.

"Location," Rafik snarled in his native tongue. "Fodl knows our location."

The terrorist got to his feet. Isphording gave a startled cry and cowered into the couch cushions, expecting to be beaten. "Please don't hurt me. Please."

"Silence!" Rafik snapped. He took a blindfold and a pair of hard plastic ear protectors from Mohammad.

"What—what are you doing?" Isphording sniveled. Tears coursed down his cheeks. They were going to execute him right here and now.

"I said, silence," Rafik roared.

Before Rafik tied the blindfold around Isphording's head, Mohammad jammed soft rubber plugs deep into his ears. Then came the blindfold and finally the ear protectors. Isphording couldn't stop shaking. He could neither see nor hear anything. He was then gagged, but surprisingly, not too tightly. One of the terrorists hauled him to his feet, and together they guided him from the office. He had no idea what was happening, couldn't tell where they were taking him. After just a few steps he smelled the exhaust from the idling van. A moment later he was unceremoniously dumped into the back. Though disorientated, he could sense the presence of the three guards charged with driving him to his court date. His ankles were bound with some kind of plastic tie, while his wrists and hands were taped as tightly as a mummy's wrappings. He couldn't wiggle a single finger, which meant he'd be unable to worry the tape off his hands. Rafik's men were as efficient as they were deadly.

Isphording imagined the guards had been similarly bound.

The doors slammed shut as soon as he was secure, and the van took off, but they went only a short distance. Judging by how he and the guards rolled across the floor, they'd made three tight turns. As near as he could tell, the Palestinians had merely stashed the van behind the warehouse. The driver killed the ignition. A few minutes passed before Isphording felt the driver slam his door.

He and the guards were isolated from each other by the gags and ties, unable to hear because of the ear protectors. He could not imagine a worse feeling of deprivation, and while he was alive for the moment, he had no idea how long it would be before the van started up again and the four of them were taken away and killed.

CHAIRMAN Cabrillo had slammed the armored van's door hard enough for the men inside to feel it, then tossed the keys onto the roof. He checked the street fronting the warehouse one more time. No one had seen him hide the vehicle behind the building. He twirled the spray bottle of bleach around his finger as he walked. Certain that no one had left behind fingerprints, he'd taken the precaution of dousing the inside of the cab with bleach to dilute any trace DNA.

Linc greeted him at the door. The ex-SEAL had unwound the kaffiyeh he'd worn to hide his black face and let the checkered head cloth drape around his wide shoulders. Artificial blood from when Julia had shot him dripped from the fringed edges.

"Well done," Juan said, and the two men exchanged toothy grins.

"You must have a thing for playing Arab bad guys, Chairman," the big man teased. "First you were Colonel Hourani of the Syrian Army, today you're Palestinian terrorist leader Rafik. Who are you going to be tomorrow, Ali Baba?"

"Only if you play Scheherazade and do the Dance of the Seven Veils."

Mike Trono, who'd taken over the role of Yuri Zayysev for Rudy Isphording's benefit, was plucking the spent remains of devices called squibs from a special vest he wore under his shirt. The squibs were made of tiny explosive charges and an ounce or two of fake blood. These devices had been a staple of Hollywood effects wizards for years. A more sophisticated device had been placed inside Linc's head scarf to make it appear that Julia had shot away half his skull. The office had also been rigged with small charges along the walls and on the furniture to further the illusion of bullets striking the plasterboard and metal. Of course all the weapons they'd used to stage the assault had fired blanks.

When Isphording and the guards were found, the story they would tell would be too bizarre to be anything other than the truth. After being grabbed by the Russian mob, the lawyer's rescuers had then been attacked by rogue members of the PLO looking for money missing since Arafat's death. The attack had been savage, and none of the Russians survived. Then the terrorists ran off when they learned one of their men might have been picked up by the police. What couldn't be so easily explained is what happened to the Russians' bodies and why the terrorists hadn't taken Isphording with them. Nor would they be able to trace how the "Palestinians" got into the country in the first place.

Juan wasn't too concerned with those details. The Swiss authorities would rattle their sabers about tighter border restrictions, but in the end they'd be satisfied because no civilians had been hurt throughout the ordeal, they had their star witness back in custody, and the world was minus a few gangsters from Saint Petersburg. And as a bonus, he thought that they would probably put pressure on Isphording to explain where the former head of the PLO *had* stashed the billions he'd stolen from his people. Who knew, maybe they'd even get some of it back.

The one thing he couldn't control was if the lawyer revealed what he'd said under interrogation. He didn't want the Swiss looking into Anton Savich, whoever he was, or a Sikh shipping mogul named Shere Singh. He could only hope that the lawyer was as frightened of Savich as he was of the PLO and would keep silent.

Dr. Huxley stepped out of the warehouse's only lavatory. She'd washed away the fake blood from her face. She'd also stripped down to a black tank top that barely contained her curves to clean the mess away from her arm. The squib that had made it appear her arm had been blown nearly off had left a livid purple bruise on her otherwise flawless white skin.

"Are you okay, Ludmilla?"

"Da," Julia deadpanned, rubbing the spot. "Is nothing." Then she arched a teasing eyebrow. "Why is it everyone but you and Hali look like extras from some zombie B-movie?"

"Because none of you either speak Arabic or look Arabic." He laughed. "Although Hali's portrayal of the steely-eyed terrorist, Mohammad, left a lot to be desired. He had just a couple of lines to learn, and he managed to mangle both. On a brighter note, I have to hand it to Kevin and his team in the Magic Shop. They really outdid themselves this time. Especially Linc's effect. For a second I thought it had gone wrong and his head really had exploded."

"Scared me, too," Julia admitted.

Juan called out to gather the rest of the team. "Okay everyone, listen up. First off I want to commend each and every one of you on a job well done. This little caper was a long shot from the beginning, and you pulled it off flawlessly."

"That mean we're getting bonuses?" Hali asked.

"You most of all, Hali. I'm sending you to a Berlitz so you can at least fake speaking Arabic." This earned a round of good-natured laughter at Kasim's expense. "Julia, head back to your hotel as soon as you're ready. You've made your flight reservations?"

"I'll be in Istanbul by two o'clock. From there I can hook up with you anywhere. Judging by what Isphording said, I take it we're going to Indonesia?"

Cabrillo nodded. "Shere Singh sounds like the next link in the chain."

"As soon as I reach Ataturk International I'll book a flight to Jakarta." She slipped into a dark blouse. "All of my disguise stuff is in a suitcase in the office."

"I'll make sure it's burned," Juan assured her and gave her a kiss on the cheek. Julia waved good-bye to the others and settled into her rental car. Linc opened the garage door, and she roared out of the warehouse.

"Okay then, I've wiped down the armored van for prints and hit the cab and door handles with bleach. Even though we're torching this building, make sure you go over everywhere you've been, especially the bathroom. Not that any of our DNA is at Interpol, but I don't want to take any chances.

"You all have your escape routes planned. Stay loose, and we'll all be on the *Oregon* by this time tomorrow."

Although he'd used disguises each time he'd made most of the rental arrangements, Cabrillo was the most likely to be identified, so he would be the next to get out of the country. While the others cleaned up the warehouse, he changed clothes and used a bucket of water and a rag to wash the concrete dust from his Mercedes SUV. By the time he finished, Hali, Linc, and Trono had finished scrubbing down the warehouse and placing incendiary bombs throughout the structure.

"How long should I set the timer?" Linc asked.

"Hold on." Juan used his cell phone to call the *Oregon*.

"Law offices of Dewey, Cheatem, and Howe," Linda Ross greeted in her high-pitched voice.

Cabrillo calculated the time difference between Switzerland and the South China Sea. "Good evening, Linda."

"Chairman, how'd it go?"

"Smooth as silk. Listen, have Murph and Eric been monitoring the news here in Zurich?"

"Sure have. Let me get them."

Mark Murphy came on the line a moment later. Juan could hear the speed metal music blaring from the headphones Murph had pulled down around his neck. It sounded like someone using a chain saw against a piece of railroad track. "Chairman, from what I'm getting from CNN and SkyNews, the Swiss don't have a clue what happened. At first they thought it was a structural failure of some kind, and then they thought they were having their own 9/11. From what I can get from local police chatter, there's been a couple mentions about the missing armored car and unknown gunmen at the scene when the explosions went off."

"Are they closing borders or delaying flights?"

"No. They think this is a local thing."

"So we're safe for the time being."

"It'll take them so long to add two and two they'll need to include interest."

"Huh?"

"It's a joke. You know, Swiss banks? Interest? Hey, that was funny."

"Stick to being a connoisseur of fine music and leave the humor to the professionals, like Max. How far are you from Sumatra?"

"A few days still, why?"

"Rudolph Isphording said the guy who controls the *Maus* is named Shere Singh. He owns a company called the Karamita Breakers Yard. Check them both out. Also track down another floating drydock called the *Souri*. Singh owns it, too."

"How do you spell that?"

Juan did and added, "It's French for mouse."

"Got it."

"Thanks, Murph. Tell Max I want you to break off from the *Maus* and make best practical speed for the Karamita Yard." Best practical speed was far slower than the *Oregon*'s top speed, but running that fast during daylight hours or without radar jamming would give away one of the ship's most important secrets.

"I'll pass it along."

"See you in a day or so." Juan killed the connection and turned to Linc and the others awaiting orders. "It seems the police don't know what happened, so we're in the clear for now. We'll all be out of Switzerland within six hours, so set the charge for eight p.m. Isphording and the guards are in for an uncomfortable day, but they won't dehydrate by the time the local fire department arrives and discovers the missing armored car."

Cabrillo fired up the SUV's throaty V-8. He had a long drive to Munich ahead of him where he'd catch his own flight out of Europe. He hoped that by the time he got there, the adrenaline still pumping through his body would dissipate, because his hands remained shaky and his stomach was still knotted. He also hoped that Mark would find that the *Maus*'s sister ship was operated as a legitimate drydock and not involved in hijacking on the open seas, but he knew the chances of that were longer than Hali Kasim giving the keynote sermon at next year's *hajj* to Mecca.

18

JUAN Cabrillo knew the type. The man behind the desk opposite him dressed poorly and took little pride in his personal appearance other than to follow the tenets of his faith. His turban was wound tightly around his head, but the fabric was frayed and stained with sweat. His shirt was of cheap cotton, and the dark circles under the arms looked permanent. Bits of food clung to his beard and mustache.

The office was also staged to present a particular image. The desk was covered with papers, and the file cabinets were filled to bursting. The furniture was cut-rate and uncomfortable, and the posters on the wall were most likely given away by the Indonesian tourist board. The computer behind the desk was old enough to be in a museum of ancient technology.

The woman who had shown Juan into the office was perhaps the only genuine article about the whole setup. She was an elderly Indonesian woman, stick thin and tired. Her clothes were as cheap as those worn by her boss, but Cabrillo suspected it was because he paid her a pittance and not because she was putting up the front of a struggling business.

After reading a complete dossier put together by Mark Murphy prior to the meeting, Cabrillo knew more about Shere Singh and his family than he'd ever wished to. He knew their estimated net worth was nearly half a billion dollars. He knew that the family's patriarch lived in a five-hundred-acre compound in a house large enough to keep his eleven children and their families under one roof. He trusted his sons-in-law only to a point. It seemed that the sides of the business they were in charge of were for the most part legitimate. It was Shere Singh's own sons who ran the illegal operations. Abhay Singh, the eldest, was the representative for the Karamita Breakers Yard.

He maintained their offices in a run-down district of Jakarta, near enough to the docks to occasionally hear a ship's horn but far enough that one had to search to find it.

Setting up this meeting with Abhay Singh had been simple. Cabrillo had contacted the company while en route from Munich to Jakarta, representing himself as the captain of a ship he wanted to sell for scrap. He wanted to know what Karamita Breakers Yard would bid for the hulk.

Juan wasn't dressed much better than the ship broker. He hadn't shaved since the day before snatching Rudy Isphording and wore a greasy black wig under a yachtsman's cap. His duck trousers had never seen an iron or a press, and the blazer stretched over his enormous gut was missing several buttons on the sleeve. If the wealthy Singh family wanted to present themselves as struggling workers, Juan could just as easily play the part of a down-on-his-luck captain.

Abhay Singh read over the report Juan had handed him on the *Oregon,* although he'd listed a false name that was currently being painted on the old freighter's hull. The papers gave her dimensions, tonnage, and lists of equipment and appointments as well as several dozen photographs. The Sikh's piggy eyes scanned the documents rapidly and thoroughly. The only sound in the dilapidated office was the rattle of a black oscillating fan and the traffic on the street one floor below the open window.

"There is one thing I do not see here, Captain, er, Smith," Singh said, shooting Cabrillo a penetrating stare. "And that is your ownership documents. It appears that perhaps you do not own this vessel you want to sell for scrap."

Cabrillo, playing the part of Jeb Smith, one of his regular personas when dealing with officials, matched Abhay Singh's dark gaze. "There is something else you don't see there." He handed over another sheaf of papers.

Singh glanced at them skeptically, got halfway down the top sheet before his head shot up, his eyes glinting with avarice.

"That's right." Juan nodded. "Her holds are filled with eight thousand tons of aluminum ingots we brought aboard in Karachi. How about we make ourselves a bargain, Mr. Singh? You forget that my ship is owned by someone else, and I forget that when you take possession I know she's carrying ten million dollars' worth of raw metal that doesn't belong to any of us."

Singh set the papers flat on his desk and folded his dark hands on top. He gave Juan a speculative look. "How is it, Captain, that you came to us at Karamita?"

Cabrillo knew what he was really asking is how did Captain Jeb Smith know that the owners of the Karamita yard were open to corruption and bribery. "Poets often write about how vast the ocean is, and that's true, Mr. Singh, but don't you know the world can also still be a small place. One hears things."

"And where does one hear things?"

Juan looked around furtively. "Different places from different folks. I can't quite recall who told me about your fine facility, but word of mouth spreads faster than dysentery and can be even uglier to deal with." His eyes settled back on Singh's, and his expression had turned to stone. Abhay Singh understood the subtext of what Cabrillo was saying: Ask any more questions, and I'll make sure the authorities take a closer look at Karamita.

Singh flashed an insincere smile. "It gladdens my heart to hear that others speak so highly of our business. I think we can come to an arrangement, Captain Smith. You must know the price of scrap steel is up in the markets, so I can see you receiving a hundred and ten dollars per ton for the hulk."

"I was thinking more like five hundred and fifty dollars," Juan countered. By rights he could have quadrupled that price because of the aluminum ingots he was pawning, but he wanted to get the negotiations over with and shower away the stench of dishonesty.

"No, that won't do," Abhay replied as though Juan had just insulted his sister. "I can perhaps go as high as two hundred."

"You can go as high as four hundred, but I will take three."

"Oh, Captain," Singh moaned theatrically, acting like Cabrillo was now insulting his mother. "I wouldn't even break even at that price."

"I think you will more than break even. We both know the value of her cargo. Why don't we say two hundred and fifty dollars a ton, and I will deliver the ship to your yard in two days."

Singh paused to consider the proposal. Juan knew that the *Maus* would most likely reach Karamita at the same time he delivered the *Oregon,* and he wondered what would win out in the Sikh's mind: greed or prudence. A cautious man would lock down the facility until after the drydock had disgorged its cargo and they'd scrapped the evidence of their piracy, but Singh would stand to make a fortune off the prize Juan was offering.

The Sikh made his decision. "The yard is full right now. Bring your vessel in seven days, and we'll have room."

Juan got to his feet and stuck out a sweaty hand. "Deal, but just in case the ship's owners have spies in Jakarta, I'll be at Karamita in two days anyway." He was out the office and past the reception desk before his comment even registered in Abhay Singh's mind.

He met George Adams at the airport, and the pilot choppered them back to the *Oregon,* where she held station well outside the shipping lanes. George had racked up twenty hours in the past few days ferrying the team Juan had used in Switzerland back to the ship. At last the whole crew was together with the notable exception of Eddie Seng.

In his cabin, Cabrillo stripped off the Jeb Smith outfit, sealing the foul clothes and wig in a plastic bag that he tossed in the back of the walk-in closet for the next time he'd need to play the part. He lathered his face with a shaving brush and carefully went over his skin with a straight razor.

In the mirror above the copper sink he saw the glint in his eye, the look he always got when he was nearing his quarry. That Singh had agreed to buy a vessel without clear title was reason enough to have the man arrested, but more importantly it told Juan that the scent he'd picked up from Rudy Isphording was running true. Abhay Singh and his father were in this up to their necks. Juan's job now was to make them expose just enough for him to track down Anton Savich and then hang them all.

After his shower and smacking his cheeks with bay rum, he dressed in a pair of charcoal trousers, a crisp white cotton shirt, and soft dark moccasins. He called down to the galley to have some food brought to the boardroom, then called all the ship's senior staff to a meeting.

The boardroom was on the starboard side of the ship aft of the superstructure and large enough to hold forty people, although the table only accommodated a dozen. When there was no need for stealth, large rectangular portholes were opened to bathe the room in natural light. Juan was the first to arrive, and he settled himself in the high-backed leather chair at the head of the cherry finished table. Maurice, the Corporation's chief steward, appeared with a steaming dish of samosas and a pitcher of his famous sun tea. He poured a glass for Juan and handed him a plate.

"Welcome back, Chairman."

Becasue the dossier on the Singh family had been e-mailed to Juan during his flight from Europe, and George Adams had met his flight in Jakarta with the Jeb Smith disguise, this was his first time on the *Oregon* since leaving for Tokyo with Tory Ballinger almost two weeks ago.

"Good to be back. What's the latest?" Maurice was an incurable gossip.

"Rumor has it that Eric Stone is currently involved with a woman in Spain over the Internet. I hear their little chat sessions are rather torrid."

Eric was a first-rate helmsman and had a mastery of the ship's systems that rivaled Juan's and Max Hanley's, but when it came to the opposite sex, he was absolutely hopeless. In a bar in London following the Sacred Stone affair, Eric had gotten so flustered over a woman's brazen approach that he'd rushed outside to be sick.

"You wouldn't be using my override to check the ship's computer logs, would you, Maurice?" Juan chided mildly.

"I didn't even know there was such a thing, Mr. Cabrillo. I merely overheard him discussing it with Mark Murphy."

That fit. Juan chuckled to himself. Murph, Eric's partner in crime, had even less luck with women than Stone, if one overlooked the occasional Goth girl he hooked up with. But a girl with more piercings than a pincushion and who was impressed with a guy who could catch air on a skateboard half-pipe wasn't much of a catch in Cabrillo's mind.

"Well, you know what they say, Maurice, any love is good love."

"Don't ask, don't tell, Mr. Cabrillo."

The steward bowed out as Max, Linda Ross, and Julia Huxley entered the room. They helped themselves to tea and plates loaded with the spicy samosas. A few seconds later Hali Kasim came in with Franklin Lincoln. Linc normally wouldn't have been in on the meeting, but he was taking the place of the absent Eddie Seng. Eric and Murph arrived last, arguing about some obscure line from an old Monty Python movie.

"First things first," Juan said after everyone had taken their seat. "Any word from Eddie?"

"Still nothing," Hali replied.

Juan cocked an eyebrow at Doc Huxley.

She answered immediately. "The subcutaneous transmitter I surgically implanted in the muscles of Eddie's thigh checked out perfectly before you and he took off for Tokyo. In fact, that one's only been in there three months."

A few key members of the Corporation had special burst locaters implanted under their skin, Juan included. The electronic devices were the size of postage stamps and drew power from the body's own nervous system. Every twelve hours they were supposed to send a signal to a commercial satellite that was then relayed back to the *Oregon*. It was a covert way of keeping tabs on operatives in the field without having them carry bugs that could be discovered and confiscated.

The technology was new and far from perfected, which is why Juan didn't necessarily trust the devices; however, in Eddie's case, there had been no other alternatives.

Hali added, "The last transmission we received from him showed he was on the outskirts of Shanghai, someplace close to the new airport."

Juan digested the information. "Any chance they planned on flying him out?"

Max Hanley tapped the stem of his pipe against his teeth. "We considered that option, but it doesn't jibe with what we know of the smugglers. Eddie's following the trail of the illegals we found in the container. By rights he should be following the same route."

"But if they were losing too many people to the pirates, wouldn't they change their tactics?" Eric Stone asked from behind the laptop he'd set on the table.

"We don't know how many the pirates have taken," Hali replied. "The ones we found on the *Kra* could have been the first batch that were intercepted."

"Or the last straw," Eric countered, "and now the snakeheads have switched to airplanes."

"If they already had seaborne resources, it would be cost prohibitive to switch to aircraft. They would need all new infrastructure."

Juan let the debate circle the table but knew there were no answers. Until they received something from Eddie's transmitter, they were just jawing in a vacuum. "Okay, that's enough," he said to end the futile debate. "Hali, broaden the number of satellites you've been checking. It's possible that somebody else's bird is getting Eddie's signal. Think outside the box on this one. Check anything capable of relaying an electronic burst transmission."

The *Oregon*'s communications expert bristled. "I've checked the logs. My people have looked at every satellite that comes within a thousand miles of Shanghai."

"I'm not doubting the competence of your staff, Hali," Juan soothed. "If Eddie was within that thousand-mile circle, they would have found him. But I don't think he is. Now I want you to double the area, search for him within two thousand miles of Shanghai, and if he's not there, expand the grid until you find him."

Hali jotted a few notes on a notepad bearing the Corporation's logo. "You got it, boss."

Juan paused until he had everyone's attention. "As for my meeting yesterday, Shere Singh, his son Abhay, and anyone else affiliated with the Karamita Breakers Yard is on our official list of suspects. They own the *Maus* and its sister ship." He caught Mark Murphy's attention. "That reminds me. Anything on the sister drydock, *Souri*?"

Murph grabbed Eric's laptop and moused through a few screens. "Here we go. She was Russian-built and bought at the same time as the *Maus* but under a different web of dummy companies. They did make the same mistake and used Rudolph Isphording to establish the fronts. Unlike the *Maus,* the *Souri* has yet to be engaged in any salvage activities. No one has rented her, no one has even seen her. She was on the Lloyds list, but the last they knew she was still in Vladivostok waiting for her new owners to take possession."

Juan opened his mouth to ask a question, but Murph was ahead of him. "Already checked. She was towed out of the harbor eighteen months ago. And no one remembers the names of the tugs."

"Damn."

Linda Ross spoke around a mouthful of samosa. "So, for the past year and a half Singh and company could have been using her for anything. Even if they didn't go around snatching ships off the high seas, a vessel that size would be perfect for all sorts of smuggling operations. They could load her with a few hundred stolen cars. Hell, they could haul a couple of big corporate jets without dismantling the wings or cram a couple thousand immigrants into the hold."

She meant her comment to be speculative, but the air in the boardroom suddenly became somber and chilled, as if a cloud had covered the sun and darkened the wood-paneled room. Everyone envisioned the massive vessel turned into a slave ship and filled with countless miserable souls destined for a life perhaps worse than death.

"*Jesus,*" someone muttered under their breath.

"Find it, Mark." Cabrillo's voice was like steel. "Whatever it takes, you find that ship."

"Yes, sir!" the young weapons specialist replied.

"Okay, back to where I was," Juan continued gravely. "For those of you who don't know, I was just in Jakarta negotiating to sell the *Oregon* for scrap." Normally this would have warranted a sarcastic remark or at least an appreciative chuckle, but everyone was too focused. "Just like Isphording said, the men who own the Karamita Yard are as corrupt as they come. Until yesterday all we had was speculation, thirdhand accounts, and the word of a convicted embezzler. I am now satisfied that Singh is involved with the pirates and maybe the smugglers, too.

"He doesn't want us to deliver the *Oregon* for a week, which would give him enough time to dispose of whatever ship is inside the *Maus,* but we're going to drop anchor outside the yard in two days. On the night the *Maus* shows up, we're going to blow the lid off this entire operation."

"What's the plan?" Linc asked.

"That's what we're here to discuss. Everyone get together with your department staff and come up with some scenarios. Mark, have you gotten pictures of the yard yet?"

"From a commercial satellite. They're a year old, and it looks like the place was under construction at the time."

"Get George to make a few passes in the chopper for some better shots. If the Robinson doesn't have the range, have him rent another helo in Jakarta. As soon as he's back, make sure everyone has copies."

"Check."

"Linc, I don't know how many guards the place will have or what kind of weapons they carry, so make sure all your gun bunnies have everything they need, up to and including shoulder-fired missiles."

"Aye, aye."

"Doc?"

"I know, I know," Julia preempted. "I'll double-check our blood supply and play vampire with the crew if we need more."

Everyone stood, but Juan wouldn't dismiss them just yet. There was one more piece of business he had to address. "Ladies and gentlemen, I want to be very clear here. This mission has gone far beyond what we were hired to do. So far we've put ourselves in danger and come out all right." He gave Linda a significant look. "You've been up against Singh's hired guns on a one-to-one and know their capabilities. The money we're making is nothing compared to the risk we face once we enter the breaker's yard. Actually it barely covers the cost of running the ship." He got a few grins. "The people under you draw salary plus bonuses. We don't. We only get paid when there's a profit.

"Each of you joined the Corporation with expectations of using your unique talents to make money. I'm afraid that there won't be much on this caper, so if any of you want out until we're done, you have my permission. Your jobs will still be open after we're through, and there'll be no questions asked and no recriminations later."

He waited for a reaction, his eyes meeting each of his senior staff's. No one said a word until Max cleared his throat.

"It's like this, Chairman. We've all had a chance to talk about this ever since we started following the *Maus*. And the truth of the matter is, some jobs are worth more than money. We all pretty much agree we'd pay for the chance to nail these bastards to the nearest outhouse door. We're backing your play one hundred percent."

The crew gave a few "hear, hears" as they followed Hanley out of the boardroom.

Juan could only smile his gratitude to his people.

SPORTING his Jeb Smith disguise again to foil casual observers on the beach, Juan leaned against the rail of the *Oregon*'s bridge wing. He'd been there long enough for the coat of scaly rust on the railing to turn his callused palms orange. The sun was a waning fireball setting slowly behind the mountains that rose in the distance behind Shere Singh's Karamita Breakers Yard. The air was heavy with the smell of scorched metal, industrial solvents, and spilled bunker fuel. While coming north along the Sumatra coast he'd observed pristine white beaches and lush jungle. Most of the land was unspoiled and primeval. But around the yard it looked as though a cancer was eating away at the earth. The beach was a tarry morass, and the sea was the color of dishwater. With the exception of a new warehouse built out over the bay, all the buildings were dilapidated and coated with black dust. He had never seen a more depressing or dehumanizing place.

The massive scale of the buildings, cranes, and pieces of construction equipment rendered the workers almost to insignificance. The derricks towering over the yard swung slabs of steel from the beached ships to fenced-in areas where grimy men attacked them with torches, hammers, and their bare hands. From Juan's vantage a quarter mile from the beach, they looked like ants devouring the carapace of some giant beetle.

And around the *Oregon* floated an armada of the damned. The fleet of derelict ships destined to be torn apart at the yard stretched nearly to the horizon. They comprised an archipelago of rusted hulks as haunted and forlorn as the spirits of the dead awaiting entrance into hell. The container ships, oilers, and bulk freighters reminded him of a herd of cattle in the pens of a slaughterhouse. The *Oregon*'s decrepit state was artful camouflage, but around her was the real thing, the consequence of salt air, raging seas, and neglect.

"Will you look at that," Max Hanley said, stepping out from the bridge. He wore a pair of grease-stained coveralls. The oil was fresh. He'd just come from the engine room. "Compared to some of those tubs, I'd say the old *Oregon* looks shipshape and Bristol fashion."

A deafening roar from inside the large warehouse reverberated across the bay and drowned out Cabrillo's reply.

"What *is* that?" Max exclaimed after the noise faded.

"Murph's new stereo?" Juan laughed. "I think there's some kind of saw inside the warehouse. I read about them once—big chain-driven machine that can cut a ship like a slicer going through a loaf of bread."

Max ducked into the bridge to retrieve a pair of binoculars from their cradle under the chart table. After a few minutes, the warehouse's landward doors cranked open. Small diesel locomotives emerged towing a twenty-foot-thick slice of a ship. The segment had a graceful flare, almost like a sculpture, and had come from near the unknown vessel's bow. A mobile crane lifted the section into the air once the train engines had reached the end of the tracks. The piece was open in the middle. Whatever ship it had come from had cargo holds rather than decks, most likely a bulk carrier or a tanker.

"Looks like a freighter-shaped cookie cutter," Max remarked.

"Big cookie," Juan said as the chunk of steel was laid on its side for workers to continue the disassembly process.

Something about his distracted tone caught Hanley's attention. "What's going on in that cesspool you call a mind?"

"We know Singh is involved. But I've been up here a couple of hours, and the place looks like it's on the up-and-up except what might be going on inside the shed."

"Where the ship saw is?"

"Uh-huh." Juan studied the building from the binoculars he'd taken from Max. "I want to take a peek inside tonight."

"What about the *Maus*?"

"She'll be here soon enough. In the meantime, knowing what ship they're tearing apart in there might tell us something."

"It's possible that it could be one of the ships the pirates hijacked before we were hired to stop them," Hanley agreed. "Could be they brought her down here inside their other drydock."

Cabrillo looked at his old friend. "I won't know until I get inside."

One of Max's bushy eyebrows went up. "Just you?"

"No sense risking any of the crew on this. I'll be in and out before they know I was there."

"Linda Ross thought the same thing when she and her team boarded the *Maus*."

"Take a look at the seaward side of the warehouse."

Max took the binoculars and studied the sprawling structure. "What am I looking for?"

"The building's built on pilings. I suspect that the metal siding doesn't extend all the way to the sea floor, and even if it does, I'm sure the doors don't. It would cause too much drag opening and closing them.

"You plan to swim under the doors."

"Once inside I should be able to identify the ship. It won't take more than an hour, and most of that is just swimming there and back."

Max stared out at the massive shed, judging odds and risk. He came to a quick conclusion. "Use a Draeger rebreather," he advised just as a horn sounded to end the workday onshore. "That'll eliminate the trail of bubbles on your way in and out."

An hour after midnight, Juan Cabrillo was in the amidships boat garage wearing a head-to-toe wet suit. The water surrounding the Karamita Yard was as warm as blood, but he needed the thin black Microprene as cover once he reached his goal. He wore thick-soled dive boots and had his fins ready on the bench next to where he sat. He was going over the Draeger unit. Unlike a scuba rig that provides fresh air for a diver with every breath, the German-made rebreather used powerful filters to scrub carbon dioxide when a diver exhaled in a closed-loop system that allowed for great endurance while eliminating the telltale stream of bubbles.

The Draeger could be dangerous at depths much below thirty feet, so Juan planned to stay close to the surface. In a slim waterproof pouch strapped under his right arm he had a minicomputer, a flashlight, and a Fabrique Nationale Five-seveN double-action automatic. The pistol fired the new 5.7 mm ammunition. The advantage of the small, needlelike cartridges was that the matte-black weapon's grip held twenty rounds with one in the chamber. Also, the bullets were designed to blow through most ballistic vests while at the same time not overpenetrate a target.

A dive knife was strapped on the outside of his right thigh and a dive computer to his left wrist.

A dive technician hovered nearby. "Just for the fun of it, I had Doc Huxley analyze a water sample," the tech said as Juan finished his inspection. "She said the sea here is more polluted than the Cuyahoga River when it caught fire back in the sixties."

"That's your idea of fun?" Juan asked sarcastically.

"Rather analyze that gunk than swim in it." The man grinned.

"You all set?" Max asked as he entered the darkened garage. Linda Ross was at his side, a slip of a girl compared to Max's looming silhouette.

"Piece of cake." Juan got to his feet. He nodded to the tech, who doused the red battle lamp.

"Eric's at the helm," Max told the chairman, "and Mark is at the weapons station just in case something goes wrong. Also Linc and a few of his SEALs are kitting up now and will be ready with a Zodiac by the time you're halfway to the warehouse."

"Good idea. But let's hope I don't need 'em."

The garage's door rattled open, and without another word Juan stepped down the ramp, slid into his fins, and silently rolled into the sea. As soon as the water enveloped him, he felt the cumbersome weight of his gear vanish. This was Cabrillo's element. Here his mind became focused. He could forget about Eddie Seng, the pirates, the smugglers, and the thousands of details it took to run his company. It was as if nothing else in the world existed except him and the sea.

He adjusted his buoyancy until he was ten feet below the surface and checked his dive computer's integrated compass. With his arms dragging at his side, Cabrillo effortlessly finned through the inky water, his breathing even and smooth. After a minute he could no longer sense the *Oregon*'s presence to his left. He'd passed her bow.

Even with the Draeger's large mouthpiece, he could taste the foul water on his lips. It was metallic, like sucking on a penny, and when he touched his wet suit he could feel a greasy sheen of spilled oil. Juan was no tree hugger—he understood that civilization was bound to have an impact on the environment. But, if for no other reason, he wanted Singh shut down for the ecological damage his operation had done to the region.

He didn't dare use a light, so he had to rely heavily on his other senses. He'd been in the water for twenty minutes, swimming against a mild tide, when he heard a hollow whooshing sound. It was water sluicing under the doors of the mammoth building. He changed course slightly to compensate for a minor drift, and a minute later his hand brushed against rough concrete. It was one of the many pilings holding up the huge building. He swam around so he was directly behind the shed. While gantry lamps illuminated a great swath of the beach, the seaward side of the structure was in total darkness. Cabrillo flicked on his dive light. The red lens produced a feeble ruddy glow, but it was enough for him to get his bearings.

He doused the light again and allowed himself to float upward, breaking the surface with the merest ripple. The doors were as tall as an eight-story building and stretched nearly two hundred feet wide. All but the largest cruise ships, container ships, and tankers could easily pass inside on their way to be broken up.

Juan ducked back under the water, kicking down only a few feet before feeling the underside of the door. He rolled under the door and resurfaced inside the hangarlike shed. He spat out his regulator and pushed his dive mask onto his forehead. The tang of scorched metal burned his nose when he took a breath.

For a moment he thought the warehouse was completely black, far darker than the near moonless night, but he realized he'd surfaced under a catwalk. Once he moved out from its shadow he could see there were a few bare bulbs strung along the distant ceiling, revealing the dark outline of a ship. He swam along its length. Unlike the vessels out in the bay, this ship wasn't scaled with rust. The hull was smooth and free of growth and had a fresh coat of either black or dark blue paint.

This was no derelict at the end of its useful life. This was a new ship that wasn't more than a few years from coming down the ways. Cabrillo's pulse quickened.

He found a set of open metal scissor stairs that rose from under the water all the way to the walkway circling the building near the ceiling. He shrugged out of his gear and tied it so it remained submerged. He transferred his silenced automatic to a shoulder holster and made sure the minicomputer had survived the trip without damage. Leading with the pistol, he slowly eased his way up the stairs, placing each foot carefully before transferring his weight. He had no idea if Singh had posted any guards, but he knew the slightest sound would echo within the metal confines of the building, so he took every precaution to maintain silence.

A metal scaffold had been laid from the stairs to the ship's main deck. He paused in a shadow, listening for the quiet conversation of bored guards or an accidental cough. He heard nothing but the low hiss of water against the ship's hull and the occasional creak as a large wave surged in from outside.

He padded across the scaffold and found cover on the ship next to one of the ship's capstans. He brushed his fingertips against the metal deck. Like the hull, it was smooth and newly painted. From what he could tell, the ship was a small tanker, what in the profession was called a product tanker because it usually hauled refined products like kerosene or gasoline rather than crude oil. The first sixty or more feet of the tanker was gone, carved away by the ship saw and hauled outside. It went against his seaman's sense to see such a new and beautiful vessel get treated like this.

Juan ignored the slight superstitious chill and made his way aft toward the superstructure. The four-story accommodation block sat right at the stern, and he could see that workers had removed her bridge wings and hacked off her funnel so she could fit into the shed. He found an open hatch and stepped inside, making sure he was well away from any portholes before turning on his light. The deck was clean linoleum, and the walls were paneled in wood. He felt along the wall. Instead of finding the plaque that would give the ship's name, registry, and other information, he found four screw holes. Someone had taken pains to erase the ship's identity.

He found a stairwell and climbed to the bridge. Keeping his light shielded, he discovered that all her electronics had been stripped out. Her radios, navigation aids, weather computer, it was all gone. The empty racks, where the gear should have been, looked like whoever had done it had taken their time. There were no torn wires or any indication the workers had been rushed.

They had also removed anything that might list the ship's name. He searched the rest of the superstructure. The galley was nothing more than a room sheathed in stainless steel. The refrigerators and stoves had been removed as well as all the pots, pans, and utensils. They'd taken the place settings as well, which usually carried the owner's corporate logo and the name of the ship. The cabins were devoid of furniture but somehow retained a hint that they had been recently occupied. One smelled of cigars, while the bathroom of another carried the aroma of aftershave.

His next stop was the engine room.

A pair of big diesels dominated the space, each the size of a bus, and fed by miles of wiring, ducts, and pipes. He checked each engine carefully, cursing where he saw someone had removed all the identification tags. And where serial numbers had been stamped into the engine blocks someone had used a hand grinding wheel to polish them away. In their wake the metal was shiny silver and smooth.

Juan holstered his pistol and began a more thorough search. It was laborious work because of the engine room's cavernous size compared to his light's puny cone of illumination. And no matter where he shone the lamp, shadows dominated his view. Still, he pressed on. He got down on the floor to squirm under a freshwater condenser only to find that someone had already beaten him there and peeled off the manufacturer's decal. He played his flashlight beam over every nook and cranny and found nothing.

Singh's people knew what they were doing, he thought. Then he spotted an area where a thick coating of spilled oil had congealed under the starboard engine. It would be next to impossible to reach the spot, which was why he felt like ignoring it, but if he was unwilling to check it out so, too, might the men who'd erased the ship's identity.

Moving his body like a contortionist, he slithered under the cold engine. The space was tight, the engine mounts barely giving him enough room to breathe, and he rapped his hand against an unseen conduit and had to suck the blood from three knuckles. Once he reached the spot, he used his hand to scrape away the tarry grime. As his fingernails peeled back trenches of thick oil, he felt the slightly raised outline of a metal plate. They'd missed one!

It took him a few minutes' more work to rub away enough grease to read the tag. It said the engine had been built by Mitsubishi Heavy Industries, and there was a fifteen-digit ID number. Juan committed it to memory and squeezed back out from under the engine. He retrieved his computer, powered it up, and began cross-referencing the number.

Their client, his friend Hiroshi Katsui, had provided a wealth of information about the ships that had gone missing in the Sea of Japan, dossiers on all the crews, including pictures, and the serial numbers of dozens of each ship's principal components. Had the pirates not swiped the oven from the galley, Juan would have been able to check his database and match it to the vessel it had been installed on by its ID number.

Using a stylus, he typed in the fifteen-character number, chose the icon for engines, and pressed the Search button.

When the ship's name came up, Cabrillo's jaw literally dropped.

"We've been had," he muttered to himself.

"Understatement of the year, Captain," a familiar voice whispered in his ear at the same time the muzzle of a gun was pressed to the back of his head.

A second later, men's voices and the dancing glow of several flashlights approached from one of the engine room's few entrances.

19

TOO many years had passed since Eddie Seng sat through his freshman lit class at NYU for him to remember how many circles of hell Dante described in the *Divine Comedy*. He was sure, though, that he had discovered one below whatever the medieval Italian poet had envisaged.

As soon as their plane landed after its six-hour flight, Eddie and the other illegals were herded inside a shipping container. By interpreting the motion that followed, Eddie knew the unventilated steel box was trucked to a port and loaded onto a ship for another ten-hour trip. The only clue that gave Eddie a sense of his location was the cooler temperatures. Factoring in the weather and a six-hour flight at roughly five hundred knots, he put their position within an arc that included northern Mongolia, southern Siberia, and the Russian coast. And since there were no lakes in the hinterland large enough to necessitate a ten-hour boat trip, he figured he was someplace on the Kamchatka Peninsula or along the coast of the Sea of Okhotsk.

The container was offloaded and dropped to the ground hard enough to tumble the men inside. Moments later the doors were opened, and Eddie got his first look at hell.

Dark mountains rose in the distance, their tops obscured by soot of some kind so the rugged peaks looked smeared. He had to blink his eyes to keep them in focus. The beach where he stood was water-worn rock ranging in size from pebbles to bowling balls. The surf made the stones clatter with each wave cycle. The ocean behind was flat and dark, gray, with a menace Eddie associated with the calm before a storm.

These details weren't what caused Eddie's mind to go numb. It was the human misery that toiled on the hill rising from sea. It was a scene out of the Holocaust. Emaciated figures, so streaked with grime it was impossible to tell if they were clothed, covered the hillside so the whole expanse seemed to be squirming, like a bloated carcass being devoured by maggots. They were rendered sexless and inhuman by their wasted condition.

There had to be two thousand people forced to work along the slope.

Some climbed up the hillside laden with empty buckets, while others staggered down under their loads. On a level section three-quarters of the way up the hill, shovelers filled the buckets with mud. They moved like automatons, as if their bodies could no longer perform any other act but scoop and dump. Farther up the hillside, others manned water cannons. The cannons were fed by hoses that snaked across the landscape to where glacial runoff from the distant mountains had been diverted into an earthen retention pond. Gravity forced the water through the lines so when it exploded from the cannons it was an arcing jet that the workers cut back and forth across a dirt embankment, sluicing away layers of soil with every pass.

Excess water from the guns poured down the hillside, gathering the topsoil until it was a liquid slurry as treacherous as quicksand. In those first moments that Eddie watched, dumbstruck by what he was seeing, a thick wave of mud suddenly shot down the slope. Those not quick enough were caught in the swell and tumbled down the hill. Some rose quickly back to their feet. Some more slowly. And one not at all. He was soon buried alive.

No one paused from their labor.

Strung over the workings on wooden poles were acres of camouflage netting that had been dyed in the same hues of gray and black and brown as the landscape, so from above, the site was completely hidden.

Near the beach where Eddie and his group gaped, haunted-eyed workers dumped their buckets into a series of mechanical sluice boxes, devices little changed from their introduction more than a century ago. The mud was washed down a long table by a gentle rocking motion. The bottom of the trough was lined with baffles that would trap and separate the heavy material from the lighter overburden. The waste fell away at the end of the boxes and eventually reached the ocean, where it spread in a brown stain, while the concentrated ore would need to be scraped away and taken for further refining.

A bucket brigade of workers formed a human chain from the tables to a three-story building a short way down the beach. Like the undulations of some enormous worm, buckets of ore that had been cleaned out of the sluice boxes were passed hand-to-hand toward the building. Eddie saw that what he assumed was the processing plant had been bolted down to a flat, oceangoing barge that could be easily towed away from the site. Tendrils of white smoke rose from a short stack next to the structure, telling him that whatever process they used to get their final product required heat.

Overseeing the sprawling site were armed men. They were dressed for the weather in thick pants and jackets. Their boots were knee-high and made of rubber to protect them from the ubiquitous mud. Most had gloves. All had AK-47s over their shoulders and carried either clubs or short whips. There were only a few guards positioned up the hill, but there were more closer to where the mining process came to its conclusion. Four men watched over each of the dozen sluice boxes, while it appeared there was a guard for every ten laborers manning the bucket brigade. The lash of whips rising and falling was the work chorus that kept the laborers in motion.

A razor-wire fence prevented the Chinese workers, and from what he could tell they were all Chinese, from approaching the far side of the building where a tracked vehicle similar to an arctic snow cat had direct access to a partially buried cruise ship that had been beached farther down the coast.

There were other beached ships on the workers' side of the barbed wire. They were small cruise ships that were so badly decayed it was astounding they had survived the trip here. They, too, had been buttressed with rubble and their decks strung with netting to break up their outlines.

Dormitories, Eddie realized, for the workers.

Even as he thought it, he corrected himself. These weren't workers. They were slaves, forced to mine the hillside in the most deplorable conditions he could have imagined.

There were only a few things on earth valuable enough for such insatiable greed. And he instinctively understood what they were after: gold.

It seemed even longer ago that Eddie had sat in a geology class, but he remembered enough to recognize that someone had discovered a gold-bearing strata up the hillside. The water cannons used hydrokinetic pressure to crumble the soil so it could be fed into the sluice boxes. From there the concentrate was spun in centrifuges to further separate out the lighter waste. The final process was to dump what was removed from the bottom of the centrifuges into mercury, the only substance in the world that attracts the precious metal. Once bonded to the microparticles of gold, the ball of mercury would then be boiled away, leaving pure molten gold.

In most modern smelting facilities the mercury vapor was recaptured, condensed, and reused in a closed-loop system that prevented workers from coming into contact with the deadly metal. Judging by the deplorable conditions of the men working the hill, he imagined the poor souls in the refinery being subjected to untold amounts of mercury vapor, one of the most savage toxins in the world.

Those few seconds taking in the enormity of the workings were the last moments he was spared the depravity of his captors. He and the others that had followed the snake with him from Shanghai were ordered into a line. An Indonesian guard locked a small chain around his neck. From it dangled a tag stamped with an identification number. Another guard noted the number in a ledger book, and the batch of them were led off to one of the derelict cruise liners. They were assigned unheated cabins. While the ship had never been luxurious by any standard, the rooms were crowded with bunk beds so ten men occupied a room designed for two. From the stench it was clear the ship's plumbing no longer functioned, and even this deep into the vessel Eddie could see his own breath. Each bunk had a single mud-caked blanket, and the mattresses were soaked through and molding. There was no place for the workers to dry themselves, so at the end of their shifts they merely collapsed into their beds, wet and covered in slime.

A guard prodded him on. He and the others were shown where they ate. It had once been the cruise ship's main dining room. All the furniture was long gone, and any ornamentation had been stripped from the walls. The floor was bare metal, and that was where the workers took their meals. The group was ordered into a line, and each took a filthy metal bowl from a pile. A Chinese man with his arm in a sling used his free hand to scoop a palm full of rice into the bowl. Next to him another disabled worker ladled in a grayish pink slop from a huge drum.

The concoction retained just a trace of warmth and was barely fit for human consumption. Eddie would later learn that the operators of the mine sent out a pair of fishing boats to drag the oceans. Anything and everything that got caught up in their nets was fed into a giant shredder to rip apart the bigger chunks and was then liquefied.

Five minutes after finding a place on the floor to choke down the sickening gruel, their guard cocked his weapon and shouted, "On your feet."

Knowing he'd need to keep his strength, Eddie tipped the remainder of the bowl into his mouth, wolfing down the rank paste as well as his own bile. Bits of fish scale scraped at the back of his throat.

"You were fed now because you are newly arrived," the guard continued. "From now on you only get food at the end of your shift."

The men were led outside once again. For the first time Eddie became aware of the wind, a constant breeze that blew in from the sea and passed through his clothes and seemed to buffet against his bones. It also carried fine particles of ash, volcanic, he guessed, which confirmed for him that he was on the Kamchatka Peninsula. They were ordered to begin lugging buckets up the hill, and as Eddie began what would be the first of a hundred torturous climbs that day, he patted the meaty part of his thigh where Doc Huxley's homing device had been implanted.

He was a long way from the *Oregon*, but he knew he wasn't alone. It would be a day, or two at the most, before Juan had a team on the ground, and the nightmare would end before it really got started.

That night he got a chance to talk to the men assigned to his cabin. There was no electricity, so the exhausted workers whispered in the dark. They all had similar stories about being smuggled out of China as illegal immigrants inside shipping containers. They had paid the snakeheads to take them to Japan, but when the containers were unsealed, they found themselves here.

"How long have you been here?" Eddie asked.

A disembodied voice replied from his bunk, "Forever."

"Seriously, how long?"

"Four months," the same man said, shifting in the dark to find a less damp spot on his mattress. "But the mine has been in operation much longer. Years maybe."

"Has anyone tried to escape?"

"To where?" another answered. "We can't swim away. The water is too cold, and the fishing boats are heavily guarded when they return, and they are only here long enough to dump their nets on the dock.

You've seen the mountains. Even if you get past the guards, which no one has been able to do, you wouldn't last a day out there."

"They own us," a third man remarked. "From the moment we said we wanted to leave China, they own us. Does it matter if we work ourselves to death here, in a textile factory back home, or in a sweatshop in New York City? This is what the gods meant for us, for all Chinese peasants. We work and then we die. I have been here ten months. All the men originally assigned this room are now gone. Go ahead with your fantasies of escape, my friend. In the end there is only one way out—and that is death."

Eddie wasn't sure if he should tell them who he really was. From what he saw as the men shuffled to the cabin, they were all in terrible condition, so he doubted the mine's overseers had planted any informants within the ranks. However, he couldn't discount the idea he'd be exposed by one of them for an extra ration of food or a dry blanket. As much as he wanted to give these wretched souls a glimmer of hope, it went against his years of training and experience. In the end he allowed exhaustion to overcome his wet bedding and the knots of pain radiating from every joint in his body. Two of his cabin mates coughed and hacked throughout the night. Pneumonia or worse. He imagined the squalid conditions and meager food rations meant disease was already rampant throughout the operation.

It was on the third day of shivering cold, and constant wet that pruned and paled his skin, and backbreaking work, that Eddie began to realize rescue might be a long time in coming. Surely Juan could have flown someone to Russia where they could rent a helicopter and at least fly over the area. But there had been no such overflight. Instead, he'd worked with the others, mindlessly hauling mud down the mountain, like ants who know nothing but to follow their instincts.

He'd already lost his shoes, and every time he took a deep breath he felt a slight rattle in the depths of his lungs. He's started off in much better shape than the others, but his body was used to regular food and rest, unlike the peasants who had lived their entire lives on a starvation diet and knew nothing but hard labor. Two of the men from his cabin were already dead. One of them had been buried by an avalanche, and the other was beaten by a guard so severely he died with blood dripping from his ears and from around his eyes.

By the fifth day, his back stinging from a particularly brutal whipping that he'd done nothing to trigger, Eddie Seng realized two things. One was that the burst transmitter in his leg had failed, and the second was that he was going to die on this forlorn coast.

On the morning of the sixth day, as the work crews were being led outside into the predawn chill, a huge ship had appeared in the bay. Eddie paused on the ramp leading to the beach to note that it was a floating drydock but mistakenly assumed it was the *Maus* and not her sister. Even at a distance the stench emanating from the black-hulled behemoth was overpowering, and flocks of gulls swooped around open ports to pluck the human waste that had spilled out from within.

As a guard prodded Eddie with a baton jab to the kidneys, he realized she was a slave ship, loaded with workers to replace the ones who'd died or were so weak they could no longer rise from their bunks no matter how hard they were beaten. How many hundreds or thousands had already perished, he wondered, only to be replaced with a steady supply of hopeful immigrants thinking they'd bought their one chance at freedom?

"That is how I was brought here," Tang, one of his roommates, remarked as they trudged up the slick hillside. Tang was the one who'd said he'd been here for four months already. His body was stick thin, and Eddie could clearly see his breastbone and rib cage through his torn shirt. He was twenty-seven years old but looked sixty. "We were loaded onto an old ship, and then it was swallowed up inside an even bigger ship like that one. If you can imagine, the journey here was worse than the work they force us to do."

By the time they'd filled their buckets for the journey down to the sluice boxes, a rust-coated ship was slowly emerging from the belly of the drydock, and workers were throwing large bundles off its deck.

"Bodies," Tang said. "I was forced to do that. We had to dump over the corpses of those who didn't survive the journey."

"How many?"

"A hundred, perhaps more. I myself had to dump the bodies of my two cousins and my best friend."

Tang didn't slow his pace, but Eddie could tell the memory was taking its toll. "So they will beach the boat and use it to house more workers?"

"First they will pile rocks around it and cover it with nets so it can't be seen from the air."

"What about the water? This whole operation is exposed to the sea."

Tang shook his head. "Other than the two fishing boats, I haven't seen any other ships since I arrived. I think we are too far from anywhere for ships to pass close by."

They had just reached the sluice boxes when Eddie suddenly fell flat on his back as though a rug had been yanked out from under him. Stunned, he looked around to see hundreds of others had also fallen. That was when he felt the ground shaking.

Even as he realized it was an earthquake, the shaking subsided, but a deep roar continued to echo like distant thunder.

He got to his feet, wiping the worst of the clinging mud from his tattered clothes. His attention and soon that of every person at the mine was drawn upward toward the central-most mountain peak that dominated the workings. Steam and dark ash gushed from near its peak in an ever-expanding cloud that would soon blot out the sun. Lightning crackled around the summit like Saint Elmo's fire.

The separating plant's door burst open, and a man rushed out, stripping off a gas mask as he ran. He was the first white person Eddie had seen this whole time at the mine.

"That is Jan Paulus," Tang whispered as the man ran toward them. "He is the overseer."

Jan Paulus was a solid-looking man, broad across the shoulders with weathered features and hands as big as anvils. He stopped just a few paces from Eddie and Tang and studied the now-active volcano that towered above the bay. He watched it for only a moment before pulling a clunky satellite phone from a holster strapped around his waist. He flipped up the antenna, waited a beat to ensure he had a signal, then dialed.

"Anton, it's Paulus," he said in English but with a Dutch or Afrikaans accent. He listened before saying, "I'm not surprised you felt it in Petropavlovsk. Shook the shit out of us. Worst one yet, but that's not why I called. The volcano above the site is active." A pause. "Because we've talked about this possibility a dozen times, and I'm looking at a bloody great cloud of ash and steam, that's how I know. If that thing really lets go, we're finished."

As if to punctuate his sentence, the ground shook again in a mild aftershock. "Feel that one, too, Savich?" the South African asked sarcastically. He listened for a beat. "Your assurances don't mean anything. It's my arse out here while yours is sitting in a hotel sauna three hundred kilometers away." He glanced around as he listened again. Eddie quickly dipped his bucket into the sluice, hoping that the mine's foreman hadn't noticed him eavesdropping. "Yeah, the *Souri* just arrived. They're offloading the latest batch of Chinese in another of Shere Singh's rust buckets. As soon as they're ready, I'm going to load the first shipment like we talked about last week."

Paulus shot Eddie a scowl. He had no choice but to move on, but still he listened for as long as he could. "We just finished another run with the mercury smelter, so now would be a good time to think about at least towing the processing plant off the beach until we know what's happening with the volcano. You have the influence to stop your fellow Russkies from sending any scientists over to have a look-see, but you sure as hell can't stop that mountain from blowing. Why don't you chopper over and take a look? In the meantime I'm going to make plans to get out of here." The miner's voice rose, as though the connection was fading. "What? Who cares about them? We can evacuate the guards using the *Souri*. Singh can get us more ships, and there's a million Chinese a year trying to get out. We can replace the lot of them . . . So what if we lose a month or two, we've already got enough raw material to keep the minters going for at least that long . . . All right, see you in a couple of hours."

Tang had gone on ahead, ascending the mountain with the dull gait of a pack animal. Eddie made no effort to catch up. He watched the ballooning ash cloud high above, digesting what he'd just heard. The foreman wanted to evacuate his people and the guards, but it sounded like he needed the permission of someone named Anton, someone with enough pull to keep Russian volcanologists from visiting the area. The South African had argued that now was the perfect time. The drydock was here with its powerful tugs ready to go, and it sounded as though they had already amassed a large stockpile of gold destined to be struck into coins. The separating plant, arguably the most important and expensive piece of equipment, could be towed to safety. The beached ships being used as dormitories were worth only their scrap price, and it sounded like they had a line on how to obtain more. That just left the workers, and as Paulus had said, with a million illegal Chinese riding the snake every year, replacing their slave force would be simple enough.

Eddie understood their twisted logic. The only thing of value they would really lose is time.

Another temblor struck. Eddie knew there was a real danger that the volcano would erupt, and he envisioned a cataclysmic explosion like the one that leveled a couple hundred square miles around Mount Saint Helens. There was no way he or anyone else left behind could escape such a blast. Over the past few days he'd resigned himself to work the weeks or even months it would take Juan to find him, and of his eventual rescue he had no doubt. The Corporation did not leave its people behind.

But the one thing Paulus and Savich could afford was the one thing Eddie Seng no longer possessed: time.

20

THE thought popped unbidden into Cabrillo's mind. *Of all the engine rooms in all the ships in the world she had to walk into mine.*

The unseen gunman pulled the weapon from the back of his head at the same time Juan shut off both his computer and flashlight. "Are you wearing night vision?" he whispered into the gunman's ear.

"Yes," came the near silent reply.

"Lead on." He took the gunman's hand. It was slim and delicate despite the leather gloves.

The lights carried by the approaching men gave just enough glow for Juan to avoid jamming a knee or bumping his head amid the forest of pipes, but he couldn't see enough to know if they were headed in the right direction. He would just have to trust someone who a moment earlier had a pistol to his skull.

He had been aboard the ship for nearly forty minutes, so he figured his presence hadn't been detected, meaning it was his companion who had drawn the guards. The smart thing for him was to separate, make his way to the side of the vessel, and swim back to the *Oregon*. However, that left too many unanswered questions. For the time being they were in this together.

They reached a hatchway that led to the steering gear room. As soon as they crossed the threshold and made a sharp turn down a utility corridor, Juan could no longer hear their pursuers.

"So who are you?" he asked as they silently padded toward the bow. "MI-6?" That was the British equivalent to the CIA. His question was met with silence. "Royal Navy?"

"No," replied Victoria Ballinger. "I'm a field investigator for Lloyd's of London, fraud division."

If Lloyd's was taking insurance hits because of the Sea of Japan pirates, it made sense they would send someone out to investigate, which explained her presence on the ill-fated *Avalon*. Most likely there had been an entire team on board to repulse the pirates and get their own answers about who was behind the attacks. Unfortunately, they had vastly underestimated the pirates' sophistication, and as a result Tory had been the sole survivor.

"How about you?" she asked. "Are you still claiming to be a tramp freighter captain with fish-finding gear, a couple of scuba tanks, and a knack for being at the right place at the right time?"

"We'll talk about that as soon as we're out of here." Cabrillo's tone was clipped. He wasn't happy about her presence or the larger implications of what he'd discovered moments before her arrival. There was time for recriminations later. First he had to get them back to the *Oregon*.

He chanced turning on his flashlight but dialed down the beam so it was as dim as a guttering candle. Tory stripped her night vision goggles from her head and stuffed them in a shoulder bag. She had to resettle her mass of black hair under her watch cap. Juan gave her a look to catch her eyes. They were blue, steady and resolved, without a trace of fear. He had no idea what kind of training she had received during her career, but the way she'd handled her ordeal on the sunken *Avalon* and her current composure told him she was ready for anything.

The corridor ended in a ladder that rose to an overhead hatch. "So, Captain, I assume you have a plan?"

"My original plan didn't include finding you and the goons who obviously followed you. I want to get past these guys without a firefight, then I've got a Draeger rebreather stashed out in the shed. Do you know how to dive?" Tory nodded sharply. "Then we'll swim back to my ship."

"I'm not leaving here until I know what vessel this is."

Cabrillo caught the stubborn lift of her chin and knew she meant it. "We're on a ship that shouldn't be here called the *Toya Maru*. She was snatched while the pirates were attacking the *Avalon*. That big ship you remembered seeing was a floating drydock called the *Maus*. They concealed the *Toya Maru* inside her and towed her here. All the while under near constant surveillance by my people, I might add."

"So why shouldn't she be here?"

"Because the *Maus* is still a couple days out."

A look of confusion swept across her beautiful face. "I don't understand."

Juan was growing frustrated. They had to get out of there, and Tory wanted to play twenty questions. But the truth was he was more angry at himself than her. Like everyone involved, he, too, had failed to anticipate the pirates' cunning. "It means they knew they were being shadowed the whole time and waited for their chance to offload the *Maru*, which came when I had to call the *Oregon* away for a day near Taiwan. They put a crew aboard this ship and sailed her down here under her own steam, while my people followed the ballasted drydock. Gauging the amount of disassembly work they've already accomplished, I'd say they've had her in this shed for a few days at least."

He touched her sleeve. "I'll tell you everything, but later. We have to get going."

Without waiting for a reply, Cabrillo tucked his pistol into his holster and climbed the ladder. The hatch wheel gave a chirp of protest as he broke the seal, then spun freely. He eased the cover up, got his gun in position, and ducked his head through to the next level. It was pitch-black and silent. He pulled his body through and waited for Tory. Once she was at his side, he risked using his light again.

He recognized the space as the main ballast control room. From here the crew could use a system of pumps to transfer their load from tank to tank in order to maintain trim. He briefly considered finding the sea suction inlet, a breach in the hull where seawater could be pumped into the ship for ballast, but it would take too long to find and open an inspection hatch. Plus there would be heavy mesh to prevent the pumps fouling on a large fish or kelp when it drew in the water.

Now that he had his bearings, he turned on his minicomputer and called up a set of the *Toyo Maru*'s blueprints. On the tiny screen the schematics were tough to make out, so it took him a few minutes to trace their escape route.

"Got it," he said at last. "Okay, stay close and stay behind me."

"Chivalry, Captain?"

"Practicality. I'm wearing body armor, and unless you dropped twenty pounds in two weeks, I know you're not."

She shot him a cheeky smirk. "Touché and lead on."

Cabrillo checked the corridor outside the ballast control room and edged out. With no light to amplify, Tory's goggles were useless, forcing him to rely on his flashlight and trust the guards would give themselves away before they saw it.

At the end of the hall they came to a set of steep stairs. Juan was halfway up when he heard voices and saw light from above. Without turning he stepped back again, feeling Tory right behind him. From the bottom of the stairs he caught a glimpse of two men armed with assault rifles passing by. He and Tory waited a full three minutes after the voices faded before making the climb again.

They had reached the level just below the main deck. Once they reached the outside, Juan planned to just jump over the side and find the rebreather. In the darkness Shere Singh's men would never spot them.

From down the hallway came the unmistakable mechanical ratchet of a weapon being cocked. Cabrillo threw Tory to the deck as lights snapped on all over the place. His finger was working the trigger before he had a target, laying down suppression fire to maximize confusion. In the first seconds of the ambush he didn't care about the danger of a ricochet. Getting out was all that mattered. Tory added her own pistol, an unsilenced 9 mm that boomed like a cannon in the metal confines of the ship.

He wanted to get back down the stairs, but when he glanced over the landing, autofire ripped up from below so close he felt the heat of the bullets and the muzzle flash was like an explosion in his face.

He fired a blind shot at the downstairs gunman and crawled across the passageway, seeking cover where the hall turned ninety degrees. Once out of sight of the ambushers, he dragged Tory to safety. He hadn't been hit, which was a miracle, and now wasn't the time to worry about the Englishwoman.

He tossed his minicomputer out into the hallway. Immediately an automatic weapon opened up. Good. The guards were jumpy. He levered his pistol out into the hall and fired three shots, moving his body as he pulled the trigger so he was exposed by the time he pulled the trigger a fourth time. He spotted his target, a turbaned guard lying on the deck and cringing behind his AK-47. Cabrillo put a pair of bullets through the top of his head, then dashed for cover as another guard farther down the hallway unloaded his magazine in a wild sustained burst.

He grabbed Tory's hand, and together they ran away from the ambush, all pretense of stealth forgotten.

Juan rounded a corner and saw the flicker of movement an instant before a rifle butt crashed into his skull. He fell flat, poleaxed, but didn't lose consciousness as Tory came up behind him and double tapped the guard as he was recovering from the swing. The guard was blown back by the kinetic energy of her nine millimeter rounds and the wall behind him was painted in his blood.

His head feeling as fragile as glass, Juan let Tory help him to his feet. His vision was blurred, and blood oozed from where skin had been smeared from his forehead. It hung like a flap over his left eye. Juan ripped away the slice in a savage jerk that caused a fresh rush of blood but allowed him to see. Tory gasped.

"I know a good plastic surgeon," was all he said, and the pair started running again.

That's when a metallic scream unlike anything Juan had ever heard began. He knew immediately it was the ship saw. A moment later the thick band of the chain saw cut into the ship just ahead of the superstructure, no more than twenty feet in front of Cabrillo and Tory. Water from the lubricating jets turned to steam, spiking the humidity to a hundred percent, and slivers of metal filled the passageway like shrapnel. The saw changed directions and began to cut horizontally toward them, shredding metal bulkheads as though they were tissue. The thick chain burst through the wall next to them, its teeth cutting the ship as easily as a can opener. The chain came at them four feet off the deck, moving through the vessel almost as fast as they could run. The stench of scorched steel was overwhelming, and an occasional filing blew off the chain and landed on Cabrillo, melting holes in his wet suit.

They came to another staircase and raced up, their focus on staying away from the deadly saw. As if the machine knew where they were headed, it started to angle up after them, chewing apart the stairwell like some prehistoric predator. The railings ricocheted off the wall as the sawing action tore them from their mounts.

Juan could barely see. The combination of the blood and what he knew was a mild concussion slowed him. But Tory didn't leave his side. Together they raced from the ravenous charge of the ship saw. They ran past crew cabins, and when they rounded another corner, both began to sprint for an exterior hatch. It was a race because they were running parallel to the thick cutting chain and could no longer see it as it sliced apart the *Toyo Maru*.

Ten feet from the open door, the wall to their right began to glow and vibrate as the chain's teeth took their first taste of the bulkhead. Because the Japanese tanker wasn't exactly square in the shed, the saw first ate through the corner they had just turned and, like a zipper being pulled, it started to split the wall.

Juan glanced over his shoulder. The chain had already cut through the first ten feet of the hallway and as he watched, another few feet were torn apart. Metal filings filled the hall like a nest of enraged wasps as the chain began to span the width of the corridor.

With five feet to go before they were clear, Cabrillo pounded Tory between the shoulder blades. The blow made her tumble, but her inertia kept her rolling. Juan threw himself after her as the thick chain passed directly over them the instant they burst out onto the open deck.

And into another ambush.

Four turbaned men had been waiting for them, eyeing the duo's fall over their AKs' iron sights. Juan and Tory had landed in a tangle of limbs that parodied intimacy. Before either could get their gun hand free, the Sikhs had weapons to their heads. The ship saw rattled to silence.

"I was hoping the saw wouldn't get you just yet," an accented voice boomed from a catwalk suspended over the ship.

Juan and Tory had their weapons taken away and were allowed to their feet, their fingers laced at the back of their heads. Cabrillo studied the man above him. Judging age and his resemblance to Abhay, Juan guessed that the man was the leader of the pirate ring.

"Shere Singh," Juan growled.

"I hope you found what you were looking for," the Sikh said. "I would hate to think of you going to your graves still filled with curiosity." He gave an order in a language Juan didn't recognize, and he and Tory were shoved toward the ship's bow.

Overhead an unseen operator was resetting the chain blade of the ship saw. Tracks built near the ceiling allowed it to be maneuvered almost anywhere within the shed. The segmented blade now spanned the deck about fifteen feet behind where the bow had been cut off, held so taut that despite its length of nearly two hundred feet, it didn't sag. And in the glare of overhead lights the tips of its special alloy teeth glinted like so many hundreds of daggers.

A moment later, Shere Singh reached the *Toya Maru*'s deck and approached, flanked by two more guards. He carried an odd metal pipe with long, perpendicular handles. Juan and Tory were each held by a pair of men in such a way that their toes barely touched the deck. Cabrillo tried to shift his weight to find leverage to break free, but each movement caused his captors to lift him even higher. When Singh was close enough to smell, he passed the length of pipe under Juan's arms and behind his back. The guards shifted their grip so they could hold him in place by grasping the handles.

Cabrillo now understood the device's purpose. This had to be a favorite way for the pirate to dispatch his enemies. The handles allowed the guards to hold their victim so when they pressed his body against the ship saw they were in no danger of being caught in the whirring chain.

When she realized the full horror of what was about to happen, Tory Ballinger screamed like an enraged lioness and jerked her body to get away. The men holding her laughed and lifted her even higher, so her entire weight pulled awkwardly against the tendons in her shoulders. The agony quickly drained the fight out of her, and she seemed to deflate.

"You're not going to get away with this," Cabrillo said.

The threat sounded as hollow to him as it did to Shere Singh, and the heavyset Pakistani laughed. "Of course I am, Captain Jeb Smith. But I must say you have lost a lot of weight compared to what my son, Abhay, described."

"Jenny Craig."

"Who?"

"Never mind. Listen Singh, we know about the *Maus,* and we know about the *Souri.* As soon as either vessel tries to enter a legitimate port, they will be seized. You're finished, so why not give up now and spare yourself a pair of murder charges."

"So you would not charge me for the deaths of the *Toyo Maru*'s crew, eh?"

Juan hadn't held much hope that the pirates were merely holding the tanker's crew, and now he had his confirmation. "In about ten minutes a special forces team is going to rush this building and kill everyone inside."

Singh laughed again. He was enjoying his complete dominance over his captives. "They will be five minutes too late for you and your nubile friend. There is nothing you can say to stop me and nothing you can do, either. I have men approaching your boat as we speak. At most you have a small mercenary force. They will be dealt with."

Cabrillo knew that even if he didn't make it out of this alive, his people would cut down Singh and all his men like so much wheat. But he wanted to keep Singh talking. Buy himself some time until he could think of a way out of this mess. "If we are going to die, at least tell me about the Chinese. How do they fit into your plan?"

Singh stepped close again. He possessed the piercing hazel eyes of a goat, and they never blinked. He smelled of cigarettes and at about six foot four stood half a head taller than Cabrillo. Using just the strength of his arm, he rammed a fist into Juan's solar plexus, a blow that expelled every molecule of air from his lungs. Had the Sikh used the full force of his body, Juan's ribs would have been stove in. It took several struggling breaths until his lungs felt at least partially inflated.

"You never knew I discovered you were following the *Maus* from the Sea of Japan. You didn't know I offloaded this ship"—Singh stamped a foot onto the deck—"when I had the chance. I have been ahead of you every step of the way, so what makes you think I would be so stupid as to tell you anything now? Knowledge must be earned. I taught my sons that. Anything given to you is worth exactly what you put in to deserve it. Nothing. What we do with the Chinese we've captured is none of your concern."

That at least verified for Cabrillo that Singh was connected to the snakeheads. "Aren't you at least curious who we are and why we've come after you?"

A lupine look crossed Singh's face. "You have me on that account, my friend. I indeed do want to know who you are, and if you came here a week ago I would have delighted in extracting that information. But now, today, it doesn't matter. I will permit you to go to your grave with your secrets as I go about my business with mine."

Singh made a spiraling gesture with his finger, and the powerful motors that drew the ship saw through its massive gears came to life. The chain soon became a blur as it whipped by just above the deck. The sound was staggering but nowhere near as bad as when it was chewing through a derelict hulk.

Juan looked around for something, anything, to forestall the inevitable. He'd come up with the germ of a plan, but at most he could hope to take out two, maybe three of the guards before he was gunned down. His only hope was that Tory would have the presence of mind to get herself over the side of the tanker and the hell away from the shed. He looked over to her. Their eyes met with such intensity that it was as if they could read each other's minds. She knew he was going to try something crazy, and her gaze told him she would make the most of his attempt. That brief exchange told him that in another world he would have enjoyed knowing her better.

The guards maneuvered Juan closer to the whirring chain saw, and no matter how he tried to resist he couldn't stop himself from taking halting tiptoe steps toward the industrial guillotine. Even from five feet away he could feel its power. Like the tingle of atmospheric electricity during a storm, it was a living force that split the air.

He tried to twist his shoulders, but that only made the guards shove him even closer.

Shere Singh moved up next to Juan, keeping enough distance that there was no way he could reach the Sikh. Singh held a length of wood in his hand. Making sure he had Juan's attention, he lowered the piece of timber onto the spinning chain. There was a brief pop and an explosion of sawdust. It took a fraction of a second for the saw to pulp the heavy piece of mahogany. Singh grinned again and stepped back, shouting over the roar of the machine, "I think I will let my men enjoy the woman before they feed her to the saw."

Juan gave no outward sign that he was about to act, but in his mind he planned out every move, choreographing the actions so when he went into motion there would be no hesitation. There was, however, a glaring variable to his plan. And that was if he survived the first instant.

He kicked both legs into the air, relying on the goons behind him to hold him steady as the limbs inexorably fell back toward the saw. His right calf made contact with the top of the serrated chain. He was dimly aware of Tory's stunned scream as the fast-moving saw bit into something hard in his leg and ripped the pole handles out of the guard's grip.

The shock and savagery nearly ripped Juan's leg from its socket and the straps securing the prosthesis below his knee were stretched to their very limit. But it had worked. The men hadn't fought the saw in a tug-of-war that would have allowed the blade to slice through the titanium struts of his artificial leg. The saw's relentless momentum tossed Juan like a rag doll fifteen feet across the deck. He landed in a perfect shoulder roll, and as his body came to rest, he was reaching into the ruin of what he called his combat leg for the Kel-Tec pistol secured within the composite limb.

The Kel-Tec was one of the smallest handguns in the world, weighing just five ounces when empty. But unlike other small pistols that were limited in their caliber to .22 or .25, the Kel-Tec was designed to fire P-rated .380 cartridges. They were man stoppers, and the armorers on the *Oregon* had hot-loaded the rounds to within a few newtons of their maximum tolerance.

As much as Cabrillo wanted to put the first bullet through Singh's head, the compact weapon only had room for seven rounds. He took aim at the startled guards who'd been holding him a second earlier and fired. The first round went wild. His breathing was coming too fast and his stump had begun to throb. The next two found their marks, and one of the guards had his throat blown open. He fell forward into the ship saw.

The chain severed his body in a fountain of blood. His head and torso fell to the deck with an obscene wet smack while his lower extremities were kicked into the air when a tooth snagged on his spinal column. They cartwheeled through the air and caught the second guard in the chest, knocking him flat and for the next few seconds out of the fight. Juan shifted his aim at the men holding Tory. They held her in such a way that he couldn't get a clean kill, so he put a round into the kneecap of one of them. As he spun away shrieking, Tory managed to twist out of the other's grasp. Juan dropped him with a double tap to the chest.

The two turbaned men that had boarded the *Toyo Maru* with Shere Singh were scrambling for cover and preparing to open up with their AK-47s. Juan emptied his three remaining rounds in slow succession to keep them down while screaming for Tory. She raced at him, and together they ran for the railing. Juan's leg could barely support him so he and Tory moved with the lurching gait of a couple entered in a three-legged race.

They reached the railing at the same time the guards took aim. The jacketed 7.62 mm bullets pinged and sparked as the men adjusted the hosing barrels of their weapons. Without pause and as ungainly as a pair of corpses being dumped from a bridge, Cabrillo and Tory allowed their speed to fold them over the railing, and headfirst they plummeted toward the water. There was nothing either could do to right their trajectory, and they slammed into the murky surface in a tremendous splash. They sank deep, and even though his lungs hadn't recovered from Singh's sucker punch, Juan made sure he and Tory stayed under as they swam away from the impact wave.

Juan could hear that someone had cut the power to the ship saw, for the building no longer echoed. He counted to ten in his head, promising his punished body that at the end of the count he would surface for air, but when he reached the magic number, he forced himself to count another slow ten and then another. It was Tory who first needed air, and they surfaced together as close to the hull as they could. Juan gulped a lungful and forced them under again, not knowing if they'd been spotted.

When they surfaced for the second time, he took a moment to get his bearings. They were less than twenty yards from the railing where he'd tied off the Draeger set. Bullets began to stitch the water around them, shooting little jets of white water into the air. The pair ducked back under without getting their breath but somehow managed to cover the distance.

Juan's mind was too fogged with the pain radiating from his leg and head to attempt untying the simple knot he'd fastened. Instead, he reached into his shattered prosthesis for a flat throwing knife. The ship saw had shredded one side of the blade, but the other still retained its keen edge. He sliced through the lines and fed the regulator to Tory as he made them both sink deeper. Because the rebreather didn't produce bubbles, the gunmen above couldn't see where they lurked ten feet below the surface. The Sikh fighters fired indiscriminant volleys into the water, hoping to get lucky but mostly just venting their anger that two of their comrades were dead and a third would limp for the rest of his life. Juan held no sympathy for any of them.

He took the mouthpiece from Tory, careful not to let water enter the system where it would cause a caustic reaction in the CO_2 scrubbers. Despite the polluted salt water, he could taste her on the rubber. He gave her hand a reassuring squeeze and then maneuvered the Draeger pack over his shoulders. The mechanical parts of his artificial limb were completely destroyed, so he fitted his fin onto his good leg, giving the other fin to Tory.

Once he had cleared water from his mask and they were both settled, he became aware of another sound: gunfire. And not the maddened fusillades fired by the guards. It was the rhythmic pulse of a weapon he knew well. He couldn't suppress a smile. Singh's men were attempting to board the *Oregon*, and he could imagine Mark Murphy ensconced behind his video screens as he opened up with the ship's Bofors 40 mm autocannon.

That's when the men above him must have seen their motion through the water, because suddenly bullets were striking all around them, cutting cavitation trails that looked like white arrows.

21

MAX Hanley ordered Franklin Lincoln and his SEAL assault team to launch their Zodiac as soon as he heard the ship saw whining from inside the shed across the bay. Max hurried from the boat garage to the operations center buried below the *Oregon*'s superstructure. The red battle lights were on, which blended with the blue computer screens to make the room glow an awful shade of purple. Why Max had never noticed this detail before was just one of the million things swirling through his mind.

With the rest of the breaker's yard quiet so late at night, Max was certain that Shere Singh had fired up the ship saw because he had caught the chairman. Eric Stone was at the helm, Murph had the weapons station, and Hali Kasim and Linda Ross were watching the threat board. Max settled in the command chair, hooking a hands-free microphone over his balding head.

"Linc, you on the net?"

"Roger, *Oregon*. We're approaching in stealth mode. ETA seven minutes."

Max was about to ask why they didn't open up the Zodiac's big outboard, because the sound of the saw would surely mask the engine's throaty roar, but then remembered that in the moonlight the Zodiac's wake would show as a white crescent on the otherwise black sea.

Lincoln continued, "*Oregon*, be advised that there is a lot of traffic pulling away from the beach. I count four, repeat, four utility boats. Thermal scan shows they're loaded to the gunnels with men."

"I have 'em," Mark Murphy called from the weapons station. His screen showed the feed from the thermal/IR/low-light camera mounted on the *Oregon*'s main mast. "I estimate fifty soldiers in total, armed with automatic weapons and rocket-propelled grenades." He typed commands into his computer to call up the ship's vast arsenal. His screen split so that each forty-foot boat approaching from the beach was on its own display. A sight reticle appeared over each dark-hulled craft. "Targets designated tango one through four. I have tracking on all inbound."

"Where's the Zodiac?" When the *Oregon*'s batteries opened up, the last thing he needed to worry about was a friendly fire accident.

"Linc's angling out of the way, but he's moving slow."

Max brought up a wide-angle camera shot on his screen. Singh's men were coming straight for the *Oregon* as the Zodiac slowly motored off to the starboard. The ex-SEAL couldn't gun his engine because the guards would open fire as soon as they saw his wake. Max was forced into a waiting game between Linc's progress out of the line of fire and the speed of the approaching utility boats.

"Incoming!" Linda Ross called out from her station. "Missile launch from the beach."

In the two seconds it took her to shout the warning, the RPG had covered half the distance to the *Oregon*, and before anyone could react, it finished the other half. The five-pound missile struck the anchor fairlead high on the bow and exploded. The Soviet-made RPG mangled a good-sized chunk of steel and blew a hole up through the deck but didn't damage the anchor chains or machinery.

"We've got more. Multiple launches!"

Wallowing this close to the beach, the range was too short for the ship's automated defensive systems to engage the incoming missiles.

Max had no other choice. "Helm, all back full!"

Eric Stone had anticipated the order, and his hands were already drawing back the dual throttle controls. Deep within the ship the four massive magnetohydrodynamic engines came to life. Like flicking a light switch, the revolutionary engines were running at full power in an instant, drawing seawater's naturally occurring electric charge, amplifying it through the cryo-cooled magnets, and creating a force wave that pumped water though her drive tubes with unimaginable power.

The backward acceleration was enough to send dishes tumbling in the galley and toss a batch of files on Cabrillo's desk into the air. But they weren't quick enough to avoid the incoming volley of RPGs.

Six of the notoriously inaccurate missiles fizzled harmlessly into the sea. Another impacted one of the *Oregon*'s dummy cargo derricks, dropping it like a felled tree. The heavy steel mast crashed against the deck hard enough to make the eleven-thousand-ton vessel shudder. The eighth missile slammed into the superstructure below the bridge. The shaped high-explosive warhead was designed to punch through a tank's thick armor, so when it exploded through the half-inch steel, much of its force remained. Two of the mock-up cabins the Corporation used during harbor inspections were gutted by the kinetic force of the explosion, but the damage was mostly cosmetic. The damage control computer activated the fire suppression system without need for human intervention, and it also directed damage control teams to the area.

"I want a report in thirty seconds," Max said over the ship's emergency channel.

He checked the GPS display and speed indicators. They were backing out of the breaker's yard at twenty knots and accelerating. A few seconds more, and they'd be out of range of Shere Singh's RPGs. But if he had more sophisticated weapons, Stinger missiles, for example, they still needed more room to shoot the rockets out of the air.

"Linc, give me a sit rep."

"They're on to us," the SEAL called back. Over the voice channel Max heard the bellow of the Zodiac's engine and the crackle of machine gun fire. "One boat is chasing us. The other three are still closing on you."

"Give us a minute to get out of those missiles' range, and we'll provide cover fire. Gomez Adams is about to launch our second UAV, so we should have a good view of the battlefield in a few minutes."

"Roger."

Arrowing across the bay at nearly forty knots, Linc couldn't hope to hit anything as he sprayed rounds at the utility boat with his M-4A1. The three-round bursts were intended to keep the pursuers from firing at him. So far, the few return volleys had been wild. The men had simply propped their weapons against the utility boat's gunwales and fired without looking.

He couldn't believe the hits the *Oregon* was taking and realized that they had been expected. But it didn't matter if the Sikh owner of the breaker's yard was on to the Corporation. What mattered now was finding the chairman and then beating a fast retreat.

The ship saw had stopped its ungodly racket a moment earlier, and Linc didn't know if this was a good sign or bad, but until the *Oregon* took out the utility boat chasing in their wake, they couldn't risk making a run for the shed. Or could they?

Mike Trono was at the Zodiac's helm, and Linc used his hands to indicate what he wanted to do. Trono nodded wordlessly and sent the lightweight boat skidding in a tight turn that would take them past the back of the huge shed.

The maneuver allowed the utility boat to cut the distance between it and the Zodiac, and the guards on board were emboldened by the opportunity. A dozen guns opened up at the same time and had Trono not juked the Zodiac, its rubber hull and the four men riding in her would have been cut to ribbons.

Linc and the others fired back. Even Trono fired his pistol with one hand while gunning the throttle with the other. One of the guards on the utility boat clutched his throat as he fell forward over the rail. He struck the roiled water of the bow wave and was sucked under. Even if the wound wasn't fatal, the props would dice his body into hamburger as the boat motored over him.

The utility boat peeled away, giving Trono the opportunity to slow as they passed behind the warehouse just as the ship saw came back to life—quieter this time because it wasn't cutting through metal.

Clutching his rifle tight to his chest, Linc rolled over the soft side of the Zodiac, absorbing the impact with the water on his massive shoulders. He was left bobbing in the wake as Mike brought the Zodiac back onto plane and rocketed parallel to the beach.

He ducked under the shed's metal skirt and came up inside the structure.

There was enough light to see that the name of the ship inside had been removed from her stern. But, with the chain saw whirring farther toward the beach, it was impossible to hear any voices that would tell him what was happening.

"*Oregon,* this is Assault One," he radioed. "I am inside the shed preparing to look for the chairman.

"Roger that," Max replied instantly. "We're almost ready to engage, so your extraction will be clear. Good luck."

Linc clicked his radio in response and began to swim down the length of the ship, searching for a way to reach the deck. Then he heard the distinct crack of a pistol up near the ship's truncated bow.

Seconds later two bodies tumbled over the ship's rail. Both wore black, one in a combat uniform and the other wearing a wet suit. It had to be Cabrillo. Linc didn't know the identity of the other person but wasn't surprised the silhouette had a woman's curves. Only the chairman could find a date in a place like this.

No sooner had the pair sunk below the water when two guards appeared at the rail, their gun barrels tracking back and forth as they searched for the two people who'd leapt overboard. The range was too long for Linc to guarantee his shot, so he silently swam on, keeping near the catwalk that ringed the shed a few feet above the tide mark. Twice he watched Cabrillo and a woman who looked vaguely familiar bob to the surface for air. Linc was sure they were headed for an open metal stairwell. *That's where Juan must have stashed his rebreather*, he thought.

The guards fired down into the water, but Linc could see they had no idea where Cabrillo had fled. By Linc's estimate, a full minute had passed since the last time Cabrillo had surfaced. He knew the chairman to be an excellent free diver capable of staying under for two minutes or more but not after a shoot-out on a ship and having fallen thirty feet from her deck. He must have reached the Draeger set.

Just as he reached this conclusion, he heard Max's voice over his radio say they were engaging at the same time he heard the 40 mm automatic cannon mounted on the *Oregon*'s fore quarter start to pound away.

Undistracted by the cannon outside, the guards began concentrating their fire at a spot about ten feet from the staircase. Something had drawn their attention. In a move that took tremendous strength because he was wearing combat boots rather than swim fins, Linc kicked his legs to thrust his upper body out of the water and brought his M-4A1 to his shoulder. Before gravity dragged him back down again, the former SEAL got off a pair of three-round bursts. One of the guards had his AK shot from his hands. The other's head vanished in a crimson mist.

He sank back down under the surface and waited for any other gunman to rake the water. What he got instead was a hand clamped around his ankle. He resisted the urge to kick it away. The chairman.

Linc felt Cabrillo thrust the regulator mouthpiece to his lips and took a few grateful breaths before passing it back. Juan must have then given it to the woman because he could feel her chest moving against his shoulder. Together the three of them began an awkward swim that was more dog paddle than any other stroke with each taking turns at the regulator. It took several minutes to retreat down the length of the tanker.

Once at the shed's rear doors, Cabrillo brought his party to the surface below the catwalk. His forehead stung from where he'd torn away the flap of skin, and his right leg throbbed from the groin all the way to the toes he'd lost years earlier.

"Your timing couldn't have been better," he told Linc. "I think my fin broke surface and gave away our position."

"Any more in here, boss?"

"Shere Singh took off the instant I pulled my gun, and if you capped the last two on the *Toyo Maru,* then that's all I know about."

"Let's not wait for reinforcements, shall we?" Tory said.

"I'm with the missus." Linc keyed his tactical radio. "*Oregon,* this is Assault One. I've got the chairman and the mermaid we pulled off the *Avalon.* We're ready for extraction by Zodiac."

"You have to wait. There's still one more utility boat out here. We're tracking it now with the eye in the sky, but we need a few minutes to try to destroy it."

Cabrillo took the Linc's headset. "Negative, *Oregon.* Shere Singh could be escaping as we speak. We need him."

"Okay, Juan. I'll vector the Zodiac to your position."

A moment later the Zodiac roared over to the spot where Linc had performed his roll-off and throttled down to a low burble. Juan abandoned the Draeger rebreather and followed Tory and Lincoln under the door. Linc's SEALs easily plucked her from the water and helped Cabrillo and the team leader into the rubber-hulled craft. Juan wasn't fully inside before Mike Trono opened the throttle gates and shot the nimble boat across the waves.

They came under immediate fire from men on the beach, their weapons winking in the darkness like angry fireflies. Trono twisted the boat away from shore and out toward the open bay where the *Oregon* was trying to find the final utility boat. The other three were flaming wreckage that would soon sink to the bottom of the harbor. The fourth had to be hiding amid the dozens of rusted hulks awaiting their turn in the shed or on the beach for dismantling.

Juan moved to the Zodiac's bow to call directions to the helmsman as they entered the flotilla of derelict ships. He'd donned a pair of night vision goggles. The outboard reverberated between the decaying hulls as they threaded their way toward the *Oregon.* With this many vessels, it was like running full speed through a maze. Trono bobbed and weaved the Zodiac, following Juan's hand signals, barreling past a supertanker that had to be a thousand feet long and between a pair of car ferries that still carried the livery of the English Channel company that ran them.

They rounded the bow of the ferry, and were angling for a gap between a partially sunken tugboat and another container ship when the last utility boat appeared from behind another ship. The Corporation team responded a second quicker and raked the utility boat from stem to stern with well-aimed fire.

The utility boat cut a tight arc in the water and took off after the Zodiac. With the tide changing, the bay was growing rougher. Both boats buffeted in the rising swells, making it impossible to engage with their weapons. In calm seas the Zodiac could more than outrun the heavily laden work boat, but the waves were acting as a great equalizer.

Every time Trono tried to break out of the forsaken armada, the utility boat was there to cut off their escape back to the *Oregon.*

The outboard coughed, dropping power for a moment before rehitting on all cylinders. Mike Trono felt around the big engine cowling and cursed when his fingers felt a bullet hole. They came away wet, and he sniffed at the liquid clinging to his skin.

"Juan, they got the gas tank," he shouted over the engine noise. "I don't know how much longer we can play cat and mouse."

The utility boat had broken off pursuit, but the Zodiac was headed away from the *Oregon* and still boxed in by so many ships they couldn't tell where Singh's men would attack from next.

"Did they head back to shore?" Tory asked.

"I doubt it," Juan replied just as the work boat leapt from behind a big commercial fisherman.

More gunfire stitched the seas around the Zodiac as Trono tried to squeeze another half a knot out of the engine. He could smell oil burning inside the cowling. The bullet had done more than hole the gas tank.

They zigzagged past the ferry boats again when something caught Cabrillo's eye.

"Mike, take us back to that sunken tugboat. I have an idea."

They raced across the bay toward the dark shape of the sunken ship. She'd settled awkwardly on some obstruction on the seafloor so that her bow was thrust out of the water and her back deck was awash. A broken crane dangling over her deck was nearly invisible in the moonlight.

Cabrillo concentrated on the course he wanted to take, ignoring all other distractions, including the fire coming from the utility boat. He had one shot to make this work. With his arms outstretched he called minute direction changes that the helmsman responded to instantly, feathering the hurtling Zodiac with a light touch.

"Okay, slow us down, draw them in."

Everyone heard the crazy order, but no one questioned it. The Zodiac dutifully slowed, which allowed the utility boat to cut their separation to seventy feet. As if senseing the moment of victory, the utility boat's driver hammered his throttles to their stops in hopes of running down their quarry.

Juan continued to feed course changes to Trono, guiding them so they would pass astern of the sunken ship. He looked over his shoulder to see the utility boat bearing down on them like a shark making its final lunge. Through his goggles' enhanced optics he could even see the delight on the helmsman's face as he prepared for the kill.

A few more seconds, Juan told himself, studying his target once again. A few more seconds. Now!

He dropped his left hand to order Mike to make a hard turn to port. The Zodiac was now racing for the gap under the tugboat's broken crane. The larger utility boat was cranked over in pursuit, its driver never seeing he was being led into a trap.

"Down," Juan shouted as the Zodiac crossed behind the tug's sunken rail and shot under the ruined crane boom. There was barely three feet of clearance, and had they not ducked to the floorboards, the rusted steel derrick would have taken off their heads.

Juan looked back as soon as they were through. The utility boat was following in their wake but at the last second the helmsman must have seen the crane. He threw the wheel to its lock, but it was too late. They were going too fast. The boat smashed into the crane, and the metal easily ripped through the fiberglass hull. A gouge was torn down her entire length, and one of her big fuel tanks was ripped from its mounts.

None of the men aboard the doomed craft had time to brace themselves, and all twelve of them on the deck were launched over the bow by the sudden deceleration. Most landed safely in the water, although one hit the crane boom headfirst and died instantly.

The diesel spilling from the ruptured tank pooled inside the filthy bilge, but before enough seawater could dilute it, a spark from the ruined electrical system detonated the mixture in a ballooning fireball of orange and black.

"Scratch the last utility boat," Cabrillo said over the tactical radio. "We're headed home."

The Zodiac's engine died when they were still a hundred yards from the *Oregon,* forcing them to man the paddles. With the motor silenced they could hear continuous gunfire from the beach as Singh's men fired blindly out to sea.

Juan threw the painter to a waiting deckhand as the rubber craft reached the ramp. By the time the last of Linc's SEALs had piled out, Juan had limped to where Julia Huxley waited with a spare prosthetic leg. He'd radioed ahead. She used surgical scissors to cut away part of his wet suit and examined the stump. Apart from some purple swelling, his leg seemed okay, so she let him strap on the second prosthesis as she examined his head wound.

"What happened?" she asked, peering at the gash with a penlight.

"Rifle butt."

She flashed the light into his eyes, checking if he had a concussion. She grunted, unsurprised that his pupils reacted normally. "You have a head like a cannonball. How do you feel? Dizzy? Lightheaded? Nauseous?"

"None of the above. It just stings a bit from the salt water."

"I bet." Julia knew that like most men, Juan was downplaying the pain. She swabbed out the four-inch-square wound, making sure that the antibacterial made him wince a few times before putting a large sterile dressing over the cut and swathing the top of his head with a gauze wrap. "That should hold you. Sorry, but I'm fresh out of lollipops."

"Then I guess I should have cried more." He dry-swallowed the painkillers she'd handed him.

Julia noticed Tory Ballinger standing nearby. "Do I even want to know what you're doing here?"

"Tory works for Lloyd's of London," Juan said, getting to his feet and testing his weight on his artificial limb. While the stump was sore, he had full mobility. "She's working the same case we are but from the other end."

"And I thought it was my bedside manner." The two women shook hands, and Julia asked if Tory needed any medical attention.

Tory was toweling off her hair. "Thanks, Dr. Huxley. I'm fine. Bit shaken maybe, but unharmed."

"Juan has a good bottle of brandy in his cabin. I'm prescribing at least one snifter."

"Chairman, you there?" It was Max Hanley over the ship's intercom. Cabrillo hit the switch mounted to a nearby bulkhead.

"I'm here. What's the situation?"

"They're still firing at us from the beach. Just small arms. No RPGs. George Adams has the UAV circling the compound. A few minutes after the ship saw kicked off for the last time, he spotted someone running from the shed. They hopped into a jeep and tore out of the facility headed for a cluster of houses a mile or so up the coast. There's a chopper on a nearby pad, but so far there's been no activity around it."

"What about our bird?"

"Crew has it on ten-minute standby," Max replied, meaning the four-passenger Robinson helicopter could be in the air in ten minutes.

"Tell George to turn over the UAV to Eric Stone. The kid has enough hours on the Microsoft flight simulator to qualify for his commercial pilot's license. I want to be airborne as soon as possible. We need Singh alive if we're going to get to the bottom of this."

"You sure you're up to this?" Julia asked.

"I'm more pissed than hurt," he told her. "Singh knew we were coming." He snapped on the intercom again. "Max, it's me. Listen, Singh's been a step ahead of us. He unloaded the *Toya Maru* from the *Maus* a while ago. Probably when you broke off at Taiwan. Hiro's tanker is already inside the shed and halfway to becoming razor blades."

"How?"

"It doesn't matter now, but I think the *Maus* has better radar than we thought. She must have known you were tailing her. Have Hali get ready to file a report with the Indonesian authorities. I suspect Singh's plugged in with the government, so he'll have to cut through a lot of red tape, but bottom line is we need this place raided by the navy or coast guard as soon as we're clear."

"I'm on the circuit," Hali Kasim interrupted. There was a manic edge to his voice. "Chairman, you're not going to believe this, but I just got a signal from Eddie's transponder."

"When?"

"Just now! Two seconds ago."

"Jesus. Where is he?"

"It doesn't make any sense." Doubt crept into the communications officer's tone.

"Talk to me, Hali."

"Russia, sir. The western coast of the Kamchatka Peninsula. What the hell is he doing there? I thought the snakeheads had their conduits running into the U.S or Japan."

Juan went still and turned his mind inward so he could no longer hear Linc and the other SEALs stowing the Zodiac and their gear or feel Julia's concerned look or Tory Ballinger's intrigued scrutiny. Eddie Seng had been taken to Kamchatka. While the question of why worried at part of his mind, the bulk of his intellect was forming a plan, calculating speed, distances, and the priorities of the mission. He factored in the

Oregon's speed, the maximum speed of the Robinson R-44 with various payloads, and the need to interrogate Shere Singh.

He was sure Eddie wasn't the only Chinese immigrant that had been taken to the isolated part of Russia, a volcano-strewn jut of land that had been closed off to the world for the better part of the past century. How many more had ended up on its rugged shores was something he couldn't know, but instinct told him there would be a great many.

What was Singh's connection? Transportation was the obvious answer. He could move men and ships inside the pair of floating drydocks with virtual impunity. He could hijack vessels carrying illegals from the open seas and make sure any witnesses, like Tory's hapless *Avalon*, never survived long enough to file a report. All Singh needed to know was which ships were carrying immigrants, and he could target them at will. That would mean that someone in China was supplying that information, Cabrillo realized, but was the smuggling the only crime taking place, or was it a means to an end?

"They need cheap labor," he said aloud.

"What was that?" Tory asked. She'd stripped off her wet jacket and wore only a thin black T-shirt. A fluffy towel was draped over her shoulders to cover her breasts. Her dark hair was damp and untamed and somehow incredibly attractive. If she had any questions about what she'd seen of the Corporation so far, she had the good sense to keep them to herself.

"This is about cheap labor; slaves. The night we saved you we also took out a pirate boat that was carrying a shipping container. We sank the ship and managed to recover the container, but not in time to save the people who'd been locked inside. We later learned they were illegal Chinese immigrants. I had one of my men follow the route those poor bastards had taken in hopes of learning what they were up to and how it related to the pirates. He just turned up on the Kamchatka Peninsula."

"We at Lloyd's only suspected Singh of hijacking shipping in the region and using his facility here to eliminate the evidence."

"There's more than that," Juan said. "He's also hijacking ships carrying Chinese immigrants and transporting them to Kamchatka. And if he needs transporters as big as the *Maus* and her sister drydock, it leads me to believe they've probably seized hundreds, or maybe thousands of illegals. They're using them as slave labor."

"What on earth for?" Tory asked.

"It could be anything." Juan hit the intercom again. "Max, make preparations to get us out of here. I'll take Linc and Mike Trono with me to find Shere Singh. I want you headed for Eddie's location with every knot the old girl can give. We'll catch a flight to . . ." He needed a second to recall Kamchatka's capital. "Petropavlovsk."

"Not gonna happen, Chairman," Mark Murphy said over the open circuit. "I've been on the Internet since Hali said that's where Eddie is. The government is reporting a major volcanic event is under way. I confirmed it through the U.S. Geological Survey's Web site. The Russians are saying there's so much ash falling that they've been forced to shut down the airport. No one's going in or out."

Juan cursed under his breath. "Okay, that doesn't change anything. I still want the *Oregon* under way as soon as possible."

"What about Shere Singh?" Max asked.

"My window to catch him just narrowed, that's all. Even with the *Oregon* moving at maximum speed, we should have a half hour here before you steam out of the Robinson's range."

"May I say something, Captain Cabrillo?" Tory asked.

Juan nodded.

"I infiltrated this facility from the landward side, and I have to say it's bloody enormous. I've been observing the place for a week, and even I don't know the full scope of Singh's operation."

"What's your point?"

"My point is that if you're only giving yourself thirty minutes to find him, then I think I can lead you to where he keeps his residence when he's here."

Juan hesitated for a fraction of a second. Tory Ballinger was a virtual stranger to him, but he felt like he knew her because he recognized a great deal of himself in her steady gaze. She'd handled herself well just moments earlier, and he still didn't know how she'd kept her wits when she was trapped aboard the *Avalon*. He saw in her the same indefatigable British spirit that had once made their island the most powerful nation on earth and had seen England through the blitz during World War Two. While in Winston Churchill that look came across as pugnacious confidence, in Tory it was alluring drive.

And to top it off, Juan thought, her own investigation had led her to the very same place his had taken him, and he doubted she'd blown up a building and kidnapped a corrupt lawyer to get here.

"You're on."

Tory had expected an argument. It was in the storm clouds building behind her bright blue eyes. Juan's quick acceptance of her offer left her off balance for a moment and her mouth agape.

"We've got about five minutes to change and kit up. Come with me. You, too, Linc. We're not done yet."

MOMENTS after the Robinson R-44 lifted from its hydraulically operated pad, the *Oregon* cut a tight circle in the bay using her athwartships bow thruster, and Linda Ross gave Eric Stone the order for full speed. Max Hanley was down in his beloved engine room. As soon as the order came through, the quad magnetohydrodynamic engines spooled up like aircraft turbines, and almost instantly the water at her stern boiled up with the raw force of her revolutionary propulsion system. Linda also ordered Mark Murphy to rake the sea just short of the beach with the Gatling gun to give the departing chopper a few moments of cover fire.

George Adams sat in the Robinson's left-hand seat with Juan at his side. Linc and Tory took up the rear bench seats. With their personal weapons and equipment as well as the Barrett .50 caliber sniper rifle lying across Linc's lap, the chopper was crowded. Adams looped them out to sea and crossed the shoreline well north of the breaker's yard.

"There's a compound up the beach about a mile," Tory said over the helo's intercom. "It's where the executives live. I watched them for a couple of days over the past week. One of the houses is much larger than the others, and now that I've seen Shere Singh up close and personal, I remember him living there."

"Any guards?" Juan asked.

"A few, but after tonight I expect the area to be lousy with them."

Juan smiled at her turn of phrase, but inside he knew to expect the worst. "What about access to the facility?"

"There is a road that runs north and south behind it. There's a hydro dam and a smelting factory to the north."

"Much traffic?'

"Mostly lorries hauling the steel plates to be melted. And almost nothing after nightfall."

"Okay, folks, we're coming back over the coastline." Adams's helmet was integrated with a night vision camera mounted on the Robinson's nose to give him greater visibility. "I see the compound she just mentioned. A lot of lights and a lot of people milling around. And, as luck would have it, a few of them aren't armed."

"Keep us out of their range and let's see what's happening."

"I see a chopper pad a little farther away from the compound," Adams said. "It looks like they've got a JetRanger, and her rotors are starting to turn."

"Can we follow them?" Tory asked.

"She's got us by forty or fifty knots and at least a hundred miles of range," Juan told her. He looked back at Franklin Lincoln. "How about it, big man?"

"I'm on it, boss."

"George, hold us steady," Lincoln said as he loosened his shoulder harness. He opened his door, ignoring the frenzied hurricane of downwash from the rotors that whipped into the small chopper's cabin. The

Barrett was an ugly weapon, nearly five feet long and heavy. In the hands of an expert the half-inch bullets it fired were accurate up to a mile.

Adams turned the Robinson broadside to clear Linc's view. A few guards in the distant compound fired at the hovering helicopter, but the distance was too great. Lincoln fitted the big rifle to his shoulder and checked the sight picture through the night vision scope. The world was an eerie green through the optics, but somehow intimate. He could see the frustration on the guards' faces as they fired at the chopper. He scanned the scene and settled the reticle on the idling JetRanger helicopter. His view was so sharp he could see the air shimmering from the heat that poured from the turbine's exhaust.

The crack of the gun sounded like a cannon, and Linc absorbed the brutal recoil without taking his eyes from the sight. The bullet arrived long before anyone on the ground heard it, so the destruction came as a stunning surprise. It struck the JetRanger's rotor mast, the most vulnerable part of any helicopter. The whirling mast came apart so that her blades were launched like a pair of deadly scythes. One cut through a cluster of men who were setting up a shoulder-fired missile. The dismemberments were something even a veteran like Franklin Lincoln had a hard time stomaching.

The other blade hit a large fuel tank mounted on stilts. The highly volatile aviation gas went up in a towering explosion that overwhelmed the scope's light filters. Linc looked over the rifle and saw flames mushrooming outward and upward. Anyone standing within a hundred feet of the tank was knocked back by the concussion. Anyone within fifty feet had been immolated.

"I've got movement," Adams called out. "Rear door of the JetRanger just opened. Guy wearing a turban is running for it."

"That has to be Shere Singh," Tory said. "Where's he going?"

"Hold on." A few tense moments passed. "Okay, he's getting into a car. Looks like a big Mercedes sedan. He's getting into the backseat. There's only him and the driver."

"Want me to take him out, Juan?" Linc asked, bringing the sniper rifle to his shoulder again.

"Not here. Let him get out onto the highway and away from all these guards."

"Singh must have radioed someone," George announced. "Another car is pulling away from the residential compound. Looks like at least three armed men inside."

"We knew this wouldn't be easy." Cabrillo checked his watch. A third of their thirty-minute window to catch the *Oregon* had gone by.

A moment later they all saw the headlights of the pair of cars race out the facility's back gate and head south. The road was hemmed in by dark jungle, so the lights reflected as though the vehicles were speeding through a tunnel. George opened the throttle to the Robinson's engine and quickly overtook the vehicles.

The drivers maintained a fifteen-foot separation. It was a little tight for what Juan had in mind, but he had no other choice. He plucked a grenade from the web harness over his shoulder and opened the small window set into the chopper's right-hand door. Optimally the grenade should have a five-second fuse; however, each incendiary's timer varied by as much as a second—not a big deal when throwing one into a foxhole or trying to take out troops advancing on foot—but with the cars hurtling at ninety miles per hour, they could cover more than a hundred feet in a single tick of a watch.

Cabrillo pulled the pin, maintaining a firm grip on the spoon, and held the grenade outside the window. The toss was more experience and instinct than calculation. He released the spoon to prime the weapon, waited a few moments, and let it drop.

The grenade was instantly swallowed by the darkness, but a second later the Mercedes swerved as the driver reacted to something heavy bouncing off the trunk. The grenade rolled off the car, hit the road, and momentum kept it tumbling down the asphalt. The trailing car raced over it as though they hadn't seen it or didn't understand what it was. Another second passed, one of the longest in Juan's life. He was sure that the guards' car had safely passed the grenade and was reaching for another when it detonated directly under the vehicle's gas tank.

The two explosions came an instant apart. First the low crump of the grenade and then the second spectacular detonation of the gasoline. The rear of the car lifted off the road, and it pivoted on its nose for a heartbeat before slamming onto its roof. It rolled seven times, shedding sheet metal and waves of burning fuel. It ended up careening off the road and slamming into a utility pole, the force of the impact bending the car in two around the teak pole.

Shere Singh's driver unintentionally slowed as he watched the destruction in his rearview mirror. This gave Franklin Lincoln all the opportunity he needed. George passed the Mercedes flying ten feet above the low jungle canopy and fifty feet to the right of the road. Linc nestled the Barrett to his shoulder and fired. While a normal bullet might have only punctured the Mercedes's tire, the .50 caliber slug shattered the spline where the front axle met the wheel. The entire assembly, wheel, hub, and tire were torn from the car. The heavy Mercedes dropped onto the shattered axle in a shower of sparks, and the car instantly began to decelerate as the driver fought to keep it on the road.

For good measure Linc put two bullets through the front of the hood and gave a satisfied nod when steam erupted from the mangled radiator.

Adams brought the Robinson over the road, keeping just behind the dying limousine, and when it finally came to a stop, he had the skids on the macadam. Even before the machine had settled onto the road, Cabrillo, Linc, and Tory Ballinger were rushing ahead. Linc and Juan carried M-4A2 assault rifles while Tory had borrowed a Beretta semiautomatic pistol from the *Oregon*'s armory.

The team had covered half of the twenty yards when the driver heaved open his door. He was out and around it before anyone could get a shot off. From his covered position behind the door, he sprayed the roadway with fire from a machine pistol. The driver was panicked, and his shots went wild, but still the trio fell to the ground. Linc opened up with his M-4, concentrating a withering stream of 5.56 mm into the open door. The high-powered rounds ricocheted off the armored door and turned the bulletproof glass opaque.

Having assumed that the big Mercedes would be armored, Juan fired under the door. His first burst missed the driver, but the second tore apart the calf and ankle of one of his legs. As he fell the door closed, exposing him to a double tap from Tory's Beretta. The impact threw him bodily into the car's fender before he slid to the ground in a disjointed heap.

Juan checked the Mercedes's rear door. Locked. He loosed his nearly full magazine into the glass at point-blank range. The first dozen bullets couldn't penetrate the tough laminate, but by clamping the barrel tightly he was able to bore a hole through the pane. Linc stepped up as Juan backed away to reload and expanded the hole, sending chips of glass arcing though the air like glittering diamonds.

Once Juan had his weapon reloaded, he tapped Linc on the shoulder to cease firing.

"Singh, I'm giving you three seconds to place both hands outside the window." There were no sounds coming from inside the vehicle. "One. Two. Three." Linc and Juan opened fire at the same instant. Bullets passing through the shattered glass started to disintegrate the opposite window. Several imbedded in the seat back, and a couple pinged off the armored plating and rattled around the back of the car until burying themselves in a soft target. A sharp cry of pain cut above the rifles' chatter. Both men held fire.

"Singh!"

"I'm shot." His voice remained strong. "Oh, praise to Allah, I am going to die."

"Put your goddamned hands outside the window now, or I throw in a grenade."

"I cannot move. My legs, you have paralyzed me."

Juan and Linc exchanged a look, both certain they couldn't trust the Sikh but knowing they had no alternative. Juan reached his hand into the car and opened the door with Linc in position to cover as much of the interior as he could. As the door came open, the interior lights came on. Singh was on the floor and as soon as he could draw a bead he fired with his own machine pistol. His aim was even worse than his driver's. The stream of bullets plowed into the armored door, saving Linc's life. The former SEAL did what tens of thousands of hours of training had instilled in him. As he dodged out of the way he put two rounds into Singh's face, one below the eye and the other straight down the man's throat. His turban uncoiled like a striking snake, and the back of his head came apart in a blooming flower of blood and tissue.

Linc cursed, twisting away in frustration and self-recrimination. "Damnit, Juan, I am so sorry. It was just—"

"Instinct," Juan finished for him, peering into the car to survey the carnage. "You had no choice. I would have done the exact same thing."

Tory shouldered past them and stepped into the back of the stretch Mercedes. Ignoring the blood she patted down Shere Singh's corpse, handing out his wallet, a leather billfold. She plucked a briefcase from where Singh had wedged it into a seat cushion, looked around to see if she'd missed anything, and backed out once again.

"Well, lads, this turned into a dead end, eh?" She wiped her hands on the seat of her pants and gestured up the road behind the idling Robinson helicopter. "It won't take long for more of Singh's forces to get organized and come looking for their boss. Discretion being the better part of valor and all that, I think we should get the hell out of here."

As they started for the chopper, George Adams added power in preparation for takeoff, choking the air with fine grit and forcing them to bend double. Juan tapped Tory on the shoulder and jerked his thumb back toward the Mercedes limousine.

"Just an investigator for Lloyd's?"

Tory intuitively knew what he was talking about. She gave him a cocky grin. "Before that I was employed by Her Majesty's government."

"Doing what?"

She placed a hand on her holstered Beretta. "Troubleshooter."

22

JUAN Cabrillo slouched in the master's chair on the *Oregon*'s faux bridge. Although the tall seat's leather was torn to make it appear as old as the rest of the tramp freighter, he'd had it custom fit so it was perhaps the most comfortable on the ship. Any watch officer was expected to use the central workstation in the op center, but this chair was reserved exclusively for Cabrillo's use.

The sun was sinking fast to port, a dramatic play of color and light made more intense by the stratospheric curtain of volcanic dust billowing from peaks far to the north on Kamchatka Peninsula. The heat of the day lingered on the bridge. Metal was still warm to the touch, and the band of Juan's shorts was damp with perspiration. He wore no shirt and had only boat shoes on his feet. With the speed the *Oregon* was making over the water, opening a door would have invited a hurricane into the bridge, so the room remained hot and stuffy.

Rather than risk running up through the East China Sea and the Sea of Japan, where shipping traffic was as thick as a Los Angeles rush hour, he had decided to vector to the east once they cleared the northernmost of the Philippine Islands and race along Japan's Pacific coast. Shipping lanes were more regulated, so he didn't have to worry about other vessels reporting a ship steaming through the region at over fifty knots. With their radar jamming on active mode, it was visual reports that concerned him. In another few hours they would cross the Tokyo shipping lanes, and traffic would drop precipitously, ending their need to steer around car carriers, container ships, and the dozens of other vessels plying the Pacific routes.

They lost only a few minutes whenever they had to detour, but time was the one thing that Juan could no longer afford. Eddie was another two days away, and already the scant reports coming from the Russian volcanologists trapped in the capital city of Petropavlovsk were disturbing. The peninsula was being rocked by nearly continuous earthquakes, and three volcanoes along the same chain were belching ash and noxious gas. So far there had been no reports of deaths, but most of the settlements on Kamchatka were so remote it might take weeks to get word.

The only bright spot, if it could be called bright, was that Eddie's transmitter continued to send out a signal that Hali could receive through the satellite umbrella. But there was a problem with even that. According to the satellite data, he was on the beach in the shadow of one of the erupting volcanoes. Juan could have asked Dr. Huxley how long the batteries in the transmitter would last after the wearer was dead, but he knew the answer already. Eddie could have died a week ago, and no one on the *Oregon* would be the wiser.

"Penny for your thoughts."

Juan whirled around before recognizing the voice, his face a mask of anger at being disturbed.

"Whoa, sorry," Tory said. "Didn't mean to startle you so."

"You didn't." He turned back to gaze at the horizon once more as if watching it would somehow bring it closer.

"I thought you might like one." Tory held out a bottle of San Miguel beer, what Juan regarded as the Philippines' only worthwhile export.

She wore a white linen skirt, a teal polo shirt, and flats. Her dark hair was brushed away from her face, highlighting the graceful curve of her high cheekbones, and artful cosmetics deepened the already arresting blue of her eyes and the fullness of her mouth. As openly as Juan studied her, he could feel her attention on him. She took in the breadth of his shoulders and the dense muscles of his chest and how even lounging in the chair, his stomach was rippled. But when her glance shifted farther south, to his artificial leg, she quickly looked away.

Because he was so adept at hiding his prosthetic limb, usually by never wearing shorts in public, Juan had encountered few awkward moments since losing the leg. Although he barely knew her, Tory's sudden discomfort made him very conscious of the leg, especially because the one he was wearing made no effort to look real. It was all tubular steel and black carbon fiber. He suddenly wished he'd either worn long pants or at least one of his legs that looked more human.

He took his feet off the rail beneath the forward windows and sat up straighter in his chair so his leg was better hidden. He was both annoyed and intrigued by why he felt Tory's opinion of him was important.

Juan accepted the proffered bottle and rolled the dew-blistered glass across his forehead before taking several healthy gulps. Julia had rebandaged his wound so he no longer looked like he was wearing a diaper on his head. He was putting off a skin graft until after the mission was over. "Thanks. Sorry about the glare of death I just shot you. I was lost in my own world there."

"Thinking about your man? Eddie, is it?"

"Eddie Seng, yes. One of my best."

"Max told me a bit about him. Actually, he told me a bit about all of you." She smiled. "Quite a collection of pirates you've put together."

He chuckled. "Brigands and privateers every man jack of them, and in all my life I've never worked with a finer team. I'm sorry I haven't been able to give you the nickel tour and introduce you around."

"I know you've been busy. Linda was kind enough to play docent." She waved her hands down the length of her body. "And to let me borrow some clothes from your Magic Shop."

"And your cabin. Is it all right?"

Her eyes went wide with delight. "All right? It's bigger than my flat in London, and if you find the marble tub missing after I'm gone, don't be surprised. You do seem to enjoy life's finer things. The food rivals Cunard, and Maurice, the steward, is an absolute love."

"Just because we're in a savage business doesn't mean we have to act like savages."

"How did you become, well, mercenaries, I suppose?"

Juan indicated for Tory to take the closest seat. This one was Max's and it seemed to swallow her. "When the Cold War ended I knew that the global polarity that had kept the world in check for a half century was over. Regional conflicts were bound to erupt, and the need to provide security services would grow. That's why I created the Corporation. As for the *Oregon,* well, rather than base my outfit in some country where I'd be subjected to their laws, I decided that using a ship would give me the freedom we would need."

"And you do this for the money?"

"I'm as much a capitalist as the next man, but I'm also particular about my clients."

"I think you are more particular than you are capitalistic."

Juan laughed again. "Maurice has been gossiping."

"He thinks the world of you." Tory smiled. "Actually, your whole crew does. I've heard you've turned down some very lucrative offers in the past few years."

"And accepted some, too."

"You know what I'm saying. This isn't all about the money."

"Let's just say it's pretty gratifying to get paid to do what you know is right. How about you, madam investigator? Did you take your job with Lloyd's because their ad in the *Financial Times* promised more pay than becoming a stockbroker?"

"Touché." She sipped from her own bottle of beer. "So, do you have any theories about what what's going on?"

"Theories, yes. Answers, no. Especially since we lost our last link in the chain."

"Franklin hasn't forgiven himself, you know."

"He and Eddie are best friends. He won't forgive himself until he knows Eddie's safe. That reminds me." Juan jumped down from his stool and grabbed a portfolio from the deck. He handed it to Tory. "The computer finished with this about an hour ago. You might find it interesting."

"What is it?" Tory asked, opening the crisp leather cover.

"Translation of what we found in the briefcase you recovered from Singh's car. In a nutshell it lists every ship his group has hijacked over the past several years from all over the Pacific. I imagine it can close a number of your cases. Most of the ships were scrapped at Karamita, but some are still sailing under flags of convenience for dummy companies Singh controls."

"Controlled," Tory corrected without looking up from the book.

"Unfortunately," Juan continued, "there's nothing about what the *Maus*'s sister ship, *Souri*, has been doing since Singh bought her. I suspect that there are other ships she's transported, perhaps a great many, that Singh kept in another ledger to compartmentalize this particular aspect of his criminal fiefdom."

She looked up. "Why would he do that?"

"No idea."

"What if he doesn't control this aspect of his criminal fiefdom?"

Juan leaned forward in his chair, sensing she might have something. "Anton Savich?"

"Max told me that's a name that has cropped up all during your investigation, although I confess I never came across his name during mine."

"All we've learned is that he was a functionary for the Soviet Bureau of Natural Resources, and after the collapse he worked for the Russian equivalent. We have no clue how he got tangled up with a smuggler like Shere Singh."

"Are there any natural resources on Kamchatka? Maybe something he came across in a report when he worked for the bureau? Like precious gems or metals or something?"

"Mark Murphy checked a bunch of databases and found nothing in any appreciable quantities."

A light shone in Tory's eyes. "What if it's something that never got reported? What if when he was working for the Soviets a report crossed his desk that indicated a major find of some kind, and he quietly buried the discovery?"

Juan nodded. "That's a distinct possibility. We all believe that they've brought a lot of Chinese labor up there. It could be he has them working in a mine of some kind." Then he got a sudden burst of inspiration. He plucked his encrypted cell phone from his pocket and dialed. On the third ring of the *Oregon*'s private cellular system, Mark Murphy answered. "Murph, it's Juan. Where are you?"

"Down in the Magic Shop fixing my skateboard," the weapons specialist said.

"Hop on a computer terminal and tell me if mercury is used in any kind of mining techniques."

Used to obscure requests, Mark said he would get right on it and killed the connection.

"What's this about mercury?" Tory asked.

"Julia found heavy doses of mercury poisoning when she performed autopsies on the pirates who tried to attack my ship—the ones who dumped the container carrying those Chinese immigrants."

"You think they picked it up on Kamchatka?"

Cabrillo nodded. "The Chinese weren't contaminated, just the sailors. If they'd been up there a lot, say dropping off other workers or on guard rotation, then its possible that's the source."

A companionable silence passed while they waited for the couple of minutes until Juan's cell chimed. He answered it by saying, "What did you find?"

"Mercury is the only element that bonds with gold," Mark replied. "It's been used to separate raw gold from ore. The practice is banned in a lot of countries because of environmental and health concerns, but it is still widely employed by indigenous miners in South America."

Juan mouthed the word *gold* to Tory. "Thanks, Murph. You can get back to your skateboard now."

Tory leaned back in her seat. "So Anton Savich is using Chinese slave labor, provided to him by Shere Singh, to mine gold on the Kamchatka Peninsula, most likely under the nose of the Russian government."

"I think that about sums it up," Juan agreed, taking another healthy swallow of his beer.

"That solves that mystery, then. We know the who, the how, and now the why."

"Appears that way."

Something in Juan's tone made Tory wary. "What is it?"

"I was just thinking, with Shere Singh out of the piracy business, your end of this investigation is over. I don't know what we're going to find when we get up there, but if our run-ins with Singh and his gang are any gauge, it's going to get bloody."

"And?" she asked, already suspecting what Juan was about to say.

"And you don't need to come with us. We'd only lose an hour or so by choppering you off when we pass the northern tip of Japan and enter the Sea of Okhotsk."

Her fury was at full gale by the time he'd stopped speaking. She came out of her chair, placed both hands on the armrests of his seat, and leaned in so her face was inches from his. "I've dedicated the last six months to this investigation. This has been my life, my every waking moment. I had to fight to get the Royal Geographic Society to let us join their expedition, only there wasn't anything I could do once the pirates hit. I had friends on the *Avalon* who were butchered by these monsters, so don't think for one second I'm not going to see this through to the bitter end, Mr. Chairman of the bloody Corporation."

For several long seconds their eyes were locked, neither giving an inch. Juan had known her strength, understood her intelligence, and now saw her passion. If he could forget that he had grown attracted to her, he would have asked her to join the Corporation right then.

"Just so you know," he said in a low, intimate voice, "I can't guarantee your safety."

Tory sensed the shift in tone, and her anger was replaced with something softer, gentler. Their mouths were still inches apart, but for both of them it was an insurmountable distance. "I'm not asking you to. I just want to be there when you put an end to this once and for all." She straightened reluctantly.

Cabrillo's throat was suddenly dry, and he needed to finish his beer. "Deal."

23

IF nothing more, Eddie Seng had to respect his captors' efficiency. The volcano looming over what had been dubbed Death Beach continued to rumble and belch ash that fell in a choking black blizzard across the facility. Earthquakes were an almost hourly occurrence, and the sea had turned into a writhing sheet of lead. Yet the overseers never relaxed the pace of work even as they implemented their evacuation plans. The boilers in the separating plant remained lit so that the last precious gram of gold could be extracted before they left. Guards exhorted the workers with clubs and whips to keep toiling up and down the hillside burdened with baskets of gold-bearing ore. And at night the slave laborers were locked in the beached cruise ships dreading the call to start working again in the morning.

Out in the bay the crew of the tugboat had succeeded in ballasting the huge drydock so that the ship in its hold could be floated free. The rough seas had caused numerous delays in the tricky operation, which explained why the evacuation had gone slower than Eddie had anticipated. He had seen a young turbaned Sikh arguing with the Russian,

Savich, and assumed that he was refusing to sacrifice the expensive drydock when the volcano finally blew. Unloading the ship meant they wouldn't have any incriminating evidence when they sailed away.

Like the other ships already littering the beach, the newest vessel brought to Kamchatka was a cruise liner. At around four hundred feet it wasn't large, but she had rakish lines, a classic champagne-glass stern, and balconies for nearly all the cabins. In her prime she would have filled a niche market for only the wealthiest passengers, those willing to pay anything for a chance to visit the Galapagos or explore the Antarctic wastes.

Today she was just another derelict, her once bright hull smeared with the excrement of those poor souls who'd endured the harsh journey to Russia. Hundreds of Chinese immigrants crowded the rail as the cruise ship was left to drift in the bay. Because her engines had been removed and she was unballasted, she rode so high that a thick band of antifouling paint could be seen above her waterline. Even the smallest waves made her roll dangerously. Eddie could hear the cries of the people trapped aboard her when a big wave sent the vessel reeling.

Fortunately, the tide was coming in, and it drove the ship closer and closer to the beach. With the winds whipping up the frigid bay, Eddie knew that a storm was coming. Hopefully the vessel would soundly ground herself onshore before it hit; otherwise she would drift back to sea. If that happened he knew the liner would turn broadside to the wind and capsize when the swells hit above ten feet. She carried no lifeboats.

Eddie switched his attention from the drifting cruise ship back to the drydock. Her massive bow doors had been closed once again, and water jetted from pump outlets along her hull. It would take several hours for her hold to be drained of seawater and make her light enough for one of the tugs to take her away. The second of the two tugs that had brought the drydock north had been maneuvered into position about a hundred yards from the ore processing building.

As Eddie had noted earlier, the processing plant had been built on a flat barge that had been towed to the bay. They had used heavy equipment to drag the large structure high above the tide line. Under the watchful eye of armed guards, workers were now clearing debris and rocks that had washed onto the beach behind the plant so the tugboat could haul it back into the sea. Drums of machine oil were standing by to be poured onto the rocky shore to ease the barge's progress back to the water. Paulus, the South African supervisor, had ordered that all the excess mercury be dumped in an area beyond the processing plant. Lakes of shimmering mercury collected in pools that eventually drained into the sea. Already wave action had claimed hundreds of gallons of the toxic metal.

The Chinese laborers given this dangerous job were those who had already been exposed to fatal doses of mercury vapor working in the plant. Most moved like zombies, their brains destroyed by the cumulative effects of mercury poisoning, while others were so afflicted with tremors they could barely stand. If by some miracle they survived the next few days, they would never recover from the exposure. And even if they did, they had received such high doses that generations of their children would suffer unspeakable birth defects.

Eddie burned the image of the brain-damaged workers splashing about amid the mercury puddles into his mind. He was so intent that he didn't realize the worker next to him had finished filling his plastic bucket with muddy ore. The young Chinese tried to catch Eddie's attention, but a guard noticed the lapse first. He lashed out with a weighted piece of hose that caught Eddie behind the knee. His leg buckled, but he refused to allow himself to fall. He knew not to even glance at the guard, because such defiance would send the Indonesian into a frenzy that in his condition Eddie didn't know if he could survive.

He hoisted the fifty-pound bucket onto his shoulder, smearing old abrasions that wouldn't heal in the constant damp. Eddie's roommate from the cruise ship, Tang, had timed his work so the two of them would trudge down the hill together. Of the original ten men crammed into the cabin when Eddie first arrived, only he and Tang were still alive.

"I think they are leaving today," Tang said out of the corner of his mouth, his eyes downcast on the treacherous footing.

"I believe you're right, my friend. The drydock will be empty soon, and it won't take them long to drag the processing plant off the beach. And have you noticed the fishing boats haven't been around for a while?"

"How can I not?" Tang replied with a sparkle in his voice. "The only thing worse than ground-up fish paste is three-day-old ground-up fish paste." They maneuvered around a particularly tricky spot before Tang remarked, "There is also what is happening around the ship the guards use as their dormitory."

For the past few days a double-ended tender had been making trips between the dormitory ship and the tug they were going to use to take away the processing plant. The area around the dorm ship had always been off limits to the Chinese, but since the transfer had begun the number of guards had doubled. Most of them were Indonesian, but there were also a handful of hard-looking Europeans who reported to Savich and not the Sikh. Judging by their discipline, Eddie thought they were ex–special forces, Russia's elite Spetsnaz. He could also tell that the Russians were as suspicious of the Indonesian guards as they were the laborers.

It didn't take a genius to know that they were transporting the gold they had already processed. Judging by how low the thirty-foot tender was in the water when she motored out to the tug, Eddie estimated they'd moved a hundred tons of bullion. The gold was being stacked in two shipping containers lashed to the tug's deck.

"What do you think will happen to us?" Tang asked.

"I told you what I heard Paulus tell Anton Savich, that they're going to leave us behind."

"So, we die on this forsaken stretch of coast whether they are here or not."

Eddie could tell from the sorrow in Tang's words that the younger man had reached his emotional and psychological limit. Like in any survival situation, keeping a positive attitude was half the battle to stay alive. In the past week Eddie had seen people endure unbelievable hardships because they would not let it penetrate their souls, while others had died in a few days, almost as if they willed their deaths to come quickly. Eddie knew that if Tang lost hope now, he wouldn't last the day.

"Listen to me; we are not going to die here."

Tang shot Eddie a wan smile. "Thank you for your strength, but I am afraid your words are empty."

"I'm not Chinese," Eddie said, and then corrected himself. "Well, I am Chinese, but I was raised in New York City. I am an American investigating illegal immigrant smuggling. There is a team of people looking for me right now."

"Is this true?"

Using his best De Niro, Eddie said in English, "You talkin' to me? You talkin' to me?"

Tang stopped and stared, unable to believe what he'd just heard. "I know this movie!" he exclaimed.

"You've seen *Taxi Driver*?"

"Yes! We were shown it in school because it was so decadent that it drove one of your people to try to kill the president."

Eddie chuckled, imagining some Communist party official putting a spin on how Hinckley's attempted assassination of Reagan related to a breakdown of our running dog capitalist ways.

"You really are an American?"

"Yes," Eddie said. "And very soon a ship's going to enter the bay."

Tang looked over his shoulder at the smoldering volcano. It was a couple miles up from the beach but seemed to blot out half the horizon. Ominously, the ash had stopped spewing from the caldera, though it continued to drift over the work site.

"I know," was all Eddie could answer to the unasked question.

"Hey, look," Tang pointed out to sea. The pair of fishing trawlers was headed back toward the beach. "Fresh slop tonight, eh?"

Eddie watched the squat boats for a moment. Gulls swarmed around their fantails. There was no logical reason for them to return. Savich was abandoning the Chinese in the shadow of an erupting volcano, so why would he bother feed them? Then he noticed that they were moving faster than normal; white foam boiled around their blunt bows, and the seabirds had to wing hard to keep pace. Their holds were empty, Eddie realized, and he saw, too, that they weren't headed for the jetty but angling more toward the tugboat in position to pull the processing plant from the beach.

Eddie's senses went on high alert, sending a jolt of adrenaline that could make him forget, at least temporarily, his exhaustion and misery. The Russian guards must have felt the same thing. They clutched their weapons a little tighter and instinctively moved to cover positions.

"Follow me," Eddie ordered.

He and Tang were near the sluice boxes, twenty yards from the separating plant. If his fears were correct, the two of them were much too exposed. He led Tang around the far side of the long metal tables and up the hillside, trying to put as much distance between them and the coming crossfire.

"What is happening?" Tang panted.

Before he could reply, automatic gunfire rippled from the nearest trawler. The dozen Spetsnaz had already found sufficient cover, so they could ignore the incoming rounds and instead concentrate on taking out the Indonesian guards who'd turned their weapons on them. The battle reached a fever pitch in less than five seconds. Tracer fire cut the smoggy air like laser beams, and laborers too slow or too disorientated to dive out of the way were cut down indiscriminately.

There had to be fifty or more Indonesians with more joining the fight in an attempt to overwhelm the Russians, but the Russians' superior training and better weapons more than evened the odds. None had been hit in the ambush, and as the fight became more fixed, they were picking off their foes with near impunity.

The timing of the betrayal was nearly flawless. Savich and Jan Paulus were on the cruise ship where the gold had been stored. The Sikh, the likely architect of the double cross, was already on the tug with a few of his guards overseeing the transfer. With the oceangoing towboat securely fastened to the processing barge by inches-thick cables, the vessel's captain couldn't make a run for it.

A jet of black smoke erupted from the funnel of the other tug, the one connected to the drydock, and the black water under her stern turned into a whirlpool as her isopod screws dug in. They were making their escape before the drydock was completely empty.

A swarm of guards came running down the hill past Eddie and Tang. They had been on duty up where workers blasted ore from the hillside with the water cannons. Hidden by a boulder, Eddie waited until one of the guards came too close. In a lightning move, he rammed the heel of his hand into the man's nose. The guard's momentum, more than Eddie's strength, shattered the nose and sent shards of bone into his brain. He was dead before he fell to the muddy ground.

Eddie checked to make sure no one had seen his attack and grabbed up the fallen AK-47.

With adrenaline still coursing through his veins, he turned to Tang and said, "Payback time."

THE *Oregon* found herself in the teeth of the worst storm to hit the Sea of Okhotsk in a quarter century. It was the confluence of two low-pressure areas, ravenous holes in the atmosphere that sucked in great draughts of air from every point on the compass so the wind shrieked with a banshee's wail and the tops of the waves were ripped clean off. The sky was an oppressive gray curtain that clung to the sea, split occasionally by electric blue forks of lightning. The temperature had dropped to the forties, so hail fell with the rain that pummeled the freighter in horizontal sheets.

The ship would rise up the backs of the tallest waves, driven by her high-tech engines until her bow pointed straight at the roiled clouds. Her bow cleaving a fat wedge through the crest was marked with explosions of seafoam that mushroomed as high as her funnel. She stood poised atop the wave for what seemed an eternity, exposed to the worst of the wind, and then her stern would rise as she plummeted down the back of the roller, her engines suddenly silenced because there was no water to force through her jets. In the sheltered lee of the towering wave the sound of the wind fell away, so an eerie quiet descended on the ship. Down the eleven-thousand-ton ship would drop so that all the bridge crew could see was the surging black of the ocean.

The *Oregon* plowed into the sea so that her bows were buried up to her first set of hatches. The sudden deceleration buckled everyone's legs and made dangling radio cords slap the ceiling. The magnetohydrodynamic engines screamed as they rammed the ship through the sea, their sheer power able to push aside the water and raise her bow. A waist-high surge of seawater raced across her deck, swamping her derricks and pounding into the superstructure with enough force to shake the entire vessel. The water sloshed over her railings and poured from her scuppers like opened fire hydrants.

As the last of the water finally drained away, the bow would begin the laborious climb up the next wave, and the cycle would repeat.

Two things enabled the *Oregon* to make any speed in the naked face of such a powerful storm: her remarkable power plants and the sheer will of her master.

Cabrillo was strapped into his command seat in the operations center. He wore jeans, a black sweatshirt, and a watch cap. He hadn't shaved since the *Oregon* plowed into the storm, so his cheeks and jaw were heavily stubbled. His blue eyes were rimmed red with exhaustion and tension, but they hadn't yet lost their predatory sharpness.

The senior bridge staff had the watch, which put Eric Stone at the helm. His station's flat-screen displays gave him a panoramic view around the ship so he could anticipate and compensate for the bigger waves. He had such a fine touch on the rudder and throttles that he could coax more speed out of the *Oregon* than her sophisticated autopilot.

Juan watched him work the ship, keeping an eye on the speed indicators above the central display screen. Her speed through the water, speed over the bottom, and drift were all measured using the global positioning system, and only when the big freighter bottomed out in the wave troughs did she lose any momentum.

Cabrillo had thrown caution to the wind, literally, in this mad dash up the Sea of Okhotsk. He was trying to outrace the fast-moving storm. The prize would go to the first to reach the coastline where Eddie Seng's transponder said he was stranded. With the storm tracking northward at eight knots, the *Oregon* and her crew had been subjected to two full days of constant punishment. Juan didn't want to contemplate the strain the engines were going through, and he'd politely told Max Hanley where he could shove his disapproval.

He'd had no choice but to suspend most routine maintenance and with it too rough to cook, the crew had subsisted on U.S. Army issue MREs, meals ready to eat, known affectionately as morsels of recycled entrails, and coffee.

But the gamble was paying off. The latest meteorological information showed them nearing the storm's leading edge, and already the barometer was rising. To his seasoned eye the freezing rain seemed to have lost its needle edge, while the swells, still towering, were coming with less frequency.

Juan called up their position on the GPS and did some mental calculations. Eddie was sixty miles away, and once they broke free of the storm, he could probably increase speed to forty knots. That would put the *Oregon* off the coast in an hour and a half with the storm barreling in on them less than six hours later. If he was right about there being thousands of Chinese laborers being used in a gold mining operation, then the window to rescue them was just too tight. They could pack maybe a few hundred onto the *Oregon*, a thousand if they jettisoned the submersibles and the Robinson helicopter, but given the ferocity of the storm, the impending volcanic eruption, and the weakened condition of the people he expected to find, the death toll could be staggering.

He had worked with guys in the CIA, mostly senior case officers, who could imagine such loss of life with the indifference of an actuary reading columns of numbers, but he had never developed skin thick enough for that. In truth he wouldn't let himself lose that much of his own humanity even if it meant paying for it with nightmares and guilt.

"Chairman, I have a contact." Linda Ross spoke without straightening from the radar repeater.

"What have you got?"

She glanced over at him, her elfin face looking even younger in the glow of the battle lights. "Storm's playing havoc with the returns, but I think it's the sister drydock to the *Maus*. I'm getting two hits forty miles out in close proximity. One's a lot bigger than the other, so I think it's the *Souri* and a tug."

"Course and speed?"

"She's headed due south from where Eddie's transponder has been pinging, and she's not making more than six knots. She'll pass at least ten miles to starboard if we don't change course to intercept."

Juan called over to Hali Kasim at the comm station. "Any change on Eddie's signal?"

"Last sweep was eight hours ago. He hasn't moved."

Again Juan ran the numbers. It was possible given the *Souri*'s speed and the amount of ocean she'd covered that Eddie was aboard her, but his gut was telling him his crewmate and friend was still on the beach.

"Ignore the *Souri*."

"Chairman?"

"You heard me. Ignore her." Juan knew he could leave it at that, and his orders would be followed implicitly, but he felt he had to give them more. Since his conversation with Tory before heading into the storm he hadn't uttered a sentence with more than five words. His concern, even fear, at what they'd find on Kamchatka had sent his thoughts inward. Now that they were getting close, he needed his crew to understand his logic.

"Once she hits the storm," he said, "the tug is going to have to haul that pig against thirty-knot winds with the drydock's hull acting like an enormous sail the entire time. Even if they ballast her down to reduce her profile, they won't make any headway in this slop. There's a good chance they even might be driven northward again. All this will give us enough time to reach Eddie, do whatever the hell we can, and then cut back south and take the *Souri* on the high seas."

Juan saw that everyone on the bridge agreed with his logic, although he could see in their faces they wanted to take the easy prey first. He expected no less from them.

"Now," he continued, "we were burned the last time we shadowed one of Shere Singh's drydocks. They have radar capabilities that probably rival our own, so I want full jamming on her, a complete radar blackout."

Linda Ross raised her hand slightly. "If they have the kind of sophisticated gear we think they do, they'll have to know they're being jammed."

"Not if we hit them now," Juan answered.

"He's right," Hali added. "Their radar is looking into the storm and is picking up so much backscatter from the waves and lightning that they can't see us yet, and if we hit the jammers, they never will."

"Hit them with everything we've got," Cabrillo ordered. "Full spectrum across the board, radar, radio, satellite uplinks, the works. Mr. Stone, I still want to give them a wide berth. Change course so they don't come within twenty miles of us just to be safe."

"Aye, aye," the helmsman replied, punching in the course correction on his computer.

Thirty minutes later the radar began picking up strong returns from the beach. There were six distinct metallic contacts. Five of them were actually grounded on the coast while another, presumably a tugboat, held station in deeper water a hundred yards from shore.

Juan wanted to send up their last aerial drone to photograph the area, but George Adams told him the light radio-controlled plane wouldn't last ten seconds in the wind. Juan considered his offer to risk a quick scout flight in the Robinson. Having the tactical data about what they were getting into was important; however, the element of surprise was just as crucial. Also, the atmosphere was still heavy with ash that would likely overwhelm the helo's air filtration system and bring the chopper down.

"Thanks, but I want to keep you in reserve," Cabrillo spoke into a pin mike headset. Adams was in the *Oregon*'s hangar. "Maintain ten-minute alert but be ready to push it to five once we engage." Five-minute alert meant the hatches over the hold were opened and the Robinson had been lifted up to the deck with her engines running and up to temperature.

"Roger that, Chairman."

"Senior staff, give me a status report." One by one his people called in. Murph at the weapons station had lowered the plates covering the Gatling gun and the 40 mm autocannon. The deck-mounted gimble .50s were locked and loaded, and a pair of torpedoes were in the twin tubes with the outer hull doors closed. He also reported all cameras were up and functioning. Hali was going to run double duty on the communications and radar systems so Linda Ross could accompany the assault team. Max Hanley was grumbling his way up from the engine room where he would take overall command as well as direct the damage control teams. Linc and his gun dogs were kitting up in the boat garage and reported Linda had just arrived. Doc Huxley was ready in the medical bay, having co-opted the entire kitchen staff for nursing duty.

Juan switched to the ship-wide channel. "Attention all hands, this is the Chairman. Here's the score. One of our own is on that beach. Each and every one of us has owed our life to Eddie Seng at some point since we started serving together, so his rescue is our top priority. Secondary to that is saving as many of the Chinese immigrants as we can. We don't yet know their number or condition, so our response to them has to remain flexible. Number three is the volcano above the site that's about as stable as the psych ward at Bellevue. That, along with the storm that's barreling down on us like the hammers of hell, means speed is of the essence. We're in and out as quickly as possible. I will not risk the ship or crew if it looks like we're running out of time.

"I'm not going to give you Henry V at Agincourt or Nelson at the gate. Each of you knows your duty and knows that every other crew member is relying on you. We're facing an unusual situation for us. This contract has gone far beyond what we were hired to do. This is no longer about pirates preying on ships in the Sea of Japan. It is about traffickers smuggling the most precious commodity on earth, human life. We're here not to line our pockets but because it is our duty as members of a civilized society to stand up and be counted among those who believe in what is right.

"All of you have had time to think about this, knowing that this moment was coming. Well, the moment is now, ladies and gentlemen. In less than an hour we engage an unknown force with the fate of untold lives depending on us. I know you will not let them down."

He clicked off the radio and immediately got back on the net. There was humor in his voice this time. "Sorry, that did come off a bit like Nelson. Now let's go out there and kick some ass."

24

CABRILLO stopped at his cabin on the way to meet the assault team. He changed out of his clothes, donning black fatigues, a Kevlar vest, and a combat harness. While most of the Corporation's small arms were kept in a weapons locker, Juan kept his in an antique safe in the corner of his office, a relic from a long-defunct railroad's Santa Fe depot. He fitted a pair of his FN Five-seveN pistols into kidney holsters, sacrificing a small amount of weight for the seconds he'd save not having to reload. Because he was leading a large force of seven operatives, they'd already decided to standardize their assault rifles. He grabbed up an M-4A1 and slid six spare magazines into the appropriate pouches. He didn't bother carrying a second knife, just the four-inch Gerber hanging inverted from his shoulder strap.

He strapped on a pair of knee pads, flexing a couple of times to settle them properly, and slid his hands into fingerless gloves with thick leather patches to protect his palms. He caught his reflection in the bathroom mirror. The determination and drive that had sustained him through the CIA and led to the creation of the Corporation was in his eyes, hewn flint-hard and focused. Game face, they'd called it, that single-minded convergence of training, experience, and will.

Once again Juan was going to step beyond himself, sacrifice for others by maybe sacrificing himself. He looked hard into his eyes, saw an unforgiving gleam, and abruptly laughed aloud.

Game face or no, Juan also knew he thrived on the danger. Why else would he be in this business? Adrenaline and endorphins were starting their siren song, humming at the base of his skull, giving him that high that only those who'd been there understand. Facing an enemy meant facing yourself. Conquering that enemy gave affirmation of what you always believed about who you are.

The boat garage was cold and clammy, crowded with men and women making final preparations. Rather than use a Zodiac, most of the garage was taken up with a SEAL assault boat, a rubber-rimmed polycarbonate-hulled craft with a modestly protected central wheelhouse and twin outboard engines. The boat could handle any sea thrown at it and could reach speeds approaching fifty knots.

The lights in the garage had been dialed down to match the outside overcast, so everyone's face looked drawn and pale. Their eyes, however, were bright and their motions swift and sure as they checked over each other's equipment. The sound of magazines being slapped home and actions being cocked was a reassuring symphony to Cabrillo's ears.

He caught Tory Ballinger's eye across the room. She had agreed, reluctantly, to stay with the assault boat when the team hit the beach. The Corporation mercenaries had trained together more times than any of them could count and been under fire more than any wanted to remember. In combat they moved and thought as one by seeming to read each other's minds. He made her realize that her presence among them would jeopardize that hard-won unit cohesion.

He couldn't dissuade her from coming on the raid, and he hadn't really tried that hard. He saw that she needed to be part of this because of her survivor's guilt over the attack on the *Avalon*. Until she'd exacted some measure of revenge, that incident would haunt her for the rest of her life. And he planned to help by making sure she'd see a little action as everything unfolded.

Tory gave him a thumbs-up and a silent nod. He shot her a cocky grin that made her smile.

Cabrillo's headset crackled. "Juan, it's Max."

"Go ahead."

"Murph says the video is about to come online. I'm piping it down to you."

"Roger."

Juan vaulted the assault boat's gunwale and flipped on the cockpit flat-panel display. Autostabilizers built into the camera mounts compensated for the constant pitching and rolling, and Murph was doing a good job zooming in on what was unfolding as the *Oregon* steamed into the bay.

The feeds flipped at a steady pace, first showing Juan an intense firefight near a large metal building built on a barge, then men who were clones of the pirates they'd taken out weeks ago attacking a tugboat that was in place to tow the barge; next he saw hundreds of Chinese workers running across the sloping moonscape of mud and boulders to get away from the expanding gun battles. He saw that the ships they'd picked up on radar were old cruise liners. All but one had settled deep into the beach, driven almost to their load lines by waves and tidal action. The lone exception might be a new arrival. Although the breakers that slammed her hull couldn't make the vessel rock, she had yet to settle into the rocky beach. Finally Murph showed him a quick shot of the volcano in the distance. Its peak was wreathed in steam and smoke.

Cabrillo quickly sized up the tactical and strategic situation and began relaying instructions. His orders sent every member of the crew scrambling. Their shouts and calls echoed down the ship's long passageways as they made their preparations. The Chairman had called for a desperation Hail Mary–type play, and for it to work he needed everyone at their sharpest.

A few minutes later the ship was close enough to the fighting to attract attention. The troops dressed in identical black uniforms, all of whom were Caucasians, ignored the *Oregon,* while the ragged-looking Indonesians fired hasty pot shots at the ship.

As soon as a pair of deckhands manhandled a large beam with lengths of chain on each end onto the assault boat, Juan ordered Eric Stone to turn the freighter away from the shoreline. While this presented a larger target to the gunmen, it allowed Cabrillo and the shore team to open the boat garage without being seen.

As the door rose smoothly upward, the shore team leapt into the assault boat, locking their arms through purpose-made restraining loops. Each team member called out as soon as they were secured. The driver, Mike Trono, fired the engine, and Juan nodded to the garage boat master. Like a giant slingshot, a series of hydraulic pulleys launched the boat down the ramp and out of the garage. The acceleration was brutal and got worse as Trono lowered the props into the water. The massive outboards bit deep, throwing a rooster tail of water back into the *Oregon* as the nimble craft came up to plane.

Cold air ripped at any exposed skin like sandpaper, and the sting of drops of water that hit them were cold enough to burn. The assault boat rocketed around the rust-streaked freighter, carving a fat wedge into the black sea. By the time anyone on the beach noticed the boat, they were moving at fifty knots, much too fast to accurately engage.

Trono constantly juked the boat across the sea as he made for the spot where Juan had indicated he wanted to land. It was in the shadow of one of the beached cruise ships, one that was so heavily grounded that workers had built a stone ramp up to the main deck. The area around the ship was strewn with trash too heavy for the surf to take away.

The boat arrowed through the breaking surf and had such a shallow draft that the team had only a couple of yards to wade to find cover on the boulder-strewn beach. Juan and Link dropped behind a house-sized chunk of stone that had been blown from the volcano during some prehistoric eruption. The assault boat had already worked its way back off the beach. Juan looked to make sure Tory had followed his orders to stay aboard, and his estimation of her rose another few notches as he saw her standing in the open pilothouse between Mike Trono and an ex-marine named Pulaski.

"What do you think, boss?" Linc asked.

"Looks to me we dropped in the middle of a little war here. I bet Singh is paying the Indonesians while Anton Savich's guys are the ones in black."

"So the enemy of my enemy ain't necessarily my friend, eh?"

"That's the attitude I'm taking."

The team worked their way up the hillside, keeping the cruise ship between them and the main area of combat. Dozens of wide-eyed Chinese workers lay on the ground, cowering. They didn't know what to make of the armed patrol. Juan tried to urge them to find cover, but they were all paralyzed with fear, and he gave up.

If he hoped to rescue any of the Chinese, he knew they'd have to put an end to the fighting.

"Chairman, we're ready," Max called over the tactical net.

The *Oregon* had shifted position. The doors covering her Gatling gun were still closed, although the ship had maneuvered to give it a clear line on the two fishing trawlers lashed to the tug.

"We're about set, too. Any luck finding Eddie?"

"Negative. Hali's taken over the cameras from Murph so he can concentrate on weapons control. He's getting good shots, but there are so damned many people on the beach that it takes a few seconds for the computer's facial recognition software to sort through them all."

"Check the area closest to the fighting. If Eddie's in any kind of shape, that's where he'll be."

"Good thinking. Hali?"

"I heard," the Corporation's comm officer said. "Shifting focus now."

Cabrillo and his people reached a level strip of land several hundred yards above the beach. Further toward the center of the site was an area that had been heavily dug up. Water cannons for blasting the tough soil lay abandoned, their nozzles pointed skyward. The ground was littered with shovels and buckets. All the workers had fled, and their guards had gone down to join the fight.

They approached the workings cautiously, weapons held at the ready, eyes never settling on one spot for more than a second.

An explosion echoed up from below, a grenade blast behind the barge that momentarily drew their attention. The black-clad body of one of Savich's men pinwheeled in a lazy arc before falling to the beach in a broken-limbed heap. At the same second came the chatter of an AK-47 firing at point-blank range.

Cabrillo dropped flat as clods of mud were thrown up all around him. He stitched the area around one of the water cannons in a reflex shot that emptied half a magazine. It was poor fire discipline but it forced the attacker to dodge for cover, and his gun fell silent.

Linc had a better bead. He fired a three-round burst that sent the Indonesian pitching backward into a coffee-colored retention pond. His body vanished under the surface while his blood stained the water. The team found cover behind an earthen berm as more Indonesians appeared out of nowhere. The sheer volume of gunfire made the air ripple.

"We don't have time for this," Linda Ross shouted over the din, changing out her magazine.

Juan looked down the hill. The assault boat was getting into position, and they would need the cover fire from the *Oregon*'s Gatling gun, but he couldn't afford to remain pinned down. The oldest adage of warfare, that no plan survives first contact with the enemy, had never felt more true.

He called the boat over his throat microphone. "Mike, can you hear me?" When there was no reply, he called again. The boat was still moving at fifty knots, enveloped in a cocoon of engine noise that made communications impossible.

He cursed and called up Mark Murphy. "Murph, we need you. There's about fifty bandits above us. We're pinned."

"Mike's about to hit the tug." Murphy pointed out.

"And the longer you question me, the closer he's getting."

"Roger that," he replied, then muttered under his breath, "Sorry, Mike."

AS soon as the last of the assault team jumped over the gunwales, Mike Trono reversed engines and drew the boat off the beach, maneuvering backward until he had the sea room to spin around.

He pulled down his headset to talk to Tory as the boat built speed. "Can I ask you something, ma'am?"

"Only if you promise to never call me ma'am again."

"Sorry." Trono grinned. "Force of habit."

"What's your question?"

"Do you know how to operate a boat?"

"I work for Lloyd's of London. My entire life revolves around boats. I'm a licensed captain on anything up to twenty thousand tons, which includes your *Oregon* before you turned it into something out of *Star Wars.*"

"So this assault craft?" He stamped the deck.

"Seems to handle as well as the Riva speedboat I rented on my last holiday in Spain. Why the inquiry?"

"Because we have a little job to do, and I need you to man the helm while Pulaski and I take care of it."

"I assume it has to do with that piece of steel that was loaded before we left your ship?"

"Captain's orders. He thinks we can salvage a bit more than a bunch of immigrants from this nightmare."

A smile lit Tory's eyes, and her cheeks blushed more than what the wind caused. "Why am I not surprised?"

They had shot across the bay, circling behind the *Oregon* again for cover, and now were headed for the tugboat. One of the trawlers was drifting away from the tug's flank, while the other remained tightly lashed. There were men scrambling all over the decks. Most were pirates, but a few were crewmen desperately trying to defend their ship. Some of the pirates had added another level to their butchery by switching to machetes to dispatch the last of the crew.

The timing was critical, but with Murph watching their back over the Gatling's sights, the assault boat charged into the battle. They were twenty yards out when Mike remembered he'd taken off his headset. As soon as he settled it over his ears, he heard the shrieking scream of the six-barreled Gatling gun, and he goosed the throttles a little more.

The expected destruction as the 20 mm shells ripped apart the pirates' boats and cleared the tug's deck never came. Instead, pirates began shooting at the lightly protected assault boat from over the tug's railing. The boat ran into a steam of gunfire. Rounds from their AK-47s punctured the inflatable curtain ringing the craft, raked the deck, and ricocheted off the outboards, miraculously missing everyone. Trono tried to wrench the wheel to get away from the tug as fast as possible, screaming to Mark Murphy to find out what went wrong.

The ground between Cabrillo and the Indonesians exploded, churned up by five hundred depleted uranium bullets. A four-foot-thick layer of earth was stripped away by the onslaught, exposing the gunmen where they'd been hiding behind the rim of the pond. Those that weren't hit directly were torn apart by flying rocks. The entire group was blown into an oblivion of bloody mist and debris.

Linc took point to check for survivors, and while his search was thorough, he also knew it was unnecessary. Nothing could have survived that.

"We're clear."

Juan drew his people together. "From here on out our element of surprise is blown, but we'll stick to the plan, flank the fighting down below, and try to find Eddie. I only hope he's built a level of trust with some of the other Chinese because if we're going to save any of them, we're going to need him."

They started off down the slope.

* * *

EDDIE Seng had remained hidden, watching to see how the fighters would react to the *Oregon* steaming into the bay. As he'd expected, the Russians ignored the distraction and continued to fight with skill and discipline. They had made a sizable dent in the number of Indonesians, but the sheer numbers were becoming overwhelming. Of the dozen who'd been caught in the initial ambush, four were dead and three were wounded, although they could still defend their position. The tide of Indonesians continued to hammer at the hillock the Russians had taken as a crude fort. The outcome of the gun battle was inevitable, and the Russians knew it. They weren't fighting for their lives anymore. This was now all about dying with honor.

Something caught Eddie's attention on the far side of the processing building. The range was extreme, but he thought he saw Jan Paulus emerge from the dormitory ship. It was Paulus, and he was starting to climb up to the helipad where Anton Savich's helicopter sat idle. He was with another man, and by the way they walked it appeared that Paulus was holding a pistol to his head. It was most likely he had taken the contract pilot hostage to fly him out. There was no sign of Anton Savich, and Eddie wondered if the South African had already killed him.

Pursuing the mine overseer was a tactical mistake, but the flame of rage that ignited in Eddie's chest blocked out any chance of rationality. The weeks of pain, starvation, and deprivation had exacted a toll on his soul that would take a long time to heal. Killing the sadistic miner would at least start him on the journey. He'd already told Tang to gather as many of the other workers as he could and head for the newly grounded cruise ship. Of any of the vessels littering the forlorn beach, it had the best chance of surviving the eruption if Juan didn't think of a way out of this mess.

His body was in no condition to chase Paulus, and yet when he started after the man, Eddie's legs felt as powerful as coiled springs and his lungs pumped air like a blacksmith's bellows. He felt alive for the first time since turning over his life to the snakeheads back in Lantan village. If any of the fighters noticed him as he dashed around rusted shipping containers and other equipment left lying about, they quickly dismissed him as just an anonymous worker trying to save himself. He'd hidden the AK-47 under the loose shirt he'd scavenged from a dead guard.

Once he was beyond the worst of the fighting he stumbled across the motor launch that had been used to transfer the gold out to the tug. It was in a secluded bay well sheltered from the rest of the beach by massive boulders, and as he stepped into the open, eight pirates who had been making ready to launch the craft looked up in unison. They should have ignored him like the others, but one went for his gun. Eddie dashed to his left as a stream of bullets chiseled at the boulder near his shoulder. He unlimbered his AK, waited for the firing to stop, and stepped back around the corner.

The gunman had turned to laugh with his comrades at the sport of it all. The first three-round burst sent his lifeless corpse sprawling into the startled arms of his friend. The second blew that man to the ground. Eddie killed one more before they got organized and made to fire back. He ducked out of the way again, quickly slinging his rifle, and began to climb the slick side of the boulder.

It was only eight feet tall, but Eddie barely had the strength to make it. His arms quivered at the strain of lifting his own diminished body weight, and the AK-47 felt like a hundred-pound rucksack. The boat's motor roared to life just as he reached the summit. He slithered over the rounded top of the boulder, trying to bring his weapon to bear. The engine's beat changed as the prop dug into the surf.

One of the pirates must have guessed his intentions, because chips of rock were suddenly blown from the boulder as at least four guns opened up from below. Eddie clamped his hands over his head as stinging chips of stone struck his skin like he'd fallen into a wasps' nest. They maintained their fire until the boat was so far away that they couldn't keep the boulder steady in their sights.

Eddie chanced looking up. The pirates were headed for the tug where a SEAL assault boat from the *Oregon* was coming under heavy fire from gunmen aboard the large vessel. Whatever plan Juan had devised had seriously come part. There were only a couple of people on the assault boat. They needed cover fire from the *Oregon* if they were going to attack the tug, and yet the Gatling remained silent.

Then the multibarreled machine gun opened up. A ten-foot tongue of flame jetted from the weapons bay, and a section of hill where there were a bunch of retention ponds high above the beach vanished in a hammering volley that sent dirt flying thirty feet or more into the air.

Unable to warn the assault boat about the approaching tender, Eddie slithered down the boulder and took off again after Jan Paulus.

FIRING with one hand while the other worked the wheel, Mike Trono added to the gunfire pouring off the assault boat as they countered the pirates' initial barrage. Tory was hunkered low on the floorboards, firing precisely aimed shots at the pirates lining the tug's rail. She had the accuracy of an Olympic marksman and the patience of a sniper.

The weapon felt perfectly balanced in her hands as she squeezed the trigger for a fifth time. Her target had ducked behind the railing's metal plating, but the shot would keep his head down for a few critical seconds. Another gore-spattered gunman raised himself suddenly, hosing the sea with his AK-47 before homing in on the fleeing boat. Tory aimed carefully, her body anticipating the wave action, and she pulled the trigger. The light bullet sparked off the railing just in front of the Indonesian and ricocheted into his chest just below the sternum, lifting him high off his feet.

"Hold on!" Trono shouted. "We're going back in. Cease fire."

He twisted the wheel once again and set the boat on a collision course with the squat tugboat. Because they weren't being fired on, many of the pirates stood up to draw a bead on the craft.

"Showtime," Murph said over Trono's radio.

The *Oregon*'s weapons officer shifted the Gatling from the hill and sent a few seconds' burst into the drifting trawler. The boat was ripped to pieces in a hail of wood splinters and shredded netting. The pilot-house disintegrated. Seabirds gorging themselves on offal left to slop on the deck took flight as their world came apart. Then the stream of bullets penetrated the engine room, tearing the big diesel from its mount before puncturing the fuel tank. The resulting explosion sent a greasy fireball climbing into the sky, and the seas were raked with shrapnel.

What little remained of the trawler sank instantly, snuffing out the flames in a gout of steam.

The destruction on the tug was less dramatic when Murph pivoted the Gatling gun and gave the trigger another squirt. As though caught by a broadside of grape shot, the pirates were scythed down by the fusillade. A hundred ragged holes appeared in the big shipping containers lashed to the deck, and glass from the aft-facing secondary bridge, used by the crew to check their charges under tow, fell in a glittering cascade that further mutilated the corpses. Murph hosed the deck with autofire, making certain that no one was left alive.

"That should hold 'em," Murph whooped.

Mike Trono danced the assault boat up to the lowest section of railing and turned the controls over to Tory. "Just hold it here. We won't be a minute."

"Why are you doing this, anyway?" she asked, standing aside while Pulaski and Trono manhandled the heavy steel girder onto the tug's low deck.

He handed her his tactical radio and gave her a wolfish smile. "Chairman thinks there's booty aboard, and not the kind a Hollywood hottie's packing."

The men levered themselves onto the deck. Hard years of training forced them to visually check to make sure no one had survived. It was a gruesome task, something out of a horror movie, because the Gatling had minced the bodies into what Trono could only describe as a sort of chunky paste. Leaving the assault boat burbling along the tug's flank, they hoisted the beam onto their shoulders and waded through the carnage toward one of the containers.

Trono pulled his Glock and shot the lock off one of them while Pulaski maneuvered the beam so they could drag it up to the top. The hinges screamed as Trono swung open one of the doors and just as quickly closed it again. Pulaski shot him a questioning look.

"Chairman's right again."

"Gold?"

"Gold."

He hoisted himself up the container with a boost from his partner, and together they levered the two-hundred-pound beam to the top. Trono looked up as they began to thread the lengths of chain through the lifting hardpoints. A small runabout was racing out from shore, hidden from Murph's vantage by the bulk of the tugboat. He counted a half dozen armed men bobbing in the craft as it crashed through the surf line and into smoother water.

"We got trouble."

Pulaski looked over his shoulder. "Damn!"

The boat would reach them in seconds, not the minutes they needed to secure the beam to the container, but they weren't about to abandon their prize. Mike shouted down to Tory, "We've got company. Bunch of goons in an open tender. Get the hell out of here."

"I'm not leaving you behind."

"We're not being heroic. We need you to draw them out so Murph can hose 'em with the Gatling."

Tory understood and slammed the throttles to their stops. The assault boat shot away from the tug, turning sharply so she passed behind the ship. She'd forgotten about the thick tow cables still securing the tug to the barge on shore. With no time to maneuver she shot under the first cable, ducking as the thick steel tore the standing cockpit from its mounts. Had her reactions been an instant slower, the hawser would have decapitated her.

The boat flashed under the second cable, angling to cut off the approaching tender. She was going so fast that the men on the boat could only stare as she bashed her boat into theirs. One of the men tumbled over the tender's side, and by the time any of them thought to reach for their guns, Tory was twenty yards away and accelerating like a greyhound.

She slalomed the assault boat as the men began firing on her. She was exhilarated by the adrenaline pumping through her veins. "I know, I know, bloody women drivers. Hit you then try to run away. How about you come and catch me, and we'll exchange license and insurance information."

She looked back to see if they'd taken the bait but was horrified to see they were intent on reaching the tug. She whipped Trono's radio set over her head. "This is Tory. I'm with Trono and Pulaski on the assault boat."

"Tory. It's Max Hanley. What's the problem?"

"There are six terrorists in a small boat about to reach the tug. Your guys are trapped on board with only pistols. They haven't a chance."

"Where are you?" Max asked in a reassuring tone to calm her down.

"On your SEAL boat. Mike wanted me to draw them away, but they weren't having any of it."

"Okay, just you hold on for a second. Pulaski? Trono? You there?"

The reply came in a faint whisper. "Max, it's Ski. We're on top of one of the shipping containers. The pirates just came aboard."

"Do you think they know you're there?"

"Negative. Mike grabbed a tarp just before they got here. Unless they check the top of the container, we're hidden. And it doesn't appear they're searching the ship."

"What *are* they doing?

"It looks like they want to release the tow cables and get out of Dodge. What do you want us to do?"

"Help them," Juan Cabrillo said over the open comm channel.

"What?" Max and Ski said in unison.

"I said help them. Ski, you and Mike hang tight. Max, I want you to cut the tow cables." Juan's radio carried the sound of the gunfight raging on the beach—the sharp crack of rifle fire, the staccato bursts from AK-47s, and the agonized screams of the wounded.

"I can do it with the Gatling," Mark Murphy chimed in. "A direct hit on the big cable drums on the tug's stern should do it."

"But why?" Max asked.

"Because there are a thousand or more Chinese workers caught in the crossfire down here, and the longer this battle lasts, the more of them are getting killed. The Russians look like they can hold out for hours still. Right now that tug is the pirates' only way off the beach, and if they see it's about ready to make way, you can bet they're going to forget all about their fight and hightail it over there."

"Which gets them away from the civilians . . ."

"Which gives Murph the opportunity to hose 'em down," Juan finished.

"What about the Russians?"

"We'll give them a chance to surrender and get off this beach alive. If they don't take it, you can take them."

As if to underscore the urgency, a tremendous crack split the air. A fresh explosion of ash spewed from the top of the volcano, billowing ever higher like a nuclear mushroom cloud. Juan had no idea how long they had. Hours or minutes. They still hadn't located Eddie, and if his plan to end the gunfight quickly didn't work, he had to seriously consider evacuating his people from the beach and making a run for it.

Hali Kasim's excited voice cut through Cabrillo's grim thoughts. "Chairman, I found Eddie! He's on the far side of the barge. It looks like he's tracking two people, one of whom appears to be a hostage."

"Where are they headed?"

"Up away from the beach. The range is pretty extreme, but I think they have a helicopter up there."

"Take it out," Cabrillo ordered, and then he and Linc exchanged a look. It was all the communication they needed. Linc was now in charge of the field team while Juan took off in a ground-eating run. He had only covered forty yards when his ankle caught on a loose stone. Had it been his real leg, the ankle would have broken or at least suffered a major sprain. All that happened was the Chairman fell hard, but his clumsiness saved his life as the air above him came alive with automatic fire. He combat rolled a dozen times to find cover behind a pile of stones. The gunman was below him, hidden behind a pyramid of fifty-five-gallon drums.

Juan checked the load on the grenade launcher slung under his M-4, steadied the rifle against his shoulder, and fired. The weapon made a comically hollow sound, and a second later the grenade impacted behind the drums. The grenade's primary explosion detonated the fuel. Three-hundred-pound drums were launched into the air like rockets, some exploding in flight, while others hit the ground and spilled their flaming contents across the beach.

Juan scrambled to his feet as a drum arced high and began to fall straight at him like a meteor. It landed five yards from him and slightly higher on the hill, so when it split, a burning lake of gasoline roared over him. He fought the instinct to run down the hill. He ran at a diagonal instead, flames licking at his knees and the heat enough to sear his lungs, but in just moments he was through the conflagration with nothing more than singed hair.

"Out of the frying pan . . ." he wheezed as he continued after Eddie Seng.

A one-second burst from the Gatling was enough to shred the steel tow cables, and the timing couldn't have been better, because the pirates on the tug had just bumped the engines to high idle, sending a thick plume of smoke from her funnel. The reaction on the beach was exactly as Juan had predicted.

The pirates almost instantly disengaged the Russian holdouts and began running for the shore. Some kept their weapons, but most dropped them as they plunged into the frigid water and began to swim out to the tug. Watching them reminded Linc of rats deserting a sinking ship. He and the rest of the shore party swept down from their position. There were a few gunmen so intent on the fight that they didn't know their ride was about to leave.

Linc took out a pair of them with a grenade and had a bead on a third when what he thought was a corpse at his feet sprang to life. The pirate knocked away his M-4 and tried to ram a wickedly curved knife into his chest. Linc blocked the blade's fatal thrust, but the knife sliced a long gash into his arm. He sank a fist into the pad of muscle under the fighter's arm, paralyzing the limb for the second he needed to cross-draw his pistol and put a bullet between the man's eyes. He ignored the torrent of blood streaming down his arm and continued his patrol.

Eddie realized he was never going to catch Jan Paulus. The burst of energy that had gripped him so tightly had now flickered to nothing. He was nauseated by hunger, and he couldn't draw enough oxygen into his lungs, but still he pressed on, driven by raw emotion. Paulus and his hostage were a minute away from reaching the MI-8 helicopter, and no matter how Eddie willed his legs to move faster, he knew he was slowing. Then from out on the *Oregon* came the distinct pop from the 40 mm autocannon. Five rounds went sailing high over the beach, passing directly over Eddie and blasting the area around the chopper. When the dust settled, Eddie could see that the cockpit had taken a direct hit. Flames licked from around the shattered Plexiglas, and the ground around the craft was littered with mangled electronics.

He looked back over his shoulder to give the ship a congratulatory salute and spotted a figure running toward him. There was no mistaking the distinctive silhouette: Cabrillo.

Paulus summarily shot his hostage as soon as he realized the helicopter was ruined and started running back down the hill, maybe thinking he could reach the tug and broker some kind of deal or maybe just in blind panic.

Knowing that Juan would have his back, Eddie started running after him, letting gravity do the work that his legs no longer could. They were thirty yards from the beach when Eddie skidded to a stop and threw the AK-47 to his shoulder. He was shaking so badly that he could barely see through the sight. He squeezed the trigger, and the rifle recoiled into his shoulder, but only one round had fired. Paulus turned at the sound, then continued on as Eddie checked the weapon. At some point he'd unseated the banana magazine from the receiver. He jammed it home, cocked the gun, and sprayed the remaining clip at the fleeing miner.

A feather of blood spurted from Paulus's calf, and he staggered and fell. He was slow to get to his feet, giving Eddie the time to cover the distance. He crashed into the South African, sending them both sprawling across the rocks. Though injured, Paulus was a big man, used to the punishing life of mining, and could absorb a tremendous amount of pain.

"You're going pay for that, mate," he said through gritted teeth, goading Eddie to hit him again.

"Don't bet on it." Eddie used the moment of confusion at his American accent to whip the AK-47 at Paulus's head. The miner ducked just in time but gave Eddie an opening for a brutal kick to the knee.

Paulus took the hit without even wincing and wrapped his arms around Eddie's chest, squeezing with machinelike strength. Eddie slammed his forehead into Paulus's nose, feeling the bone crackle, but the miner only seemed to redouble the pressure. Eddie hit him again, and this time the South African roared in pain, loosening his grip enough for Eddie to get one hand free. He grabbed the man's ear and gave it a savage yank. Paulus let go. Eddie got one leg behind Paulus's and shoved him back. Paulus reached out as he fell, taking a handful of Eddie's shirt.

Hitting the ground with Eddie on top of him should have driven the air from Paulus's lungs, but it didn't. The impact had been cushioned. It reminded Eddie of falling on a waterbed. To his horror he realized they'd landed in a huge puddle of mercury.

Before Paulus could recover, Eddie rammed his knee into the man's crotch at the same time he forced his head below the surface. Paulus involuntarily gasped at the pain, sucking in a mouthful the toxic liquid metal. He started going into convulsions, but Eddie stayed on him like a cowboy riding a bull. Paulus managed to wrench his head above the surface. He coughed up great silvery globs of mercury before Eddie jammed his head back under. It took a minute more for him to stop struggling. When Eddie got off the body, it rose back to the top of the pond. Paulus's mouth and nostrils were little glimmering pools of mercury, and his eyelids looked like someone had already laid coins over them.

"That is definitely on my list of top ten ways not to die," Juan said, placing a hand on Eddie's shoulder.

"For a while there," Eddie panted, "I thought I had to take on all these goons by myself."

Juan helped him to his feet. "What, and deny us a share of the glory?" He nodded at the corpse. "Anton Savich?"

"No, a South African hired to oversee this nightmare named Paulus, Jan Paulus."

"Any idea where Savich is?"

Eddie shook his head. "Last I knew, he was in that big cruise ship down the beach. Paulus had Savich's pilot hostage, so I think he's already dead."

"Damn."

"Why? Saves us the trouble."

Cabrillo went silent for a moment then said, "The fence."

"Fence?"

"Like the guy who buys stolen goods from a thief," Juan explained. "Until gold is properly assayed and stamped by an official mint, it's worthless. No one legitimate will touch it. Savich had to know that before putting this caper together, which means he already has someone lined up to buy it from him. Someone who could get the gold authenticated and trickle it into the system. It has to be someone big to handle this much, a major banker with serious connections."

"Sorry, boss, I've got no idea who it is."

Juan smiled. "Don't worry. We'll find the greedy bastard."

Linc called Juan over the radio. "Beach is secure, Chairman. The Russians saw the writing on the wall and surrendered in exchange for a ride out."

"It's time for us to get out of here." Cabrillo looked around. Hundreds of Chinese workers seemed to have materialized from the ground. They'd found cover among the boulders, and now that the fighting had stopped and the tug had motored a mile down the bay, they were milling around in shock. "All of us."

ONCE Juan issued his orders it took only a few minutes for the word to spread that the workers were to board the newest ship to arrive on the beach, but it would take an hour or more for them to climb the only ladder tall enough to reach the ship's rail.

Juan was waiting at the pier the trawlers used when Tory motored up in the assault boat. "Going my way, sailor?"

He jumped down into the deck and impulsively kissed her mouth, but the kiss was interrupted by another booming explosion from the volcano that sent foot-high ripples dancing across the water.

"My, my, you made the earth move." Tory laughed huskily.

For Juan the mood had already passed. They were in a fight against the clock, and every second counted. Tory correctly read his expression and gunned the throttles.

On Cabrillo's orders, Max had swung the *Oregon* around so her stern pointed at the grounded cruise liner. Deckhands had run out the ship's own towing cables from recessed hatches under her fantail. Using a pair of Jet Skis, thick ropes attached to the cables had been transferred to shore where a hundred of the most able-bodied Chinese immigrants were in position to haul the big hawsers to the cruise ship.

"Max, you reading me?" Juan called over his radio.

"I'm here."

"What's the situation?"

"They're about ready to haul the cable over to the cruise ship. Her name's *Selandria,* by the way. Linda and Linc are over there directing everything. She says the bollards are nothing more than mushroom-shaped rust, so we're going to thread the cable around her anchor capstans. They should be able to handle the strain."

"Okay. I'm almost back. As soon as they have the cable secure, I want all our people back on the *Oregon.*"

"I'm going to have to sit on Doc Huxley. She wants to take a team over there right now and start helping the worst of the Chinese."

"Then sit on her," Juan snapped. "If this doesn't work, the grim truth is we're going to leave those people behind and pray we can get some help up here before the volcano blows its top."

"On that front, once the fighting stopped I tried to raise the Russian Coast Guard, but the mountain's pumping out a lot of electrical interference. All our communications are out except the short-range tactical net."

"We're on our own."

" 'Fraid so."

"I want you to stay in the op center. I'll be up on the flying bridge. Have someone meet me there with some clean clothes." He shot Tory a glance, and she nodded enthusiastically. "Some for Tory, too."

Juan stripped out of his filthy battle jacket as he made his way through the ship, feeling bad that the housekeeping staff was going to have a hard time getting his muddy boot prints out of the plush hallway carpets. He reached the flying bridge just as Maurice stepped off the elevator from the op center. He was pushing a silver mess trolley. He handed a bundle of clothes to Juan and another bundle to Tory. Tory stepped into the radio shack to change while Juan undressed where he stood.

"That feels better," Juan said.

Maurice pushed back the trolley's gleaming cover, and the aroma of hot food made Juan's mouth swim. "Shredded jerked beef burritos and coffee."

Around a mouthful of the spicy, foot-long Mexican specialty Juan said, "Maurice, you just doubled your salary."

The elder waiter then tipped a flask into Juan's coffee cup. "From my stock of brandy. Just enough to take the edge off."

"Tripled it."

The storm they had raced up the Sea of Okhotsk had caught up with them. Rain began to pound the windscreen, and lightning crackled overhead. From under the trolley Maurice pulled out a matching pair of rain suits, baseball caps, and Juan's rubber sea boots. "I had a feeling, sir."

Juan slipped into the slicker as Tory came out of the radio room. She wolfed half a burrito in just a couple of bites. "God, I didn't know how hungry I was."

"Chairman?" Max was calling through a walkie-talkie.

"Go ahead."

"They have the cables across. Linda says she needs ten more minutes."

"Tell her she has five. This storm's about to hit, making a tough job near impossible." He stepped out onto the flying bridge and into the gale. The wind had picked up to force five, and volcanic ash mixed with the storm so clots of mud fell from the sky. He looked aft. The heavy cables had been fed through the *Selandria*'s fairleads, and all looked in order—except that the *Oregon* had drifted in the wind and wasn't straight on to the cruise ship. He called a correction down to Eric Stone and looked to see the swirl of water at the bow thruster port.

"That's good. Stations keeping, Mr. Stone."

The assault boat roared off into the choppy sea to pick up the shore party, her rubber pontoon flexing as she crashed through the waves.

"Think we can do it?" Tory asked, joining him out in the open.

"We can generate the horsepower of a supercarrier with our engines, but if that hulk is stuck fast, we'll have the classic dilemma of immutable force and immovable object."

"Would you really abandon them?"

Juan didn't answer, but that was answer enough. Despite what he'd said earlier, she could see the determination in his eyes and knew he'd tear the guts out of his beloved ship and risk his people for the chance of saving even one of the Chinese immigrants.

A couple of minutes later the SEAL boat pulled away from the beach, loaded with the last of the Corporation people left behind. Juan waited until it was clear of the tow cables before bringing the walkie-talkie to his lips.

"Okay, Eric, put some tension on those cables."

The *Oregon* crept forward, and the cables slowly rose out of the sea, sheeting water as the bundles of wire clamped tighter and tighter.

"That's it," the helmsman reported. "Speed over the bottom is zero. We're at full stretch."

"Dial us up slowly to thirty percent and hold it."

There came the distinctive whine as the magnetohydrodynamics spooled up. The angle of the tow and the power of the engines made the *Oregon* settle heavier into the sea so that waves split over her bow in raging sheets.

"I've got movement," Eric cried. "Gaining five feet a minute."

"Negative, we're just stretching the cable a bit more." Juan had spent a summer on a tugboat during college and knew how easily cable stretch could look like they were already under way. "In a minute you'll find we're sliding back. When that happens bring us up to fifty percent."

Juan watched waves slamming into the *Selandria,* trying to see if she was riding them or just being punished by them. There was some movement as walls of water passed under her bows, but each time the foreward section of the ship rose up on a wave meant her stern was being ground deeper and deeper into the beach.

"Fifty percent," Eric announced a moment later. "No movement."

"Bring us to eighty."

"I can't recommend that," Max Hanley warned. "You've beat my babies pretty bad already."

Theoretically there was no limit to the power output from the magnetohydrodynamics, but there was a weakness in the system: the high-speed pumps that kept the banks of magnets cooled to superconductive temperatures with liquid helium. The extreme cold played havoc on the impellors, and after the prolonged abuse they endured to reach Kamchatka, their failure weighed heavy on Max's mind.

"Those engines are maintained by the best engineer afloat. Bring us to eighty."

The *Oregon* dug in even deeper, allowing waves to wash over her railings. The water at her stern became a boiling caldron as the pump jets forced hundreds of tons a minute though the tubes.

"Nothing," Eric reported. "She's stuck fast. We're never going to haul that pig off the beach."

Juan ignored his pessimism. "Give me full starboard lock."

Eric complied, wrenching the controls so the *Oregon* sheered off a straight line like a dog straining at a leash, adding a couple more tons of pressure to the tow.

"Port lock!"

The ship swung around, straining the cables so they vibrated with tension. A haunted moan escaped from the *Selandria* as her hull pivoted on the rocks and then came a rending scream of metal as she shifted further.

"Come on, baby. Come on," Juan urged. Tory had her hands to her mouth, her fist clenched so tightly her fingernails were a bloodless white. "Anything?"

Eric sent the *Oregon* careening back to starboard before answering. "No. Speed over the bottom remains zero."

Max interrupted. "Juan, I've got temperature spikes showing in engines three and four. The coolant pumps are starting to go. We've got to shut down and try to get as many of those poor souls aboard as we can."

Juan looked back. The Chinese had been warned to stay off the deck—a tow cable parting under tension would whip back with enough force to cut a man in two—however, the *Selandria*'s bow was a sea of pale, frightened faces, huddled and shivering in the cold rain. A rough count put the number of immigrants on the liner at over three thousand. The *Oregon* could take maybe a third of that number. "Okay."

Max must have had his hands on the engine controls because they wound down to low idle the instant the word left Juan's mouth. Free of the strain, the *Oregon* bobbed up, shedding water like a spaniel.

Tory gave Juan a sharp, disapproving look, a stinging rebuke at his giving up so easily, but she hadn't let him finish speaking.

"Take the tension off thc cables and spool out another hundred yards. Creep us ahead and prepare to weigh both anchors."

"Juan, do you really think . . ."

"Max, our anchor winches are powered by four-hundred-horse-power engines," Cabrillo pointed out. "I'll take every pony we can muster."

Down in the op center Max used computer keystrokes to disengage the clutch on both cable drums, allowing them to run free while Eric Stone engaged the engines again to move the ship farther out into the bay. When they reached the hundred-yard mark, Max let go the anchors. They sank quickly to the bottom, which was only eighty feet deep.

"Now back us gently and set the flukes," Juan ordered.

The big Delta kedging anchors dragged along the rocky bottom, cutting deep furrows in the loose rock and boulders until their hardened steel flukes snagged bedrock. A computer control automatically adjusted the tension on the anchor chains to keep them from slipping.

"We're ready," Max announced, but his tone was less than enthusiastic.

"Tension the tow cables, then bring us up to thirty percent." Juan snapped a pair of binoculars to his eyes, purposefully avoiding looking at the men at the *Selandria*'s railing. Waves continued to pound the ship's bow, causing her to saw up and down, grinding her stern ever deeper.

"Thirty percent," Eric announced. "No movement over the bottom other than stretching the cables."

"Ramp it up to fifty," Juan said without taking his eyes off the cruise ship. "Anything on the anchors?"

"Zero recovery on the winches," Max answered. "Heat's already building in three and four. We're thirty degrees from red line and automatic shutdown."

The forces acting on the tow were titanic, brute horsepower against twenty thousand deadweight tons of steel that had been pounded into the beach. Pulled taut by the cables, the *Selandria*'s bow stopped responding to the waves, so water washed under her, causing volleyball-sized rocks to dance back and forth.

"Anything?" Juan called.

"No recovery on the winches," Max said grimly, "and zero movement over the bottom."

"Eighty percent!"

"Juan?"

"Do it and take the safeties off the engines." Juan's voice was charged with anger. "Bury them past the red line if you have to. We're not leaving those people."

Max complied, typing a few commands that told the computer to ignore the heat building up in the massive cryo pumps. He watched his screen as the columns indicating temperature turned red and then climbed above the safety limit. He reached out deliberately and shut off the computer monitor. "Sorry, my darlings."

Juan could feel his ship's torment through the soles of his boots as she fought the tow. The vibrations were tearing her apart, and each shudder sent a lance into his chest.

"Come on, you bitch," he snarled. "Move."

A rumble built across the bay, so deep and resonant that it was a feeling across the skin rather than a sound that hit the ears. The top of the mountain was hidden by a dense cloud of ash, and the ground shook so strongly that the beach seemed to become a liquid. This was it. The main eruption. The volcano was going to blow like Mount Saint Helens, and a wall of superheated ash and gas would tear down from the summit in a deadly avalanche that scientists called a pyroclastic flow, one of the most destructive forces on earth. Juan had gambled all and was about to lose everything. It was too late to go back and save any of the Chinese. Tears stung his eyes, but the firm line of his jaw never slackened.

"We've got to cut the tow," Max said.

Cabrillo said nothing.

"Juan, we've got to go. We need a couple of miles between us and that volcano if we're getting out of here alive."

He didn't doubt the words. The pyroclastic flow would reach far out to sea in an enveloping noxious cloud that would smother anything in its path. But still he remained silent.

"Movement!" Eric shouted. "Port winch is recovering, five yards a minute."

"Must be slippage," Max countered. "She's dragging across the sea floor."

It was as if the sun had been eclipsed. Darkness came so swiftly that it left Juan's eyes swimming. He could barely see the *Selandria* through the swirling ashfall. Hot ash stung his bare hands as he held the binoculars to his face. He just couldn't tell if the liner had moved or whether Max was right and the anchor had slipped.

No one spoke for what felt like an eternity. Stone's eyes never left the speed indicators, which remained stubbornly at zero.

Then over the sound of the eruption, the *Selandria* screamed, a mortal, almost human sound, as if she could no longer endure the tremendous pressures of tow and storm.

"Got her," Eric shouted as his speed indicators tickled ever so slightly.

Max turned his computer screen back on. "Recovery on both winches."

"Speed over the bottom is ten yards a minute. Fifteen. Twenty."

As more and more of the ship's weight felt the buoyancy of her natural element, the speed continued to increase. Tory clutched Juan's hand as they watched the *Selandria* get drawn back to the sea, her hull plates shrieking in protest as she was dragged over the rocks. And when a particularly large wave pounded the beach, she gave it a squeeze as the ship rode up its face, her stern coming high in her first moment of freedom.

"She's free," Juan called down to the op center and heard a roar of approval from his crew. Someone, probably Max, who was a rank sentimentalist under his tough veneer, sounded the ship's horn—a keening celebratory note that echoed and echoed.

"We're not out of the woods yet," Juan said and led Tory back inside the bridge. They descended into the op center. Another cheer rose from the throats of his people, and his back was slapped black and blue.

Now that the *Selandria* was refloated, Juan ordered the power output cut to fifty percent and had the view from the aft-facing cameras brought up on the main screen. Already water frothed along the liner's waterline as the *Oregon* continued to accelerate down the bay.

"Dear God," Tory gasped.

The top of the mountain had been vaporized. A solid black wall of ash was pouring down the mountain, a swirling, choking mass that seemed alive. Everything before its fury was cut flat. Trees that had stood for a hundred years were ripped from the ground and tossed like matchsticks. A second later the sound of the explosion reached the ship, a painful assault on eardrums that was the loudest yet.

Workers on the *Selandria* scrambled to get back inside the ship as the pyroclastic flow finally reached the surf line in an explosion of steam, and still the ash roared onward, spreading outward so it swallowed the other ships left abandoned on the beach. One of the smaller ones was blown onto its side, while the barge carrying the processing plant was flipped completely upside down.

"Hold on," someone said unnecessarily as the ash enveloped the *Selandria* and completely filled the camera's view.

It hit the *Oregon* like a sledgehammer blow, a hurricane of ash and pumice that shattered windows and heeled the ship over so her starboard rail was buried into the sea. But she kept driving, shouldering aside the fresh onslaught of nature's fury until she burst out of the cloud and into shadowy daylight.

No one moved or even breathed as they watched the screen. Seconds dribbled like molten lead. Then suddenly the bow of the *Selandria* emerged through the curtain of ash like a ghost becoming real. Her hull was covered in clinging dust, but she'd never looked more beautiful. But still the crew waited, watching. A tiny movement caught everyone's attention. Mark Murphy quickly zoomed in as a door on the upper deck opened tentatively. A small figure stepped out, looked around, and then motioned at someone inside the ship. In seconds there were a dozen people on the deck, kicking up clouds of ash in a spontaneous game to celebrate their survival.

Maurice appeared in the op center as if by magic. The tray in his hand held a trio of Dom Perignon bottles and enough cut crystal flutes for everyone on duty.

Amid the raucous celebration, Tory whispered into Juan's ear, "So who was the bitch?"

"Huh?"

"When we were on the flying bridge you said, '*Come on, you bitch, move.*' Who was the bitch you were talking about? The *Oregon* or the *Selandria*?"

"Neither."

The corner of her mouth turned downward as she thought about his answer. And then her lips parted in a beaming smile. "Max is right. You are a crafty bastard. You were talking to Mother Nature."

He couldn't keep the satisfied smile from his lips. "I knew there'd be a major earthquake just before the main eruption. Water-saturated soils undergo what's called liquefaction. Basically, the shaking causes the ground to turn into quicksand. That broke the suction that had built under the *Selandria*'s hull and allowed us to drag her off."

"Cutting it awfully close, weren't you?"

"You only get the big rewards when you're willing to face the big risks."

"Chairman." Mark Murphy was still at his weapons station. "I've got a radar contact six miles dead ahead, moving at seven knots."

"The tug," Max said.

"Speaking of rewards."

Even with the *Selandria* in tow it took the *Oregon* only fifteen minutes to come within visual range of the fleeing tugboat. Juan scrambled the deck crew to get in position as he ordered Eric to take the squat tug down the port side. There were only a handful of pirates on the tug, so they were almost on top of them before anyone realized they weren't alone. Two of them raced out onto the tug's flying bridge with their AK-47s, but they quickly ran for cover when Murph opened up with one of the gimble-mounted fifty-calibers housed in hidden bunkers on the *Oregon*'s deck.

"Mike, Ski, can you hear me?" Juan called over the radio.

"I thought you'd forgotten all about us," Pulaski replied over the tactical communications channel. "Mike and I were thinking we were in for a long cruise vacation."

"Sorry, boys. You're not up for leave for while yet. I can see the two containers on the tug's stern. Which one are you on top of?"

"The rearmost."

"And the lifting assembly?"

"Ready to go."

"We'll be alongside in about one minute." Juan then addressed Murphy. "Disable the tug's rudder assembly, would you please."

"With pleasure."

He called up the Bofors 40 mm autocannon, waited for the weapon to be deployed from its concealed bay, and put a half-dozen rounds under the tug's fantail. Her speed dropped off instantly, and a trail of oil began to seep from where her hull had been penetrated.

Eric Stone kept his hands loose on the controls as he brought the *Oregon* alongside the tug, slowing to match speed as the gap between the two ships shrank to just a few feet. He used rudder and bow thruster to keep the vessels in virtual lockstep. Murph never took his eyes off his cameras, waiting to provide cover fire if any of the pirates showed themselves.

Up on deck, a pair of deckhands swung the boom of the *Oregon*'s main derrick across the gap, feeding out line so the hook dangled scant inches above the shipping container. Trono and Ski finally emerged from under the tarp and attached the hook to the beam they'd secured to the metal box. Mike made a circular gesture with his hand, and the crate came free of the deck.

Mohammad Singh, Shere Singh's second-eldest and therefore second most trusted son, had survived the initial assault on the tug because he'd hidden in a cabin while his father's men fought and killed the crew and were later gunned down by the Gatling. Fighting was something that his father paid others to do. However, when he saw the crane swing over the side of his ship, he immediately understood that someone was trying to rob him. He raced down from the bridge, brandishing a pistol, and burst out on the afterdeck, screaming curses at the top of his lungs.

Mark Murphy saw the man dash across the deck but was a fraction too slow training one of the .50 calibers.

Singh leapt for the container just as it began to pendulum from the wave action. He scrambled to find a grip and was forced to drop his pistol in order to hold on tight.

The winchman drew back cable so the container cleared the railing and had just started to pivot the boom back over the *Oregon* when a heavy rolling wave surged past the two ships. Stone did an excellent job of keeping the vessels from crashing against each other, but the deckhand couldn't stop the container from arcing across open space and slamming into the tug's bridge with a wet slap. When it swung back, all that remained of Mohammad Singh was a meaty red stain.

Most of the crew not on duty assembled in the hold where the container had been lowered once the *Oregon* was well beyond weapons range of the floundering tug.

Ski and Trono doused everyone with a cascade of champagne froth when Maurice handed them each a bottle.

"It's kind of anticlimactic," Juan shouted over the revelry, "because these two clowns had to sneak a peek on the tug, however . . ." He drew the word out as he swung open the big doors.

The lighting in the hold wasn't particularly conducive for examining treasure, but the golden reflection that radiated from the container was the most beautiful color any of them had ever seen.

Juan hefted one of the bars, pumping it over his head like a trophy, while around him the men and women of the Corporation went wild.

25

JUAN Cabrillo leaned back in the sofa with an exhausted sigh and took a sip of the brandy he'd bought from the duty-free shop at Zurich's airport. For the first time in nearly two weeks he felt he could finally relax.

He gazed into the fire burning in the open hearth, losing himself in the flames' hypnotic dance.

When they'd dragged her off the beach, the *Selandria*'s hull had been holed by sharp rocks. They managed to tow her twenty miles down the Kamchatka's west coast before maneuvering her into a shallow inlet and letting her sink. They transferred as much food as they could spare and emptied nearly all the supplies from the medical bay. Juan allowed Doc Huxley and her team just twenty-four hours to evaluate and treat as many people as she could before he ordered the *Oregon* to continue south.

They came across the second tugboat and the drydock *Souri* only 150 miles from what Eddie said the workers called Death Beach. As Cabrillo had said, she'd had a hard time making headway in the storm.

They put a torpedo into the *Souri* as they passed her by without so much as a warning and blew the rudder off the tug's sternpost with a blast from the 40 mm.

It was only then that Cabrillo contacted the Russian Coast Guard. He routed the radio call through a half dozen satellite relays to mask their position and reported that there were several ships in distress in the Sea of Okhotsk and gave their GPS coordinates. He explained about the Chinese refugees, which the operator he spoke to didn't seem all that concerned about, and how there was a fortune of illegally mined gold on one of the tugs, which seemed to get more of a reaction.

News of the dramatic rescue and incredible find following the worst volcanic eruption in Asia for a decade broke as the *Oregon* limped into Vladivostok. They turned the Russian mercenaries over to the authorities and laid up the ship for much-needed repairs.

It was there that Juan phoned Langston Overholt, their principle CIA contact, and told him the whole story. He also called Hiroshi Katsui to inform him that the pirate menace that had overwhelmed the waters off Japan was over and gave instructions for their final payment.

He considered the fortune in gold they'd made off with a bonus that their client didn't need to know about.

Two weeks after the eruption, Lang sent Juan an e-mail. The first rescue workers to reach the bay reported that someone had survived the eruption aboard one of the cruise ships. He'd barricaded himself in a food locker as the pyroclastic flow buried the vessel under five feet of searing hot volcanic ash. Lang thought Juan would like to know the survivor gave his name as Anton Savich, a volcanologist well-known in the region. Savich was currently staying at a hotel in Petropavlovsk

Juan wanted to go himself, but he felt that Eddie Seng needed it more. Franklin Lincoln went along for the ride. They were back two days later with the name Bernhard Volkmann. He was the banker who was going to fence Savich's gold.

"How'd you do it?" Juan had asked his two officers across the desk in his cabin.

"Simple, really," Eddie had said. "Once we broke into his room and kidnapped him, we drove him to the airport and promised that we wouldn't kill him if he told us what we wanted to know."

"And?"

"He had nothing to lose and everything to gain, so he told us."

"*And?*" Juan repeated, feeling like he was pulling teeth.

"Well, when the Russians rescued the Chinese off the *Selandria*, there weren't enough beds around Petropavlovsk to house them, so they put about a thousand men into a hangar at the airport until they figured out what to do with them. So after Savich told me the name, I went into the hangar with him, explained to a few of the men there that Savich was responsible for what had happened to them, and, well, let nature take its course."

Juan glanced at Linc.

"Like the man said, we promised not to kill him. Never said anything about turning him over to his victims. Guy had already stopped screaming by the time we were out of earshot."

That was what had sent Juan back to Switzerland for a meeting with Bernhard Volkmann, which, as Juan recalled while sipping at his brandy, had gone as well as he'd expected.

Volkmann had agreed to buy the sixty tons of gold that had followed Juan to Switzerland in a couple of airfreight containers. He agreed to establish a trust with half the proceeds on behalf of the Chinese workers who'd mined the gold, and he agreed that he would then sell his bank and retire to the slums of Calcutta, where he would devote the rest of his life to charity.

For his part, Juan agreed not to put a bullet through the greedy bastard's head.

A light knock on his door jerked Juan back to the present. The press interest in the explosion and kidnapping of Rudolph Isphording had long faded, and he looked nothing like the dark-haired, dark-eyed, and mustached Spaniard he'd pretended to be when he'd rented the safe house, so he walked calmly across the living room and swung open the door.

"Hi, sailor, remember me?" Tory wore her hair up, accenting the long line of her neck, and her blue eyes captured the glow of the fireplace and reflected it back at Juan. She wore a loose gray suit over a white oxford shirt buttoned low enough to catch his attention. Her lips were brushed with gloss and were poised in an unsure smile.

"I never expected to see you again," Juan finally stammered. She'd disappeared soon after the *Oregon* docked in Vladivostok without so much as a word of good-bye.

Her smile faded slightly. "Are you going to invite me in?"

"Sure, sure."

He fixed her a drink and was careful to sit opposite her in a chair rather than next to her on the couch facing the fire.

"I didn't think you *were* going to see me again," she began, "but Max called me in London and dispelled some of my preconceived notions. I saw you as the rakish sea captain with your merry band of swashbucklers and figured you would have a girl in every port. I realized that I didn't want to be another notch on your sword belt, so rather than let myself get hurt for falling for the wrong kind of man—again—I decided to go home and spare myself a touch of heartache.

"Then Max called me. He told me that you don't keep a woman in every port, and in fact in all the years he's known you, he's never seen you even go on a date. He told me you were widowed and that your wife was killed by a drunk driver. He says you don't have a single picture of her and only told him about her one night years ago, but that since her death you've cut yourself off from relationships."

Juan made to speak, but Tory silenced him by crossing to the chair and placing one delicate finger across his lips.

"Max also told me that since I left, you've been an insufferable sod, which is why he called me. He seems to think you might like me, and was pretty certain I liked you. So here I am, flying in on a wing and a prayer. How about it? Remember what you told me. Only big risks can bring you big rewards."

"Only Max ever knew I was married, and I didn't tell him the whole truth," Juan said softly. "She was killed by a drunk driver, but what I didn't say is that she was the drunk. It was ten, no, eleven years ago. She had been to rehab twice already, but it never really stuck. I didn't know she'd relapsed this time. When I saw the cop standing outside my door that night, I knew immediately what had happened."

"I'm sorry." Tory's hand rested on Juan's chest. "And you still carry a torch."

He stared into her eyes. "I still carry the anger."

The silence stretched for several seconds. "You're not angry at her, are you." It wasn't a question. "It's yourself you blame."

"Who else can I?"

"Her, for one." Tory shrugged out of her jacket. "Listen, Juan. Max told me you've already have another job lined up, and I've only a week's leave from Lloyd's. I'm not asking that you drop everything and marry me. I'm not even asking that you love me. I'm asking that for once you stop taking the blame for everything bad in the world and let yourself enjoy some of the good. When was the last time you were intimate with a woman?"

The frankness of the question sent a stirring jolt through his lower body and inside him a dam he'd spent half a lifetime erecting crashed down in a swirl of emotion. His hand wrapped around the back of her head of its own volition, his fingers entwined in her hair. "Since . . ."

"Don't you think it's about time?" she asked and kissed him.

Juan lifted her easily from the chair, cradling her in his arms as he moved to the bedroom, his heart beating like a trip-hammer. "It was never about time," he whispered in her ear. "It was just waiting for the right person." He smiled against her skin. "And I have to warn you I'm probably a bit rusty."

"Don't you worry. We'll work the kinks out." Tory gave a throaty chuckle. "And maybe even work a few kinks in."